WICKED WIVES

Anna-Lou Weatherley was born in Hampshire and grew up in London where she still lives with her partner and two children. An award-winning journalist and women's lifestyle writer for over fifteen years, she is the former editor and acting editor of *J-17* and *Smash Hits* respectively and has written for all the major glossies including *Grazia*, *More*, *Company*, and *Marie Claire* among others.

She is the author of two teen titles, *Ibiza Summer* and *The Wrong Boy* (Piccadilly Press). Her first adult novel, *Chelsea Wives*, was published in 2012.

By the same author:

Chelsea Wives

ANNA-LOU WEATHERLEY

Wicked Wives

AVON

AVON
A division of HarperCollins*Publishers*
77–85 Fulham Palace Road,
London W6 8JB

www.harpercollins.co.uk

A Paperback Original 2013
1

First published in Great Britain by
HarperCollins*Publishers* 2013

A catalogue record for this book is
available from the British Library

ISBN-13: 978-1-84756-332-3

Set in Sabon LT Std by Palimpsest Book Production Limited,
Falkirk, Stirlingshire

Printed and bound in Great Britain by
Clays Ltd, St Ives plc

MIX
Paper from
responsible sources
FSC˜ C007454

FSC.org

Well, here it is, the difficult second novel all my fellow writers warned me about that (thankfully) turned out to be a complete joy to write, though it would be fair to say it would never have got off the ground without Sammia Rafique and Claire Bord at Avon (HarperCollins) – I can't thank you enough for all your continued passion and support. Also, special thanks to Becke Parker and indeed all the Avon team for all their hard work and dedication. You're the best!

I have the greatest agent ever, Madeleine Milburn, without whom I would not be writing these words. Maddy, your belief, support and advice has been essential in helping me get to this point. Thank you so much for all your faith and confidence – I look forward to our continuing journey together.

Thanks as always to my dearest friends (in no particular order), the amazing Laura Millar, darling Susie Ember (Rabbit), my girl Sarah Quefs (and the boys), Andie Redman, Michelle Langan and Nyree Boardman. Also, Maya, Christina, Karen and the lovely Limor Katz (you wanna come in my house?). You're my inspiration and mean so much to me. Also a special mention to the Mykonos crew, LM, Daniel, Chris, Katrina and Pauline – happy memories guys!

I would also like to thank all the wonderful magazine girls who have supported me including Jane and Marianne at *Grazia*, Marina Gask, Wendy Rigg, Ally Oliver, Suzy Cox and Chantelle Horton – and anyone else I might have missed. Can't tell you how much I appreciate it.

As always, thanks to my lovely family, Mum, Pops and Sheila, Hannah and our kid, Marc – Vegas this year kiddo, woop woop!

A special mention to net-a-porter.com for fashion and outfit inspiration (and a wonderful, if expensive, distraction from writing), ditto matchesfashion.com. I would also like to thank the beautiful and stylish women of Italy – those girls really know how to work it!

And last but never least, my amazing boys, Louie, Felix and Alan for everything you do for me, for all the support, cuddles, encouragement and late night runs to the off-licence. I love you!

For Mum and Pops. Respectively, of course.

'I generally avoid temptation unless I can't resist it.'
— Mae West

PROLOGUE

The view from the yacht was superlative. The ocean, a faultless shade of azure blue, stretched out as far as the eye could see, its perfect blue ubiquity broken only by the crystal-white shoreline of St John's Bay. The sun had begun to set in the distance, a mix of blood-red orange and purples erupting seamlessly into a rich ombre pattern, painting the sky like an oil canvas.

Tom Black peered over the top of his mirrored Ray-Ban Aviators and rested his forearms lightly on the shiny chrome edge of the smart Sunseeker 75, appreciating the final rays of the Antiguan sun on his tanned skin. He took a cursory glance at the diamond-encrusted Rolex on his wrist – a welcome reminder of just how far he had come in recent months. It was 8.28 p.m.

Casting a critical eye around, he admired the shiny teak wooden deck and opulent white leather furnishings of the yacht with a fleeting sense of satisfaction. A huge, cocoon-shaped day bed took pride of place on the sun deck, affording its lucky recipients both seclusion and exposure to the best of the day's rays as they relaxed – or otherwise – on the sumptuous white cushions. On one side of the bed a magnum of Dom Pérignon Vintage Rose 1959 was chilling to -25 degree perfection in a solid silver Tiffany champagne bucket. On the other, a matching bowl filled with the finest Beluga caviar and two silver spoons nestled on crushed ice. Tom silently congratulated himself. It was a miracle he'd made it here, all things considered; he knew he was on borrowed time, that it wouldn't take long for them to find him, but he just needed tonight. *Just one more night to make things right*.

A light breeze caught the fine, silk curtains that draped provocatively from the vast dome-shaped bed, lifting them in a ghostly manner, and, finally satisfied that all was to his exacting standards, Tom made his way down to the master suite below and showered quickly but thoroughly in the lavish, marble and sandstone floored en-suite bathroom, anxious to admire himself in his new, custom-made Tom Ford suit. Only the best for his imminent guest.

Stepping into a fresh pair of white Calvin Klein briefs, he spritzed himself liberally with Grey Vetiver and slid into a crisp, white Richard James shirt that he'd picked up on Savile Row. Enjoying himself now, he slipped on a pair of flawless gold and diamond Cartier cufflinks, pulled on the midnight-blue trousers and single breasted jacket, and added a thin black silk tie. Alluring and glamorous, it was the perfect blend of American minimalism matched with Italian class. Seductively whispering (rather than screaming) wealth and sophistication, it suggested the wearer was a no-nonsense kind of guy who knew his way around the boardroom *and* the bedroom, the kind of suit that stopped women dead in their tracks. The kind of suit Tom Black liked.

Surveying his masculine, gym-honed reflection in the full length Venetian mirror, he resisted the urge to say aloud, 'the name's Bond . . . James Bond,' grinning childishly as he ran his thumb and fingers across his well-defined jawline, forgetting himself. For a moment he felt a flutter of excitement, a brief transient state of happiness that was swiftly replaced with one of sharp guilt as he thought of Jack . . . of Loretta . . . of *her*.

Tom forced himself to smile at his reflection. How he would do it all so differently given the chance again. Introspection; waste of fucking time that was. He knew he was a prime candidate for therapy, a psychiatrist's dream; but who needed a shrink to tell them what a fuck-up they were and pay for the privilege? Screw that. He adjusted the lapels on his five-hundred dollar shirt in the mirror; his thoughts had begun to coast towards the moribund and he distracted himself by examining his features. He might be what society deemed 'middle aged' – a term he despised – but he sure as shit didn't want to look it. All that ageing gracefully bullshit was for people who couldn't afford to look good, or worse, for those who'd already given up on life. He was neither. In a bid to bolster his withering ego, he told himself that after tonight, after he'd done what he knew he had to do, he would find another playground; start again while he still had the looks to get by. He'd go younger this time; the younger ones were so much easier. They were less demanding, more malleable, easier to please and deceive. They didn't yet possess that haunted expression, one that spoke of broken hearts and shattered dreams, of wasted years and bitter disappointments. These days, when he looked into the eyes of women of a certain age he found himself having to look away. Sometimes it was too much like looking into a mirror.

Tom pulled a white-tipped Marlboro Light from a soft pack on the table and lit it with a vintage 1973 Cartier lighter, a little agitated. Inhaling deeply, he felt the knot of tension in his gut ease a little as the nicotine hit his system, caressing his blood vessels into submission. He'd kicked the weed years ago but tonight he needed something to take the edge off. She would be here soon.

Extinguishing his cigarette in a Lalique glass ashtray, he

made his way to the lower deck to sluice with mouthwash and top up with Grey Vetiver. Pride; it always came before a fall. No wonder it was one of the seven deadly sins. It had prevented him from following the path of true happiness his entire life. Tonight though, he knew he would need to remove the mask once and for all, lay his soul bare, finally tell her what he should have told her all those years ago. Then it would be over.

The unmistakable sound of footsteps along the jetty caused Tom to look up, and with a rapid heartbeat, make his way back up to the top deck, conscious of each step his hand-stitched Italian loafers made.

As the figure came into view, Tom's eye was immediately drawn to the outstretched hand and the .9 mm Glock it shakily held, the metal glinting malevolently in the last of the sun's fading rays as it pointed directly at him. Registering surprise and confusion, his heart beating aggressively beneath his pristine suit, he felt a violent surge of adrenalin flush through his system, loosening his joints to the point of collapse.

'Well, well,' he heard himself say as the sharp cracking sound of the gun discharging split the balmy, almond-scented air; only it did not sound like his voice at all, it was the voice of a stranger, low and detached. 'I wasn't expecting to see *you* . . .'

4

CHAPTER 1

'Mmm, looks delicious,' Ellie Scott murmured appreciatively as she looked down at the eggs Florentine that had just been placed in front of her by a smiling, if a little harried-looking waitress. Lindsay, her PA, sitting opposite her, nodded enthusiastically as she threw her copy of the *Daily Mail* down onto the table and carefully pulled out a large document from her new Chloe Marcie tote. Ellie's dance school was due to open in less than two months and there was still so much to organise. Just looking at the to-do list brought her out in a cold sweat.

'Any news on a venue yet?' Lindsay tentatively asked, between mouthfuls of her eggs Benedict.

'Linds, I've been on to every estate agent in London,' Ellie gave a despairing sigh as she swished her long, honey-highlighted hair from her face, wondering if it was too early for a quinoa-vodka Bloody Mary; it was practically one of your five-a-day.

'. . . And? Any luck?'

Ellie momentarily abandoned her knife and fork with a clatter. She felt like crying.

'Something will come up,' Lindsay reassured her boss brightly. After all, Ellie's husband was synonymous with luxury estates all over the world. Surely if anyone could pull a few strings for his wife it was her billionaire business tycoon, a man who made Philip Green look like Del Boy Trotter from *Only Fools and Horses*.

Truth was though, Ellie hadn't actually told Vinnie about the collapse of the venue, at least, not yet. This was exactly the kind of situation she had hoped to avoid; running to her husband at the first sign of trouble.

'I'm viewing a place after lunch,' Ellie lied in a bid to put an end to the conversation. 'In the meantime, I think we should just carry on with the plans as discussed, get everything organised so that as soon as a new venue is found, it's all systems go.'

It had taken the best part of eighteen months to source and secure the Soho venue that Ellie had planned to transform into her flagship dance studio, so it had been a bitter blow to have been gazumped at the last minute. Now she had less than eight weeks to find another venue and turn everything around or she stood to lose a lot of money, and more importantly, face. This dance school was her life's dream. Her childhood ambition of becoming a professional ballerina had long since passed, fate had put paid to that some years ago, but this school was a chance to give something back; allowing other girls, talented girls like she'd once been, to achieve what she herself wished she could have, if only life had taken a different path.

'And—' Lindsay scanned her to-do list for the umpteenth time in case she'd missed anything important, '—while we're still on the hunt for a new venue, we should think about drawing up a guest list for the opening night, and then there's the . . .' she had gone into full efficiency overdrive now, but Ellie had stopped listening. Her concentration had been broken by a commotion taking place at the front of the restaurant. A waiter was busy ushering a female wearing the darkest Dior shades and a vintage Pucci

6

headscarf through the doors and away from a swarm of paparazzi that had gathered outside like locusts.

'OMG! Don't turn round, but you are never going to believe who's just walked in . . .' Lindsay's jaw was practically swinging on its hinges, 'only Miranda Muldavey.'

'*Nooo*!' Ellie hissed. 'But she lives in LA.'

Lindsay tapped her copy of the *Daily Mail* with a chewed fingernail and gave a conspiratorial nod. 'It says she's back in London, come to see her family apparently, you know,' she leaned in towards her boss, '*before the trial starts*.'

Miranda Muldavey was bona fide Hollywood royalty, a global icon who had regularly graced the covers of glossy magazines and newspapers the world over. Or at least she had been, until she had made an ill-fated decision to go under the knife and been left a butchered mess.

Miranda's sensational story had brought Hollywood to a standstill. Overnight, one of the most celebrated actresses on the planet had been reduced to little more than a freak sideshow, a figure of ridicule and pity, her career – and face – in tatters.

Of course, the rumour-mill had practically spun into overdrive with such force that you could see smoke. This was the 'handiwork' of a cosmetic surgeon. But whose?

'And she was so beautiful as well,' Ellie sighed. 'Just goes to show that you should never mess with what's God given. But then again, I'm not an A-list Hollywood actress. All that pressure to look half your age and have the body of a teenager . . .' Ellie glanced over at the lone, hunched figure, hiding behind her oversized shades as she perused the brunch menu. 'To her credit, she's remained very dignified about the whole thing – even if she's a virtual recluse now.'

Lindsay raised a sardonic eyebrow.

'. . . More's the pity really.'

'So, does the paper drop a hint on who the culprit is?'

Ellie asked. Miranda's story had been the source of much dinner-party debate during the past six months. Even Vinnie had shown an interest in it.

Lindsay thumbed her copy of the *Daily Mail*, 'not exactly, though interestingly, there *is* a story right next to it about Doctor Ramone Hassan, you know, the celebrity surgeon who's always on those before-and-after TV shows? It says here that he's due to fly back to LA from his holiday in Santorini in a few days' time, *just* as the trial begins . . .' She widened her eyes, continuing to read aloud. '"Dr Ramone 'Ramsey' Hassan, one of the most successful and celebrated – not to mention richest – plastic surgeons on the planet, a man who has helped countless Hollywood actresses turn back the clock, seen here with his new wife, Lorena, looks relaxed as he holidays on the picturesque Greek Island of Santorini."'

Ellie looked up from her plate.

'Let me see that,' she said, taking the paper from her PA's grasp. She looked down at the grainy paparazzi shot of an older-looking, dark-skinned man standing on a boat, his unsightly paunch visible over the top of his tight Speedo briefs, but it was the woman next to him that caused her to drop her fork in alarm and her heartbeat to gallop like a racehorse inside her chest. Draped over a sun lounger with a champagne flute in one hand and a thin, white cigarette in the other, was a Dolce & Gabbana bikini-clad woman with pneumatic breasts that were struggling to free themselves from the miniscule triangles of fabric that strained to conceal them. Wearing a matching turban and blowing cigarette smoke from her enormous, plumped-up lips, it was unmistakably *her*. Loretta Fiorentino, or Hassan as she now was. The press might've misspelt her name, but it was her alright. Ellie would never forget those eyes; as dark and soulless as a shark about to attack.

'Well, well, well. *Loretta*,' she murmured underneath her

8

breath, transfixed by the surgically enhanced face of a woman she hadn't seen in over two decades – and was all the better for it.

'Ellie . . . *Ell-liiee*,' Lindsay's voice cut through the fog of her thoughts with all the subtlety of a meat cleaver.

Ellie suddenly stood.

'Actually, I've got to run, Linds,' she said, snatching up her iPhone from the table. 'I've got this appointment . . . and I promised Tess I'd see her before she flies off to Ibiza.'

'OK, but before you go . . .' Lindsay held up the mock invitations, head cocked to one side in apology. 'What do you reckon; the red or the black?'

'Black,' Ellie said as she leaned in to kiss Lindsay on both cheeks, throwing her Chanel Caviar bag over her shoulder in a deft swoop. 'Let's play it safe.'

Ellie pasted on a smile as she left the café. The press clipping had thrown her. Loretta Fiorentino was someone she had hoped never to have to think about ever again. She was part of a past that Ellie had long ago buried and had no plans to resurrect; at least not in this lifetime. The news story had said that 'Lorena' and her husband were at the end of an extended honeymoon and were imminently due to head back to LA, potentially making a brief stop off in London first, 'if the mood takes us.' Ellie hoped it wouldn't. In fact, she hoped they'd get on a one-way plane back to LA as soon as possible and stay there permanently, because if Eleanor Scott knew one thing, it was that wherever Loretta Fiorentino was, trouble was never far behind.

CHAPTER 2

'*Cazzo imbecilli*!' Loretta Hassan jabbed at the picture of herself in the paper with a long pointed red fingernail. 'The press, they are fucking idiots!' she screeched, incredulous, her Italian accent thick with protest. 'I mean, for the love of God they are journalists! *Journalists*! And they cannot even spell my name correctly!' She slammed the offending paper down onto the silk Versace sheets, causing Bambino, her white teacup Chihuahua, to yelp in alarm. 'The British press,' she hissed, 'they are the worst in the world – *Lo-rena*,' she elongated the name contemptuously from her collagen-filled lips, as though it were poisonous. 'Who the fuck is *Lo-rena*?'

'My darling,' Ramone 'Ramsey' Hassan, Loretta's husband of two months, rolled off his wife's naked body with a sigh. 'You must not upset yourself,' he said softly, patting her hand like a child. 'You have not long recovered from your operation. It is not good to put your body through so much stress, not at your ag –' Loretta shot him a fierce glare and he wisely refrained from finishing the sentence.

'Do you not realise what this means, you stupid man?' she snapped, snatching the offending newspaper up again and waving it in front of her husband's weary face.

'You see how they have positioned us next to the Muldavey story? This is not an accident, no?' her eyes narrowed into menacing slits. 'You must get onto the lawyers as soon as possible! We'll sue their sorry asses to kingdom come!'

Furious, Loretta threw back the fine silk sheets. Swinging her short but slim coffee-coloured legs over the edge, she began to pace the room.

Ramsey, smarting a little from the 'stupid man' comment, watched her stalk the length of the palatial master suite, her delicate feet leaving imprints in the cream Persian rug.

'Come back to bed, Loretta, darling,' Ramsay sighed. He had neither the emotional strength nor the energy to calm her down today, especially after the aggressive sex session they'd just had. He was exhausted.

Though he was at great pains to disguise it from his new wife, Ramsey was feeling the pressure of his impeding trial. The super-injunction he'd managed to take out against the actress speaking out had afforded him a modicum of protection, for now at least, but such tremendous stress was beginning to take its toll on his health. In recent weeks his headaches had reached the point of being unbearable and the heart palpitations he was increasingly experiencing were giving him great cause for concern. He had never felt worse.

Ignoring him, an incensed Loretta, newspaper in hand, flounced out onto the enormous patio. The view was without doubt as arresting as any she'd seen before and for a moment it was all she could focus on.

Villa Adonia was situated on a sequestered and tranquil section of the western tip of the picturesque Greek island of Santorini. Perched on a cliff top with a horseshoe-shaped beach below, private and completely secluded, it enjoyed exceptional 360-degree views of the crystal clear Aegean sea and was by far the most exquisite hideaway on the entire island.

'*Merda, fa caldo*! It's hot!' Loretta purred, allowing her Missoni kaftan to slide from her shoulders to the floor, exposing her naked, olive-skinned flesh. It had to be tipping one hundred degrees at least.

Loretta had turned heads from an early age. She possessed a magnetic beauty; all large brown eyes encased in dark lashes, luscious thick lips that seemed to part naturally in an overtly sexual pout, and an abundance of thick, jet black hair that tumbled down her back in corkscrew curls. But it was Loretta's body that was her greatest asset. When, at the age of fourteen, it met with puberty, she became the talk of Naples.

The young Loretta spent her days behind the meat counter of her father's store, dreaming of escaping the slums of Naples to Hollywood, where she would become a star of the silver screen, just like her idols, Ingrid Bergman, Sophia Loren, and Greta Garbo. After her father was tragically shot dead in a bungled robbery and her mother followed him to the grave less than two years later, there was nothing left to prevent her from pursuing her dreams. Loretta had quickly decided that the fastest, most effective way of getting to the top in Hollywood was to screw her way there, and as a result, it was not long before she got a break starring in a string of low-grade adult movies, ultimately going on to marry the director – a man she neither loved nor particularly liked – at just eighteen years old. Naïvely, Loretta saw her foray into the soft porn industry – and her marriage – as a stepping stone to achieving her lofty ambitions. But the union was a disaster, and just eighteen months later she was left penniless and pregnant. Disillusioned but still determined, Loretta had made the decision to abort her unborn child and vowed never again to fall foul of a man. The next time she married – and she had no doubt there would be a next time – she would make sure it was for the right reasons: money; bags of it.

Although it had been a strategic move on her part, seducing and marrying one of the richest plastic surgeons in Hollywood, Loretta *did* care about Ramsey in her own unique way. He was perfect husband material and she planned to stay with him for as long as it suited her, which she estimated to be somewhere around the five to seven year mark, give or take, figuring this would be long enough to entitle her to a generous slice of his substantial wealth; and possibly the Tuscan house, if the judge was having a good day. Love was not part of Loretta's repertoire. As far as she was concerned, love was a losing game played by fools. And Loretta Fiorentino was *nobody's* fool.

Leaning over the whitewashed wall, she looked out across the perfectly blue Aegean sea, watching as the sunlight glittered and danced across the ocean like God himself had scattered it with diamonds, and wondered if it was champagne o'clock yet. She needed a drink to help compress her thoughts. The paparazzi would be crawling all over them thanks to such a libellous piece of tabloid juxtaposition.

'*Merda*,' Loretta cursed under her breath. When she had called her husband 'stupid' she had meant it. Ramsey had royally fucked up; his would be the most precipitous fall from grace and now it looked as though they would both have to pay the price.

'I did it for you my angel,' he had pleaded when she had demanded to know the truth. 'I know how you've always felt about Miranda Muldavey; how it should have been you who'd had her career, how unfair life has been to you . . . I made sure she'll never set foot in front of a movie camera again.' He had paused, pensive, staring up at her with impassioned dark brown puppy-dog eyes. 'I thought you would be happy . . .'

Ramsey was a great surgeon, perhaps even the greatest of his time, with an unblemished reputation and a fiercely loyal clientele. Yet the afternoon Miranda Muldavey,

13

arguably the most notorious face in Hollywood at the time, had walked into his surgery, Ramsey had seemingly abandoned all his senses and a lifetime of impeccable ethics and, blinded by obsession, committed an unspeakably diabolical act.

It made Loretta shudder to think of what her husband had done. It was true; she *had* always been insanely jealous of Miranda Muldavey and couldn't help but compare herself to the beautiful actress. After all, they were of the same age, background, and they even bore similar physical attributes, yet one had gone on to achieve a level of success that the other could only dream of. Muldavey was famous for playing the romantic lead alongside some of Hollywood's hottest men – she was revered and respected, while Loretta was notorious for her outlandish dress sense and being photographed bending over next to swimming pools – little more than a joke, fodder for third-rate gossip rags. But she had never wished the actress any *real* harm. Maiming her had been entirely Ramsey's own twisted idea.

Loretta lit an L&M and forcefully blew smoke from her glossy pursed lips. Even with the best lawyers her husband's money could buy, things were looking grim. If there was the slightest suggestion that this was something more sinister than simple negligence then it wouldn't just be Ramsey's livelihood and unblemished career on the line; it would be his liberty too.

Loretta looked down at the copy of the *Daily Mail* in her hand and felt her fury re-ignite like embers of a bonfire. If Ramsey lost everything, then what would be left for her when she came to divorce him? After all, everyone knew that half of nothing is nothing. 'Whatever happens, we've still got each other,' her adoring husband had said that morning as he had pumped away on top of her, with his usual lack of finesse.

Sighing heavily, Loretta looked out to sea. What she

needed was a plan; one that would exonerate Ramsey and protect her investment. It struck her that maybe the two nurses who planned to give evidence at the trial could be bought off. After all, everyone had their price, as she herself knew only too well. And if that didn't work then there was always blackmail. As well as a price, everyone had a past and she vowed to start digging into theirs to see if she couldn't locate a few skeletons to use as leverage.

'Dahling,' Loretta strutted from the patio back into the bedroom with a renewed sense of purpose, her mood visibly buoyed. 'Call the butler will you? Have him bring up some more vintage Krug. The '92.'

Ramsey did not answer her.

Glancing over at her husband in bed, his large bulk buried beneath the Versace sheets, Loretta made her way towards the Moroccan-themed en-suite.

'Did you hear me, dahling? I said I want champagne . . . and order some bellinis and beluga while you are at it. I'm a little, how do you say . . . *peckish*?'

Receiving no response, Loretta sighed a little irritably, making her way over to the bed where she gave her husband a less-than-subtle poke. He did not move.

Loretta felt the first icy flutters of fear settle upon her stomach like fresh snow on grass. 'Ramsey dahling, are you ok?'

Peeling back the sheets, she audibly gasped, causing Bambino to give a skittish jump.

'*Cazzo merda*! Fucking shit!' she sprang back from the bed, her heart knocking painfully inside her chest as though it were made of brass. Ramsey's lips were formed in a perfect 'O' shape; his eyes open wide in a ghoulish mask of surprise and despair. Paralysed to the spot, her heartbeat pulsing loudly in her ears, Loretta glanced at the telephone on the bedside table. With a shaking hand she went to pick it up but changed her mind, instead tentatively pressing a red manicured finger against her husband's neck to check for a pulse. His skin still felt warm to the touch and although overcome with revulsion, she held it there for a few moments. Detecting nothing, she took his wrist between her thumb and forefinger; again, nothing.

He was dead.

Jesus. The poor bastard must've gone and had a heart attack. Lightheaded with adrenaline, Loretta looked down at her dead husband with a mix of shock, repulsion and pity. And then it struck her with all the force of a swinging axe; the trial! Even she knew that a dead man cannot be tried. And no trial meant no compensation to be paid, or no list to be struck off, or no reputation to be sullied. It also meant that as his wife, his next of kin, she stood to get the lot; the houses across the world stuffed with priceless furniture and antiques, fleets of luxury cars, a private jet, and enough diamonds to put Switzerland out of business . . . It would all be hers.

Snatching up Bambino from the bed with a squeal, Loretta dramatically threw herself down onto her husband's lifeless body.

'Oh my poor dahling,' she said, covering Ramsey's rapidly paling face in scattergun kisses as tears began to track her cheeks. She had been wrong to call him stupid earlier. The man was a fucking genius. In that moment, Loretta truly loved her husband for the first, and last, time. 'Grazie tesoro bambino,' she sobbed, as she finally reached for the phone. '*Grazie . . .*'

CHAPTER 3

Victoria Mayfield stared at her computer screen; it was as blank as her mind. She had been sitting at her antique shabby-chic Parisian desk inside her study for just over an hour now, her fingers hovering precariously above the keyboard.

She looked up to the ceiling, ran her hands through the top of her glossy chestnut hair and took an audible breath. Her agent would be expecting the first few chapters of her much-anticipated new novel by next week and she had not written so much as a line.

Following the success of her debut novel, *Mirror, Mirror* some ten years ago, and the equally lauded sequel, *Broken Glass*, the name Victoria Mayfield had become synonymous with young, hopeful and desperately romantic women the world over – and it had made her ridiculously rich and famous in the process. Such accolades meant nothing to Victoria now though. She would have traded it all in a nano-second to have her life back to how it had been a couple of years ago when CeCe was alive.

Abandoning her laptop, Victoria left the room and wandered out onto the landing of her four-storey Notting Hill mews house and found herself hovering outside CeCe's

17

bedroom, staring at the brightly coloured wooden letters that spelled out her daughter's name: CECELIA.

Stealthily looking around as though someone were watching her, Victoria pushed open the white door and tentatively stepped inside. Her therapist had advised against spending time in the nursery, had even suggested that she might clear it out and re-decorate as 'part of the healing process' but she would not hear a word of it; these small things, they were all she had left.

Victoria inhaled the clean, baby-like scent of the room. Staring at the assortment of soft toys, she picked up CeCe's favourite rabbit, clutching it to her chest. On the wall to her left, white wooden photo frames containing professional black and white shots of her daughter, her bright-eyed, tiny chubby face all gummy smiles, hung from the picture rail by pink silk ribbon.

'Hello sweetheart,' she spoke softly. She ran her finger over one of the pictures, stroking her daughter's tiny face through the glass. She moved towards the beautiful antique white sleigh crib that CeCe had once slept in and smoothed over the soft patchwork quilt that she'd had made by French artisans in Paris and for a split second she felt as if everything was normal; a mother preparing her child's bed for her mid-morning nap. The painfully fleeting feeling gave her such an intense rush of pleasure that she almost gasped out loud.

Picking up a blanket, a brightly coloured cashmere affair by Brora, Victoria held it up to her face and inhaled deeply. She was sure she could still smell the newness of her daughter on it and an involuntary cry of anguish rose up in her throat and escaped her lips in a low moan.

'Why, God?' She shook her fist up at the ceiling, choking back sobs. 'Why did you take her?'

Victoria Mayfield was the kind of woman who had it all; good looks, talent and intelligence. A loving daughter, a giving friend and a loyal wife, she had always been aware of her privileged background (Daddy was a hedge-fund manager and Mummy, a well-respected stage actress), and had never taken any of it for granted. It wasn't in her nature to be ostentatious. Daddy had said she was just like his own mother, Cecelia, a woman she had never met but sensed had had kindness running through her very core.

Victoria Sheldon (as she had been before marriage) had seemingly inherited all the good of her grandmother, as well as the aesthetically pleasing Sheldon genes. Hers was a natural beauty. Her face, perfectly symmetrical, was a compilation of both her stunningly attractive parents; she had her father's intense, deep green eyes and large red lips, and thanks to her mother she had also inherited a mane of thick, glossy, chestnut hair – which she had only recently, at the age of thirty-seven, felt the need to maintain with a few highlights – and a small upturned nose that sat in perfect proportion to the rest of her slim, oval face.

Her eleven-year marriage to Lawrence Mayfield, a handsome, talented film director, had been, by and large, a blissfully happy one. Perfectly matched, they complimented one another perfectly; his natural vivacity offset by her quiet charm.

On the surface, to an outsider who happened to be looking in, Lawrence and Victoria Mayfield had the lot; an enviable marriage, success and acclaim in both their chosen professions, plus a personal fortune that ensured they had the very best of everything. There was just one blot on their sublime landscape: they could not conceive.

'Give it time,' others said when month after month, Victoria's unwelcome period had arrived with all the regularity of a baddie in a fairy tale. Five years down the line however, with numerous failed IVF attempts behind them, it transpired that they had what a glut of specialist doctors referred to as, 'Unexplained Infertility'. Devastated that they might not ever be able to consolidate their love for each other with a child of their own, they had made the painful decision to stop with the treatment and let fate dictate. And so it had. Less than a year later, Victoria had found herself expecting.

Victoria sat down in the large comfortable nursing chair, a chair she had sat in to cradle her daughter's tiny body as she fed her, and looked down at the small, soft rabbit she held in her hand, its beady black eyes shining up at her. Every cell in her body wanted to scream with anguish. It was all so cruel and unjust. There was a world of unwanted and unloved children out there, neglected and abused by their parents, and yet God had not seen fit to take *their* children from *them*, had he? Deep down in Victoria's shattered heart, she knew that God had had nothing to do with CeCe's death; she just needed *someone* to blame, and He seemed as good as anyone.

It had been uncommonly cold that night of the 16th July. Victoria remembered this because she had felt the need to wear a pair of light cashmere pyjamas to bed – unusual for the time of year.

After giving five-month old CeCe her bedtime feed and placing her down into the beautiful crib, she had watched her tiny daughter kick her chubby baby legs and coo, happily fixated on the mobile of bees and butterflies that gently danced above her, lulling her to sleep. Victoria had felt an overwhelming rush of love for her daughter as she watched her drift off in her crib. She was so adorable! Her saucer eyes were sapphire blue and twinkly, fine platinum curls settled at the nape of her sweet-smelling neck and her rosebud lips were as pink as the flowers themselves. CeCe was her greatest achievement; a baby made all the more precious by coming into the world against the odds.

Lawrence had been in Guatemala the night of the 16th July. He had been filming a documentary on drug mules, a somewhat dangerous assignment, and one that had caused Victoria some consternation at the time. Still, she had slept soundly that evening, a fact she felt guilty about to this day.

CeCe looked peaceful when Victoria had approached her in her crib the following morning. She had slept seemingly soundly and Victoria marvelled at what a clever little girl her daughter was; she had never suffered the torture of sleep deprivation like so many of her fellow new mothers who bitterly complained, bleary-eyed and tetchy, over strong cups of espresso at NCT classes. It was only when she got closer to the crib that Victoria realised that something was wrong. *Terribly wrong.*

CeCe's perfect face was tinged blue and when Victoria snatched her up from the crib her body felt cold and rigid. The logical part of her brain immediately told her that her daughter was dead but her heart steadfastly refused to concede this fact, even for a second. And so she had run, clutching the child still wrapped in her soft cashmere blanket, down the stairs, her hysterical, bloodcurdling screams so desperate and piercing that they alerted her housekeeper way down in the basement of the house almost instantly.

'Oh please, God,' she had screamed. 'No . . . *nooooo.*'

Marney O'Brien would never forget the look of pure despair etched on her employer's face that morning. Her low primeval screams would haunt her till her death.

*

From that day onwards, inside her own mind Victoria Mayfield had never really stopped screaming. Even Lawrence struggled to reach her. Though Victoria still loved her husband, their union was now forever blighted, defined by heartache and loss. This feeling was exacerbated by the fact

21

that the doctors had said they were 'unlikely, if ever' to conceive again. As if fate hadn't bestowed them a cruel enough blow, Lawrence had suffered a crippling bout of mumps in the year that had followed little CeCe's death, rendering his already dwindling sperm count virtually non-existent.

'Perhaps you might consider adoption?' the US specialist had gently suggested, his five-thousand-dollar-a-pop fee affording them the soft touch at least. It was an option Victoria had flatly ruled out. She had felt the feet and elbows of flesh and blood inside her belly; her creation, *their* creation, and knew there could be no substitute.

Two years had passed since CeCe's death, and with still no baby, Victoria was getting desperate. She couldn't afford to wait five years like she had done before; she wasn't getting any younger. As far as she was concerned, a life without children would be no life at all.

From the comfortable confines of CeCe's nursing chair, Victoria was dragged from her thoughts by the sound of her private phone ringing in her bedroom next door. She heard the incongruous sound of her own cheerful voice as the recorded message kicked in.

'Tor! Hi! It's Ellie. Fancy a little lunch this week, if you're around? I was thinking Nobo perhaps? Or The Belvedere? Your call . . . I don't know about you but I could do with the company – and a glass of something alcoholic! Actually, sod it, make it a bottle with the week I've had . . .' Ellie laughed, though Victoria's intuition detected an edge to her friend's tone. 'Anyway, if you're about, give me a shout. Otherwise, catch up soon. Hope all's well, darling. Call me . . .'

Victoria's friendship with Ellie Scott was the best thing, the *only* good thing that had come out of all the wasted time they had spent at the fertility clinic. It had

22

been comforting to meet like-minded people who understood the emotional ups and downs of endless fruitless IVF cycles and heartbreak, and through it the Mayfields and the Scotts had forged a strong bond.

Victoria made to pick up the phone but hesitated as the image of her daughter's coffin bubbled up in her mind; a beautiful white solid oak casket adorned with a stunning array of pink flowers that spelled out the word 'Angel'. It had looked so small as it disappeared through the burgundy velvet curtain of the crematorium that she had wanted to run after it, to rescue her daughter's tiny body before she turned to dust, to hold her hand, be with her, like a mother should be. She had become hysterical at that point and a doctor had been called to give her a shot of something that had made her sleep, a sleep in which she prayed to a God she despised that she might never wake from.

Victoria abruptly stood. Kissing the rabbit on its soft fluffy face, she replaced it carefully onto the shelf and left the room, taking one sorrowful last look around before closing the door behind her.

Making her way into the vast walk-in wardrobe in her bedroom, she drew back the bespoke sliding doors and began to pull various dresses from their padded hangers, only to instantly discard them in a pile behind her.

Getting pregnant was no longer merely something she hoped for, but a base need within her that had to be filled, as essential as the very oxygen she breathed. Picking up the pile of dresses and throwing them onto the bed, Victoria knew what she had to do. She could no longer wait for fate to chance its arm any more than she could face another year of bitter childless disappointment. She could almost feel her eggs drying up with each second that passed, her empty womb growing less and less accommodating by the

23

day. With all options exhausted, she had made the decision to take matters into her own hands. She *would* be pregnant by the end of the year and if the doctors and her husband couldn't help her, well, then she would have no choice but to help herself.

CHAPTER 4

Driving through Sunset Strip in a shiny black Lamborghini Gallardo, Tom Black had the countenance of a man who'd lost a cent and found a dollar. It was a beautiful day; the sun shone high in a cloudless late May sky and the sidewalk was teeming with hot women, all dressed appropriately for the biting heat in Daisy Dukes and cute summer dresses that barely covered their tight little asses. It gave him a tangible buzz as they all looked up as he roared past, sound system up, soft top down, the Black Eyed Peas blasting out of the Bang & Olufsen stereo. Fuck, man, this was why he loved LA. The broad streets lined with palm trees, the cool bars and eternal sunshine where women strutted their stuff; fake tits and bikinis by the truckload. No one looked old here. It was like Peter fucking Pan's playground and it was one of the main reasons he had decided to call it home. In reality however, LA couldn't have been much more of a departure from the rough East London streets Tom had started out on. Back then, 'home' had been wherever his womanising drunk of a father's heart – or dick – had been. Invariably this meant temporary accommodation at one of his many 'auntie's' houses, as they were always referred to. Tom struggled to remember any of them; one was much like the other, a hazy blur of blonde hair, raucous laughter and lipstick. Until Charlene O'Connor that is. The O'Connors had changed everything . . .

The Lamborghini purred loudly as Tom pulled up at a set of lights and he smiled as a particularly arresting blonde with enormous shop-bought tits teetered along the crossing, her denim mini skirt leaving little to the imagination. He revved the engine almost subconsciously as she strutted past and looked up, flashing him a megawatt white smile in recognition of his appreciation.

'Cool whip, dude,' she said in a high-pitched Californian drawl, eyeing the Lamborghini with approval. She couldn't have been much older than twenty-three and Tom could tell from the glint in her violet blue eyes that she was just his type: up for anything. He rested his elbow on the side of the car, peering at her eagerly from beneath his mirrored Ray-Bans, giving her a peek at his arresting dark brown eyes. She was sure she had seen this dude somewhere before, in one of the magazines she'd read during one of her more prolonged stays in hospital, or on TV perhaps? She looked him over with caution, though this was largely for effect. The car alone was worth more than her apartment and yearly salary combined.

The car, however, didn't actually belong to Tom. It was on loan from a gambling pal he played poker with and he was damned sure he was going to make the most of it.

'Wanna see what she can do?'

'Sure,' said the blonde after the briefest hesitation, 'why not?'

Tom grinned as he leaned over to open the passenger door, moving the Louis Vuitton holdall to one side. Just as he'd thought; up for anything.

'What's in the bag?' she enquired, curious as she

effortlessly slid into the passenger seat, her mini skirt riding high up her lean, tanned thighs.

'Ask no questions, and I'll tell you no lies,' he replied, raising a provocative eyebrow as the lights turned to green and they roared off along the boulevard, the G-force of the powerful engine pulling her back into the cream leather seat. She squealed with delight. His accent told her he was British. And already she could tell this was going to be one hell of a ride.

'Hey bud, your phone's ringing.' He saw the girl's lips move as her platinum-blonde hair whipped about her face, sticking to her fruity lip gloss, but he hadn't heard a word above Kanye West and the loud hum of the Lamborghini's powerful engine. 'Your phone,' she mouthed in an exaggerated gesture, pointing to his Blackberry Bold which was buzzing angrily on the smart leather dashboard.

'Well, answer it then,' Tom replied, turning the stereo down a couple of notches. She shot him a quizzical look, but did as she was told.

'Hi!' she giggled into the receiver breathlessly.

'Yeah, er . . . hello . . . who is this? Can I speak to Tom?'

'Sure, I'll just put him on,' the girl purred in her best telephone voice. 'Hey bud,' she held out his cell. 'Like, I think it *might* be for you.'

Tom laughed. He liked her. She had a sense of humour. Rarer than rocking-horse shit in LA.

'Tom Black,' he pressed the loudspeaker button, careful to keep his hands on the wheel of the ridiculously expensive car that he didn't own.

'Don't tell me,' the voice said, deadpan, 'you got yourself *another* new PA?'

'I found her on the sidewalk,' Tom winked playfully at the girl and she collapsed into more giggles. She sensed they were gonna have some fun together. And having just been

27

sacked from yet another dead-end waitressing job, fun was *just* what she was looking for.

'Yeah? Guess it's her lucky day,' the deadpan voice retorted, breaking into a violent coughing fit. It was Jack, Tom's oldest friend and business partner.

'Jesus my friend, you sound like shit.'

'Have you taken that dough to the bank yet?' Jack immediately shot back, letting Tom instantly know that this wasn't going to be a friendly, chew-the-fat kind of conversation. 'I want that money safe, Tom. We need to make sure we got our shit in order if we're gonna win that goddamn auction . . .'

'Auction?'

'Christ Tom, *I told you*, don't you listen to a goddamn word I say?' The irritation in his voice was clearly audible now, 'that fucker Constantini is refusing to do a deal so we're gonna have to take it to bids like everyone else, so unless we've got the cold hard cash we can forget about it. The dream will be over before it's even begun.' Jack was already beginning to regret entrusting Tom with such a large sum of money. He'd been laid up in bed for five days with some evil Asian flu bug thing and had become seriously twitchy about having that much green lying around in his apartment, which was why he'd instructed his oldest friend to do him a favour and take it straight to the bank that morning, all three million dollars of it.

'Whatever the fuck you do, Tom,' a red-eyed Jack had said with real gravitas, handing his friend the heavy Louis Vuitton holdall, 'don't lose it; everything I got is in that bag. So I want you to go straight to the bank, *OK*? No diversions, no detour via a casino . . . you got me?'

'I'm on my way boss,' Tom replied with such jovial nonchalance that it had caused Jack to see red, prompting a further, more violent coughing fit this time.

'I'm fucking serious, Tom!' he struggled to breathe. 'If anything should happen to it . . .'

'I'm almost at the bank right now,' Tom replied breezily. He put his foot down harder on the accelerator and the girl squealed again. He imagined she was probably a screamer in the sack too. He looked forward to finding out.

'Yeah, well hear me loud and clear, bro,' Jack's hacking cough sounded like machine gunfire, 'I need to know all's cool your end of the deal, that you'll bank the cash and get your share of the green – we fly out to London in three weeks.'

Tom and Jack had been in the 'entertainment' business for the past fifteen years, with varying degrees of success. The story was usually the same; Jack would initially stump up the cash, generally prised from his exasperated but wealthy father, and together they would attempt to turn some rundown old gin joint on the wrong side of town into a hot, happening new hang-out for the young, beautiful and rich. And sometimes it had even worked; at least until either Jack lost interest or Tom gambled away the profits, both of which had been the case on more than one occasion. Now, however, it was time to get serious. This latest acquisition was to be their defining moment, a transitional leap from small fry to legitimate players, and having exhausted New York, Vegas and LA, from a business perspective at least, it was time to cast the net a little wider.

'Jeez man, I thought you'd be pleased,' Jack had responded to the lukewarm reception Tom had given him upon informing him about the 'near-as-damnit perfect' venue he'd found for them in the heart of London's West End. With a dense population of young, affluent, and fashion-conscious prospective clientele, it seemed like an appealing prospect, especially for the particular concept they had in mind – a hybrid mix of a lavish premier super club and casino, combined with fine dining and themed table dancing. 'London is the epicentre of cool right now, man. It's hot to trot.' Jack had insisted.

Tom had reluctantly acquiesced. London was his birthplace but it had long ago ceased to be his home. Besides, the city held bittersweet memories for him and he had made a promise never to return again. But then, Tom had never been much good at keeping promises . . .

Now all that was standing in the way of their dream was the auction for the rundown but ultimately perfect old warehouse in Soho; that, and the small matter of six million dollars, three of which were sitting in a Louis Vuitton case in the back seat of the Lamborghini.

'No stress, bud,' Tom smiled. 'I got everything in hand on that front.'

There was a pause on the line as Jack digested this information, his chest wheezing like an old boiler on its last knockings. If this deal came off they'd make their money back ten-fold within twelve months. But they were still a little shy of three mill of the recommended auction price, which was where Tom came into the equation. Jack was relying on him to make up the shortfall, which was a little like relying on a politician to come good on his promises; hit and miss.

'You're telling me you already got your hand on three big ones? And you didn't care to mention that small fact to me this morning?'

The girl's ears pricked up. *Three million bucks*! *Jeez*!

'Just trust me, OK?' Tom winked at his passenger and she grinned in return, uncrossing her long, slim legs in a consciously provocative move.

'Yeah right! Look what happened the last time I did that?'

Jack Goldstein was the closest thing Tom Black had left to family. They had been friends since his early Vegas days, bonding instantly by their shared interests of making money and chasing pussy. Ultimately though, ups and downs aside, theirs was a friendship that had been built on the essential elements of trust and respect, and as a result, it had stood the test of time.

'Well then, just chill out. We'll go to the auction; we'll get our casino. We'll make our millions. Simple.'

Jack sighed. Tom was being evasive.

'I'm serious, Tom,' he said earnestly, between short, violent bursts of deep chesty coughs that made him sound like a sea-lion attempting to mate. 'I don't plan to return back to the States without that venue.'

'Jesus Jack, stop breaking my balls will you?' Tom suddenly snapped, causing the girl to look over at him. 'I'm pulling up outside the bank right now . . . and we're gonna get our casino, OK?'

Jack was unfazed by his friend's sharp outburst. He'd heard it all a million times over.

'We've got a couple of weeks' grace to get our shit sorted then it's all systems go,' he said, pausing to sneeze three times in succession.

'Jeez bud, you need to get yourself to a doctor.'

'Get that bread banked and I won't need to,' he snapped back, although he knew he was right; Jack couldn't remember a time when he'd felt this goddamn awful and it was worrying him. But he hated quacks. Quacks were wack as far as he was concerned – messengers of doom. His late grandfather had been the same. First doctor he ever saw in almost seven decades told him he had less than six weeks left. Jeez. You were better off not knowing that kind of shit. 'And don't let me down, Tom,' he added seriously, 'I'm counting on you. Three million and counting . . .' Jack said flatly, blowing his nose loudly before hanging up.

Turning his attentions briefly back to his passenger, momentarily distracted by her perfect form and abundant peroxide hair that couldn't possibly be all her own, Tom's mind began to click into overdrive as his forced smile faded faster than a fake clairvoyant's apparition. Truth was, Jack had every reason to worry. There *was* no cash; Tom owned the princely sum of nothing. Somehow, he needed to find a shortfall of at least three million bucks in less than seven days if he wasn't about to renege on his word and lose face.

A thought bubble appeared above Tom's head and he grinned at his passenger again. He was under no illusion that to make that kind of money in such a short period of time he would need a spectacular show of luck . . .

'You doing much this weekend . . . ?' he made to address the blonde, realising he didn't even know her name.

'. . . Candy,' she prompted, returning his grin with a broad smile of her own, showcasing her ice-white veneers, *de rigueur* in Beverly Hills.

'Of course,' he gave a knowing nod. What *else* would she be called?

'And yeah, I was kinda planning to hook up with some girlfriends, you know, hit the bars, a few jello shots . . .' she'd added, not wanting to make it sound as if she was too available.

'Well, *Candy*,' Tom said, turning to her earnestly and fixing her with an intent gaze that immediately held her intrigue, 'cancel your plans.' He had a sixth sense about this one; she had fortune on her side, he was convinced of it.

'And why would I wanna do that?' She cocked her head to one side, her fake eyelashes sweeping her cheeks as she blinked rapidly at him.

'Because we're going to Vegas, baby!' he announced with a little whistle, the tyres of the Lamborghini screaming in objection as he accelerated around a corner.

After all, what did he have to lose?

CHAPTER 5

Ellie was finding it difficult to concentrate as her driver, Wesley, weaved through the Notting Hill traffic in her carbon-black Aston Martin V12 Vantage. She couldn't get the earlier conversation she'd had with her wayward daughter out of her head.

'Jesus, Mum, chill out already. I'm not a child anymore. I'm *eighteen*!' Tess Scott had stood before Ellie with a defiant hand on her skinny jean-clad hip, rolling her eyes at her mother in over-exaggerated exasperation. 'I'm pretty sure Allegra's mum isn't giving her the whole "make sure you use a condom" routine and banging on about ecstasy pills! It's all so . . . *embarrassing*.'

'Maybe that's because Allegra's mother doesn't give a toss, Tess,' Ellie had sharply replied. 'I happen to care about what *my* daughter gets up to. I've *been* to Ibiza, remember . . .'

Tess rolled her eyes. Yeah, and no doubt her mother had sampled *all* that was on offer while she was there too. She was such a goddamn hypocrite sometimes it was unreal.

Ellie hadn't wanted to fall out with Tess just before she left to catch a plane but her feisty daughter seemed to have a knack of rubbing her up the wrong way. 'I'm only looking out for you,' she'd said, her tone softening. 'You'll feel the same when you have your own kids one day.' She had reached out and touched the tip of her daughter's nose with an affectionate finger. 'It's just that you're young and beautiful . . . I know what all the men out there will be after and I want you to be careful . . .'

Tess had thrown her limited-edition Mulberry Alexa onto the chrome and leather bar stool of their pristine designer kitchen with a loud exhalation. Frankly, she bloody well *hoped* that's what they were after. It was partly the reason she was going, after all.

'If I'm so beautiful, how come you're so against me testing for that model agency I told you about?' Tess had folded her arms and fixed her mother with a defiant stare.

'Oh Tess, not this again, please,' it had been Ellie's turn to roll her eyes. 'I've *told* you. That agency supplies glamour models and no daughter of mine is going to splash her half-naked body on billboards all over London. Not while she's living under my roof. Can you imagine what your father would say?' Ellie shook her head, dismissing the idea. 'Once you've got a degree behind you, well, I can't stop you if you want to pursue a career in modelling. But please, Tess, get your education first,' she'd pleaded. 'You've got a brain in that head of yours. I wish you would use it sometimes.'

Ellie stared out of the window as they turned out of Holland Park onto Abbotsbury Road where they immediately hit a slew of rush hour traffic and pulled her iPhone from her Miu Miu clutch.

Hey darling ☺ Hope you've landed safely. Watch out for snakes in your boot!

She smiled as she sent the text. Tess would know what she meant. The *Toy Story* catchphrase was a code word they used when asking the other to tread carefully.

'Shit.' Ellie looked down at her platinum and diamond

Chanel bracelet watch in irritation. She would be late to meet Vinnie now.

'Wesley, would you mind turning the air con up?' she asked politely. All this business with Tess had left her feeling hot and bothered.

Tess was a bright girl. Smart. She'd been described by the principal of her ridiculously expensive private school as 'a naturally high achiever', though she'd also added 'diva' and 'troublemaker' to that list too. Ellie knew her daughter had a bit of a wild reputation; she had seen how she acted up around her friends. Tess loved being the centre of attention, especially where the opposite sex was concerned. It worried Ellie that her daughter seemed naturally drawn towards drama and chaos, something she herself understood only too well. Men had always found the O'Connor women alluring and she knew that such a disposition invariably had the potential to bring trouble. Tess seemed to feed off male attention, soak it up like a sponge.

Ellie knew her daughter was no virgin but she didn't like the idea of her being easy pickings either. Tess was more vulnerable than she thought she was; and certain men could smell vulnerability like a shark senses blood. Not that it was entirely Tess's fault; she was the classic only child of exceedingly wealthy parents. Always the centre of attention, she had been sheltered from any kind of negative influence her entire life; beautiful, adored and spoilt rotten, that was Tess Scott. It was a bitter regret of Ellie's that she had been unable to give her only daughter a brother or sister. More than anything, Ellie had hoped to give her husband another child. It was the least she could do after everything he had given her. But life had denied them, and Ellie secretly wondered if it had seen fit to punish them both for her sins. Sins that she and Vinnie never spoke of . . .

Ellie's early life had been the antithesis of her daughter's; all Tess had known was extreme wealth and the protective

36

blanket that it afforded. She had had the very best of everything money could buy, and yet in an odd twist of fate, it wasn't *in spite* of her mother's impoverished provenance that she had all these things; it was *because* of it.

Ellie thought of her own mother and felt a terrible pang of sadness resound inside her chest. Charlene O'Connor had been beautiful once, with peroxide-blonde hair and emerald green eyes that sparkled when she smiled. Her aesthetically pleasing appearance was her greatest asset, and with bills to pay and mouths to feed she had put it to good use as an 'exotic' dancer in an East End gentleman's club. Though frankly, that was a misnomer if ever there was one. 'Never once seen a gentleman walk through those doors in all the years I've worked here!' she would joke. Ellie could still remember it now. The low, amber lighting inside that dingy club; the omnipresent smell of cigarettes and cheap perfume in the air. It had been Charlene's intention to make enough money to put her talented daughter through ballet school, give her the chances she'd never had to make something of herself. Her mother had always been so proud of her. 'You were pirouetting before you learned to walk!' she would say. 'I knew the moment you were born that you had a special gift.' It still pained Ellie to this day to know that she had ended up following in her mother's footsteps into the clubs and dive bars of Las Vegas. Sure, she had become a dancer alright, only it wasn't quite the kind her mother had hoped for. *Nothing like keeping it in the family, eh Mom?*

Ellie never knew her father and wondered if he was even aware of her existence. But Charlene had always had enough love to compensate for his absence; she had been an attentive mother once, caring and protective – and she had worked hard to pay to put her talented daughter through ballet school. And then she had met Ray Black, and everything changed. From the moment Ray Black had set foot inside 'Dirty Harry's' spit 'n' sawdust club, all shiny flash suit and wide grin, Charlene O'Connor had been completely bowled over by his good looks and charm. It had raised more than a few eyebrows when she had agreed to up sticks and accompany the handsome stranger on his quest for the big time in Las Vegas with the young Ellie in tow. It was only a pity Ray had failed to mention his burgeoning gambling and alcohol addictions *before* they'd boarded the flight. And so Vegas had not quite turned out to be the fresh start Charlene O'Connor had hoped for. She soon found herself stuck in a cramped prefab on the wrong side of the Strip, working the dive bars, only for Ray to drink and gamble away her earnings. Life was no different from how it had been in London; in fact it was worse. And then of course there was Ray's son, Ellie's new surrogate step-brother. His name was Tom. Tom Black.

*

With the traffic finally dispersing, Ellie looked down at her YSL python hobo bag on the passenger seat and chewed her glossy lip tremulously. Unzipping the inside pocket, she glanced at the small newspaper cutting she had kept of Loretta and her surgeon husband, with mixed emotions. She was still debating whether or not to show Vin. She knew it would only resurrect terrible memories for both of them and she had no desire to spoil the evening they had planned. But she didn't like to keep secrets from her husband. All those years ago, she had made a promise she intended to keep; one where she swore she would always tell the truth, no matter what. She owed him that much. Truth was, she owed him everything.

Pulling up outside the Michelin-starred L'Atelier de Joel Robuchon restaurant in Covent Garden, Wesley switched off the engine.

'Mrs Scott,' he gave an impeccably gracious nod as he opened the car door.

Ellie momentarily stared at the grainy image of Loretta Fiorentino – a woman who had inadvertently changed the course of her life – before screwing it up into a tiny ball and dropping it into the gutter as she stepped from the Bentley.

As far as she was concerned, it was the best place for it.

CHAPTER 6

Ibiza. A hedonist's paradise; a twenty-four-seven party island where the young and beautiful flocked in search of sex, drugs and debauchery. The kind of decadent place where anything went. The kind of place Tess Scott had been looking for.

Tess grinned enthusiastically as she looked out into the busy crowd of party-goers; topless girls parading around in outrageous costumes that barely covered their modesty, half-naked bodies drenched in sweat writhing up against each other, painted faces gurning in time to the relentless beat . . .

'Makes Boujis look like Sunday school,' she remarked to Allegra, as a dancer wearing gold pasties on her nipples and an enormous feathered headdress shimmied past. Allegra raised an eyebrow and they both collapsed into a fit of giggles. Tess had heard that some pretty risqué stuff went down in Ibiza; live sex shows, boat parties that turned into all-night debauched drug orgies, and frankly she couldn't wait to discover whether the rumours were true. She was so over the whole London Sloane scene; there *had* to be more to life than getting trashed on Treasure Chests in Mahiki on a Friday night. Besides, right now, the further she was away from London the better. Her parents were practically suffocating her, trying to run, and ultimately ruin, her life by insisting she finish her A-Levels before going off to university, Oxford ideally. Just the thought of it bummed her out big time. Fact was, she had absolutely no intention whatsoever of attending university, Oxford or otherwise. After all, her family were loaded, like, *seriously stacked*. It wasn't as if she *needed* to work, at least, not right now. Right now, she just wanted to have fun while she was young and free of responsibilities. Ultimately she would eventually settle down and marry someone rich or famous anyway. Then she'd knock out a couple of sprogs and no doubt end up having to sacrifice whatever career she'd carved out for herself, rendering all those years of studying a complete and utter waste of time and effort. That's not to say that she lacked ambition; quite the contrary, just not the kind her parents approved of. Being famous; that's what Tess Scott aspired to. She was already fairly illustrious among the cliquey West London party set as it was, but now she wanted to cast the net a little wider, and the idea of having her every move documented by the likes of *Heat* and *HELLO!* magazine was the pinnacle of such aspirations.

'Come on, babes,' Tess grabbed Allegra's arm, forcibly pulling her in the direction of the stage, where two go-go dancers were spinning tricks on the poles. 'Let's show these amateur bitches how it's *really* done.'

The MTV party was in full swing now, sweat-drenched bodies bouncing and moving in unison as if they all shared the same heartbeat. Tess, looking every inch the rich, beautiful socialite that she was, jumped up onto the stage and started writhing provocatively around the pole to a pumping Rhianna and Drake remix. As she wrapped herself around the pole, indulging the rampant exhibitionist within her, she felt an intense pair of eyes upon her and was pleased to note that they belonged to an attractive looking dark-haired dude, standing left of the stage, sipping champagne. Conscious of his lingering eyes burning holes in her skin, she ramped up the raunch factor another notch, furiously snaking and gyrating her hips, shaking her tight little booty in an over-exaggerated manner that wouldn't have looked out of place in a particularly salacious gangsta rapper's promo.

Like what you see, huh babes? Well, get a load of this!

'Shit, girl,' Allegra said, wide-eyed, as Tess, pumped up on adrenaline, jumped off the stage, her curtain of lustrous honey-blonde hair swishing behind her. 'When did *you* learn to pole dance?'

'There's *a lot* you don't know about me, babes,' Tess shot back cryptically.

'Another mojito?' Allegra shook her glass.

'You really need to ask?'

Making her way to the bar, Allegra Kennedy-Ling attempted to suppress a slight pang of jealousy. Tess Scott was her best friend; she had known her since junior school and they had practically grown up together, but she was also an insufferable show-off, made worse by the fact that whatever she seemed to put her mind to she excelled at. Tess's recent appearance in *Tatler* magazine had launched her already sizeable ego into a whole new stratosphere and had seen her swanning around London as if she were the Next Big Thing.

'How come *she* gets her mugshot in Tats?' Calista Clinton, a mutual 'friend' had remarked sourly, poring over Tess's pictorial debut in the fashionable society glossy one afternoon over a skinny soya latte in Shoreditch House.

'She probably blew the photographer,' Poppy Fox had chipped in, somewhat uncharitably, given her own dubious reputation.

'Who *hasn't* she blown?' Calista rolled her eyes, dunking her biscotti in her froth and simulating a blow job with it.

They had all collapsed into fits of giggles, Allegra included, if a little sheepishly.

'Pretty impressive stuff,' the dark-haired guy approached Tess with a raised eyebrow and a smile, handing her a glass of champagne, which she took with a breathtaking sense of entitlement. She raised her glass, automatically slipping into flirt mode. The dude was older, but he was still pretty hot.

'Where'd you learn to dance like that?' he fixed her eyes with his own just long enough to build a flicker of tension between them.

Tess gave a nonchalant shrug. 'It's in the genes.'

She was pleased with this response; she thought it made her sound sexy and mysterious.

The stranger held his hand out. 'Marco. Marco DiMari.'

'Tess.' She shook it vigorously. Daddy had once told her that a person's handshake was indicative of their personality; Marco's was hard and fast – promising. On closer inspection he didn't disappoint either, even if Tess did suspect that he was the wrong side of thirty. Tall and dark, he had a well-defined jawline complete with designer five o'clock shadow and an ice-white smile that appeared almost luminous under the fluorescent lighting of the club. The shirt was expensive, *definitely* Prada, and the cufflinks real diamond. She had seen enough up close in her life to be able to tell the difference.

'So, you're Italian?'

'*Si*,' he grinned. 'You like Italian men?'

'I haven't made up my mind yet,' she replied, tartly.

Marco smirked.

'You here with someone?'

'A friend,' Tess drained the champagne glass and handed it back to him.

'A *boy*friend?'

'A *girl* friend, actually,' she nodded in the direction of

43

Allegra, who was making her way back towards them from the bar, fresh mojitos held like trophies in the air as she weaved through the bobbing masses, trying not to spill any of the precious liquid.

Marco surreptitiously surveyed his prey, enjoying the electricity that crackled and fizzed between them.

'You and your girlfriend fancy coming to a pool party later? Me and some friends have got a villa just up near San Lorenzo.'

Tess nodded as if she knew where he was talking about, though really she didn't have a clue.

'Where are you girls staying?'

'At the Ushuaia Beach Club,' she replied coolly, adding for good measure, 'the Presidential Suite.'

He looked impressed, just as she had anticipated.

'So, how about it then, Tess?' Marco said, eyeing her miniscule Pucci bikini top with expertly hidden lasciviousness. She had the most amazing set of tits he'd ever seen. Everything about her reeked of wealth; the glossy hair, the natural tan, the designer ensemble and expensive jewellery . . . he'd struck gold.

'Here's my number,' Marco said, placing something in her hand with a sly wink. 'Call me. We'll have a car come pick you up.' Tess gave a nonchalant nod, though privately she was ecstatic. There was something irresistible about the sexy-looking Italian, an air of danger that instantly intrigued her.

Having successfully navigated the crowds, Allegra approached, handing Tess a Mojito as she eyed the stranger a little cautiously.

'We'll see,' Tess smiled coquettishly, lowering her eyes at him. She had every intention of calling him and suspected he knew as much.

'Ladies,' Marco dipped his head before disappearing back into the buzzing throng.

44

'Who was *that*?' Allegra asked.

'Marco . . . Marco DiMari,' Tess said looking down at his glossy, black and gold embossed business card. 'Director of Photography by all accounts . . . Picasso Films.' It was then that she noticed the little wrap of white paper behind it and felt a frisson of excitement ripple the length of her body. *Was that what she thought it was*?

'He's invited us to a pool party later,' she added, quickly closing her hand lest Allegra see what was in it. A party girl she might be, but Tess had never been into drugs. Truth was, she'd always been scared of them.

'We gonna go?' Allegra asked tentatively. Hot or not, she sensed there was something seriously shady about that Marco character, something that had made her feel instantly uneasy.

'Babes,' Tess raised a finely arched tattooed brow as she surreptitiously slipped the small wrap of powder into her sparkly Mui Mui clutch. 'I wouldn't miss it for the world.'

CHAPTER 7

'Stand back! I said stand back!' Loretta Hassan's bodyguard snarled menacingly as he opened the door to the chauffeur-driven Rolls Royce and attempted to navigate his client through the swarm of awaiting journalists and paparazzi that were buzzing like wasps around her, flashes popping like champagne corks.

'Mrs Hassan!' A bespectacled man pushed his way to the forefront of the gathering throng. 'Peter Phillips, *LA Daily*. Is it true that your husband was responsible for Miranda Muldavey's botched surgery? Was that why she turned up at his funeral?'

A TV camera zoomed in on Loretta's face and she half-heartedly attempted to shoo it away.

'I'm afraid I cannot possibly comment,' she purred demurely in her thick Italian accent, turning away from the camera for dramatic effect. She couldn't afford to let the grieving widow act slip. Not with the beady eyes of the nation's press all over her.

Ramsey's gloriously A-list funeral had taken place the previous week in Malibu and Loretta, dressed head to toe in black McQueen couture, her creamy breasts spilling out of her tight corseted dress like boiling milk, had made for a tabloid feeding frenzy. Under normal circumstances, she would've relished such excessive media attention, but on this occasion she had been seething by such intrusion; she had personally assured her husband's celebrity mourners of a complete press blackout. After all, Hollywood was all smoke and mirrors. Everyone wanted to give the illusion that their youthful good looks were down to impressive genes alone and not the skilful handiwork of her husband.

However, the journalist had been misinformed: Miranda *hadn't* shown up at the funeral. Not even a glimpse. Loretta had thought it odd that the actress had yet made no formal statement to the media. After all, now that Ramsey was in his box what was to stop her from naming and shaming him?

Loretta reached the top of the stone steps towards her attorney's Bel Air office but just as she was about to disappear inside, her path was blocked by an attractive female journalist.

'How concerned are you about Miranda Muldavey's private lawsuit, Mrs Hassan?' she inquired, displaying an all-American white smile.

Loretta felt her cheeks flush and her heart skip a beat. *Lawsuit? What lawsuit?*

The astute journalist's eyes widened. 'Oh! So, you didn't know!' Her glee was almost palpable.

'That's enough! Stand back, or one of yous is gonna get a serious clump,' Loretta's lump of a bodyguard's patience had finally run out as he pushed his client through the revolving doors of the imposing gothic building.

*

Loretta threw her studded leather Valentino clutch onto Randy Mumford's desk with such force that it bounced. 'If this is a joke, Randy, it is not a very fucking funny one.'

She was incandescent; her cheeks flushed crimson, her ample chest heaving up and down with an influx of adrenalin.

'Please, won't you sit down?' he gestured to the vintage leather Chesterfield opposite. 'A brandy perhaps?'

'I don't want a fucking brandy, *Randy*,' she snarled, though in all honesty she could murder a drink. In fact, she could *commit* murder, if what that bitch journalist had said was true. Randy fixed her one anyway. The word 'no' invariably meant 'yes' where women like Loretta Hassan were concerned. It was little wonder old Ramsey's heart had given out in the end. Poor bugger.

As an attorney to some of the Platinum Triangle's richest and most famous there was little he hadn't seen and heard when it came to tales of excess and debauchery. In a few years' time when he retired, Randy planned to write a tell-all book on his years of digging celebrities out of the murky holes they invariably dug for themselves; sell them all out for a fat publishing cheque and then fuck off to Thailand to see the rest of his days out in the sun getting pleasured by ladyboys.

Ramsey and Randy had been golfing buddies, and as genuinely remorseful as he was about his friend's sudden demise, it had crossed his mind that with him out of the picture he might be in with a shot at this year's club trophy *and* a chance to get to know his formidable wife. He wasn't sure which idea appealed most.

'You mustn't let them get to you, Loretta,' he instructed, pulling at the collar of the new Armani shirt he had worn especially for their meeting, wishing he'd gone up a size now. 'Those hacks will say anything to get a rise out of you.' Truth was, he had half hoped she would drop the whole grieving widow façade and they might crack open the bottle of Krug he had chilling on ice in advance of her arrival. He had even indulged in a little fantasy of fucking her over his desk. After all, Ramsey had managed it. And

48

what had Ramsey done that he hadn't, aside from a handicap of five and last year's club trophy?

'I want you to give it to me straight, Randy,' Loretta demanded, chin raised in defiance.

Randy stifled a lascivious grin. Frankly, he'd like nothing more.

She lit a cigarette without permission.

'Is it possible for Miranda Muldavey to come after me for compensation, even though my beloved Ramsey,' she clutched her chest dramatically as smoke billowed from her plump lips, 'is no longer with us?'

Randy sighed, his ridiculous notion of an afternoon of champagne and sex rapidly diminishing by the second.

'Well, it's possible,' he shrugged, 'but unlikely. She would need to prove your husband's negligence beyond reasonable doubt and, as you know, a dead man cannot stand trial. I suppose she could take out a private lawsuit, come after you that way, but again, the chances of her succeeding, in my opinion you understand, would be pretty slim.'

'Slim you say?'

Randy downed the remainder of his crystal tumbler and pulled his lips over his teeth, before fixing her with an earnest stare.

'Lady, I'd say they were fucking anorexic.'

Loretta visibly relaxed. Randy was right. These journalists would say anything to provoke a reaction. A reaction made headlines. And headlines sold newspapers. But still, Muldavey's silence niggled at her.

'I've had my secretary prepare copies of all the documents,' Randy said, sliding a brown envelope across the oxblood-leather covered desk. 'And I have the originals here for you to sign.' He held out a Mont Blanc ink pen, poised, ready for her to take it.

Loretta took the pen from him and began to sign in her florid handwriting.

'Congratulations, Mrs Hassan,' Randy said dryly, quickly adding, 'if that's the right word to use, given the circumstances.'

Loretta was cross that she didn't feel as euphoric as she had imagined she would, inheriting a touch over 500 million dollars.

'There will be nothing left to celebrate if that crazy bitch comes after *my* money,' she thumped her ample chest with such a breathtaking sense of self-righteousness that even Randy was a little taken aback, and he'd certainly seen more than his fair share of avarice over the years. 'You cannot let Muldavey take it away from me.' Loretta held his gaze from across the desk as she expertly slipped back into her helpless little girl routine, the one men seemed to drink down like a particularly fine vintage Châteaux Margaux.

Randy cleared his throat and watched as Loretta crossed and uncrossed her slim, tanned legs in slow, deliberate movements. The woman was certainly no spring chicken, but then again, neither was he, and she *was* wearing incredibly well for her age, whatever that might be. It was difficult to tell, given all the work Ramsey had done on her.

'Well,' he said softly, enjoying the switch in her demeanour as it dawned upon him that this was probably a woman who would do *anything* to save her fortune. 'I'm sure we can come to some sort of *arrangement*. Let's crack open that champagne,' he grinned, the twitch inside his Armani slacks now a fully-fledged hard-on as he imagined her bent over his desk, skirt above her waist as he went at her like a jackhammer from behind.

Loretta smiled thinly as she surreptitiously opened the top button of her blouse.

'You know, if you want my advice,' Randy said, leaning back in his seat and trying to stop himself from imagining his bald head sandwiched between her impressive cleavage, 'I would spend as much of that money as you possibly can, as quickly as you can. Invest in something; property, a legitimate business . . . the more you spend, the less there will be for her to take . . .' Loretta pulled her chin into her chest, indignant.

'Take? What do you mean, *take*?'

'Not that this will happen, you understand . . .' he added quickly, not wanting to spoil the upturn of her mood. 'I'm just saying that if the worst *did* come to the worst, there are ways of protecting your *assets*.'

'Go on . . .' he had her interest now and this pleased him.

'You could always transfer it all into someone else's name. Someone you trusted, obviously, a family member, a lover perhaps . . . if it belonged to someone else, in name at least, then Muldavey could never make a claim on it.' He paused for a moment to open the bottle of vintage Krug, decanting the amber bubbles into matching Tiffany flutes, adding, 'I realise it's far from ideal, but it would be one way of protecting your money.'

Loretta stifled a snort. The man was *cazza loca*. She would rather cut out her own eyes. Besides, she trusted no one. Sometimes not even herself.

She had made that mistake once before, trusting a man who had managed to peel back her tough outer layers and uncover a softness beneath she had never even known existed; a man who had gone on to shatter her heart and destroy her faith in everything good. A man named Tom Black.

'If I were you,' Randy continued, a look of self-serving cheer creeping across his booze-bloated face, 'I would take myself off somewhere. You know, have a holiday – a long one; I'm sure you deserve it. Why not charter that new jet of yours? Start ridding yourself of some of that cumbersome cash,' he smirked broadly, displaying a set of yellow teeth. 'Let me deal with Miranda Muldavey this end.'

Loretta visibly recoiled. She could smell his fetid breath from where she sat; a revolting mix of halitosis and cognac.

'Do you know, Randy, I think you might be right,' she smiled, genuinely this time. Randy had just given her a fantastic idea, and in doing so unwittingly blown any chances of her dropping to her hands and knees and pleasuring him under the desk in the process. 'I will fly off somewhere; somewhere no one will find me. At least not without looking . . .'

Randy came from behind his desk to join her and she stood. Vertically challenged and about forty pounds overweight, he looked as if his suit had shrunk in the wash and Loretta wondered, incredulously, how anyone could manage to make bespoke Armani look so disgustingly cheap. She lunged forward and kissed him then, caught him clean off-guard, and he struggled to regain his composure as her long hot tongue played with his short wet one. She felt for his erection, only to be met with more disappointment. Pulling away from him sharply, Loretta suddenly snatched up the signed documents from the desk and stuffed them inside her Valentino clutch.

Randy looked at her, crestfallen. 'But I thought . . .'

'You thought *what*, Randy?' she raised a dark, arched eyebrow at him that was sharp as a poisonous arrow and made him instantly lose his erection. 'I would rather join my husband in the grave,' she hissed, disgust dripping from her lips. 'If Ramsey could see you now,' she shook her head, slowly tutting with disapproval as her eyes swept the length of him.

Suitably rejected, Randy bristled.

'You can save all the grieving widow crap for someone who buys it, lady. I know what an ageing, gold-digging piece of trash you are underneath all the plastic surgery.'

'Sticks and stones, Randy, as the English say,' Loretta cackled, checking her lipstick in her diamond-encrusted Dior compact before turning sharply to leave. Though he was right about one thing; she *did* need a holiday. Somewhere hot, somewhere fabulous and fun, somewhere she could embark upon the most epic shopping spree of her life without the press tracking her every move. She knew just the place.

CHAPTER 8

'Where *are* you taking me?' Ellie giggled girlishly as Vinnie guided her precariously along the narrow Soho street, his hands covering her eyes.

'Not far now,' he promised, barely able to contain his own excitement. 'And no peeking!' He knew his wife only too well.

'Have you *seen* these heels?' she protested, referring to the six-inch Pierre Hardy sandals she was wearing, squeezing his arm tightly in a bid to steady herself against the cobbles that were proving tricky to navigate. Vinnie laughed. It had not escaped his watchful eye that his wife had seemed a touch subdued over dinner tonight; it was the first time he had seen her genuinely smile all evening.

'So then, are you going to tell me what's bothering you?' he'd eventually asked her, tentatively sipping a glass of the Chateau La Mondotte Saint-Emilion 1996 wine he'd just ordered and watching as she had unenthusiastically picked at her plate of caviar, crab meat and lobster jelly.

Ellie had given a small smile. Her husband was such an intuitive man; he'd always been able to see straight through her like a pane of glass.

'I'm sorry, darling,' she'd apologised. She hadn't meant

54

to be so sombre, especially not tonight; she had wanted to show him how glad she was to have him home. 'Ignore me, it's nothing . . . I'm just a little worried about Tess, that's all.' It wasn't a lie exactly; Ellie had heard from her daughter just once since she'd landed in Ibiza and she'd had to physically stop herself from phoning every five minutes to check up on her. But since she'd seen that damned photograph of Loretta Fiorentino in the newspaper, and then of course there was the collapse of the business venue weighing heavy on her shoulders . . .

Vinnie had looked at his wife from across the table. She looked so beautiful tonight; her long hair hung in loose waves around her smooth, naked shoulders and the dress she was wearing, a strapless black Helmut Lang number, off-set the shamrock green of her eyes and caressed her delicate curves, modestly displaying the swell of her breasts and décolletage. Even after all the years that had passed Ellie could still manage to stop his heart in its tracks.

'Tess will be just fine,' he'd reassured her. 'She can take care of herself; she's her mother's daughter, remember? And, well, you know, she's not a kid anymore. In fact, if I remember rightly, *Mrs Scott*,' he'd taken her hand in his, lightly played with her delicate fingers for a few moments, '*you* were just a year or so older than Tess yourself when we met.'

Ellie had narrowed her eyes at him playfully, taking another generous gulp of the expensive wine, though it wasn't quite taking the edge off her mood as she'd hoped.

'That was different,' she'd objected.

Vinnie had given a knowing smile.

'I was more . . .' She'd thrown her husband a thoughtful look, trying to find the word she was searching for.

'. . . Streetwise?'

'Yes! Streetwise.'

'I remember,' he'd said, eyebrows arching provocatively. She'd jokingly pushed his arm away. 'Anyway, I'll still never know why you picked me that night out of all those beautiful girls . . .'

'There were other girls?' Vinnie had clutched his chest in faux-shock as he'd held her gaze from across the table.

There had been a big buzz at the Venus Club that night twenty-one years ago as Vinnie and his entourage had strolled through the door, all sharp suits and expensive-smelling cologne.

'I want first dibs on this one,' Mercury, a tall, skinny black stripper from Des Moines had firmly stated, applying a thick coat of plum-red lipstick, her third since clocking on. 'He's got Big Tipper tattooed on his ass and *this* black ass wants to get me some of that.' As the girls had begun to bicker amongst themselves, each vying for the handsome stranger's attention in the hope of making a good earn, Ellie had continued to dance, lost in the moment, imagining she was performing on stage with the Royal Ballet, just as she had done as a child. It enabled her to block out the reality of what she was doing; displaying her goods to sleazy men in a tawdry strip joint for a few dollars.

Yet still he had asked for her out of all the others.

'The name's Angel,' she'd told him with a fixed smile, slipping into the booth opposite him. He had a handsome face, the look of a young George Clooney about him and something had instantly told her that this was no ordinary punter.

'You don't say,' he'd replied, with a smile. Only, it wasn't the kind of smile she was used to; the kind that belied those base thoughts underneath. It was a smile that had reached his sparkling blue eyes.

That night Ellie O'Connor had felt unusually self-conscious as she had begun to peel the straps of her tiny dress from her smooth, slim shoulders. She had actually *wanted* to put on a good show for the man in the sharp suit, had *wanted* him to find her attractive.

'I'd just like to talk,' he'd said softly, holding his hand up to prevent her from going any further, 'if it's all the same to you.' As powerful and ruthless in the boardroom as Vincent Scott was, and ultimately attractive to women as a result, he had never been one for strip clubs and had only attended that night out of courtesy for his hosts.

Ellie was dumbfounded. This was a first; no one had ever paid for her to keep her clothes *on* before.

'Suit yourself,' she'd shrugged, yanking her bra straps back up. 'It's your money.'

And so they had just talked, and Ellie had learned that at thirty-six years old, sixteen years her senior, Vincent Scott was the eldest of three siblings born to wealthy, upper-class parents and had been brought up on an affluent country estate in Wiltshire, England.

By all accounts, Vincent, or Vinnie as he had insisted she call him, had been close to his father, a kind and loving man who had taught his eldest son to hunt, shoot and fish. When he'd died, some five years previously, Vinnie had taken over at the helm of his father's property development business, Great Scott Properties. He'd been modest about his accomplishments; crediting great timing and the property boom of the late eighties for his subsequent global success. But Ellie sensed that underneath his soft veneer lay a steely determination. Inherited money or no, a man didn't become a successful billionaire without an iron will.

'But enough about me,' he'd said, modestly. 'Tell me, how does a young woman such a long way from home come to be working in a place like this?'

He had listened attentively as Ellie had recounted the story of how she had been just seven years old when her mother had upped sticks from the East End and followed her heart to Las Vegas.

'I still miss it,' she'd smiled a little ruefully, 'London, I mean. It'll always be home to me.'

'And your mother?' he'd enquired, watching as a deep sadness had seemed to descend upon her, dulling the brightness of her eyes. Ellie had shook her head as she'd thought of Charlene; she had often wondered what might have been had her mother never met Ray Black, for she was in no doubt that it was their tempestuous and abusive relationship that had led to her subsequent demise. The real tragedy was that in spite of everything – the gambling, the womanising and the drinking – Charlene O'Connor had truly loved 'her Ray'. But it had been the worst kind of love; the kind that tore right through you like a cyclone, destroying everything good in its wake, and it had left her mother an empty shell of a woman; hard-faced and bitter, dependent on alcohol just to make it through the day.

'So I've had to put my dreams of becoming a professional ballerina on hold for a while. Just until I make enough money to put myself through dance school and make ends meet, you know how it is?' she'd casually explained, realising that he probably didn't have the first idea. 'Now that Tom's no longer on the scene, I've got to look after myself, hence the reason I'm here,' she'd looked around the low-lit club filled with drunken leering men with a resigned sigh.

'Tom?' he had quizzed her.

Even now Vinnie could recall the pause she had given, that she had looked down at her cheap stiletto-clad feet as if she hadn't quite known how best to answer the question.

'. . . Tom's my . . . step-brother.'

Vinnie had left the Venus Club that night on a high of the like he'd never experienced before. On the surface he was incredibly modest, unassuming even, but it belied the sharp business mind and hard-nosed determination that lay at his very core. He was certainly no pushover, as some had learnt to their detriment, and he wasn't the type to lose his heart without careful consideration, especially to a young stripper from the wrong side of the tracks. And yet on the night of July 18th, almost twenty-one years ago to the day; call it fate, destiny, or whatever you liked, he had made the decision that he could not leave Las Vegas without her . . .

*

'Oh Vin,' Ellie looked across the table at her husband with a deep fondness. He was older now, in his mid-fifties, his salt and pepper hair now more salt than pepper, and the faint lines around his eyes had turned into deep creases; years of laughter etched on his face like a timeline. She knew how lucky she was; Vinnie had taught her everything she knew. They had never had a cross word their entire marriage, and yet deep down Ellie had an instinctive fearfulness of her husband. There was another side to his gentle, caring nature, one that he kept hidden from her at all costs, but that she knew existed all the same. Vinnie had given her wealth and status of the like she had only ever been able to imagine; the chance to be somebody and make something of herself. She felt forever indebted to him because of it, and yet she had come so close to nearly losing it all . . .

It had been a mutual decision not to reveal to anyone the truth about Ellie's former occupation. Not that Vinnie was ashamed; quite the opposite in fact, he had been proud of the way his young girlfriend had dealt with the hand she'd been given in life, but he was nobody's fool; he had known how it would look. Beautiful young stripper meets older, billionaire businessman. By burying Ellie's past, Vinnie had only ever wanted to protect her. After all, when they had married in a lavish ceremony in the lush grounds of his family's Wiltshire estate some thirteen months later, people had whispered about the union between him and his lowly, if beautiful, secretary. Ha! If only they had known the *real* truth!

'Ta-da!' Vinnie dropped his hands from her eyes and stood back to survey her reaction.

It was dark now and the narrow cobbled Soho street was lit only by the rich amber glow of a singular street-lamp. Ellie blinked up at the dark, boarded-up building in front of her that she assumed was some kind of disused warehouse and wondered what exactly it was she should be looking at. 'Number twelve Starling Street, W1; your new dance school . . .' he announced with a theatrical wave.

Instinctively Ellie put a manicured hand over her mouth to stifle a gasp.

'Now, before you say anything I want you to listen. You have to understand that a man of my, how shall I say, *standing* in the property business, gets to hear things on the grapevine . . .'

Ellie's heart thumped against her ribcage.

'So you already know about me losing the venue then?' she had looked at him with a mix of indignant relief, 'about those bastards gazumping me at the last moment?'

He put a finger to her lips to prevent her from continuing and felt the softness of them against his skin. 'Ah, now none of that matters now,' he reassured her, 'what *does* matter is that we find you another venue, a better one; this one.' He pulled her close to him and felt the warmth of her skin against his own.

'We're going to bid for it at auction next week, and

we're going to win it. So tell me, Mrs Scott, what do you think?'

Ellie kissed him then, small scattergun kisses over his clean-shaven face and then deeply, her tongue exploring his.

'I think, Vinnie Scott,' she breathed, 'that you are the most wonderful husband in the world.'

CHAPTER 9

As much as she didn't care to admit it, Allegra was feeling out of her depth. The pool party resembled a scene from a bad porn movie. There were naked girls everywhere; tanned bodies draped like mercury over blue and white striped sunbeds and couples openly having sex in the pool and on the terracotta patio outside. To her left she noticed a tall, naked brunette with shiny fake tits and tattoos willingly administering a blow job to some greasy-looking long-haired guy as another guy pumped away at her from behind, grinning manically as he frenziedly grabbed at her breasts for purchase. Allegra turned away in disgust, glancing over at a group of people brazenly snorting cocaine from a glass coffee table, dancing to the deafening sound of David Guetta like demented maniacs as they swigged from champagne bottles.

She nervously scanned the room for Tess. That shady Marco character had sequestered her off somewhere inside the sprawling hilltop villa, leaving Allegra to her own devices.

'Hey hunny, wanna hit?' a sinewy-looking black girl with the longest weave she'd ever seen held out a joint as she shimmied over. She was naked, save for a tiny fluorescent pink Pucci G-string that barely covered what little modesty she had left, and a pair of transparent, ridiculously high platform sandals, the like of which you could only buy in sex shops.

Allegra shook her head nervously. 'Suit yourself,' the girl had shrugged, kissing her teeth as she sauntered off towards some guy, collapsing on top of him, brazenly sliding her hand inside his boxer shorts and getting to work.

Allegra self-consciously pulled at her tiny designer denim mini skirt and wished she had worn her maxi dress instead. This was a bona fide fucking sex and drugs orgy; a world away from the occasional flash of G-string she'd indulged in after one too many cocktails at Funky Buddha on a Friday night back home – and it was scaring the shit out of her. She anxiously checked her iPhone. She would kill Tess for abandoning her like this. *So much for fucking friendship*. She'd been on her own for the past hour and a half, nervously fending off the unwanted attention of various freaks. Bloody Tess Scott . . . why did she always have to play the wild card?

As she made her way up the stone steps, discarding her cumbersome pair of patent Louboutins in haste, Allegra fought back the urge to burst into tears. In a moment of rare clarity she suddenly felt exactly what she was; a little girl playing at being a grown up and she wanted her daddy.

'I'm looking for a girl . . .' she stammered in a small, nervous voice to a guy who was propped up against the wall in the hallway, audibly dragging on a suspicious-looking cigarette, 'long, dark blonde hair . . . white hot pants . . . Gucci bikini . . . ?'

The pockmark-faced guy grinned, a horrible self-satisfied smirk that only served to accelerate Allegra's rapidly burgeoning sense of unease. He thumbed the door behind him.

Shaking as she pushed past him, Allegra opened the door

63

to the bedroom and instinctively put both hands up to her mouth to stifle a shocked scream. It was dark inside, the unremarkable room lit only by a small undetectable light source but it was enough to see that Tess, who was sprawled out across the bed, was completely naked save for a bottle of tequila in her hand, which she was proudly holding up like an Olympic torch. There was a guy on top of her, also naked, while another was knelt behind her, his erect cock visible as she giggled with delight, tequila spilling from her glossy lips. There was a third guy too, Allegra recognised him as Marco from the club, who appeared to be filming it all. He was shouting out words of encouragement, 'yeah baby, you look so hot baby, ooh yeah, show us what you got . . .'

Stunned into silence, Allegra watched in horror as one of the three men grabbed a giant, obscene-looking dildo from a repertoire of sex toys on the bedside table.

Tess began to moan in pain or ecstasy, Allegra couldn't be sure which. Her eyes were as wide as saucers. *Jesus, was she on drugs?*

Suddenly alerted to Allegra's presence, the guys in the room all looked over in her direction.

'Hey sweetheart,' Marco acknowledged her, his voice a forced saccharine sweet, 'you come to join in the fun?'

Paralysed to the spot, Allegra vigorously shook her head in the negative. Tess, seemingly oblivious, didn't even look up.

Marco watched Allegra for a long moment, momentarily allowing the camera to drop to his waist, his dark, beady eyes boring terrifying holes into her.

'Well, close the door on your way out then if you're not staying, yeah?' he snapped coldly before turning his back on her towards the action. 'Come on guys, I wanna get this all in one take.'

Tearing through the villa like her life depended on it,

Allegra finally found herself outside on the dusty road track where she ran, barefoot, sandals in hand, in the opposite direction of the villa. As the noise gradually faded and, deciding she was probably no longer in any imminent danger, Allegra collapsed against a small stone wall and slumped to the ground. Her heart was beating a song inside her chest and she struggled to catch her breath; she thought she might pass out. What the fuck did Tess think she was playing at having a gangbang with all those guys? And filming it too! Tess had always been a bit crazy but this time she'd taken it *way* too far. *Stupid, selfish bitch*. Yet as angry as Allegra was, a small voice inside her said that there had been something horribly wrong about the scene she'd just witnessed; something dark and sinister. Still, if Tess had been stupid enough to put any of that shit up her nose then as far as Allegra was concerned she deserved all she got.

With her fear gradually subsiding, Allegra started to relax a little, her thoughts beginning to take a new turn. Wiping her nose with the back of her shaking hand, she reached inside her Mulberry clutch bag for her phone.

'Daddy!' she said, her voice cracking with emotion as she finally broke down in tears, sobbing like a little girl. 'Can you send a plane for me? I want to come home.'

As far as Allegra Kennedy-Ling was concerned, Tess Scott was on her own.

CHAPTER 10

Tom had been right about Candy; she was definitely a screamer in the sack.

'Ohh yeah, baby! I'm almost there! Keep going . . . like that, yeah! Oh . . . *ooooh* . . .'

They'd been going at it ever since they'd checked into the penthouse suite at The Player, and she'd been 'there' at least twice already.

Tom looked down at the young woman bucking and squirming underneath him as he ploughed himself into her in long, slow strokes; her long blonde hair fanning the pillow like a yellow blanket as she laid it on a bit heavy with the vocals. She was very young and extremely sexy, yet he felt absolutely nothing as he blithely pumped himself inside her, running his hand over her toned stomach and shiny, albeit impressive, fake tits. Candy Wilson could hardly believe her luck. What had commenced as one of the shittiest days on record, getting fired from her deadbeat job at the diner by her asshole of a boss – strike that, *ex-boss* – had ended up here; in a luxury penthouse suite of a hotel in Las Vegas, *Las fucking Vegas*, with vintage champagne on tap and a rich, good-looking dude who was hung like a fucking horse and gave great oral. Jesus, the man's tongue should come with a 'Parental Advisory' sticker. What's more, he had promised to take her shopping in a limo later, maybe catch one of them fancy shows after a lobster and champagne dinner somewhere really posh. It was like something straight out of a frickin' Julia Roberts movie! Life had been pretty shitty lately, Candy thought, what with the court case and a spell in the hospital thanks to those bastards she called parents. It looked as if things were finally beginning to go her way.

Candy had already sussed out that Tom had to be something of a high roller, simply by the unorthodox reaction they'd received upon arrival. The hotel staff had practically fallen over themselves to accommodate them in the penthouse suite – *the frickin' penthouse suite* – it was at least ten times the size of her poky studio apartment back in LA and the soft furnishings were like something from one of those glossy interior magazines her mom was always reading; all gilt baroque gold mirrors, sumptuous Persian rugs, tactile suede couches, and a huge, gothic-looking bed with a ceiling mirror above it. *Hel-lo Sin City!*

'This place is *awesome*!' she'd squealed, wide-eyed, suddenly seeming her age as she had thrown herself down onto the bed, the pure silk and goose eiderdown making a satisfactory whoosh as she impacted onto it. 'You some kind of face around here?' Candy had enquired, intrigued. 'Seems like everyone can't do enough for you . . .'

Tom had smiled with a hefty display of false modesty.

'Welcome to my hometown, honey,' he'd laughed, throwing himself down on top of her, pushing her legs apart as his hands began to explore her young, tight body. 'Welcome to Vegas. Playground of the rich!'

Tom had always enjoyed the physical release he experienced during sex, the rush of endorphins as he came, flooding his body and brain with dopamine and other feel-good chemicals – in fact he was addicted to it, but as with any kind of addiction, it was always such a transient, fleeting state, void of any real depth, the ultimately short-lived high making way for the inevitable crashing low.

Tom had only ever felt that deeper level of connection with a woman once in his life before, the kind of connection that transforms sex into the act of making love; the kind that touches you deep inside, leaving you with the feeling of having grown closer to another human being. Although the intensity of it had frightened the crap out of him, he had never since been able to replicate such a feeling with anyone else, though it would be fair to say he had certainly given it his best shot over the years.

As Candy loudly came for the fourth time that afternoon, Tom kept one surreptitious eye on the Louis Vuitton holdall next to the bed. It wasn't too late to do the right thing and bank it, his voice of reason told him as he threw her around the bed like a rag doll – this one liked it on the rough side. But the *other* voice inside his head, the one that always seemed to lure him into trouble, was already attempting to talk him out of it. *It's just a little game of cards*, it whispered to him, seductively, *one that would allow you to double your money and make good your end of the deal with Jack*.

No one played Five Card Draw like Tom Black; he'd been notorious in his day, a charming trickster who'd outsmarted the pros, even with the worst hand imaginable. Hell, not even Lady Gaga could read *his* poker face.

The internal phone unexpectedly rang, causing a post-coital Candy to jump.

Tom rolled off her spent young body and picked it up. He was convinced this one was a lucky talisman. He could see it in her eyes. When he won big tonight he'd treat her to a little spree in Gucci and Victoria's Secret. Give her something to really scream about.

'Tom Black.'

'*Tom*! Jesus buddy! It's been a while . . . they told me you were in town! How the fuck are you . . . ?'

It was Marvin Katz, manager of The Player. The pair went way back to when Tom was a ten-dollar slots guy and Marvin was making his name on the tables, something of a player himself, or at least he would have everyone believe.

'Jesus, how are you Marv?' Tom stood naked, placing the phone between his ear and shoulder as he began to pace the room. 'I hear you're the big cheese these days . . . good for you buddy,' he said, with as much sincerity as he could muster. The Marvin Katz he'd known back in the day could only just about manage to string a coherent sentence together, let alone run a chic, quality establishment like The Player.

'It's good to hear you, Tom,' Marvin said, in his nasal New York accent that hadn't seemed to soften with the passing of time. 'I hope the guys have been looking after you with the comps so far . . . listen, whatever you want Tom, champagne, a limo, hookers . . . you just let me know, OK?'

'Thanks Marv,' Tom glanced at Candy who was now busy helping herself to the contents of a deluxe heart-shaped box of Godiva chocolates. 'I appreciate it,' he said, wondering just how far his offer of such generosity might stretch. *Like a few million dollars' worth of generous.*

'The guys tell me you're looking for a big game, Tom.'

'That's right, Marv. I'm hoping you can hook me up.'

'We've missed you, Tom,' Marvin said with a healthy dose of sycophantic smarm that Tom immediately saw straight through.

'Hey! Have you seen this?' Candy's shrill LA accent cut through the conversation like a shard of glass as she held up the glossy, gold-embossed menu card, her eyes wide and her exposed tits standing to attention like torpedoes. 'It says here we got our very own butler, 24/7, like, you gotta be shitting me?'

Tom heard Marvin guffaw.

'I take it you won't be needing any *extra services* tonight then?'

'Oh I don't know, Marv . . . the night's young,' Tom reposted.

'Yeah, but not as young as the broad I'll bet,' Marvin shot back, and Tom forced himself to laugh. Marvin Katz wasn't nearly as amusing as he thought he was, but if laughing at Marv's lame attempts at humour meant he would look into sorting him a game, then he'd suck it up all day long.

'You kill me, Marvin,' Tom chuckled, rolling his eyes at Candy, who giggled as she popped a truffle between her glossy blow job lips. 'Let's have a drink together later, celebrate my big win.'

'I like your confidence my friend,' Marvin replied dryly, with forced good humour. Some things never changed. Tom Black had always been a cocky little English fucker; way too big for his size nines, that was his problem. Gamblers like Black might think they're the shit, but the house always won at the end of the day; they were just too fucking arrogant to want to believe it.

'Leave it with me, Tom. I'll put the word out, see who's in town.'

'I appreciate it Marv . . . And make mine a Bourbon on the rocks . . . a large one yeah?' he added before hanging up.

Tom felt the first trickles of adrenaline stirring inside his guts, the kindling of that euphoric rush he always got right before a game. He'd played for money in the past, big money too, but nothing in this league . . . it was a heck of a lot of green that wasn't even his to gamble but as far as

Tom was concerned, what choice did he have? He'd given Jack his word he would get his share of the money and Tom's fierce pride meant that he'd rather skip town than lose face in front of his friend. Tonight there could be no room for error; it was shit or bust.

CHAPTER 11

Walking through Portobello Road on a beautiful summer's afternoon, Ellie Scott struggled to think of another place in the world she would rather be. It was Friday, market day, and the whole place was alive with tourists and shoppers perusing the eclectic mix of antique shops whose contents spilled out onto the pavement like a giant treasure trove. She loved the paradox of Portobello, the glitz mixed with the grime; struggling artists and buskers sitting alongside media moguls, wealthy fashionistas and banker's wives. There was something uniquely unpretentious about it and it reminded her of the streets she had grown up on as a child.

Hearing her iPhone beep inside her white Birkin, Ellie dipped a manicured hand inside, blindly searching as she became sidetracked by a vintage Vivienne Westwood corset dress in a boutique window. She hoped it was Tess; call it a mother's instinct, but Ellie felt an unsettling sense of unease that her daughter might be in some kind of trouble. But it wasn't Tess. It was Victoria messaging to say she was already on her way to the charity event at the Cobden Club where they were due to meet. It was to be the third social event she'd attended that week and

Ellie wasn't entirely enamoured by the thought of yet another afternoon of making polite small talk with vastly over-privileged women, who she suspected cared more about making their hair appointments than they did about the charity *du jour*. But this was her life now, and had been for the past two decades. The polo, Glorious Goodwood, Cannes, the Henley Royal Regatta, Ascot, Glyndbourne, not to mention all the hundreds of other global events and private charities Vince was a patron of – she accompanied him to all of them. Always impeccably dressed, always impeccably polite and if she was brutally honest, always impeccably bored shitless . . . sometimes her jaw physically ached from it all. But what could she do? Her husband topped the *Forbes* rich list every year, and with money and position like that came great responsibility.

Victoria Mayfield was already at the Cobden Club by the time Ellie arrived and had helped herself to a Kir Royale and a small plate of sushi before squirreling herself away at a small table at the back of the room. Looking around her, she surveyed the scene of gossiping, overly preened society women with a heavy heart. The last thing she felt like doing was socialising. That morning her period had arrived, regular as fucking clockwork, just as it did every goddamn month. Victoria greeted her monthly cycle like a personal affront; Mother Nature sniggering at her inability to do what came naturally to most women. It was all just so *unfair*; Lawrence, her husband, had been home more than usual this past month preparing for a big trip to South Africa where he was due to film a documentary and, ensuring the extra time they'd had together had not been wasted, she was convinced this month would be the month she'd finally see that line turn blue.

'Jesus Tor, not again!' Lawrence Mayfield had smiled wearily at his wife as she'd led him into the bedroom for the third time in less than forty-eight hours. 'You're wearing me out!'

'And you're *complaining*?' she'd replied, giving him a mock-disdainful look as she tore off her Agent Provocateur underwear in haste, eager to get down to business. Lawrence Mayfield had inwardly sighed. He enjoyed nothing more than making love to his wife. After all, she was beautiful and he adored her, but not like this, not on demand; it was all way too forced and unspontaneous, not to mention deeply unromantic. His wife had become hell-bent on producing, to the point of obsession, and Lawrence was seriously beginning to doubt her mental state. There was a darkness to Tor now; places inside her mind he knew he could no longer reach. And the worst thing of all was that he had not a goddamn clue what to do about any of it.

Victoria threw back her Kir Royale and swiped another from an attractive waiter. He was young, twenty-one at most, and she found herself blushing as she imagined herself naked on top of him, riding him furiously. Would his sperm be better than her husband's? Would it swim harder, faster stronger, towards her willing eggs?

'Tor!' Ellie Scott was making her way towards her, two Kir Royales in hand and a beaming smile on her radiant face. 'Wow! Check *you* out! You look *amazing*!' Ellie said, kissing her warmly on both cheeks and standing back to admire Victoria's choice of attire, a colourful, eye-catching Mary Katrantzou body-con dress that displayed her slim, curvaceous figure to its finest. It was somewhat of a departure from her usual demure and understated look.

'I *reckon* if I didn't know you were a happily married woman, Tor Mayfield, I would think that you were on a cougar hunt!' Victoria gave a hollow laugh. Her friend had no idea just how close to the truth she really was.

'So, how's the book going?' Ellie took a seat opposite her friend and glanced around the room at the sea of designer outfits and expensive handbags. 'Ah, the book!' Tor replied, swiping a soft-boiled quails egg and Beluga caviar crostini from a passing waiter and slipping it between her glossy Chanel nude lips. 'Well, let's just say it's not exactly writing itself.'

'Oh?' Ellie placed her white Birkin on the table for maximum exposure. She'd been on the waiting list for the much-coveted bag for almost six months and couldn't resist showing it off. She knew it was childish – it was just a handbag at the end of the day – but sometimes it was difficult not to become embroiled in the one-upmanship that was so blatantly rife at these types of affairs.

'My publishers are on my case about it, but this one's going to have to wait,' Tor announced stoically, glugging more Kir Royale. 'After all, it's not like I've not made them a fuck load of money, now is it?'

This didn't sound like Tor at all. She'd always been so highly professional, so dedicated to her writing and the loyal legion of fans that ferociously devoured her books.

'And Lawrence?'

Tor drained the remains of her champagne flute and began to eye the Grey Goose vodka cocktails that were doing the rounds.

'He's off to South Africa soon, for six weeks, possibly more. Filming bloody elephants . . .' She paused for a moment and looked up at Ellie with a doleful expression, adding quietly, '. . . And I'm still not pregnant.' For the briefest moment she wondered if she might confide everything in her friend, divulge the secret little plan she'd recently been cooking up in her head, but Tor knew that to say it out loud meant making it a reality and she wasn't sure she was quite ready for that yet.

Ellie slid her hand across the table and placed it on top of Tor's.

'Oh honey, I'm so sorry,' she said with genuine regret.

Tor swallowed down a lump as sharp as glass. She knew that Ellie meant it, that she above all others most understood the pain and disappointment that had become a seemingly permanent fixture in her life these last couple of years. After all, they had spent a long time under the same fertility doctor, a man who had been hailed as a so-called miracle worker, yet so far had been unable to work his magic where she and Lawrence were concerned. Or the Scotts, for that matter.

'Your husband's sperm count is seriously diminished, Mrs Mayfield,' Doctor Fouad had gently reminded her during her last, and final visit. 'I'm not saying it's impossible – I believe nothing is impossible – but I am saying that it *is* very unlikely that you'll ever conceive with your husband again.'

With your husband. Those words had haunted Victoria ever since.

'There's still hope,' Ellie said in a bid to pull her friend out of her obvious black mood. 'You've got to keep trying, keep believing. You're still young . . .'

Tor gave a derisive snort as she drained the remains of her fourth Kir Royale. All that sweet cassis was beginning to make her feel a bit nauseous now, but to hell with it. On the fertility drugs, she had never imbibed more than one glass of fizz on a special occasion; fat lot of good it had ever done her. She was sick of remaining positive and 'turning the frown upside down' as Lawrence was always reminding her; she wanted results, not kind words. You couldn't love and feed and nurture kind words. 'Anyway,' Tor straightened herself out before she unravelled completely. 'How's the venue search going? Found anywhere suitable yet?'

Ellie welcomed the conversation's change in direction.

'Now that you come to mention it . . .' she said, beginning to explain all about the amazing old warehouse in

Soho that Vinnie had found. '. . . It's completely perfect – everything I've been looking for.'

Tor forced a smile; it was the only way she knew how these days.

'So it's all systems go!' she said, mustering up her best excited face.

'Provided we win the auction,' Ellie interjected.

'Well, surely being married to a billionaire property developer *must* have its perks.'

Their giggles were interrupted by a horse-faced blonde woman wearing a Jil Sander paisley skirt suit that did absolutely nothing for her robust frame.

'Ladies,' it was Lady Davinia Sexton-Lloyd, one of today's hostesses, and arguably one of the most prolific gossips this side of the Thames. She was married to Lord Sexton, a bloated old buffoon whose name suited him.

'Lovely to see you, Davinia,' Ellie stood to shake the woman's diamond-encrusted hand. 'I trust you're well.' It was all the opening Davinia needed as she plonked her cumbersome bulk down to join them.

'Marvellous, darling,' she replied, displaying a little red lipstick and canapé between her teeth as she smiled brightly. 'You know how busy it is at these events; I think I need to clone myself.' Ellie balked at the very idea. '—And this is . . . ?' she turned to Victoria, precariously placing her copy of *HELLO!* magazine on the glass table which had been lavishly decorated with scented Jo Malone tea lights and tiny Swarovski scatter crystals. No expense spared for the orphans of Uganda.

'Victoria Mayfield – a very good friend of mine.'

'*The* Victoria Mayfield?' Davinia looked impressed. 'Of *Mirror, Mirror* fame?'

'The very same,' Ellie sang, giving Tor a surreptitious wink.

'Well, Victoria, this *is* a pleasure,' she gushed, her gaudy Bvlgari jewellery rattling as she shook her hand vigorously.

'I'm an avid reader of *all* your books. Took *Mirror, Mirror* with me to Courcheval last year, couldn't put the bloody thing down.' Tor thanked her politely, finally releasing her hand from the woman's vice-like grip.

'It's been a week from hell, I tell you,' Davinia placed a palm over her shiny botoxed forehead, 'trying to organise this lunch on top of Seaton's wedding. I ask you,' she rolled her eyes in exaggerated exasperation, 'I really should've gone into events management you know,' she turned to Victoria. 'Seaton's my son,' she explained as an afterthought.

Tor looked at Ellie with an expression that begged the question, *Seaton Sexton*? She called her son *Seaton Sexton*! 'He's getting married in Monaco next week and there are still a million and one things to organise. I mean, he's left *everything* to me and his father – good job we've still got all our faculties!'

Debateable, Tor silently thought as she watched Lady Seaton throw her head back with a roaring laugh. 'Kids eh? You know how it is?'

Victoria shifted uncomfortably in her seat. *Actually, two years ago I found my baby girl dead in her crib and now my husband has crippled sperm so, no, actually I don't know 'how it is' and probably never fucking will!*

'Tell me, are any of the glossies going to cover it?' Ellie interjected, in a bid to steer the conversation back towards Lady Sexton's favourite subject: herself. Davinia's delight at the opportunity to brag was almost palpable.

'Funny you should mention but yes! They've even given it a plug in this week's issue of *HELLO!*,' she said, the magazine miraculously falling open to the well-thumbed exact page in question. "An exclusive peek behind the scenes at Lord Seaton Sexton-Lloyd's wedding to Florence Corbett-Wellesley!" It's marvellous isn't it?' she gushed with such pride that Ellie thought the woman was about to explode.

'I take it she won't be using her full name,' Tor smirked, the Kir Royales loosening her tongue. Lady Seaton shot her a sideways glance but Ellie missed it, her attention having been caught by the news story opposite. *Loretta Fiorentino*. Jesus, there she was again! And this time there was no mistaking her. The small photograph showed her standing outside a church dressed in a jet-black couture dress, unmistakably McQueen, her enormous comedy breasts spilling over the top like rising dough. She was holding a small Chihuahua underneath her arm as though it were a clutch bag, its tiny face peering out at the camera. The headline read: 'Widow Grieves for Top Plastic Surgeon Husband as Muldavey Rumour Mill Continues . . .' Ellie stared at the face of a woman she had once, a long time ago, thought of as a friend, and felt a tight knot of nausea form in the pit of her stomach.

'Terrible business, that,' Davinia remarked, having clocked Ellie's interest in the story. 'Poor Miranda. She's an old friend of the family's actually,' she pulled her mouth into a thin line, pleased to be able to make such a topical namedrop. 'Says there that she's going after Hassan's wife for a spot of compo for the *disastrous* mess he made of her face . . .'

'Serves the old bitch right,' Ellie shot back, forgetting herself. Just the sight of Loretta's face seemed to rancour far more than she had expected. Davinia's eyes widened, her gossip antennae twitching wildly.

'Someone you know, darling?' she carefully enquired.

Ellie quickly closed the magazine.

'Oh no,' she lied, watching the look on Davinia's face slip with disappointment. 'She just reminds me of someone I once knew. Someone a long, long time ago . . .'

CHAPTER 12

Tess woke with a heart-stopping start, and for the briefest moment felt a sense of relief as she realised she was alone. But it was a fleeting state, and was soon replaced by a rod of ice-cold fear as it rapidly dawned upon her that she was not in her own bed. Her head was audibly pounding, a sickening, resounding throb either side of her temporal lobes, causing her vision to blur and the nausea in her belly to instantly rise to her throat.

Disorientated, she made to stand. It was then she felt the searing pain shoot through her body, sharp as a splintered arrow. Groaning, her joints felt brittle as glass, like her bones were about to shatter with her weight upon them and the soreness she felt *down there* caused her to wince aloud in pain. She felt as if she'd been hit by a truck and dragged for ten miles. Tess sat back down onto the bed and it was only then she realised that she was completely naked. *Jesus fucking Christ, what the hell was going on?* Gripped by fear and panic, she hurriedly covered her modesty with a white bed sheet, her eyes darting around the room as she tried to piece her shot-to-shit memory back together again. The room was unrecognisable; rudimentary bare white walls and terracotta tiles, a double bed

80

with a pair of small wooden tables either side of it, and a tiny shuttered window allowing only the thinnest sliver of sunlight to creep into the darkened room. She glanced at one of the tables in search of something to drink, her thirst was such now that she felt at the point of collapse, and was horrified to see that among the discarded empty bottles and wine glasses there was an assortment of sex toys; ugly, giant, life-like dildos staring back at her in an array of different shapes and sizes and colours. Rubbing her temples in angry frustration, she forced back tears as she desperately tried to locate her clothes, her bag, her phone, *anything* . . . And then she remembered; oh my God! Allegra! She was sure she had been with her friend the previous evening, but where the fuck was she now? And why was she here, in this room, naked and alone? It was as if someone had torn a page from her memory; it was all just a gaping black hole, and she had a gut-sickening feeling it wasn't something she'd want to put on a postcard to her parents back home. *Jesus, what the fuck had she done?*

Burying her head despairingly in her hands, Tess heard voices approaching and instinctively threw herself back down onto the bed and feigned sleep.

'Jesus, man,' a male voice said. 'She's still sleeping . . . exactly how much of that shit did you give her last night?'

'Too fucking much, probably,' a gruff voice shot back. It sounded familiar, though she did not know why. 'She'll wake with one motherfucker of a headache, I can tell you that.'

'And the rest . . .'

'I told you I'd found us a wild one didn't I?' He sounded pleased with himself. 'They're all the same those posh chicks . . . filthy little bitches, up for anything. All that dough corrupts them you know . . . turns them from convent schoolgirls into game little whores. I have to say though; this one gave a pretty special performance last night.'

81

The pair of them gave a chuckle that made Tess want to throw up. She could sense their presence from underneath the thin bed sheet and could hardly breathe through her terror.

Don't panic. Stay calm.

'You think we'll make top dollar on that video then . . . I mean, everyone loves to watch a good roasting don't they . . . ?'

Tears were escaping the corners of Tess's eyes now. *They'll be gone in a minute* she reassured herself. *Then you can get your stuff and get the fuck out of here, fly home and forget any of this shit ever happened, right?* Only she didn't need to forget because she couldn't actually remember in the first place, and judging by what she was hearing, it was probably just as well.

'Nah, I've got something better in mind for this one,' the familiar voice said. 'I did some research, found out who she is . . .'

'What, is she, like, famous or something?'

'Her pops is none other than Vincent Scott my friend . . .' the voice sounded triumphant.

'Vincent Scott?'

'Fuck me, Fabrizio, anyone would think you lived in a fucking cave under the sea. Vincent Scott . . . of Great Scott Properties,' Tess heard the antagonism in his voice and it scared her. They knew her father's name . . . this was bad; *really fucking bad.*

There was a slight pause.

'And?'

'And you fucking prick, he's a billionaire. One of the richest dudes in the whole of fucking Europe!'

The other voice began to laugh then, a horrible manic chuckle that suggested the owner was a little unhinged.

'Bingo!' it said.

'Bingo indeed my brother; *bingo in-fucking-deed.*'

CHAPTER 13

The tension inside the private poker longue at The Player was thick enough to cloud judgement.

'I'm out,' the cowboy said, flatly. 'I fold.' He slammed his glass down onto the table, causing the ice inside to crack in objection. Howard Stanley shook his head and quickly followed suit, abandoning his cards with reluctance as he looked over at Tom Black and the two remaining players, Willy Grey and the Japanese businessman who, flanked by two burly minders, looked as if he had more money than sense and would probably need a generous slice of both before the night was over.

'How about you, Willy?' Tom remarked, deadpan, his poker face an expressionless blank as he made eye contact with the old man opposite.

Willy returned his stare, his left eye twitching.

He eventually nodded after a long moment's pause. 'And I'll raise you another million,' he casually added, pushing a pile of neatly stacked burgundy chips across the table towards the dealer.

'That's three million in the pot,' the dealer announced without emotion, accustomed to hearing such high numbers; it was all in a day's work for him.

Willy Grey carefully peeled back the corners of his cards, only briefly breaking eye contact with Tom. Nothing would give him greater pleasure than screwing Tom Black to the wall tonight.

Candy rubbed the inside of Tom's thigh from underneath the table. At his insistence she had worn a long bubblegum pink sequinned Cavalli dress with a plunging neckline that stopped at the navel, displaying her enhanced young breasts like a pair of perfectly round globes. It had been a calculated choice of attire, aimed at distracting his fellow players, and one that seemed to be working its magic this evening to great effect.

She took a tentative sip of her Dirty Martini cocktail, her sixth and counting, and played with the diamonds around her neck seductively.

'We win big tonight baby and you get to keep the lot,' Tom had promised her as he'd fastened the delicate clasp of the Graff pink and yellow diamond waterfall necklace around her slim neck earlier that evening. 'I want you to dazzle 'em tonight,' he had instructed. 'Smile and flirt, make like you're *available* . . .'

'Jeez, I ain't no hooker . . .' she'd pouted.

'It's just a game, baby,' he'd reassured her, kissing the back of her creamy neck, giving her goose bumps. 'It's all about distraction . . . if those guys start thinking about their dicks, it means they ain't thinking about the game, you get me?'

Candy had responded with a conspiratorial giggle. Frankly, she'd be prepared to do *anything* if it meant keeping hold of all this awesome bling.

Tom looked down at his cards as the tension in the room escalated.

'I gotta go pee,' Candy stated a little too loudly, her caustic LA twang breaking the tension.

'I dunno why you bring broads to the table, Tom,' Willy

84

gave him a wry smile, once Candy was out of earshot. 'You know what they say about women and poker . . .'

Tom raised an eyebrow.

'Call,' he said in response, stacking his burgundy chips in a tall pile and carefully placing two blue gaming cheques on the top '. . . and I'll raise you another million . . .' he paused, 'no, you know, what?' he signalled to the dealer, 'make it two.'

The room fell silent but for the sound of the oscillating fan churning above them. Tom's raise had just taken the game into new territory.

'That should just about cover the girl's agency fees for tonight, eh Tom?' the sarcasm dripped from Willy Grey's voice, his left eye twitching manically.

Tom remained silent. True to his name, Willy Grey was always trying to get a rise out of people.

'Your old man was the same, Tom,' Willy surmised, as his left eye went into some kind of spasm. It was an affliction he'd had since his teenage years and it still drove him fucking nuts. 'He was a good hustler, all flash suits and Cartier cufflinks, much like yourself, but it was the pussy that ruined him in the end.' The corners of Grey's thin little mouth turned outwards, like he was imparting the gospel of the Lord himself.

Tom didn't much care for the man's overfamiliarity. He may have done the casinos with his old man once upon a time, but frankly who in Vegas hadn't?

'Yeah, pussy and bourbon eh, what a way to go?' Tom replied tightly as he held his gaze, hoping it might throw the miserable, twitching prick off kilter.

Candy returned from the restroom, refreshed from a little line of coke from the wrap Tom had given her earlier and immediately felt the palpable pressure in the room, her initial stride reduced to a tentative tiptoe.

'Something to keep your energy levels up,' he'd said

85

earlier as he'd handed her the small wrap of powder. 'But don't go overboard eh?' Tom hated to see women strung out on coke, and Candy, with her Barbie doll looks and high-pitched voice, was sailing dangerously close to the edge.

'Gentlemen,' the dealer cleared his throat, 'your hands please.'

Tom instinctively squeezed Candy's thigh, convinced it would bring him extra luck. If the cards were on his side tonight all his worries would be over.

Candy held her breath in anticipation, her heart pumping rapidly from adrenalin mixed with grade-A cocaine.

As the Japanese businessman turned over his cards Tom took a silent intake of breath.

'A flush,' the dealer said, clinically, 'two cards; king of spades and ten of spades.'

Willy Grey's eye was flicking like a faulty light bulb. This was in the bag, he thought smugly as he flipped his cards.

'High full house,' the dealer announced evenly as Grey continued to study Tom's expression. *Gotcha*!

Tom sat back into the comfort of the padded Louis antique gold chair and linked his fingers together, his knuckles cracking as he stretched them. He *wanted* Grey to see that he was worried. He *wanted* him to walk blindly into a false sense of security.

'Your hand, sir,' the dealer prompted Tom.

Sighing, Tom looked over at the Japanese businessman and then at Grey; the two men, so utterly physically opposite from each other, were now wearing the same pensive expression and could've been mistaken for brothers.

'Do the honours Candy, will you?' Tom nodded at the pair of playing cards lying face down on the table.

'Me?' she squeaked.

'Yeah you,' Tom winked at her and so, shrugging, she did as she was told and turned the cards over.

There were gasps and claps in the room. The Cowboy whistled.

'The five of spades and seven of spades – that's a straight flush my friend – highest cards.'

Willy Grey felt all the air leave his body as if he'd just been punched in the stomach. He was fucked; royally, regally fucked. In that split second he realised his life was over; finished, finito. His new wife, the greediest of the lot so far, would leave him after this and his business would be dead in the water. He'd lost *everything*.

'OH. MY. FUCKING. *GAAAAD*!' Candy Wilson leapt into the air like a rocket had gone off underneath her and threw her slim arms and legs around Tom's body, attaching herself to him like a limpet.

'You did it, baby!' her voice was high and tight with euphoria. 'You just won over ten . . . million . . . dollars,' she said the words slowly, over and over again, like a child learning to speak. Laughing, Tom twirled her to the ground before draining the dregs of his Courvoisier. He nodded at the Japanese man, who graciously returned the gesture. Grey, however, looked like he'd been dead for a week and someone had just dug him up.

'Willy,' Tom proffered his hand; he could feel the old man's hatred coming off him in waves. The prick had always been a bad loser.

Tipping the dealer twenty-five thousand dollars' worth of chips, Tom turned to Candy, her face lit up like a picture as she played with the Graff diamonds around her neck; *her* new necklace.

'So then,' Tom said, buzzing with adrenaline, a smile as wide as the Thames, 'looks like the first round is on me.'

CHAPTER 14

Ellie Scott couldn't sleep. She'd been tossing and turning for most of the night, drifting in and out of a shallow, fitful slumber.

She still hadn't heard from Tess and her concern had now, in the grip of a sleepless night, escalated into full-blown paranoia. Her maternal instincts were screaming that her daughter was in some kind of trouble.

Slipping in and out of consciousness, Ellie restlessly rolled onto her side and wished that Vinnie were here and that she could shuffle into the familiar reassuring warmth of his body; her very own comfort blanket. But Vinnie was in the US on business and so once again she found herself alone with her thoughts, thoughts that had begun to coast towards the moribund.

As a shallow sleep eventually threatened to claim her, Ellie's subconscious mind took her back to the summer of 1989. It had been the hottest summer on US record for over fifty years and she could still recall the stickiness of her skin against the thin, cheap polyester bed sheets that she'd slept in. She had been about to turn sixteen years old . . .

*

'Stop it! You're hurting me,' Ellie yelped as Tom pulled her roughly down onto the bed and pinned her by her arms. 'I told you,' she said breathlessly, 'not until my birthday, and that's not until *tomorrow* in case you've forgotten.'

'Bloody cock tease, that's what you are.' He pulled a face.

'It's not that I don't want to, Tom,' she pleaded, rolling into his back as he turned away from her, spooning him. He was naked from the waist up and his skin felt soft and smooth against her chest. 'It's just that I want it to be right, you know, proper.'

'Whatever,' he sulked. 'But I might've found a replacement by the time you make up your mind.'

'Big head,' she said, giving him a playful slap on the back. But she knew he was right. Tom Black could have anyone he wanted. With his dark Latino complexion, hypnotic eyes, and cocksure smile, he was as close to perfection as a man could get. Or at least Ellie O'Connor had thought so. And it would be fair to say she wasn't alone.

She stared at him, unblinking, and wondered what it was about him that made her love him so much. It wasn't just his movie-star looks; she came alive whenever he was near her, but she knew him inside out. Tom Black had more front than Blackpool Pier, as her old Nan would've said. He could be cruel and dismissive but it was all just a ruse at the end of the day, an elaborate disguise to cover up the insecure little boy underneath, the one who just wanted to be loved.

'I don't see what difference a day makes anyway,' Tom said, continuing to push. He wanted her; badly. Ever since he'd noticed the swelling beneath her t-shirt, how her hips had become rounder and smoother, he couldn't get her out of his head. His little Eleanor had grown into a woman right before his eyes and he wanted to be the first to sample the goods. 'It's just a day; just another number,' he gave a casual shrug. 'You'll not feel any different tomorrow, birthday or otherwise.' He sat up on the edge of the bed, his back still towards her, and she noticed a freckle on his shoulder that she'd not seen before.

'It makes a difference to *me*,' she replied, sharply jabbing him in between the shoulder blades. 'And that, Tom Black, is all you need to know.'

He was smiling, she sensed it.

'Tomorrow you could get run over by a truck,' he turned his body to face her then, grinning. 'Then you'd be up there,' he pointed to the ceiling, 'kicking yourself in heaven, thinking "if only I'd done it with Tom!" You could die a virgin, Eleanor. Imagine that, going to your grave never having known the pleasures of the flesh.'

Ellie gave an uneasy laugh. He could love her and destroy her in the same breath.

'Yeah, or I do it with you, get hit by a truck and end up down there,' she pointed to the floor, 'burning in hell for my sins!'

'Hell sounds like my kinda place,' Tom snapped the ring pull from a can of Colt 45, discarding it on the threadbare carpet with a sniff, 'more fun.' He got up from the bed and made his way over towards the stereo, stopping to open the small window a little wider, a wall of cloying Nevada heat smothering his face like a blanket.

'Anyway, it's hardly romantic is it?' Ellie threw him a look, 'what with your dad and my mum tearing lumps out of each other downstairs.'

The muffled voices from the room below, they had both noted, were getting progressively louder and Ellie knew it wouldn't be long before it reached a messy, bloody crescendo. She knew the drill only too well.

'They'll kiss and make up in a minute, they always do,' Tom said, sensing the despair in her voice and wanting to say something to make it better. He pressed a button on the stereo and Simply Red's *A New Flame* began to play as he flopped back down on the bed next to her. She really was quite something to look at now, all bright green eyes that sparkled when the light hit them, pillow lips and long, honey-coloured hair that felt as soft as cashmere to stroke. He certainly wanted to fuck her, but it was more than that. They'd been thrown together through circumstance and it was something unspoken between them, a silent understanding.

Ellie was distracted by the almighty row taking place between their beloved ma and pa downstairs. She was sensitive underneath all the streetwise swagger and he knew the fighting really got to her. It got to him too, only he was much better at hiding it.

'Sweet sixteen and never been kissed,' he teased, wrapping his arm around her as the bloodcurdling screams downstairs reached new heights.

'I *have* been kissed, I'll have you know. Plenty of times, actually,' she bristled.

Tom sighed as he stared up at the peeling artex ceiling above them; it was a depressing grey colour, matching the grubby net curtains that gently lifted from the sticky breeze outside.

'I remember my sixteenth birthday,' he said, a little wistfully. 'I got drunk on 20/20 and screwed Chasey Grey in the parking lot behind the Walmart.'

'Wow, a regular romantic.'

'Well, she seemed to enjoy it,' he retorted, placing his hand on her belly, the feel of her naked skin beneath her crop top giving him an instant hard-on inside his battered Levi 501s.

They were silent for a moment, the sound of their respective breathing barely audible above the music and muffled cries below.

'I wanna get out of here, Tom,' Ellie said suddenly, her

voice cracking slightly. 'I don't just mean this shitty room, I mean this life. I feel like I'm dying a slow death here.' She sat up with purpose, stretched her long, slim legs out in front of her. 'I wanna do something with my life. My dance teacher thinks I've got what it takes to make it big, you know, the ballet, Broadway! Be *someone*.'

Tom watched her intently as she made her speech. He wanted so much to be able to say something to make it better but as always, something stopped him; at the end of the day, kindness felt just too much like weakness.

'Face it, kiddo,' he snorted, 'this time next year you'll be in the clubs shaking it for men like my dear old dad downstairs.'

Ellie pulled her knees into her chest and hugged them. She vehemently resented this remark, if only for the fact that she feared it might be true.

'You know nothing, wanker!' she spat back.

Tom laughed, amused by her outburst. He liked that she was feisty. They were similar that way. He pulled her back down onto the bed next to him. 'Well, if it's any consolation, I believe you'll be someone, someday,' he said, keen to get her back on side. 'Though whether you'll ever be as successful as me . . . now that's debatable.'

'Oh really?' she raised a sarcastic eyebrow.

'In ten years' time I'll be a multi-millionaire.' He propped himself up on his elbow, looking down at her with an arrogance that she found irresistible. 'The boats, the jets, the houses and cars, the jewellery . . .' he raised his hands in demonstration. 'The whole fucking enchilada . . . I'll have it all. I'll call them *Black's*. Have hot girls dancing for *me*, on *my* payroll . . . king of the fucking clubs.' He jabbed his chest with his thumb.

'What, like your old man, you mean?' She grinned facetiously.

'Watch me, you'll see. Actually, me and Jack are onto

92

something as we speak,' he tapped his nose with a conspiratorial finger. 'I might even give you a job if you ask me nicely. Pay you to shake your little ass in *my* club.'

Ellie hit him with a pillow. 'You're disgusting,' she made to turn away from him, but he was too quick for her and held her there, her strength no match for his.

'So *easy* to wind up . . .'

Ellie had grown used to Tom's unpredictability over the years they had lived together. In fact, as far as she was concerned, it was all part of his appeal. The proverbial sunshine and showers; that was Tom. You never knew what you were going to get.

A sickening thud from downstairs stopped their conversation mid-track and Ellie winced.

'Sounds like they're really going for it tonight,' Tom remarked after a long moment.

He held her then and she felt a genuine tenderness in his touch.

'I mean it, Tom,' she said, fighting back tears as she buried her face into his warm chest. He smelt of cheap aftershave and fags. 'I'm going to get out of here and make a good life for myself one day; be rich and successful; be *happy* . . .'

'We're gonna be winners. I know it.'

Ellie loved Tom when he said things like this. Things that gave her hope for the future, a future she could not envisage without him. 'We'll make it together. You'll get out of this festering shit pit and make something of your life, fulfil your dreams, because that's the kind of woman you are.' He paused for a moment, allowing his carefully chosen words to resonate.

Ellie was floored. He had never referred to her as a 'woman' before.

'I love you, Tom,' she whispered the words just loud enough for him to hear them.

She would marry Tom Black and they would make a life together. Her, a famous ballerina, him a lauded entrepreneur, the kind of couple that women envied and men wanted to be. It was their destiny, she felt sure of it.

Tom's hand moved gently upwards of her thigh, gently resting between her legs. This time Ellie did not move it. Maybe he *was* right after all; what difference did a day make?

*

Coming round from her shallow slumber, Ellie sat up in her bed and, rubbing her gritty eyes, brought her knees up to her chest and hugged them tightly, cursing herself. She felt the heat pulse between her legs, a dull ache for him. Even dreaming of Tom felt like a terrible betrayal of her husband and yet there were times when she could not prevent it; it was times like this, in the dark of a lonely night, that he dripped into her psyche, resurrecting feelings she had spent a lifetime trying to bury.

Though she attempted to deny it to herself, Ellie knew she had loved Tom Black with a deep, intense passion and burning lust that regrettably she had never mimicked with her husband. With Tom it had been instantaneous and all-consuming; she had wanted him with a base ferocity that had scared her, if only for the fact that deep down she suspected it would one day destroy her – a supposition that had nearly turned out to be correct in the end. It had always bothered Ellie that it had not been the same way with her husband. A husband who she knew would walk the world barefoot twice over to make her happy and give her what she wanted in life. She heard her mother's familiar voice resounding inside her mind, 'the heart wants what the heart wants, Eleanor,' she would say as if to justify her own dubious choices. 'You don't choose love; it chooses you.'

And yet Tom had turned her over without a backwards glance the moment Loretta Fiorentino had strutted into the Venus Club, all tits and lips and cheap costume jewellery, seducing him with her exotic accent and talk of going places. Loretta had set her cap at Tom Black that night and had promised him the earth in a bid to lure him into her lair; money, clubs, contacts, 'the whole enchilada', as Tom had put it. Not that Tom had needed much persuading. He was going places, with or without Ellie in tow, and had abandoned her without a second's thought; though some years later he would vehemently deny this betrayal, attempting to prove his love to her one final time . . .

It was no good. Ellie threw back the fine cream silk sheets and flung her long, slim dancer's legs over the side of the intricately carved four-poster Fratelli Basile bed that in a twist of irony her husband had imported from Italy, her Agent Provocateur lace chemise sliding down her naked body as she stood. Making her way over to her dressing table, she sat down on the cushioned stool and blinked at her reflection; seeing herself as a stranger would. Ellie pulled at her skin absentmindedly, poking her tongue out before reaching for her Crème de la Mer serum. Eye bags she could cope with; she could have them removed tomorrow if the fancy took her, it was just her past that wasn't so easily erased.

Ellie snapped herself out of her thoughts by applying a dollop of Laura Mercier Fig hand cream, inhaling the deep, earthy sweet scent as she rubbed it into her skin. She had to stop this; no good had ever come out of raking over the past.

It was that bloody bitch Loretta's photograph that had triggered all of this. Ellie had spent decades repressing her past with an iron will that would've flawed a heavyweight champion, and so tonight felt like a defeat, though if she was honest, it had also been cathartic. Thinking of Tom had allowed her to remember the girl she had once been, someone she had denied for the past two decades. A girl that, in an odd way, she missed being.

Ellie's iPhone suddenly beeped, and alarmed, she snatched it up from the bedside table.

'Oh thank God,' she breathed aloud as the message came into view.

Hi Mom, Dont worry bout me. Havin a GR8 time. B in touch soon. Tx

She stared at the text for a moment. Something was different somehow but she couldn't quite put her finger on what it was. The use of the word 'Mom' perhaps.

Ellie slid back into bed. She was just being paranoid. Tess was OK, and even though she could not quite shake the sense of unease that had stalked her these last few days, for now, it was one less thing to worry about.

CHAPTER 15

Marco DiMari discarded the phone onto the bed without so much as a second thought as he rifled through Tess's belongings. There had to be a fair few grand's worth of designer gear here he thought happily, as he inspected the contents of her Louis Vuitton holdall with gusto. The suitcase alone was worth a small fortune and he could just see himself passing through customs with it. He grinned at the thought.

Marco DiMari's real name was Tarik Valmir and although he had people, women largely, believe that he was a real Italian stallion from Rome, he was in fact born in a small city called Lezhe in Albania and had grown up largely on the peripheries of East London, Bethnal Green, to be exact. The Italian thing was simply a ruse to entice women; it certainly got you into their knickers a lot quicker. Ever tenacious, he had even learnt to speak the language fluently, fooling Italian women themselves on occasion. Oh yes, Tarik liked his alias. He liked it a lot.

Hoping that he might've thrown Tess's mother off the scent with his text message, Marco came across Tess's passport.

'Bingo,' he said underneath his fetid alcoholic breath.

He was sure there was big money to be made from this one and he wasn't about to let such an opportunity slip through his nimble fingers. He'd seen a new opportunity in Tess Scott, the billionaire's fragrant daughter. One that was far too good to pass up.

Marco heard the pounding on the wall next door again. The girl had been going at it on and off all morning, hammering at the door and walls, crying and screaming like a banshee. He knew he would have to give her something to drink soon before she collapsed with dehydration. He didn't want a stiff on his hands – she was worth far too much for that.

He heard Tess's muffled cries through the wall.

'That's right love, you carry on. We're halfway up a fucking mountain in Spain you dozy bitch, no one can hear you.' He banged his fist against the wall in retaliation, laughing, 'no one at all!'

CHAPTER 16

Tom watched as Candy threw herself around the dance floor like an epileptic on acid.

'Come on!' she beckoned to him above the deafening sound of Lady Gaga's *Born This Way*. 'What's wrong with you? You've just won ten million bucks! If I were you, buddy, I'd be on the tables doing the frickin' can-can.' Tom raised a distracted smile. Truth was, Candy Wilson was beginning to grate on his nerves; it was coming up for three a.m. and, flying off her tits on coke, she was showing no sign of calling it a night.

Deep down Tom knew he should really get the fuck out of Vegas, pronto. Access to this amount of ready cash was way too much of a temptation for the likes of him. It was like putting a dope addict in a field full of poppies.

Agitated, he pulled at the collar of his bespoke white shirt. It was hot inside The Paradise Club, The Player's resident hot spot which attracted the young, beautiful and rich from far and wide. He delicately sipped at a chilled glass of Cristal champagne from the magnum he'd bought earlier and took a pinch of coke from his snuff box in a bid to distract himself from the pull of the casino tables downstairs. Surely a little flutter on the roulette or the craps wouldn't do any harm, the small voice inside his head whispered, besides, it would give him a breather from the coked-up Candy. He'd quite happily bung her a thousand bucks and her flight home if it meant getting shot of her. However, Tom had promised the girl a shopping spree with a champagne and lobster lunch thrown in and he was pretty sure hell would freeze over before she allowed him to renege on his word.

'I'm going down to the casino for a bit,' he shouted in Candy's ear above the melodic voices of Pitbull and Ne-Yo. 'You stay here, have some fun. Do some more coke.' He handed her a fat bunch of hundred dollar bills and watched as her eyes lit up like diamonds. 'I'll meet you back at the suite – no rush, baby,' he adding disingenuously, pressing his lips against hers and sliding his long tongue deep into her glossy, willing mouth.

'Mmm,' she made an appreciative noise as she merged back into the dancing throng. 'I'll be waiting for you,' she cooed, lowering her eyes seductively.

*

Throwing back a tumbler full of bourbon, Tom swallowed hard. He'd only been at the craps tables for an hour and was already $750,000 down. He was thoroughly pissed at himself.

'Another bourbon, sir?' the overly made-up waitress in the tiny dress enquired as she hovered over him.

'Make it a double, sugar,' he winked. Tom ran his fingers through his dark hair, fighting back his agitation. This was just a little blip on what had otherwise been a momentous occasion and he wasn't about to let it unduly concern him.

'I hear you've had a pretty good night tonight, my friend,' Tom looked up to be greeted by Marvin Katz's familiar grinning mug, 'congratulations.'

100

Tom clapped Marvin's shoulder with a victorious smile that made him look even more handsome than he was.

'What can I say, Marv?' he said with a hefty dose of false modesty, 'you know how it goes; you win some you lose some.'

Marvin took a seat next to Tom at the craps table and the waitress reappeared with a bottle of Maker's Mark and two fresh crystal tumblers.

'Cheers,' the men knocked glasses, ice chinking.

'Indeed,' Marvin replied, careful to conceal his emotions. That Tom had just won big irked him, just as it did whenever anyone won big in his casino. The trick now was to make sure he stuck around and shared it all back out to the house again.

'I've organised it for you to keep the Penthouse Suite for a further couple of days, Tom. Give you and that little piece you brought along time to get to know each other better.' He gave a good-natured laugh that was as flimsy and transparent as a cellophane wrapper.

Tom took pleasure in the knowledge that Marvin Katz was seriously pissed; pissed that he'd won big and pissed that he had a pretty, insatiable twenty-something on his arm who would quite happily suck his dick all night long without breaking a sweat.

'And how's your wife these days, Marv?' Tom carefully enquired, wondering how Marvin would react if he knew that Tom had once given his wife, Elaine Katz, a mercy fuck in the back of her Mercedes a decade earlier. Not that he'd been given much choice in the matter. She'd practically lampooned herself on his dick, almost chewing half his ear off in the process.

'Can't complain,' Marvin replied tightly, grimacing as he swallowed back the bourbon.

'Send her my regards, won't you?' Tom said. 'Is she still driving a Mercedes these days?'

101

Marvin glanced at him, thinking it a strange question. How did Black know what car his wife drove?

'Yes,' he nodded, suspiciously, 'E-class cabriolet. She upgraded to a new model some years ago – never looked back.'

'Bet you wish you could say the same thing, eh Marv?' Tom clapped him on the back again. Marvin Katz detected the lightest smirk upon Black's face and felt an urgent need to wipe it off.

'Anyway Marv,' it's been a pleasure as always, but I'm off first thing. Got a few business details to attend to,' he shook the man's hand with vigour. 'You know what they say; best to leave the party while it's still in full swing.'

Marvin Katz secretly hoped Tom Black would be met with a sudden, and ideally painful, death. Yet somehow he knew he would end up having the last laugh tonight. The thought cheered him up no end.

CHAPTER 17

'I've got absolutely nothing to wear!' Victoria exclaimed as she stood inside her vast walk-in wardrobe, staring at the colour coordinated rails of designer clothes.

Lawrence Mayfield shot her such an incredulous look that even she managed a smile.

'OK, well, nothing I *want* to wear then!'

Lawrence sighed.

'You could wear a sack cloth and still be the most beautiful girl in the room.'

Victoria smiled her response but found herself having to turn away from him. Such sentiment from her husband did not sit comfortably with her these days. However well meant, it somehow felt forced and unspontaneous, as if he was trying too hard to please her, to make up for their shortcomings – namely their ability to have another child. 'Anyway, it's only dinner with the Scotts, wear what you want.' Lawrence hoped he'd managed to hide his reluctant tone about tonight's little get together. It wasn't that he disliked the Scotts, far from it. Eleanor was especially easy company; it was just the fact that the common ground they shared at being 'reproductively challenged' was always the great big elephant in the room whenever they got together. Lawrence knew how the evening would go as if he'd written the script himself; they would get the usual friendly catch-up banter out of the way, and then once the expensive wine began to flow, it would only be a matter of time before Tor began recounting their shared experiences at the clinic, quoting the doctors verbatim and comparing notes. Lawrence screwed his eyes tightly together with impending dread.

'How about this one?' Victoria held up a red lace Erdem dress for inspection.

'It'll show that wonderful figure of yours off perfectly,' he flashed a boyish smile. 'You know you've got the body of a twenty-five year old.'

'Shame I don't have the ovaries of one though . . .'

Lawrence felt his whole body sag. 'Look, why don't we skip dinner with the Scotts tonight,' he said jovially, ignoring her last comment. 'I'm off to Africa soon and I want to spend as much time alone with my wife as possible.' He went to her, put his arms around her waist from behind, inhaling the soft powdery scent of her neck. 'Why don't we order in some greasy food, grab a bottle of something chilled and watch old black and white movies, you remember, like we used to do before . . .'

'. . . Before CeCe was born,' she added.

Lawrence let his chin rest on his wife's slim shoulder. He felt utterly defeated. There was nothing he could say to make it better, however much he continued to search for the words. In fact, the more he opened his mouth, the more he seemed to put his foot in it.

'It's a lovely idea Lol, but I've promised Ellie now and it's a little late in the day to cancel. Besides, we'll have plenty of us time at Foxgrove next week.'

Lawrence inwardly sighed but acquiesced.

'The red dress it is then,' he said resignedly, his fingers sliding down her arm as he made his way from the room, careful not to allow her to see the defeat etched onto his handsome face.

*

'So, what is it this time my man, hanging out with giant pandas in China, or getting down with buffalo in the Zambia?' Vincent Scott slapped Lawrence Mayfield's back good-naturedly as he signalled to the housekeeper to pour him a large scotch on ice.

'Actually it's elephants in Africa,' Lawrence replied. 'Goldie Hawn's the VO – she's a big fan of them you know, elephants.'

'Beautiful creatures,' Vinnie nodded earnestly. 'Seen a few up close myself, ridden one on safari . . .'

'Really . . .'

Of course Vincent Scott had been up close and personal with elephants, Lawrence thought.

There was nothing particular about Vincent Scott that Lawrence Mayfield found offensive per se. He was undeniably affable, impeccably polite and the perfect host, and over their years of shared experience at those unbearable fertility clinics he supposed you could say they had become friends. Only, Lawrence suspected that Vincent Scott didn't really have friends, at least not in the true sense of the word. Ironically, he imagined he was the kind of man who couldn't afford them. There was a cold air of detachment about him and Lawrence could honestly say that he knew no more about who Vincent Scott was now than he'd done the day they had met over two years ago. He was a dark horse, as they said.

'Just make sure one doesn't step on your toe!' Vinnie laughed, and Lawrence forced himself to join in. He shuffled in his antique Chesterfield chair. A priceless heirloom no doubt.

'And you?' Lawrence found himself asking out of politeness. 'How's life in the property game? Is Donald Trump quaking in his boots?' He didn't know why he was so pleased with this remark. It was a backhanded compliment and a little uncalled for.

'Got something big coming up down under,' Vinnie tapped his nose with his forefinger.

Lawrence nodded disingenuously. What was it about Scott that got up his nose so much? Lawrence wondered if this might not be his own insecurity, yet he couldn't quite shake the feeling that Scott somehow deemed himself superior. Ellie looked over at Lawrence Mayfield and her husband chatting, and smiled.

'It's great that they get on so well, our men.'

'Isn't it,' Victoria agreed, running her finger along the rim of her gin and tonic. Her thoughts were elsewhere, something that was becoming a bit of a habit these days.

'Maybe we should all think about going away together for a holiday somewhere? The Maldives perhaps, or a little break in Biarritz. Actually, forget the men; let's sod off somewhere stunning and hot for a girlie break!' Victoria giggled, unable to stop herself from imagining a little holiday romance, or, more accurately, dalliance, with some virile, exotic Latin type.

'It's a great idea, hun,' Ellie conceded with a grin. The idea of escaping London for a bit greatly appealed. The sticking point however was her husband's business schedule. Making money was an addiction for Vinnie, an affliction. The greater the risk, the bigger the high he seemed to obtain. In that respect he was no different to Tom Black. Tom. There she went again, thinking of his name. Ellie glanced over at her husband, and for the briefest second his face became Tom's.

'Darling, are you OK?' Vincent's voice popped Ellie's thought bubble abruptly and Tom's face dissipated back into her husband's. 'What's the odd look for?'

'Look? What look?' Ellie smiled nervously, 'Tor and I were just talking about how nice it would be to get away for a bit. After all, it doesn't look like we're in for much of a summer here, does it?'

'You can say that again,' Tor agreed. 'I doubt my new Victoria's Secret retro bikini will even get a look in if it carries on like this.'

'Now that *would* be a shame,' Lawrence winked at her. So far so good, he thought to himself. No baby talk as yet. He wondered if this might be a turning point. He hoped so.

'Well, here's hoping I won't be tied up Down Under for too long eh?' Vinnie remarked. 'Perhaps we can think about organising something when I'm back.'

'And when might that be?' Ellie found herself asking, though frankly she knew better than to. She had long accepted that whatever her husband said went, and not to question it. It wasn't that he was despotic, or that she was particularly subservient, it was just the dynamic between them; how it had always been. Vinnie was the one in the driving seat. In some ways he had become almost like her guardian, a father-figure if you liked.

'I can't say, Ellie,' Vinnie said, smiling, though there was a detectable tightness to his tone.

Victoria glanced over at her husband and saw his eyebrow twitch.

'So, what's on the menu tonight then?' she asked. 'I'm famished.'

'My good friend Gordon and his team of sous chefs are busy in the kitchen as we speak,' Vincent said theatrically, seizing the opportunity to change the subject. 'He likes to surprise, so I'm not even sure myself to be honest.'

'Well, I do like surprises,' Victoria smiled, smoothing her hands down her red lace Erdem dress and suddenly realising that she hadn't taken her daily dose of folic acid. 'Oh Lord!'

her face took on a mask of horror. 'I forgot my folic acid!' she exclaimed, her mouth forming an O shape as the panic welled up inside her.

'Well, I'm sure it'll be OK if you take it when we get home,' Lawrence said tremulously. He knew it had been too good to be true, knew they wouldn't make it through the night without some kind of reference to their 'affliction' as she called it.

'But you know what the doctor said!' Victoria's raised voice resounded around the high ceiling of the Scotts' vast and impeccably designed dining room. 'He said I must take it with strict regularity otherwise . . . well, you never know it could be the difference between . . .'

Vincent duly poured himself and Lawrence another scotch to busy himself.

'For goodness' sake, Tor . . .' Lawrence felt his cheeks flush.

'I'm sure I have some somewhere,' Ellie touched her friend's arm lightly as she glanced over at her husband and Lawrence. 'Let me go and have a look.' She stood, her Roland Mouret crepe evening dress hugging her slim, delicate curves as she made her exit.

Bloody elephants, Lawrence Mayfield thought miserably as he braced himself for the inevitable awkward silence that followed. The room was full of them.

CHAPTER 18

Candy Wilson heard the knock at the door and rolled her violet-blue eyes. She had just immersed herself into a deep hot whirlpool bath filled with expensive Michael Kors beauty products and wasn't inclined to move for anyone.

The enormous bathroom was like something straight out of MTV's *Cribs*; all floor to ceiling marble, his and hers sinks with matching gilt gold taps, ornate mirrors and a deep, sunken, oval bath which could've doubled as a mini swimming pool. This was Candy's first real taste of the good life and she was loving every second of it; only there was still no sign of Tom.

It had been five a.m. by the time she had fallen out of The Paradise Club, admittedly higher than a rogue helium balloon, and had practically crawled back to the suite, where she'd promptly passed out. She had awoken, fully clothed, some hours later and had been disappointed to find that she was alone. Tom's belongings were still there though so Candy assumed, a little indignant, that he must've slipped off to lunch without her. Her first thought was to call him but it had suddenly struck her that she couldn't. She'd been so swept away by the events of the last twenty-four hours that she hadn't even thought to ask for his cell.

Squeezing a generous dollop of Michael Kors shampoo onto her blonde hair Candy began mentally planning out her day's shopping expedition; she could hardly believe her luck. Just a day earlier she'd been mooching along the Boulevard, with nothing but unemployment and prejudice to look forward to. Her stint in the nut-house had proved a real sticking point when it came to getting decent paid work. Her parents had been on her case round the clock, yet it had been those pair of treacherous fuckers who'd had her sectioned in the first place. Well, all that shit was behind her now. All thanks to a chance meeting with Tom Black. Jeez, perhaps she *was* some kinda talisman, or whatever it was he'd called her.

The knocking on the door was getting progressively louder and more urgent now.

'Holy crap!' she'd highlighted the Do Not Disturb button, so what the fuck was this guy's problem? 'Hey buddy!' she called out, irritably. 'Like, durrr . . . can't you read?'

Candy closed her eyes once more and thought of all that money Tom was about to spend on her, and then it struck her that it might actually *be* Tom who was pounding on the door. Maybe he'd lost his room key or something.

'OK, I'm coming, *I'm coming*,' she sighed resignedly, reluctantly hoisting her toned body from the scented water and, grabbing a fluffy white hand towel that barely covered her modesty from the heated rail, she opened the door.

'Wassup, you lost your keycard?' she said, expecting to see Tom. Instead she was greeted by a strange angry looking man in a suit and four enormous security guys who looked like they snacked on kindergarten kids for lunch.

'Oh!' Candy physically recoiled in alarm, pulling her towel tightly around her chest like a shield. 'I thought you were . . .'

'Is Mr Black with you?' the man interrupted, looking past her into the suite. Candy shook her head.

'No, I haven't seen him since . . . sorry, *who are you?*'
That she even had the clarity of mind to ask the question
surprised her just as much as it did him.

'*I'm* Marvin Katz, floor manager here at The Player,' he
shot back. 'When did you say Mr Black would be back?'

'I didn't,' she retorted, a little put out by the man's abrupt
tone. Marvin cocked his head to one side, his whole countenance softening. He parted his thin lips into an affable smile.
If this little tramp was lying to him she'd be out on her
butt faster than a bullet from an AK47.

'I mean it,' she reiterated, sensing that Katz didn't believe
her. 'I've been waiting for him myself. He left me in the
club around three a.m. and said he would meet me back
here . . . anyway, why the urgency?' she enquired, leaving
the door open as she nonchalantly strutted back into the
suite, her damp blonde hair swishing behind her in tangled
knots. Marvin Katz followed her, nodding at his entourage
to stay put.

'Oh, it's just a small matter of an unpaid bill, that's all,'
he shook his head as if it were of little importance. Candy
gave a derisive laugh.

'Well, I'm sure there'll be *no* problem settling it; don't
know if you heard but my friend won big last night,' she
couldn't help boasting. 'And when I say big, I mean, like
real big.' Marvin Katz stifled a contemptuous snort. *Don't
know if you heard* . . . If someone farted in his casino
Marvin Katz *heard* about it. He gave the girl a patronising
smile.

'Oh really?' he replied, the sarcasm in his voice lost on
her completely. Katz scanned the room with beady eyes,
wondering for a brief moment if Black might be hiding in
the cedar closet, or under the bed perhaps. Candy grabbed
a silk robe from the bathroom and slipped into it, allowing
Marvin Katz a fleeting glimpse of her naked behind.

'He's taking me shopping today,' she called out from the

111

bathroom, her delight almost tangible. 'Can I give him a message when he returns?'

Marvin suddenly felt a small twinge of pity for the young woman. *When* he comes back? Try *if*, sweetheart. The slippery fucker was probably half way to another state by now, a thought that made him want to commit murder.

Tom had played directly into Marvin Katz's hands. As predicted, the lure of the tables had been too big a pull for a compulsive gambler like him. Now he was in debt to the house to the tune of five million and Katz had come to collect. Only it seemed Tom had been one step ahead of him.

'Just tell him I was asking after him,' he flashed her a quick sinister smile before turning to leave. 'Hope you've enjoyed your stay here at The Player, Miss,' he said disingenuously without turning back to look at her, adding sharply, 'you've got twenty minutes to clear your stuff out and leave.' Candy Wilson stood behind the door, dazed, as it slammed in her face, her Gucci dreams rapidly evaporating like the steam from her luxury bath.

Her luck, it seemed, had just run out.

CHAPTER 19

Pulling sharply over to the roadside, Tom opened the door to the Lamborghini and violently threw up. He looked like shit; his usual perfectly styled hair was a ruffled mess and his $2000 suit now looked as if it had been picked up at a thrift store for ten bucks, but it was nothing compared to how he *felt*. It was almost as if he was having an out-of-body experience; watching the nightmare from the outside, looking in as though it was happening to someone else. His chest heaving, he wiped his wet mouth with the sleeve of his designer suit and desperately tried to piece together the events of the previous evening, trying to figure out at what point it had all gone so diabolically wrong.

Blessed with the benefit of perfect hindsight, Tom knew it was a mistake ever to have come to Las Vegas. Vegas was like a faithless lover, luring him back over and over again.

Tom's thoughts coasted towards Candy then and how he'd abandoned the girl; she was probably still sleeping in the penthouse right now, clueless as to the shower of shit that was about to rain upon her from a lofty height. He'd given security the slip with relative ease, all things considered, turning back only to look at the magnificent, imposing hotel with nothing more than his car keys and a half empty bottle of Maker's. He didn't even have a firm destination in mind to run to; all Tom knew was that he'd had to get the fuck out of Vegas, make some distance between himself and the unholy mess he'd left behind. And yet his diminished conscience, what was left of it, was now beginning to gnaw at him. The look on Candy's pretty young face when he'd promised to take her shopping, how her eyes had lit up like neon signs and the megawatt smile she'd given him, bright enough to power the Strip. Tom inwardly cursed himself. Maybe if she'd been at his side on the roulette table then none of this would've happened. By leaving his lucky charm behind he had broken the magic spell of his good fortune, and it had been the worst decision of his life; a life that was soon to be cut spectacularly short if Jack got wind of what had just happened. *Jesus fucking Christ*; Jack. Tom wondered how he was going to react when he realised that he had lost his three million bucks. Tom's stomach lurched again and he took an intake of breath as the bile rose up in his throat.

With the unforgiving morning Nevada heat prickling at his skin, he reached inside the glove compartment of the Lamborghini and sighed with relief as he located the small bottle of Evian. Gulping back the warm contents like his life depended on it Tom looked at himself in the rear view mirror. His eyes were bloodshot and unsightly spittle had settled in the corners of his mouth. Perhaps he would be better off dead, he reasoned, engulfed by a wave of self-pity. At least he would leave a good-looking corpse behind.

It was in his most dark and desperate moments like this that he always thought of *her*. Here in Vegas he felt her ghost like the breeze around him. She had always been his first point of call whenever he'd been in a tight spot;

something he'd never had with a woman before or since, and he was besieged by the sudden urge to see her. He gave a wan smile. He wondered if age had been kind to her and if she was still as beautiful as he remembered. Not that it really mattered because in his mind she would be forever young, for that's how he remembered Eleanor O'Connor, the only woman who'd ever understood him.

With an audible intake of breath, Tom started up the Lamborghini's engine. As he drove he thought of what Marvin Katz might do to Candy when he discovered that he had skipped town, leaving behind a five million deficit. He knew the vindictive old fucker probably wouldn't think twice about having her pretty little ass thrown in jail, if only by association. Still, he attempted to convince himself, what the fuck did it matter to him? After all, he hardly knew the girl. Anyway, he'd shown her the time of her young life; plied her with champagne and coke, given her a posh dress and diamonds to wear while partying the night away in the VIP area of one of the world's most exclusive nightclubs; what more could a girl want?

Hitting the brakes, the wheels of the exquisite sports car screaming in protest, Tom did a swift U-turn.

'Fuck, shit and fuck again,' he cursed aloud as he slammed his fists onto the leather dashboard. It was no good; he would have to go back.

CHAPTER 20

Loretta wondered if the day could possibly get any better. Having spent the morning buying up Versace's entire Spring/Summer collection and a mountain of Graff diamond jewellery, she was now having lunch with a prominent Hollywood agent in the three-star Michelin restaurant, Il Luogo Divino, on the high end of the strip.

'So, darling, tell me what little gems of beauty you treated yourself to this morning,' Artie Maynard blinked at her with earnest watery blue eyes from across the dinner table, clasping his papery hands together in prayer as he admired the vast collection of shopping bags nestled at Loretta's spike-embellished Christian Louboutin heels. 'Gems being the operative word, I see,' he raised a perfectly manicured eyebrow approvingly at the Graff logo emblazoned on her shopping bags.

Artie Maynard was one of Hollywood's most infamous and influential celebrity agents and as such had represented some of the greatest celluloid faces of all time. He was a tiny slip of a man with a fearsome reputation, his diminutive size belying his sheer ruthlessness when it came to securing the best deals for his clients, and ultimately himself. Camper than Christmas, Artie had styled himself upon the late and unrepentantly flamboyant Quentin Crisp, all cravats, blue rinse and choice head gear, but as fey as he was, no one fucked with Artie Maynard. Not if they wanted to work in Hollywood again.

'Dahling,' Loretta purred, batting her lashes in deliberately coy over-exaggeration, 'you know me so well.'

This was not strictly true. Although their paths had crossed at various functions and events over the years, it was in fact the first time Artie Maynard and Loretta had ever sat down to lunch face-to-face and she could barely believe her luck. He was notoriously difficult to pin down, and if anyone could give her a heads up in Hollywood it was 'Smartie Artie', as he was known in prominent circles.

'Oh, just a little trolley dash in Graff, you know how it is,' she waved a glib be-jewelled hand. 'And I picked up the most divine pair of leather studded shorts in Versace. Donatella closed the store to allow me a *private* view of her new collection,' she casually boasted. 'I was thinking of wearing them to the Oscars this year with the matching biker jacket and a pair of her perspex wedges, what do you think?'

'I think you'll stop traffic darling,' Artie gushed, *for all the wrong reasons*.

'Grazie, *tesoro*,' she preened, stroking Bambino who was hidden beneath the table on her lap.

'Sir, madam,' a young and attractive liveried waiter politely addressed them. 'Can I get you some drinks?'

Il Luogo Divino was the glamorous house restaurant at The Player and boasted a hot-bed of culinary talent from around the globe. Booked out months in advance, Loretta had demanded the best seats in the house today next to the vast floor-to-ceiling glass window, affording them a sublime, panoramic view of the Strip, and thanks to the little mix up with the penthouse suite earlier she had made sure she got them.

'The Ruinart champagne for me, darling.' Loretta purred.

'. . . And I'll have a glass of the Chateau Suduiraut 1er cru classe,' Artie said in a perfect French accent as he perused the exquisite menu, deciding to opt for the soft-poached egg with Beluga caviar to start, followed by the royal of hare with parmesan cream. It would play havoc with his cholesterol levels but what the hell. She was paying.

'So, doll,' Artie cut through Loretta's train of thought with his distinct effeminate New York accent. 'I've been thinking about our little chat on the phone and I've come to the conclusion that . . .' He paused for dramatic effect '. . . I'd be happy to represent you!'

Loretta almost choked on her glass of Ruinart.

'Oh Artie, darling, that's fabulous!' she gushed, genuinely thrilled as she leaned forward to kiss him on both cheeks, affording him a close-up of her enormous enhanced breasts that were fighting to escape her strapless Alaïa dress.

'I've had *my* peeps draw up a little contract; standard stuff, plus a few other clauses you might want to have *your* peeps look through, but otherwise baby girl, I think we got ourselves a deal.'

Artie Maynard had been inclined to tell Loretta Fiorentino to go and play with the traffic when her initial call asking for representation had come through. He knew the woman had the reputation of being a pugnacious bitch. But he could not argue that she represented a new kind of challenge. She was a car crash waiting to happen and whether he liked it or not, this kind of 'celebrity' had mileage these days.

Toasting their mutual success, Loretta beamed.

'You won't regret it, darling,' she purred, getting straight down to business. 'When the Muldavey *merda* hits the fan I will need someone with experience to take care of business, make sure I come out of it all smelling of Fracas, *si capisce?*'

Artie nodded sagely. He understood alright.

'So the rumours *are* true then?' he cautiously enquired, knowing that Loretta was the type to go off like a faulty firework after one wrong word, 'about your husband and Miranda, I mean?'

Before she had time to think of a magnanimous answer to Artie's question, Loretta was distracted by the sound of a loud commotion going on outside on the sidewalk.

'What on earth's happening out there?' Artie enquired, practically launching himself across the table to get a better view.

'An arrest or something,' Loretta remarked, watching with barely concealed delight at the drama that was unfolding on the entrance steps to The Player.

A man had been pinned to the floor by four of the hotel's burly security guards and was shouting obscenities at the top of his voice; he seemed to find such treatment highly objectionable.

'Get these fucking gimps off me, Marv, I mean it!' the man's muffled cries resounded through the glass atrium of the restaurant. 'I've said I'll come quietly! What more do you want?' Diners were standing now, gravitating towards the bay window for a better look at the source of discord. Artie smirked. It was as he had suspected; people adored a real-life car crash.

'A thief,' Arte surmised, taking his seat again, his interest waning now he realised there was no blood and gore on offer.

'A *well-dressed* thief,' Loretta's antenna was twitching wildly; something about the man on the floor had pricked her interest.

'Perhaps he's a dangerous fugitive on the run – wanted by the FBI!' Artie squealed dramatically.

Loretta watched with morbid interest as the man was forcibly dragged from the steps and inside the hotel lobby, past the restaurant. At one point he tried to stand and she almost got a glimpse of his face but he was kidney punched by a member of the security team and buckled over before she had the chance.

'I fucked your wife, Katz,' the man shouted through his obvious pain, 'and boy was she grateful. She said she hadn't come in years!' Gasps began to emanate among the stunned diners. This was not the kind of show that one expected from such a world-class establishment, but it was thrilling nonetheless.

Loretta threw her head back and gave a delicious laugh, enjoying every uncomfortable moment.

'Well, I say! Did you hear that?' Artie covered his mouth in shock, although in truth nothing shocked him these days, after all, he'd worked with actors for over four decades. 'I should have known it would be over a woman – it always is.'

Loretta was distracted.

'Will you excuse me, darling?' she suddenly announced, handing Bambino over to him from across the table. 'I need to use the little girl's room.'

She flounced off, leaving Artie holding the dog.

Once out of sight, Loretta swerved the restroom and made her way towards the lobby. She couldn't help herself; she was naturally drawn towards chaos like a moth to a naked flame. Upon seeing her approach, Maurice, the man behind the desk, visibly flinched.

'You'll be very pleased to know the penthouse suite is free now, Mrs Hassan,' he said, pre-empting her question. Maybe now the woman would finally shut up and stop bugging him. 'The former occupants have, er . . . *vacated.*' He glanced across the lobby at the security guards who were struggling to restrain the man on the floor, his legs sporadically kicking out at them as he attempted to break free.

120

'Get your dirty fucking hands off me!'

'I must apologise for the noise, Mrs Hassan,' Maurice simpered.

'The man is a thief?' she enquired.

'Of sorts . . . the cops will be here any minute. Once again, I must apolo—'

But before he could finish the sentence, the man suddenly broke free and made a run for it across the lobby towards them.

'Oh no you don't, buddy!' Maurice gasped as the most nimble of the security team rugby tackled him to the floor, where he landed with a sickening crack at a startled Loretta's feet.

'Jesus fucking Christ, my nose . . .' he groaned.

Loretta looked down at the man rolling on the ground in pain, a pool of dark burgundy liquid forming on the marble floor where he had fallen and felt a bolt of electricity shock her system as she finally caught sight of his face.

'Well, well, well . . .' she smirked, her heartbeat accelerating inside her chest as she peered down at him, 'if it isn't Tom Black.'

Some days it seemed, just kept on giving.

CHAPTER 21

Pulling up outside Livedon, the sound of gravel crunching satisfactorily beneath the tyres of the chauffeur-driven Aston Martin, Ellie turned to her husband and gave a wan smile as she looked up at the imposing house in all its spectacular, neo-classical Georgian glory.

Hidden behind a wild meadow perched on the brow of a hill, the Grade I-listed Livedon's location was more than idyllic. Having been lovingly and painstakingly renovated back to its former glory by Vincent over a number of years, the nine-bedroom, seven-bathroom house set within thirteen acres of lush grounds boasted two formal dining rooms plus three separate receptions, its own vestry, servants' quarters, an outdoor and indoor swimming pool, in-built gym, walled rose gardens and an ornamental lake.

Due to his hectic business schedule, Vinnie didn't make it out to Livedon as much as he would've liked and rather than leave the house desolate, save for the skeleton staff that maintained its daily upkeep, he often hired it out for various propitious corporate and social occasions, the most recent being a *Vanity Fair* party.

'Livedon was meant to be *lived in*,' Vinnie would often remark. 'I'd rather hire it out to a bunch of strangers than

122

watch it turn ramshackle and unappreciated.' Ellie only wished she could share her husband's enthusiasm for the place, but the truth was Livedon held bad memories for her, memories she would rather not revisit. She wondered how long Vinnie had planned for them to stay.

'I've ordered dinner on the terrace for eight,' he said, nodding his gratitude to a member of staff who had relieved him of their plentiful Smythson luggage. 'So, plenty of time for a nice relaxing bath, or a long walk if you prefer . . .' he linked his arms around Ellie's waist and pulled her closer to him, his lips lightly touching the tip of her nose as he raised his eyebrows. 'Or we *could* just go to bed . . .'

Ellie forced another smile and silently followed her husband up the stone steps towards the front door, briefly looking back over her shoulder out towards the orchard. There were ghosts here. She could feel them everywhere.

*

Scouring herself in the shower until her skin burned, Ellie chastised herself. She was being selfish beyond comprehension and told herself to snap out of it. They would only be here for a couple of nights at most, and after everything her husband did for her surely she could do this one small thing to make him happy?

By rights Livedon should've held happy memories for Ellie; after all, it was where she and Vinnie had been married in a lavish ceremony almost twenty years ago to the day. But the day itself, purported to the best of a bride's life, had been overshadowed by events that took place the night before.

It had been a beautiful evening, the night of June 15th 1990; the sticky heat of the glorious summer's day had melded into a sultry evening and the night air had been perfumed by the scent of Livedon's lush flower gardens in full bloom.

Ellie had taken to her bed early, exhausted; the day had seen an army of people march in and out of the house in a human conveyor belt; chefs and caterers, florists, lighting technicians, silver service staff, musicians, photographers, all flapping like the proverbial headless chickens. It had made Ellie's head spin. She was nervous enough as it was; in less than twenty-four hours, wearing a Vera Wang couture dress that had cost more money than most people earned in a decade, twenty-year-old Ellie O'Connor would pledge her wedding vows to Vincent Scott in front of thousands of important strangers – to love and to cherish him, to forsake all others . . .

That night Ellie had eventually drifted off into a fitful slumber, only to be awoken by the tapping sound of gravel against glass. Initially she had thought it might be Vinnie playing some kind of joke but he was staying with his best man at a luxury hotel some ten miles down the road and besides, he knew it was bad luck for the groom to see the bride on the eve of her wedding . . .

Wrapping her nakedness in a thin robe, her curiosity pricked, Ellie had approached the window to investigate and it was then that she saw him disappear behind the trees into the orchard.

Convinced that her eyes must've deceived her, she had stealthily tackled the long winding staircase and, pulling on a pair of Hunter wellingtons that were by the door, she grabbed a torch and slipped, unnoticed, outside. As she made her way through the inky blackness with some purpose, the scent of summer filling her nostrils, Ellie suddenly wondered what she would say or do if it really *was* him.

The sound of a match being lit behind her caused her to spin round in alarm.

'Tom?' she breathed, suddenly terrified.

He had stepped out from behind an old oak, crossing one foot over the other as he leaned against the tree, nonchalantly lighting a cigarette, his face aglow from the dim light of the match. Fighting the urge to run to him, she watched as he inhaled deeply on his cigarette before expelling the smoke from his lips up into the night air.

'You thought I wouldn't come, didn't you?' he eventually spoke, the sound of his voice causing a hairline fracture in her heart. 'You thought that I would let my girl marry someone else without saying goodbye?'

Ellie recalled how she'd been besieged by a simultaneous mix of anger and excitement; the nerve of the man! There he was, bold as brass, standing before her after all this time; after not so much as a phone call from him since the day he had absconded with that Italian slut, standing in the grounds of her husband-to-be's stately home on the day of her wedding as if it was the most natural thing in the world.

'How dare you come here, Tom!' she said defiantly, adrenaline pouring into every crevice of her being. 'It's a bit late in the day for recriminations, isn't it?'

He had looked at her then in that familiar amused way that suggested he knew all her innermost secrets.

'I had to come, kid,' he eventually said, his dark eyes shining like marbles as they devoured her, 'when I heard you were getting married . . .' Standing there in a thin white robe that stuck to her obvious nakedness beneath, the tops of her slender legs peeping out of her wellingtons, he thought how she had never looked more beautiful and was struck by a terrible sadness that she would never truly know how he had missed her.

'. . . Oh, I see,' she mocked, 'when you heard I was getting married you thought, I know, I'll fly halfway across the world and try and screw it up for her!' her arms were folded tightly like a shield around her. 'Well, that's so typical of you Tom, isn't it? Can't bear to see anyone else happy . . .'

'Oh! So you *are* happy? Could've fooled me . . .'

Ellie shook her head wearily in response.

'Why Tom?' she pleaded. 'Why are you here? You made your choice. Now you think you can just turn up here like this and . . . and . . .' he watched her as she crumbled; she was choking back tears now, her brow furrowed in distress '. . . the night before my *wedding* . . .'

He made to go to her but she sprung backwards, recoiling from him. 'Come any closer and I'll scream,' she warned him, her chest heaving beneath the thin cotton robe. 'The whole place is alarmed to the hilt; one scream from me and they'll set the dogs on you.'

'Impressive,' he shrugged, backing off nonetheless. 'Well, you've certainly landed on your feet, kid,' he nodded, the corners of his mouth turning outwards as he looked around the orchard and up towards the house. 'Little Eleanor O'Connor, the East End stripper done good . . .' he was mocking her now, unable to hide his passionate jealousy. 'If your old mum could see you now . . .'

Enraged, Ellie launched herself at him, tears streaking her face as she pounded his chest with her fists. 'How dare you!' she growled, her face a tight ball of anger. 'You think you can just come here out of the blue, waltz back into my life unannounced like this . . . insinuating that it's *me* who is the gold-digger? *Me* who would be so shallow as to marry someone for money and status?' She was ranting now, 'and all this from a man who sold me down the river for five minutes of fun with some old porn star well past her sell-by date because he thought there might be a quick buck in it for him. You're a fucking hypocrite Tom Black. A liar and a cheat and a hypocrite . . .' She had fired the words from her lips like sharp tacks, her face a mix of heartbreak and rage. 'Well hear this; you're not even half the man I'm due to marry tomorrow.' She was circling him now, tears streaking her

126

face, her eyes burning with outrage as he watched her, his heart aflame. She jabbed at him with a pointed finger. 'Unlike *you*, the man I'm marrying understands the meaning of the word loyalty and would never betray me because, do you know what, Tom? He loves me!' she shrieked, borderline hysterical now. 'Yeah! He really fucking loves me!' She began to pummel at his chest again then but he had grabbed her slim wrists and held them together tightly, pressing his knee between her legs as he pushed her up against the oak tree, taking her breath away with the force of the impact.

'But do *you* love *him*, Eleanor?' he'd whispered, his breath hot and sweet in her ear as she gently whimpered, ferociously fighting the tightening in her groin. His lips found their way to hers and he kissed her deeply with an urgency that took her breath away.

'You arrogant bastard,' she had groaned, feebly attempting to push his hands away as they explored her exposed skin, the tips of his fingers lightly circling the outline of her stiff nipples, his breath hot against them. 'Please Tom . . . don't . . .' She ached for him so fiercely now, a pulse between her legs so acute that she felt at the brink of collapse.

'You know it's me you've always loved,' he breathed, and the tragedy was that he'd been right. She could feel his hardness against her thigh and the last of her resolve evaporate with despair. 'You can marry your billionaire tomorrow,' he'd said, his chest heaving in time with her own, 'be my guest. But it'll be *me* you'll think of when he's making love to you; it'll always be me, kid . . .' She gasped as he tore open her robe, instinctively wrapping her legs tightly around his waist. 'It was always just you and me . . .' he whispered as he plunged himself deep into her, over and over again, unable to stop himself, deep and hard until she cried out his name, begging him not to stop as the intensity of her orgasm threatened to engulf her. '. . . Just you and me . . .'

*

Vinnie would never truly forget Ellie's tearful confession to him on the day of their wedding. He remembered listening to her with heavy heart as she had nervously explained Tom Black's unexpected arrival on the eve of their much-anticipated nuptials.

'And?' he had asked her with a tightness in his chest, his spine stiffening, 'did you say your . . . *goodbyes*?'

The word was loaded with connotation and they both knew it.

She had nodded silently, unable to meet his gaze. When she had finally looked up, the pain and remorse he had seen in her doleful expression had answered all the questions that he'd been too frightened to ask. Vinnie had silently nodded his understanding with a desperate resignation, a look that had near shattered her heart.

'I will understand if you don't want to mar—' she started, but he had silenced her by taking hold of her arms.

'Can you promise me one thing?' he had looked into her glassy eyes and she had nodded as tears silently spilled down her beautiful young face. 'After today, we never mention that man's name again.' He had shaken her forcibly. 'From this moment on, Tom Black no longer exists. He is dead to us both.'

She had nodded before falling into his arms.

'I'm so sorry,' she'd said, over and over again. 'I'm so, so, sorry . . .'

Vinnie had held her shaking body and comforted her like a child. He'd chosen not to allow this one moment of indiscretion to destroy everything good he knew could be between them. As he had held her he made her a silent promise that he would teach her the true meaning of love and loyalty. He would marry Eleanor O'Connor and give her the life he knew she felt she didn't deserve. He would bury what he had suspected had taken place here the night before, for the simple reason that he loved her more than anything else in the world and could not bear to lose her. Deep down however, following the events of that one night, Tom Black had become a ghost in their marriage, a memory that neither could quite erase. And it was the start of Vinnie's poisonous hatred for a man he had never even met.

Vinnie had never asked his wife to recount the details of what had transpired that night at Livedon and he never would – some things are best left unsaid. Even when, six weeks later, she had come to him, wide eyed, and nervously announced that she was pregnant he'd refused to question her. As far as Vincent Scott was concerned, the child growing inside his wife's belly was, and always would be, his. And the years had happily proved him right, for two decades had now passed to the day and here they were, not a moment of real discord between them ever since. Vincent Scott was a proud man; his pride was his honour, especially when it came down to business. But Eleanor was his one weakness. He might have forgiven her for her indiscretion that night, but he certainly hadn't forgotten.

CHAPTER 22

Tess was rudely shaken awake from her drug-induced coma by a young woman whose face she had never seen before.

'Shhh,' the girl brought her finger to her lips as a disorientated Tess slowly sat up and made to speak, rubbing her dry, gritty eyes. 'Just do as I say and I will get you out of here, *d'accord*?' Frightened though she was, Tess had instinctively nodded. 'Here,' she handed her a cold bottle of Evian which Tess proceeded to drain in seconds without stopping for breath. It tasted better than liquid gold.

'Don't worry,' the girl spoke in a low voice, her accent was strong – French, Tess thought – 'you're not losing your mind. It is the drugs, that's all; he puts them in the water; GHB, sometimes Valium, sleeping tablets . . . whatever,' she shrugged, sucking deeply on a white-tipped Gitane. 'You will feel like this for a few days, *non*? Then it will be out of your system. Then you will remember.' She had sighed in resignation, as if this was not necessarily something to look forward to.

Tess struggled to comprehend what was happening to her. Was she dreaming? Every fibre of her being was screaming at her to run; to just get the fuck out of there, but her limbs felt as if they'd been tied down with lead weights.

'How long have I been here?' she croaked. Her voice was a dry rasp and when she swallowed it felt like a thousand razor blades dragging across her throat.

'Three days,' the girl casually responded, blowing smoke rings into the air, her left leg swinging over her right. 'You were here at the party . . .' the girl looked at her and nodded, in a bid to jog her memory. 'You don't remember?'

Tess shook her head and felt the tears begin to come.

The girl produced another bottle of Evian from her bag and handed it to her. Tess gulped it back. 'What am I doing here?' she pleaded. 'Shouldn't we call the police?'

'We won't fucking need to if you keep shrieking like this,' came the sharp response. 'They will hear us from Paris.' She stood then and Tess got a better look at her. She was tiny, all of five feet nothing and her short, dark gamine crop would have given her the appearance of a little boy were it not for the fact that she had the most beautiful, feminine features Tess had ever seen; enormous almond-shaped brown eyes with the longest lashes, cheekbones you could cut yourself on and rosebud cupid lips that were the kind of shape women requested from their plastic surgeons.

'I want to go home,' Tess croaked, attempting to stand.

The girl's expression softened a little.

'Get dressed, Cinderella,' she commanded, tossing some clothes onto the bed.

'My passport!' Tess cried. 'He has my passport!'

The girl shook her head once more and smiled, exposing a set of small, neat white teeth with a gap in the front two, like Madonna's.

'Not anymore he doesn't,' she waved the small burgundy document triumphantly in her hand. 'So come on; *vite, vite*!' she ventured, 'we've got a plane to catch.'

131

CHAPTER 23

Loretta looked on with palpable glee as Candy Wilson was summarily ejected from The Player by two burly security guards with all the finesse of a couple of monkeys flinging shit around a cage.

'Time's up sugar tits,' she smirked, forcefully blowing cigarette smoke in Candy's direction as she looked down at her contemptuously. 'You've had your fifteen minutes of fun, now it's time to hit the road.' Loretta wanted rid of this girl pronto; she had waited years for the opportunity to have Tom Black right where she wanted him and she didn't want any distractions, especially young and pretty ones.

Candy brushed herself down as if trying to erase the fingerprints from the two lunkheads who'd manhandled her, 'and who the fuck are you, his goddamn mother?'

The comment stung Loretta like a slap in the face. She'd been in half a mind to throw a couple of hundred dollar bills at her to see her on her way quietly, but she'd well and truly blown that now, the garrulous little slut.

'Make sure she stays out,' Loretta hissed at the two meaty security staff, who duly nodded. 'I'm a good friend of Marvin Katz and I don't want this little tramp anywhere near the casino, you understand?' Loretta hissed, with the intention of Candy hearing every word.

'So how the fuck am I supposed to get back to LA?' Candy whined, her long blonde hair extensions still damp from that morning's rudely aborted bath. 'I don't have a red cent to my frickin' name.' The brevity of the situation was only just beginning to dawn upon her, panic swelling up inside her guts like yeast.

'*Non è il mio problema* – not my problem.' Loretta watched the girl with a cold eye. It was the fact that the girl had spent the night with Tom, and that he'd risked his liberty by coming back for her, that made Loretta's jealousy spike.

'Tom doesn't want you here, so if I were you I'd start looking for another meal ticket and move your pretty little ass along,' she shooed her away irritably as if swatting a bug, 'off you go . . . nice and quiet now.'

'You can't do this to me you fucking goddamn bitch!' Candy screeched, scrabbling around on the pavement.

Loretta laughed nastily, flicking her Vogue cigarette butt onto the sidewalk, just missing Candy as she turned on her high heels and strutted back inside The Player.

'Ciao!' she said without turning round.

'Yeah, and fuck you too,' Candy muttered as she slunk off in the opposite direction.

This was bad, real fucking bad. She had just one buck to her name, not even enough to make a call to her parents. Not that she'd call on those two treacherous assholes for help. Jeez, talk about extremes. Just a few hours ago she'd been throwing back Cristal cocktails and shoving coke up her nose while dressed in diamonds and couture. Now she was on the bones of her ass without the means to get home. Candy felt her mood curdle. She should have known it wouldn't last. Good things happened to other people, not Candy Wilson. She was destined for a life of rejection and shit.

She lit a crumpled Lucky Strike miserably. She was done with Vegas – and with that schmuck Tom Black. Jeez what a frickin asshole, humiliating her like that, running out on her after everything he'd promised.

Candy had met some cold-hearted fuckers in her time but this guy took the frickin' cheesecake. She felt the injustice of her predicament burn in her chest, misery leaking into her psyche like acid.

Candy needed to think, get a grip on the precarious situation she was now in, her bitter disappointment slowly making way for blind resentment. Screw Tom Black, and his freakin' fairy godmother. She'd hitchhike her way back to LA through the desert if she had to. Some trucker dude was bound to give her a ride.

Purchasing a bottle of water and some Reece's Pieces with her only remaining dollar, Candy strutted along the sidewalk, her thoughts turning uglier with each step. She could not go back to that dark, debilitating place inside her mind again, *would not*, and yet she felt it calling to her. As black and scary a place as it was, it was also somehow familiar and reassuring too.

Candy had only been walking for about five minutes when she heard a vehicle approach, the sound of heavy rock music and male banter growing closer as it pulled up alongside her, the satisfying sound of tyres on gravel as it ground to a halt. She hid a small knowing smile across her pretty young face.

'Well lookey here guys!' the driver rested his elbow on the car door, turning to the lascivious grinning faces of his fellow passengers as his eyes scanned her undeniably hot young body. 'Need a ride, baby?' he nodded towards the passenger seat. 'Me and my pals got room for one more.'

Keeping her smirk in check, Candy gave the dude the once-over, weighed up the situ; bunch of frat guys on a

Vegas bender, rich college kids; nothing she couldn't handle. A sense of relief washed over her.

'Hell dude,' she smiled, displaying her perfect all-white American teeth, her ruptured confidence returning with each passing second, 'I thought you'd never ask.'

CHAPTER 24

Stemming the flow of blood from his nose with a linen napkin, Tom reflected on what a difference a few hours could make. This time yesterday, he'd been naked on top of Candy on this very bed where he was now sitting, facing a smug-looking Loretta Fiorentino. The absurdity of the situation was not lost on him.

'So then,' Loretta began, an L&M in one hand, the other balanced precariously on her rounded hip, 'are you going to talk or am I supposed to play some kind of guessing game?'

Tom looked at her through rapidly swelling eyes.

'The girl?' he asked.

Loretta rolled her eyes, indignant.

'If you mean *Candy*, that little tramp you were with,' Loretta elongated her name with a saccharine smile, 'I have dealt with her,' she said evenly. 'She is no doubt on a flight back to LA as we speak.'

Tom nodded. It had not been his intention to leave the girl high and dry like that, however irritating she had become, and was grateful to Loretta for seeing her right, but he couldn't quite bring himself to thank her.

Bambino jumped up onto the bed and placed his tiny

shivering body next to Tom's. He knew how the animal felt. After all, Loretta had been his mistress once upon a time too.

'It's good to see you, Loretta,' Tom said though it had sounded so disingenuous that he had felt compelled to quickly add, 'you're looking well.'

Loretta raised an arched brow, ribbons of smoke escaping from her over-plump lips like coiled snakes.

'*Well*? Is this the best you can do, Tom? You must be losing your touch.'

Tom had a mind to simply get up and leave. He wasn't sure which fate was worse; being thrown in jail or stuck in a hotel suite with Loretta Fiorentino.

'Never . . .' he shot back, wincing through his pain.

Loretta pursed her lips and continued to watch him carefully, absorbing his every movement. Tom Black: well, fancy that. For two decades she had fantasised about the moment their paths might finally cross again, only she hadn't expected it to happen quite like this.

'How's your nose?' She smirked.

Even up to his neck in a quagmire of shite, Tom's primary concern was that his good looks might be spoiled. 'Perhaps you could recommend me a decent surgeon, Loretta,' he retorted with a raised brow as he finally found the strength to stand.

Loretta watched him with a lascivious eye. Even twenty years on he was still one of the most attractive men she'd ever set eyes on. The dark hair had remained thick and free of grey, assisted or otherwise, and his body – *that body* – she could tell had been well tended to and preserved over the years. Loretta felt the resurrection of familiar stirrings.

'Drink?' she suggested, halfway to pouring a large Courvoisier. Walking towards him, she unexpectedly and violently threw the contents of the glass in his face.

'That's for walking out on me fifteen years ago,' she hissed.

'Jesus fucking Christ!' he jumped back in agony, feeling a searing white hot pain as the alcohol sunk into his broken and bloodied skin. 'Well, it's good to see you're not bitter, Loretta,' he remarked sarcastically, grabbing a hand towel and patting his face with it. 'You're a real fucking bitch, do you know that?'

'And you are a real fucking bastard, Tom,' she shot back. 'A match made in heaven, no?'

He gave a little derisive snort as he looked at his reflection in the mirror, the alcohol stinging his eyes, but he was pleased to see that his injuries were more superficial than he'd first thought.

He watched her as she stalked up and down the suite, blowing smoke rings above her. As much as Tom cared not to admit it, Loretta *did* in fact look good. She was older now of course – pushing fifty he estimated – and it was patently obvious she'd had work done; plenty of it. But her body was still in good nick, squeezed as it was into a skin-tight cream bandage dress that exposed her voluminous chest to the point of indecency. He had not expected her to grow old gracefully and she had certainly not disappointed.

Sensing his eyes upon her, Loretta straightened out her spine and sucked her stomach in.

'I've bought you an extra hour, Tom,' she said, pouring him another Courvoisier, handing it to him this time.

'*Salut*,' he said dryly, watching her carefully over the rim of the glass. Loretta had met her match in Tom Black. In fact, they were more similar than either cared to admit and such a dynamic had once made for a truly explosive union – in every sense. But then Loretta had gone and committed the ultimate sin; she had fallen in love with him, and with that love came the beginning of the end.

138

It had not escaped Tom's thoughts over the years that had he never have met the woman then perhaps he would still have Eleanor O'Connor in his life, and it was for this reason he hated her the most. Not that he'd let it show; his sharp survival instincts told him that eating a little humble pie might just be the best path in this instance.

'Truth is Loretta,' Tom said, looking up her with those dark, dangerous eyes that she had always found so irresistible, 'I'm in a fuck load of trouble and I need your help.'

CHAPTER 25

Armed with basic provisions, Marco returned from the supermercado and, throwing the shopping onto the kitchen table, made his way through the villa with a sense of purpose. He was feeling on top of the world this morning and didn't care who knew it. Three days had passed since the night of the party and Marco had decided it was time for phase two of his little plan. He'd been slipping the posh bint GHB and roofies for the last seventy-two hours and knew she'd still be feeling groggy and disorientated, which was all part of the plan.

Glancing around the main part of the villa he was pleased to see that Monique was nowhere to be seen. The junkie slut had probably nodded off in one of the bathrooms somewhere, which was just as well. She was like a rancid fart that lingered around the place. He only allowed her to breathe the same air as him because every now and again she had her uses, such as the occasional blow job. Anyway, he was glad to see she had made herself scarce. This allowed him to crack on with the job in hand, namely convincing the British chick that he'd done her a favour, looking after her these last few days. Marco had planned his manipulation of Tess Scott down to the letter; he'd make out that she'd been well out of it at the party and that he'd let her stay and sleep it off. If she queried it, he'd claim the door had never been locked – he'd explain that's what drugs did to you, they fucked with your mind. And then, once she'd started to regain her faculties, he'd show her the little home movie they'd made, act like she'd been a more than willing participant in all of it – in fact, he would go so far as to say that *she'd* been the instigator and that there were internet distributors fighting to get their hands on her exploits. He'd tell her that she was going to be a big star, a household name by Christmas. Of course, he would act the innocent when she started to kick up a fuss, pretend he was genuinely surprised by her objections. Then he'd tell her that the only way he could default on the deal with the distributor was if she came up with the bread to buy the bloke off and get the video back. He'd make out like he was doing her some sort of grand favour. It was fucking genius, even if he said so himself.

Smiling happily, Marco practically skipped towards the bedroom. This was going to be easier than taking candy from a baby.

Turning the key in the door while balancing a bottle of water and some pre-packed sub rolls, Marco observed that it had locked instead of opened. That was odd, he thought as he entered the room. Immediately seeing that it was empty, he quickly checked the small en-suite bathroom. Realising Tess was gone Marco dropped the provisions in a white hot rage, and, bringing his fist back, punched a hole through the door. He screamed just one word as his hand made painful contact with the wood. 'MONIQUE!'

CHAPTER 26

'*Il mio, mio*,' Loretta shook her head, swishing her long peroxide mane, and tutting like a school mistress, 'hasn't someone been a very bad boy . . . a very bad boy indeed.'

Tom Black sipped at his fourth glass of Courvoisier and was already contemplating a fifth. He'd told Loretta the whole sorry story and now he would have no choice but to suck it up as she gloated and mocked his predicament with barely concealed delight.

'*Non so*, Tom,' Loretta sighed, a self-satisfied smirk plastered across her taut, heavily made-up face, 'you were always inclined to such impetuous behaviour; I always said it would be your downfall . . .' He could tell she was loving every minute of this, vindictive bitch.

'Even by your standards this is a mess,' she continued unhelpfully, 'and we all know what *low* standards you have, Tom.'

Tom turned away from her, lest he said something he might later regret. He'd read all about the Muldavey affair and her recent inheritance – who hadn't? A husband in the morgue and a fortune in the bank; nice work if you could get it, and much as it had galled him to think he might have to appeal to the woman's better nature, if indeed there was one, right now he saw no other way out of this gargantuan holy mess he was in. Only he knew that Loretta would not make it easy for him.

Loretta decided she must have been a thoroughly decent human being in a previous life because as far as comeuppance went, it didn't get much sweeter than this. She had Tom Black by the short and curlies; right where she wanted him, like a bug trapped inside a glass. It might have taken two decades to get here but so far, watching him inwardly squirm, it was proving well worth the wait. Winning big and losing bigger in the space of a few hours was vintage Tom Black; impetuous, impulsive, reckless . . . that it wasn't even his money to lose had amused her further still. Jack would put a bullet through him if he found out he'd squandered his life savings on the roulette table and lost him his precious opportunity to become a fêted London casino owner. When it came to that kind of money, friendship fell by the wayside.

Still, Tom would be of no use to her dead and Loretta was not about to let such a golden opportunity slip through her painted fingers.

'This is the way I see it,' she spoke carefully as she lit another L&M and picked up Bambino who had trotted out onto the balcony to join her. 'You are in debt to the house to the tune of five million dollars, this is correct?' She didn't give him time to respond, 'and you need at least another six million or so to secure the London business?' Loretta's mind was revving like a formula one racing car, so much so that you could almost see steam coming from her ears. The more information Tom had given her on the London casino that he and Jack had planned to buy, the more the idea had begun to gather momentum inside her head. From a business perspective it sounded like quite an appealing prospect. After all, she'd been advised to protect her money by investing it into something and she liked the idea of owning her own club and casino; somewhere chic and fashionable. Watching her from the bed, Tom dropped his chin in despair. Saying it aloud simply confirmed the gravity of the situation and he had the grace to suddenly feel ashamed of himself.

'The venue's going to auction tomorrow,' he said flatly, 'the reserve price is five million, though it's anticipated to go for twice that amount at least,' he palpated his nose. 'It was a sound business idea, and still *could* be,' he added, carefully.

With her back still towards him, Loretta allowed a small smile to escape from her lips.

As much as Loretta wanted to exact revenge on him for breaking her heart all those years ago though, she also just wanted him all to herself. Tom Black was the ultimate prize, and in suggesting what she was about to she knew she would get what she wanted, because Loretta Fiorentino always did, in the end.

'Today is your lucky day, Tom,' she said blowing smoke up into the air with moue lips. She turned to him then, observed those dark eyes of his glistening like black cherries in the low light of the room. They still held mystery and excitement for her, just as they always had. 'I'll settle your debt with Katz.'

'And the casino?' he asked quickly.

Loretta smirked. She admired the man's chutzpah; it was so much like her own.

'Jack need never know of any of this,' she said by way of an answer, extinguishing her cigarette in an antique marble ashtray and immediately lighting another. 'I'll even pay for you to get your nose fixed,' she added with a laconic smile.

Tom waited for a 'but . . .

'Well,' he raised his eyebrows in a cocky fashion that simultaneously both turned her on and repelled her. 'I always knew you were a generous woman, Loretta. Only what might be the conditions of such an altruistic offer; my soul on a platter, perhaps?'

Loretta threw her head back and laughed garrulously.

'What soul?' she shot back.

'Surely you're not telling me you're going to loan me a little over eleven million bucks out of the goodness of your heart?' Tom was careful to keep the sarcasm from his tone. She was his only way out now and he knew it.

Loretta parted her lips provocatively, sipping on her champagne as she devoured him with her eyes.

'Whoever said anything about a loan?' She wanted him now, felt the heat pulsing between her legs. She wanted to straddle him right there on the bed, impale herself on his big dick, slide up and down on it until she cried out; remind herself what she had been missing all these years. Tom gave her a bemused look. 'That's right, Tom,' she whispered, 'I'm going to *give* it to you; call it a gift – for old time's sake. After all, I am a very rich woman now . . .'

Catching the amorous look in her eyes and realising what was expected of him, Tom obligingly slipped the straps of her dress from her shoulders. Screwing Loretta Fiorentino for eleven million was a pretty fair deal he thought, but still, as he brushed his lips against her skin and heard her sigh with pleasure, he couldn't help thinking how much he'd rather not have to.

'What's the catch, Loretta?' he said, watching as she closed her eyes in pleasure at his touch.

'There is no catch,' she moaned, mock-offended by the very suggestion, but of course this was not strictly true. 'It's simple; you get the money in exchange for your name.'

'I'm not sure I follow you,' he pulled at her dress until her ridiculous breasts bounced free of the fabric's restraint. Taking one of her large nipples in between his lips, he continued to watch her cautiously as she closed her eyes and allowed her head to roll back on her shoulders.

145

'I pay your debts; I buy you and Jack the casino – legitimately. It would be in your name, it would be your business; I would have nothing to do with it. It would be a gift from me to you; a *wedding* gift.'

Tom blinked up at her, her nipple still between his lips, and felt his blood run cold. 'All you need to do is marry me, Tom,' she added flippantly, as if this were a very natural conclusion to the conversation. 'You get the money and the club, I get the man and the name,' she met his eyes. 'Take it or leave it.'

'You're serious?' he could barely disguise his horror.

Loretta's black eyes shone like marbles as they met with his.

'Deadly,' she said

CHAPTER 27

'An argument? What sort of an argument?' Ellie stood in her ultra-luxurious £300,000 Colosseo Oro, Marazzi-designed kitchen, one of only ten in the entire world, and blinked at her daughter in disbelief. It had been nothing if not a shock to find Tess was back from Ibiza upon their return from Livedon. Moreover, she looked like shit and was being unusually reticent.

'Over a boy, was it?' Vinnie had interjected, trying to make light of the tension that was building in the air between mother and daughter.

Tess sighed, crossing her long, slim legs as she sat down on one of the crocodile-embossed leather kitchen stools, running her fingers through her straggly blonde hair that hadn't seen a brush for a few days and looked like it.

'Look, I don't really know what it was all about, OK?' she explained with the lightest irritation in her voice. 'I wanted to go to a party and she wasn't up for it and things were said and, oh you know how these things start, Mum. It was something and nothing, it was no biggie . . .'

Why hadn't she called to let them know all of this, Ellie thought? It didn't make any sense.

Tess recognised her mother's need to make herself busy whenever she wanted to prevent an argument and such familiarity caused her to have a little wobble. Part of her wanted to just crumble and confess all, fall into the protective warmth of her mother's arms and sob uncontrollably, tell her what a disaster it had all been. Only it all sounded so disgusting and absurd that she just couldn't. Besides, she could almost certainly forget about getting her own place if she did come clean – her mother would deem her incapable of looking after herself.

'"No biggie"?' Ellie admonished, raising a perfectly arched eyebrow. 'So let me get this straight,' she fixed her daughter with a hard stare, holding a packet of Lavazza in her hand like a weapon, 'you fell out with Allegra – your best friend of many years – over something as insignificant as a party and decided to fly home early, *separately*, then your bag was stolen and the airline lost your luggage. That is right isn't it Tess?' Put like that, it did sound a stretch too far and they both knew it.

'Yeah, that's about the size of it,' Tess said breezily, sticking to her story. 'Look Mum,' she cocked her head to one side, her voice softening slightly, 'Ibiza wasn't quite what I'd hoped it would be, OK? And before you say anything, I've already been onto the airline about the lost luggage and they're looking into it. Don't worry; I'll make sure I'll get compensation from them,' she said earnestly.

'It's not about the money,' Ellie replied unconvinced. Tess's countenance told her that she was lying. Her daughter was a natural drama queen, prone to histrionics; had she been speaking the truth Ellie felt sure she would've heard her screams from the airport. No. Tess was acting far too calm, far too laidback and philosophical about such a run of misfortune, and this worried her.

Vinnie watched his wife and daughter size each other up; they were so alike in many ways, stubbornness being one of them, and felt he should step in as peacemaker before the underlying tension exploded into a row.

'Well, it's good to have you home safe, darling,' he said, kissing the top of her head. 'I'm just sorry Ibiza didn't live up to expectations,' he flashed her a conspiratorial wink, 'but I am with your mother on this one,' he added with a fatherly concern. 'You could have at least called us. We would've helped you.' Tess leaned into her father's kiss and swallowed the diamond-hard lump that had formed in the back of her throat. His kindness almost undid her completely and she forced herself to take a deep breath.

'I'm sorry, Daddy. I didn't want to worry you,' her voice was tremulous. Tess decided there and then that whatever happened, her parents must never discover the truth about the events that had taken place in Spain. It would destroy them to know that she had taken drugs and put herself in such a stupid, vulnerable position.

'Actually, while you're both here, there's something I want to ask you,' Tess said evenly, glancing at her mother's furrowed brow and concerned expression. 'I'm thinking of moving out.'

Now Ellie knew something was *definitely* wrong. She glanced over at Vinnie and he gave her a look that suggested that they should at least hear her out.

'Was that a rhetorical question?' Ellie enquired.

Tess rolled her eyes.

'OK then Mum, I am *telling* you that I'm going to be moving out,' she turned to her father then, her expression softening, 'and I need to find an apartment, Daddy.'

Vinnie could see that Ellie was shaking as she began to decant fresh coffee into small bone china cups.

'Leave it with me, darling,' he half-whispered, nodding in Ellie's direction, signalling that he would do his best to try to talk her mother round.

'And what's brought all this on?' Ellie spoke without

turning to face her daughter. Something had happened in Ibiza; it was as if her daughter had returned home a different person.

'It's just that I'm eighteen now, Mum,' she replied, 'it's time I got my own place; got my arse in gear and stood on my own two feet like you're always telling me to.'

Ellie felt the panic rise inside her like a swelling river.

'I can't see what the rush is, Tess,' she said quickly, managing to keep the confrontation from her voice. 'You have all the privacy you need here, plus your laundry done for you and your meals cooked; you don't have to worry about bills or household chores . . . all of which you will have to take into consideration if you move out.'

'So, I'll get a maid,' Tess shrugged. 'And I'll go to college, maybe even uni,' she added by way of attempting to appease them. 'That's what you want, isn't it?'

'It's not just about what we want, Tess,' Ellie shot back sharply.

Vinnie rested his arm gently on his wife's as if to silence her.

'Let's just think about it shall we?' he said softly.

Taking this statement as a given that she would get her way, Tess grabbed a pain au chocolat from the freshly baked selection of pastries on the table and bounded out of the kitchen, careful not to catch her mother's eye.

'Thanks Daddy,' she said with a plastered-on smile. 'I knew I could count on you,'

Once she was in the safety of her bedroom, Tess chucked the pastry in the waste paper basket and allowed her fake smile to fade. It was only then she threw herself down onto the bed and allowed the tears to finally come.

CHAPTER 28

Ellie spun herself across the shiny wooden floor of the dance studio, perspiration trickling down her face and prickling the skin on her neck, her body, graceful and powerful as she twisted and turned in time to the music, lost in the moment. Amy Winehouse's smooth soulful tones rang out from the Bang & Olufsen speakers. *Back To Black*. The irony was not lost on her. In fact, listening to the lyrics properly for the first time, Ellie wondered if the song had not been written for her. After all, she and Tom had never really said goodbye. She had simply come home one day to an empty apartment. Ellie still felt the sting of such abandonment, even now.

Instinctively she put her hand up to her chest, as if to prevent such memories from breaking her heart again, like it had all those years ago. She had never felt pain like it, nor would she again. His absence had left behind a white hot searing ache inside her chest that had taken many, many years to finally soften. The months after Tom's desertion had become nothing less than basic survival for Ellie. She'd barely been able to sleep or put food in her belly, such was her daily torment. She had felt herself slipping into a deep depression, numbing her pain with gin and cigarettes, repeating the pattern of her mother's life like a *fait accompli*. And then Vin had rescued her. He'd given her a way out, another option; he had promised to love her and take care of her, free her from a life of hardship and struggle. And she'd seized the opportunity to emancipate herself from such pain. It had been the best decision she'd ever made, only in doing so she had felt forever in debt to her husband, the relationship never quite equal as a result.

'Encore! Bravo! I'm burning calories just watching you!' Victoria's voice was amplified by the acoustics of the studio.

'You startled me!' Ellie stopped dancing, breathlessly making her way over towards the stereo, cutting Amy off mid-flow. 'Come to join in have you?' she grinned at her friend, pleased to see her, grateful for the distraction from her troubled thoughts.

'Have I buggery,' Victoria snorted. 'I've come to tell you there's a table at Sheekey's and a bottle of vintage fizz with our name on it. So get showered quick sharp. I'll be downstairs, waiting in the car.'

*

Sheekey's was as busy as you would expect for a Friday lunchtime, but Victoria liked its old-school London glamour, its lack of pretension and of course, its fabulous oyster bar, so it was worth a little squash and squeeze.

'Where did you learn to dance like that?' Victoria sipped her champagne delicately as she perused the menu. She had never seen Ellie dance before and had been remarkably impressed. She knew her friend had a passion for it, hence how keen she was to start up her own school, but she hadn't realised the extent of her talent. In fact, watching Ellie as she'd spun gracefully around the studio, it had struck Victoria that she knew very little about her friend's past at all. When it came to Ellie's preferences for restaurants, designer labels and lipstick she could write you a list, but she knew practically nothing of her provenance or upbringing. And Victoria wasn't the type to push – it was Ellie's prerogative if she didn't want to offer such information; though she was intrigued, the writer in her instinctively telling her there was an interesting back story.

'I had lessons as a child; then dance college when I was fifteen but . . .' Ellie thought how best to answer without having to talk about her mum, about Ray Black and Vegas, about Tom . . . 'But then I . . . I had an accident and that put paid to any career aspirations.' She speed-read the menu casually, hoping such an answer would be suitably sufficient to prevent too much further questioning.

'Well, you've certainly got talent!' Tor smiled. 'I never knew.'

Honey, there's a lot about me you don't know.

'Well, I don't get down to the studio as much as I would like these days,' Ellie replied in her usual self-deprecating manner. 'But once I get my own place up and running I plan to teach some of the classes, maybe for the younger ones, you know, baby ballet, that kind of thing.'

Victoria gave a wan smile as an image of CeCe dressed in a little pink leotard and tutu flashed up in her mind. How beautiful her girl would've looked in a get-up like that; it was like a bruise on her heart just thinking about it.

'Well, fingers crossed for the auction next week; I'm looking forward to it almost as much as you are. I've never been to a property auction before.' Victoria signalled to the waiter, 'We'll have a dozen of the Fines de Claires please.' He duly nodded his appreciation of their choice.

'Very good, madam.'

'So, looks like things are looking up,' Victoria forced herself to sound upbeat. She was getting good at it these days.

153

'Let's hope so,' Ellie flicked her long silky hair from her face and smiled brightly in return, 'though I am a little worried about Tess.'

'Of course you are,' Victoria sniffed. 'She's eighteen years old. It's a worrying age.'

'She wants to move out.'

'Really? That's a bit sudden isn't it?'

'Sudden indeed,' Ellie raised an eyebrow. 'You know Tor, I swear something bad happened in Ibiza.'

'Best friend's tiff, wasn't it?' Victoria mused, subconsciously scanning the restaurant for anyone of note, or more pointedly, anyone with *prospects*.

'No, it's more than that . . .' Ellie's voice trailed off. As much as her daughter had attempted to appear as if everything were hunky-dory, Ellie knew her too well. For all her smiles and forced vivacity, Tess was hiding something, and her hasty decision to move out seemed to be born more from a need to escape than a genuine desire for autonomy.

'Have you tried talking to her?'

Ellie raised an eyebrow and sighed. It was an obvious question, but she knew she'd never get a straight answer from Tess.

'She's so defensive Tor; there's really no talking to her.' She shook her head in despair. 'It's so bloody difficult being a parent sometimes. You can't do right for doing wrong.'

Victoria gave her friend a small reassuring smile and squeezed her hand gently.

'You just your best, that's all any parent can do.'

Ellie suddenly remembered herself.

'Oh God, Tor, I'm sorry, here I am blathering on . . . I didn't mean to be insensitive.' She inwardly cursed. She knew how terribly sensitive her friend was when it came to the subject of parenthood and children, though she was far too kind and polite to ever show it. Ellie could've kicked herself.

'Don't be daft,' Tor chided her, though inside she felt like screaming herself hoarse. 'I can't expect you never to talk about your daughter again just to spare my feelings.'

'All the same, I should've thought . . .'

There was a moment's pause between them.

'Well,' Tor shuffled in her seat, taking one of the oysters from its bed of crushed ice and giving it a good tobacco basting before throwing it down her neck. She wanted to change the subject before the hard lump in her throat morphed into tears. 'I've decided I'm going to be pregnant by the end of the year.' It was a statement of fact as far as she was concerned.

Ellie smiled, following suit, the creamy oyster gliding down her throat.

'Well that's the spirit, honey,' she smiled. 'Optimism is a good thing. What does Lawrence think?'

'Lawrence? Well, he doesn't know yet,' Tor replied suddenly desperate to tell her friend all about the idea that had dominated her entire waking thoughts these past few weeks. 'And I probably won't tell him.'

Ellie looked puzzled. 'You won't tell him?'

'Yes, I think he might have something to say about my plans to take a lover . . .'

Ellie almost dropped her champagne flute.

'*Whaaat*?'

Victoria felt her heartbeat accelerate behind her ribcage like a psychotic baboon in a cage. She'd been playing devil's advocate but Ellie's expression had told her to abort mission.

'I'm just kidding!' Victoria shrieked, 'your face!'

Ellie felt herself instantly relax.

'You had me going there for a minute, you minx,' she gave a nervous giggle, lightly smacking the tips of her friend's fingers.

'As if,' Tor shot back. 'I might be desperate for a baby, but I'm not *stupid*.'

'Glad to hear it,' Ellie chuckled. 'Though frankly even if

155

you were thinking of taking a lover I'd wish you luck finding someone half decent in this city. I mean, imagine being a woman over thirty on the dating scene in London,' she pulled a face. 'Thank God we're married because all my single girlfriends tell me the men in this city are either gay, married or emotionally unavailable.'

They both laughed.

'Tell me about it,' Tor giggled, spilling a little of her champagne between lightly shaking fingers.

Though in fact as far as she was concerned, any one of the above three would do rather nicely.

CHAPTER 29

Jack Goldstein stood, stony-faced outside Sotheby's auction house, and checked his BlackBerry for the millionth time. He would kill Tom Black for this. And he'd do it with a smile on his face and a clear conscience too, because that bastard he had spent a lifetime calling a friend had stitched him up good and proper.

Tom had been missing in action for three days now, two of which he'd spent calling him on constant redial only to be frustratingly met with an unctuous voice message. *'Hi, you've reached Tom Black . . . leave a message and I'll get right back to you . . .'* Slippery fucking bastard.

At first Jack had forced himself to remain calm; reassuring himself that there was no way on God's holy earth Tom would betray *him*, someone he had known since childhood and who had stood by him through thick and thin, bailing him out of numerous scrapes and placed a caring arm around his shoulder when his father had died. But gradually Jack had been forced to entertain the idea that this counted for the princely sum of fuck-all. How could he possibly have been so stupid? Tom had a sickness; he was a gambler, and an impulsive one at that. Leaving him in charge of a lump of notes like that was like asking an alcoholic to watch your drink while you slipped off to the rest room.

Jack pulled his Armani suit jacket around his chest and watched the thick London traffic, the sound of horns hooting in frustration as it ground to a halt. It was supposed to be the start of summer on this godforsaken little island he thought irritably, it was June after all, and yet he'd been unable to get warm ever since his arrival. Deep down he knew he wasn't well. The chest pains and persistent cough, the dull ache in between his shoulder blades, it was indicative somehow and he knew he would soon have no choice but to pay a visit to the quacks. But the inevitable could wait as far as he was concerned. He had more pressing matters to attend to, i.e. the one he was dealing with right fucking now.

The sound of his phone ringing caused Jack to snap back to reality and, suddenly recognising the number, he snatched it up with an accelerated heartbeat.

'Well,' he said, his voice a low, menacing growl, 'this had better be fucking good.'

CHAPTER 30

Settling back into the plush and roomy cream leather seat of Loretta's private jet, Tom couldn't help thinking how he had as good as signed his own death warrant. Loretta may have settled his debt with a rather crestfallen-looking Katz, but in doing so he had agreed to betroth a woman he could barely stomach being in the same room with, let alone promise to love and cherish for all eternity.

'We'll make an announcement in the press once we're in London and the casino opens,' Loretta mused, as much to herself as anyone else.

'Do you really think that's wise?' Tom attempted to stall her. 'Wouldn't it be best to wait until all the Muldavey business has blown over? Besides, aren't you worried how it might look; the supposed grieving widow already planning her next trip up the aisle? Hardly a way to endear yourself to the public is it?'

He did have a point, irked though she was with the passion that he made it. 'The paps will be all over us like a cheap suit as it is.'

Loretta was silent for a moment, that sharp mind of hers turning over like a brand new Ferrari. The mention of Miranda Muldavey's name always killed her good mood. She had spent a lifetime training herself to ignore her conscience; a conscience simply complicated things and prevented you from getting what it was you really wanted. Yet when it came to that damned actress . . .

'Perhaps you're right, *dahling*,' she reluctantly agreed. 'It's just that I want to make our engagement official as soon as possible,' she stretched her body provocatively out across the chaise longue. 'I want the women of the world to know that Tom Black is very much *off* the market.' She pouted at him in a manner she perceived to be childishly sexy.

Tom gave a disingenuous smile.

'Of course you do,' he smiled, adding carefully, 'but we must choose our moment carefully. Let the Muldavey scenario play itself out first, eh?'

Loretta placed Bambino next to her and rolled onto her front, her ample chest supporting her weight like an inbuilt inflatable, and allowed the pile of magazines to slide onto the plush black and cream Versace logo embossed carpet. She wished he wouldn't keep mentioning that woman's name.

'Speaking of which,' Tom allowed his head to flop back against the cream leather which creaked in objection, 'was Ramsey really behind it all? I mean, from what I could tell he seemed like such an unassuming man, hardly a Sweeney Todd type.'

She fixed him with narrowed eyes.

'Sweeney Todd? I have never heard of this person,' she shrugged. 'Anyway, since when have you ever cared much for the truth?'

'Oh, I don't know,' Tom lamented, 'just curious. Besides, I didn't think married couples were supposed to have secrets.'

Her frown dissipated into an amused smile. This is what

she had been missing all these years; a man she could banter with, someone who could keep her on her toes.

'I like your attitude, Tom,' she purred, examining him through cold eyes. Loretta had wasted no time instructing her people to hastily draw up a contract of marriage in which it clearly stated that in exchange for bailing him out, Tom was to honour his part of the agreement and marry her in a lavish ceremony of her choice in no less than three months' time. Once married, he would have to remain that way, for divorcing her would automatically mean forfeiting ownership of the precious club that they were imminently about to purchase. It would also mean having his debt at The Player reinstated. It seemed Loretta had calculated everything down to the finest detail, using her potent powers of persuasion to their twisted and wicked best. She had even agreed to have Jack's name put on the official deeds of the club alongside Tom's, ergo arousing no suspicion when it came to signing the papers. Only what Jack would not know was that his signature wouldn't be worth the paper it was printed on and that the club they were about to procure would only ever belong to *him* all the time Tom was married to *her*. Which brought them nicely onto the adultery clause; an inspired little twist on her part. If Tom was to ever be caught *in flagrante* with another woman then everything automatically defaulted straight back to Loretta. No second chances. As perverse as it all was in the cold light of day, Tom couldn't help admiring her; after all, this was Loretta at her Machiavellian best.

'Jack's seriously pissed,' Tom said, his mind churning over at the stilted conversation he'd just had with his friend on the telephone. 'He's outside Sotheby's right now, waiting to go into the auction.'

Loretta spoke without looking up from the magazine. 'We'll make the bid by phone.'

161

'He doesn't trust me,' Tom grumbled. 'He thinks I've made off with his millions.'

Loretta raised an eyebrow, continuing to read.

'Good job you ran into me, wasn't it?' She resumed flicking through her limited-edition copy of *Couture Bride* with a deep sense of satisfaction. It was a complete myth what people said about money not buying you happiness. Thanks to her inherited fortune, right now she had everything she could possibly want; money, power *and* Tom Black – the only three things she'd ever really cared about in her entire life.

Tom swallowed down a bourbon on the rocks and signalled to the steward to cut out the middle man and bring him the bottle. With no immediate way out of the mess he was in, he decided that anesthetising himself was, for now, the most appealing option. He stared out of the small tablet-shaped window at the cloudy abyss and wondered how many bottles he would need to sink before he blacked out.

'The pilot wishes to inform you that it's one hour to landing, sir,' the perma-tanned, obviously gay steward informed him, gently placing the bottle of Maker's Mark on the table.

'Damp, cold little place, London,' Loretta remarked sourly as she watched the pastel-blue sky from the window fade to a cloudy grey. 'Still, I have arranged for us to stay at The Lanesborough at least, the Royal Suite, of course,' she added.

'Perfect,' Tom remarked disinterestedly as he poured himself another bourbon, savouring the hint of vanilla oak as it hit the back of his throat. 'We'll celebrate the auction win with dinner at Apsleys, shall we? Head off to Bond Street the following morning, have a little look in Graff or Tiffany's for your engagement ring.' Tom knew exactly the right thing to say to Loretta; understanding her was second nature.

'Ooooh *magnifico*,' she purred, discarding the dog, who yelped in surprise. 'Now pass me the phone darling; I have some bidding to do.'

CHAPTER 31

'This is *so* exciting,' Victoria Mayfield squealed in a hushed whisper as she took her seat inside the auction house. 'I've never been to an auction at Sotheby's before.'

'Me neither,' Ellie replied from the corner of her mouth. 'It can't be too much different from buying art and antiques though, can it?'

'I suppose not,' Victoria shrugged as she flicked through the glossy brochure until she came to the disused Soho warehouse.

'Look at it! If that place doesn't have dance school written all over it I don't know what does! I can see your name above the door already,' Lindsay chipped in, carried away by the whole sense of occasion. She was pleased as punch to have been invited along today; it made her feel as if she was an integral part of the set-up that was to be *Ellie's Angels*.

'Ladies and gentlemen,' the buzz in the room fell silent as the auctioneer, somewhat dapper and eccentric-looking in a tweed three-piece suit and cravat, introduced himself. 'I'm Arthur Winstanley, your auctioneer for this afternoon, and may I take this opportunity to welcome you all to Sotheby's and wish you all the very best of luck!'

Jack Goldstein sat at the back of the elegant Georgian-themed auction room, sandwiched between a rather portly looking gentleman wearing too much cologne and an emaciated elderly woman who looked like she had more money than minutes left on the planet, and willed his phone to ring. The conversation he'd just had with Tom, if you could call it that, had left him feeling even more anxious and confused than ever.

'Before you explode, just hear me out, OK?' Tom's voice had sounded different somehow; low and serious, quite unlike his usual obsequious self. 'We're going to bid via phone,' he had continued. 'Just trust me, OK. I'll call you back in five.' Jack had opened his mouth to speak but Tom had already hung up on him. It was all he could do to stop himself from throwing his phone onto the floor in a blind rage.

Arthur Winstanley turned his attention towards the Soho warehouse.

'OK ladies and gents; lot five. Swift Street, West One – prime real estate positioned in the beating heart of London's most vibrant area, rich with heritage. This is a commercial property of overwhelming development potential, boasting over . . .'

As Winstanley waffled on about the obvious merits of the place, Ellie nervously glanced around the auction room. This was it; her big moment had arrived and she suddenly felt under intense pressure to get the outcome she desperately needed. Keep calm, she inwardly told herself, remembering Vinnie's advice. She heard a phone ring from the back of the room but kept her eyes firmly on the auctioneer, not daring to look round. *Stay focused.*

'Alrighty then, good people,' Winstanley cleared his throat. 'Who's going to start the bidding off at four million?'

CHAPTER 32

Winstanley nodded at Ellie in recognition of her bid. 'Thank you madam, do I see four and half . . . four and a half million in the room for the fabulous Soho warehouse, anybody?'

Jack duly raised his hand.

'Keep your cool, buddy,' Tom carefully instructed him from the other end of the receiver, which only served to stimulate Jack's irritation. 'Let the small timers play themselves out first before we go in big.'

'Big?' Jack shot back, careful to keep his voice low and monotone. 'We've only got six million to play with for fuck's sake.'

He heard Tom laugh then and felt like hanging up on him.

'You have a lot of explaining to do my friend,' Jack said between clenched teeth, though he realised, somewhat prudently, that now was probably not the time to go into it in detail.

'Four and half it is at the back. Do I see five? Yes, thank you in the middle. Shall we say six? You sir, at the back?'

Jack duly nodded. Six was the most he'd expected to pay to secure the place, with a little change left over for decoration.

Victoria squeezed Ellie's hand, thrilled by the sheer pace of it all; money was being thrown around like a hot potato, millions bouncing off the walls in a squash court.

'Eight million,' Ellie suddenly blurted out immediately alerting Winstanely's attention.

'Fantastic, madam. Eight million to my right . . . that's a fair jump . . . do I hear an increase on eight?'

Ellie held her breath as the room fell silent.

'Some broad at the front's just called eight mill,' Jack hissed tightly into the receiver. 'We've fucking lost it,' he could hardly swallow, such was his fury and disappointment. He'd been through so much worry and concern these past few days, only to be outbid by some posh totty holding her husband's chequebook.

'Bid twelve,' Tom glanced at Loretta, stretched out as she was on the chaise longue dressed in exotic nude and black lacy La Perla underwear that would make a mockery of the word modesty in any language. She nodded her agreement as she cautiously sipped on a chilled glass of pink vintage Laurent-Perrier champagne. 'Don't argue Jack, just do it.'

'Any advance on eight? Do I hear maybe eight point one perhaps?' Winstanley suggested hopefully, things were beginning to hot up now and he felt the usual rush of adrenaline loosen his old joints.

'Twelve million!' Jack called out, half standing, as if he couldn't quite believe what he was saying himself. Gasps emanated from the room as everyone turned in his direction.

Winstanley was ecstatic; he really did love his job.

'Amazing! Twelve million! Thank you sir, now this is more like it; twelve million for the Soho warehouse it is. I say twelve million, any advancement . . . Twelve point five? . . .' he announced, as if he was doing them all a favour.

'You, madam?' he nodded at Ellie who could barely breathe, her chest was so tight.

'Thirteen,' she said confidently, glancing at her PA who looked as if she were about to explode with the sheer weight of the tension and drama. Winstanley was working himself up into an epic lather.

Loretta looked over at Tom's phone. Jack was on loudspeaker and up until now she had shown marginal interest, assuming twelve million would be more than enough to secure a place that was valued at half of that. Now, however, she realised that there was a stumbling block. Someone else wanted the club – and they seemed to mean business.

'Ask him who the other bidder is,' Loretta instructed.

Jack heard a female voice in the background but this was hardly a surprise to him. It was no doubt some little tart Tom had picked up along his travels.

'It's a woman,' Jack glanced over in Ellie's direction.

'Fifteen million,' Loretta said, forcibly flicking the pages of the magazine that she had by now stopped reading. She wasn't about to allow a woman, any woman, stand between her and the path of true happiness. *Let's see what the bitch has got, shall we?*

'Fifteen fucking big ones?' Jack shook his head, incredulous. 'Forgive me, Tom,' he whispered down the phone, 'but might it be wise of me at this stage to enquire just where the fuck you think we're gonna find fifteen million pounds from? You do know it's illegal to bid at an auction without the means to pay the fucking bill at the end?'

'Just bid,' Jack figured he had little choice at this stage other than to do just that and so he raised his hand.

'Fifteen!' he called out, beginning to wonder if perhaps he had underestimated the situation; maybe Tom *had* somehow come good. Ellie looked at her friend.

'What do I do?'

Victoria shrugged apologetically and chewed her lip.

'Should I ring Vinnie?'

'Fifteen million pounds!' Winstanley announced the figure

168

as though he were saying the name of his first-born son. 'Madam, can I take any advancement on fifteen?'

Ellie felt light-headed with adrenalin. Damn Vinnie! She needed him here with her right now; would he advise her to carry on bidding or cut his losses and bail?

'Seventeen million,' the words came from her lips but it was as if someone else had said them.

Victoria glanced at her with wide eyes. Was she insane?

Winstanley thought he might be about to explode.

'Seventeen million pounds ladies and gentlemen! Just about enough to keep my wife in wigs and false teeth for the year.' The room erupted into laughter and it was a clever move on his part, for it broke the tension.

'What now hot shot?' Jack deadpanned. 'This broad is prepared to pay seventeen million fucking big ones,' he whispered into the handset. Tom turned to Loretta, who had now deemed the situation serious enough to abandon her wedding magazines. 'Well?' he raised an eyebrow.

Winstanley heard the figure when it came but couldn't quite believe it.

'Twenty. Million. Pounds,' he expelled the words from his lips as if addressing visiting royalty.

Panicking, Ellie thought back to the conversation she'd had with Vinnie the night he'd surprised her by taking her to see the old warehouse.

'. . . Fifteen million tops should secure it,' and she wondered if that had been her husband's way of letting her know that she shouldn't exceed that amount.

She shook her head at Winstanley, her heart sinking so hard and fast to her YSL shoes that she felt rooted to the floor.

'The lady's shaking her head,' Winstanley nodded his understanding reluctantly. 'In that case, can I say for twenty million pounds, going once . . .' he paused for a deliberate length of time, allowing any second thoughts to be realised,

169

'going twice . . .' he added, holding his breath, 'madam?' He looked over at the woman's beautiful, defeated-looking face for the last time '. . . Sold to the American gentleman at the back for twenty million!' The hammer fell and the room erupted into rapturous applause. 'Congratulations sir!' Winstanley threw his arms theatrically into the air like a manic preacher in prayer. He was really quite exhausted.

Hearing the sound of Jack's muffled euphoric screams from the loud speaker Loretta grinned and raised her champagne flute.

'Complimenti, darling!' she knocked the tip of Tom's glass with her own. She had paid way over the odds for this London casino but as she eyed her husband-to-be with careful consideration, she would make sure that Tom Black would be worth every penny.

CHAPTER 33

Victoria Mayfield dived into the water and allowed herself to float, weightlessly, to the top of the heated swimming pool. She stared up at the vaulted glass ceiling. The sky above it looked overcast and white, not a sliver of blue to be seen. Summer, it seemed, really was taking its time in coming.

Victoria had forgotten what it felt like to wake up happy. To feel a lightness of heart and mind as she opened her eyes each morning. Now when she awoke it was always the same; the sense of unease, the dull ache in the pit of her belly. Lifting her head from the water, the weight of her thick, wet hair causing her some resistance, Victoria turned on her front and began to swim, a slow, gentle breast stroke at first, gradually gathering momentum and speed until she was powering through the water in a front crawl.

She had always loved it here at Foxgrove Hall, their vast seven-bedroom country house in Surrey that they had acquired largely on the back of her inheritance and collective bestseller sales. As with everything in her life now though it was filled with painful memories from the past, and perhaps worse, of ones that would never exist.

Foxgrove was a house that needed the laughter of children

to truly bring it to life, to give it warmth and vibrancy. As it was, Lawrence and Victoria rattled around in it; its vastness only exaggerated by their loss. She was getting nowhere fast waiting for something to happen and those fertility specialists that she'd been handsomely paying had been as much use as an ashtray on a speedboat. She had no other choice than to take matters into her own desperate hands. After all, if Mohammed won't come to the mountain . . . isn't that what they said? But could she really betray Lawrence in such a calculated way, making love to another man, a stranger, in a sole bid to impregnate herself? She recalled the look of horror on Ellie's face when she had casually mentioned taking a lover and inwardly winced.

Victoria knew that to go ahead with an affair would be gambling with her marriage, the only thing she had left in her life worth holding on to, yet she couldn't stop herself.

Lawrence, dressed for the gym in smart navy Lacoste track pants and matching blue and green striped t-shirt, waved at his wife as he entered the pool area and took a seat on one of the large padded wicker loungers. He watched her as she pulled herself up and out of the pool, a vision in a deep red Heidi Klein bathing suit, her finely honed curves and the swell of her naturally voluptuous breasts filling him with desire for her.

'Good morning, my darling,' he smiled at his wife lovingly. 'Fancy skipping breakfast and going straight back to bed?' he raised his eyebrows comically, Groucho Marx-style, though he was deadly serious.

'At least let me have some eggs Benedict first,' she smiled as one of the housekeepers brought a tray of fresh coffee, orange juice, toast and eggs to the table.

'Keep your strength up,' he added with a grin.

He glanced up at her as she towel dried her hair, wrapping it around her head in a complicated fashion. She shot him an amused look.

He was so cheered to see her smiling that he reached out to her, pulled her close to him and gave her a lingering kiss that she lovingly reciprocated.

'What was that for?'

'You're my wife. Am I not allowed to kiss you for no reason?'

'Of course,' she smiled again, pulling her robe around her as he poured them both some coffee. 'It suits you,' he said, thinking how he had not seen her look so relaxed in ages.

'The towel?'

'No, silly, being here, at Foxgrove. We should try and make it down more often. It's not as if we both couldn't do with the break, is it?'

'You can say that again,' she said. Lawrence was soon to be off on location again. It was little wonder she wasn't pregnant. 'Anyway, I want to hear all about Goldie Hawn, if she's as adorable in the flesh as she is on screen . . .'

Lawrence laughed.

'Even if she is,' he replied with a cheeky grin, 'she won't be a patch on you, Princess.'

It had been a long while since he had referred to her in this vernacular, an affectionate pet name he had once given to her and CeCe, his 'pair of princesses.'

Lawrence berated himself, him and his big bloody mouth. She was still so fragile, even now.

'I'm looking forward to seeing the elephants though,' he said, changing the subject and taking a large slurp of the hot black liquid, almost taking the burning sensation like a punishment as it slid down his throat. 'You know they can actually pass knowledge down from generation to generation. Apparently it's quite something to see up close.'

'I'll bet,' Victoria cut into her eggs Benedict and watched as the runny yellow liquid filled her plate. 'But just make sure you get the lowdown on Goldie!'

Lawrence was going to be in Africa for three weeks, filming what was tipped to be an award-winning documentary on the plight of the African elephant. He had even managed to get a bonafide Hollywood heavyweight on board, a real coup for his film production company.

Lawrence had thrown himself into his work these last few years; it had been his saviour really, a constantly changing and challenging environment to keep his mind active. He missed Tor whenever he was away, which was becoming ever more frequent these days, but since CeCe's death he had wondered if it was easier to miss her than it was to actually be with her.

'Enough about her,' Lawrence said with a mouthful of egg. 'I want to know what my beautiful wife has been up to and what you've got planned while I'm away.'

Victoria smiled thinly. *If only he knew.*

'Well, I attended that auction with Ellie. She was hoping to buy that old warehouse in Soho, remember, I told you about it? Only someone pipped her to the post at twenty million.'

'Twenty million! Jesus. That's insane.'

She nodded, biting into her toast.

'She was devastated. It was her life's ambition,' she added, suddenly wishing she had been more supportive of her friend at the time. She, above all people, understood the pain of losing something you really wanted.

'Someone must've been pretty keen to shell out that kind of money,' he reasoned. 'Who was it?'

'Nobody knows,' she replied.

The corners of Lawrence's mouth turned outwards.

'Well, Scott's a billionaire himself. A sum like that would be a drop in the ocean, surely?'

Victoria shrugged.

'You'd think . . . still, I felt terribly sorry for her. Apparently whoever bought the place is planning to turn it into an exclusive casino-cum-nightclub-cum-restaurant type place. Like the city needs another one of those!' She swallowed her toast.

Lawrence nodded his agreement.

'Anyway,' he changed the subject. 'I've got a whole week before I have to go again, so what do you fancy getting up to my precious? Anything you like; I am but your humble servant and master after all.'

She laughed, wishing she could say what it was she *really* wanted – a baby; *any* baby. Did it really matter at the end of the day whether Lawrence was the biological father or not? He would never know any different, and ignorance is bliss after all. She would find herself a lover; someone discreet, someone who didn't know who she was, with no connection to her family and friends, and he would need to retain her husband's dark, pleasing features, so that it would not be a stretch to imagine that the child was his. Not that anyone would ever question such a thing, least of all Lawrence himself. He trusted her implicitly.

Victoria smiled, pushing her plate away from her, her stomach churning a little with the thoughts she had dancing around in her head.

'We've been invited to the grand opening,' she said, 'they were sent to my agent; it's in three weeks' time. It's already the talk of London . . .'

'Sounds like my idea of fun.' Lawrence was being facetious.

'The invitations were printed on gold leaf paper and encrusted with Swarovski crystals – obviously no expense spared.'

'Well, aren't we the lucky ones?' he rolled his eyes. Lawrence much preferred the eclectic, quirky company of creative types to the jumped-up pomp and splendour of all those celebrities and socialites. 'Shame I won't be here,' he said with a healthy dose of sarcasm and she slapped him playfully.

'Perhaps we can jet off somewhere before I go,' he suggested. 'Just pack a bag and chase the sun. After all, doesn't look like we're going to get much of a tan here.' He suddenly seized his wife's hand, causing her to blink in alarm. 'I've missed you so much, Tor. I want to make it up to you . . . all this time away; it's not been good for us.'

'Oh Lol, darling, shhh,' Victoria cut in. 'Stop apologising for doing your job. I have been perfectly fine on my own.'

Lawrence smiled at her gratefully. She had always encouraged him in his profession endlessly and selflessly.

'And the book? How's it coming along? Writing itself I'll bet . . .'

'Great,' she lied convincingly. 'I'm almost halfway through. It's been like a gift, this one.'

'So, what *shall* we do today then?' he reiterated his earlier question.

'Actually, I quite like your original idea of going back to bed,' she said, flashing him a mischievous smile. Victoria grinned, her eyes alight with the possibility that with a little help from a person yet unknown, she would soon feel the unmistakable pleasure of a galloping heartbeat and tiny kicking limbs inside her belly. All she needed now was to find the perfect stranger. But who?

That was the twenty million pound question.

CHAPTER 34

Marco DiMari boarded the EasyJet flight to London Gatwick alongside a bunch of frazzled looking party-goers.

'Don't suppose there's any chance of an upgrade, eh babe?' he smarmed at the young, plastic-looking stewardess who was almost as orange as her uniform.

'If only,' she blinked her false eyelashes in double time and grinned, exposing a little red lipgloss on her protruding teeth. 'Though I might be able to swing a complimentary packet of peanuts if you play your cards right.'

Marco winked at her with a lascivious grin. Women, they were all the same; whores, every goddamn last one of them. He was in no doubt he could have this one bent over the stinking chemical bog with the gentlest of persuasion. In fact, now he thought of it, it might help take his mind off a few things, namely his desire to break Monique's neck and dump her useless body in the Thames, which incidentally was exactly what he planned to do when he got his hands on the treacherous cunt. Not before she'd given up the posh bitch first though; Tess Scott, the fragrant, spoiled, little daddy's princess. Reaching inside his jacket pocket, Marco located the small USB stick. The pair of them must've thought they'd really had him over, doing a bunk like that.

As if he'd ever have been stupid enough to make one copy of his little film.

Marco had been more than prepared to play it straight with Tess Scott, would happily have given her the original copy in exchange for a fair sum, but it seemed dumb and dumber had thought that two brain cells were better than one, and now both of them would have to pay a much higher price for double-crossing him.

CHAPTER 35

It had been a little over three weeks since the auction disaster and although she was putting on a brave face, Ellie was still no closer to getting over it. The worst part had been explaining it all to Vinnie in a fraught transatlantic phone call.

'Twenty million,' Vinnie repeated the words again as if they were foreign to him. 'You'd have to be a fucking madman to pay over the odds like that!'

Vincent Scott was a businessman and he didn't like to lose. Losing put him in a bad mood and this was nothing short of a fucking disaster. Prime real estate like the Soho warehouse only ever surfaced once in a blue moon and he could've kicked himself for being so short-sighted.

'Well exactly,' Ellie grumbled, crestfallen. 'A madman; you said so yourself.'

He felt her bitter disappointment as if it was his own, and inwardly cursed. 'That's twice now I've been gazumped. Maybe someone somewhere is trying to tell me something,' she added miserably, pulling her lightweight Zac Posen knit across her shoulders, suddenly a little chilled.

'Look,' he lamented wearily, 'this is totally all my fault. I should have been at the auction with you but I thought we were home and dry. No one is more upset for you than I am.' Vinnie's tone was soft and reassuring but it belied the anger and injustice bubbling up inside his guts like a cauldron. He had promised Ellie that place and now he'd lost face in front of his wife. He was not a happy bunny.

Ellie had nodded silently, questioning whether she even deserved such kindness from her husband. Was karma finally catching up with her?

Vinnie pushed aside his emotions for a moment and allowed his business brain to kick into gear. Who on earth would be crazy enough to have forked out an inflated fortune on a place that wasn't worth even a quarter of what they'd paid for it?

He didn't know. But he was damned sure he was going to find out.

CHAPTER 36

'What is *she* fucking doing here?' Jack roared as he'd sat behind his makeshift desk in a small backroom of the building site that was soon to be their casino.

'And it's great to see you too, Jack!' Loretta smirked.

Jack's heckles had risen faster than a phoenix from the flames. Fact was, Loretta on her own was a waking nightmare. Attractive as she was in an obvious way, coupled with his old friend, it was a duo that spelled nothing short of cata-fucking-strophic disaster. 'A little souvenir from Las Vegas,' Tom had explained with a whimsical smile that he had noted fell instantly flat. 'I picked her up in duty-free . . . not bad huh?'

'Give us a minute, Loretta, will you?' Jack had said, though it was not so much a request rather than a command.

Loretta wisely did as she was told, careful not to shut the door entirely so that she could eavesdrop on the conversation.

'You had better tell me that she has got nothing to do with the casino, Tom,' his mouth was spirit-level thin and his voice low, 'and tell me fucking quickly.'

'Relax, buddy,' Tom had said with his favoured convivial tone that had never washed with his oldest friend. 'I told you. I won that money fair and square in the poker game of my life . . . I mean, you should've seen it . . . Marvin Katz looked like he was going to shit a cardboard house.' Tom figured that the most authentic lies were always the one's which sounded closest to the truth. Jack looked at him, unconvinced. 'And that's another thing . . . gambling that money, Tom . . .'

Tom rolled his eyes. They'd been through this a million times already.

'It came good, didn't it?' he gestured around the place as if to drive the point home.

'Must've been some game.'

'Katz set me up with a high roller; I borrowed from the house and held my nerve. There's nothing else to know.'

Jack picked at a piece of loose skin on his lip. He knew Marvin Katz of old; that man wouldn't lend you a light if his house was on fire. He watched Tom with narrowed eyes.

'Look, I promise never to do anything crazy like that again so will you give me a break, huh?' Tom paused. 'I mean, do you see her name on the papers? Huh, do you? No. It's like I told you. I bumped into her in Vegas the day I was due to fly home. She was out there spending some of that dead husband's money of hers. I was celebrating, she was celebrating . . .'

'. . . And so we decided to celebrate together . . .' Jack joined in the final part of the sentence, nodding his head in an over-exaggerated fashion, and yet there was something not quite right about any of it. Tom had turned up in London with a busted nose, which he'd since got fixed thanks to one of Loretta's many contacts in the surgery world. He'd claimed to have fallen over drunk while celebrating, but Jack didn't buy it. Jack had never seen him get into a fight in all the years he'd known him; he would rather run the risk of looking like a pussy than jeopardise his good looks. If Tom had fallen over and broken his nose,

Jack was sure as shit he would've received a fucking telegram letting him know about it.

Still, what the fuck did it really matter now? Jack had signed those papers in front of a legitimate brief. It was all legal and above board; fifty-fifty, straight down the line between them.

'So, what *is* she doing here?' Jack hissed, repeating himself as he glanced towards the door. Loretta was undoubtedly listening in on the conversation. Frankly, he'd have been a trifle disappointed if she wasn't. 'You *know* the woman is trouble, Tom. She's like a fucking poisoned chalice; a robot with tits. She brings a bad feeling to proceedings, you know what I'm saying?' he said, embarking on a manic coughing fit until he was bent double and gasping for breath. 'I'm telling you,' he rasped, 'somewhere along the line that broad had all her blood transfused with battery acid – she's poison, Tom. Get rid of her,' he spluttered, expelling the last remnants of his lungs into a paper napkin. He looked down at the bloody tissue and threw it in the wastepaper basket, not wanting to accept what his insides were desperately trying to tell him.

Get rid of her. Tom only wished it was that simple. If Jack knew the truth he'd cough himself six feet under.

'What, Loretta? Come on, she's OK. She's just a bit of skirt. I can keep that one in check. Besides, Artie Maynard's just got her some bit part in Guy Bentley's new movie by all accounts. She starts filming in a few weeks; she'll be flying back out to the States the day after the grand opening and will be out of our hair.' He eyed him carefully, wondering if he was making any headway. 'Look, we open this place in a few weeks. Then the world's our oyster. It's just you and me buddy, like we always said. This place is going to put us on the map,' he threw a triumphant arm across Jack's shoulder. '*Black Jacks*,' he said with a bright smile. 'It's got a great ring to it, my friend. So let's just crack on with getting this place straight, right?'

183

'Yeah, OK,' Jack said, wiping the spittle from the corners of his mouth. His chest hurt and he felt short of breath. But then, Loretta Fiorentino had that effect on a person. Tom saluted him before making to leave.

'You want to get down to the quacks with that cough of yours you know,' he called out behind him, 'and get him to prescribe you a chill pill while he's at it. All that stressing will be the death of you.'

Jack nodded with a thin smile as Tom closed the door behind him. He had a horrible feeling he might be right.

CHAPTER 37

Loretta only had a few more weeks to go before filming commenced in LA – the eternal sunshine state – and had decided to make the most of it; after all, she had much to celebrate. Artie Maynard had positively surpassed himself by securing her a substantial speaking role in Guy Bentley's latest flick. Loretta had been given the part of a garrulous and sophisticated high-class madam; a role she'd not even needed to attend a casting to secure.

'Darling, the part was practically written for you.' This wasn't a lie. Guy Bentley had called Artie up with the request that he find him 'an older actress, someone who's obviously past their sell-by date who doesn't mind sending themselves up.' And there was only one person who'd instantly sprung to mind.

'A *madam*?' Loretta wasn't sure whether to be elated or offended. But at least she would make a tidy sum off the back of it, which would certainly help cushion the financial blow that had been the auction. '*Proprio qui . . .* just here's fine,' she barked at her driver who duly pulled the cream Rolls Royce up outside the entrance to Dolce & Gabbana. She felt at home here among the obviously monied European women who stalked the pavement in their dark shades and fur coats, clutching their oversized totes while laden down with designer shopping bags – it reminded her of her beloved Milan.

Befittingly dressed in a pair of Dolce & Gabbana leopard print, skin-tight jeggings, Loretta wrapped an ocelot-print Alexander McQueen silk chiffon cape around her smooth shoulders, impervious to the sartorial rule of never teaming two sets of different animal prints together and, scooping Bambino up into her arms, waited for her driver to open the door.

The paparazzi were already waiting as she stepped out onto the pavement and she inwardly sighed as their flash-bulbs popped and exploded like fireworks around her. The Muldavey story was still big news and it seemed the scandal-obsessed Brits couldn't get enough of it – or her interesting sartorial choices. She had been in London less than a fort-night and had already topped some of the weekly 'worst dressed' lists. *Il nervo*!

*

The wife of a billionaire had myriad perks, and shopping for designer outfits was most certainly one of them, Ellie thought as she surveyed the rail of delightful dresses in the lavishly decorated Dolce & Gabbana boutique. She was indulging herself today; Tess had just moved out into her own apartment, an apartment, incidentally, that her husband had been instrumental in acquiring. Vinnie had set Tess up in one of his Number One Holland Park addresses, one of the most exclusive in London, if not the world, but it felt like a world away from their family home

'Is there something particular that you're looking for Mrs Scott; a special occasion perhaps?' The assistant knew Ellie by name; she was a regular visitor and a highly regarded customer.

'Just browsing, thank you, er . . . Lavinda,' Ellie replied, surveying the girl's name badge as she pulled a silk crepe embellished plunging dress from the rail and inspected the intricate design detail. A little black dress would be just the thing to cheer her up, despite having a whole section of her vast walk-in wardrobe dedicated to them already. Well, a girl could never have too many.

'I think I'll try this on,' she said as Lavinda duly led the way towards the private changing area.

De-robing inside the plush curtained dressing room, Ellie stood in her beautiful Agent Provocateur underwear and studied her reflection in the mirror. Her body was still in excellent shape for a woman fast approaching forty, though modestly, she would never have admitted as much to anyone else.

'Look, just put them all in there, *capicse*?' she heard a shrill voice call from the adjacent changing room as she stepped into the £5,000 dress. 'And what do you mean the dog is not allowed? Bambino comes with *me*, and if there is a problem then I will happily speak to your superior. And make sure you keep those paparazzos away, yes?' the voice continued garrulously, 'do you know how lucrative a shot of me in my lingerie would be to them?'

Ellie felt an icy chill run the length of her spine as she hovered behind the curtain. The voice sounded frighteningly familiar.

'I need something for the opening of my fiancé's casino,' it continued, 'and if it *must* be pret-a-porter then it has to be . . . how do you say . . . show-stopping? I want colour and splendour; I want sheer and thigh-high splits, sequins and crystals . . . I want something *Italian* . . .'

Ellie instinctively brought her hand up to her chest and held her breath. It couldn't be, could it? That accent . . . the familiar waft of Fracas perfume . . .

Simultaneously pulling back the curtains, Ellie and Loretta

stepped out of the changing rooms in their respective dresses and looked each other directly in the eye.

'*Scopami*!' Loretta instinctively sprung backwards, unable to disguise her initial shock. Instantly re-gaining her composure, she raised an eyebrow. 'Eleanor O'Connor!' she said. It had sounded like an accusation.

Ellie took Loretta's instant recognition to be a compliment of sorts and she squinted back at her in the pretence that her own was not quite so obvious.

'*Lorena*, isn't it?' Ellie said as she brought her finger to her lips, patting them gently. While she would recognise that woman's face at a hundred paces, she wasn't about to give her the satisfaction of knowing as much.

Loretta carefully disguised her dented ego with a smirk.

'It's *Lor-et-ta*,' she was forced to correct her. 'Don't tell me you have forgotten your old friend?' She gave a ridiculous childish pout, somehow incongruous on the face of a fifty-something woman.

Old being the operative word, Ellie thought as she felt Loretta's cold, calculating eyes travel the length of her body. 'I almost didn't recognise you with your clothes on,' Loretta remarked, barely able to contain the envy that was mapped across her face. Ellie O'Connor, the young stripper from whose clutches she had stolen Tom Black from some twenty years ago. What on earth was *she* doing here?

'I almost didn't recognise *you* either, *Loretta*,' Ellie commented, with a laconic smile of her own. At a glance Loretta looked passable as an attractive woman in her forties, but on closer inspection you could see that she had merely attempted to stave off the inevitable accumulative years by dabbling in an awful lot of surgery. Only her eyes remained the same; cat-like dark holes that seemed to disappear into the back of her head.

'What are *you* doing in London?' Loretta asked accusingly, scooping Bambino up from the floor where she had noticed he had lovingly deposited a little 'gift' upon £4,500 worth of clothes.

'I *live* here, Loretta,' Ellie responded with an air of facetiousness that masked her discomfort, 'though I could ask the same of you.' It was nothing short of a miracle that the pair had never crossed paths in all the years that had transpired between them. Loretta saw her opportunity and seized it.

'I'm here with my fiancé on business,' she mused with mock-nonchalance as if such a thing were an everyday occurrence for her. 'You might have heard through the grapevine . . . The old warehouse in Soho? He's just bought it; plans to transform it into a Las Vegas-style casino. Bring a little much-needed,' she hesitated, visibly giving Ellie the once over, '*glamour* to the city.'

Ellie felt her blood turn to ice. So Loretta was involved in the procurement of *her* dance school?

Ellie composed herself, remembering who she was now; she had money and status and was no longer that ten-dollar Las Vegas stripper that Loretta had once known. Yet somehow, standing there in the harsh gaze of the woman's cold, soulless stare, that's just how she was made to feel.

Picking up on Ellie's distress, Loretta felt her spirits lift.

'Oh, don't tell me you had your eye on the place too?' she purred, practically submerged in schadenfreude. Eleanor O'Connor had been the woman at the auction who had pushed the price up? The thought made Loretta's victory that much sweeter; twenty million pounds sweeter, in fact. 'Well, I wouldn't worry too much,' she attempted to screw her nose up but the tautness of her skin wouldn't allow it. 'You could always get a job there; I hear they're looking for strippers – of all ages.'

Ellie stiffened but decided not to bite, conscious that someone might overhear them.

'How long are you staying in London?' Ellie enquired with forced sweetness.

'Until the grand opening, then it's off to LA to begin shooting my new film. Guy Bentley's new picture actually, you'll have heard of it,' Loretta said with no attempt at disguising a lack of modesty.

'Congratulations,' Ellie mused with mock-sincerity, adding, 'actually I read about it in the papers. You'll be playing the part of a madam, won't you?'

'That's right,' Loretta replied tightly.

Ellie raised an eyebrow, 'that should be a real test of your acting ability.'

Loretta decided to ignore the sour remark and play her ace instead.

'So, you're married these days?' she cast her eye down towards Ellie's De Beers diamond-encrusted platinum wedding band, wishing she had tried on the red body con number first now; realising the neon yellow and leopard print Cavalli gown did little for her figure as she caught sight of herself in the mirror. 'Who's the lucky man?'

Ellie sniffed.

'His name is Vincent Scott,' she remarked confidently. The Scott name was a buzz word for exquisite luxury and quality the world over. A name she knew would stick in Loretta's throat like a knife.

Loretta pursed her inflatable glossy red lips. Well, well, well. He'd been on Loretta's hit list himself once upon a time. She'd met him once; attractive in a stand-offish typical British sort of way.

'Anyway, I'm awfully sorry to hear about your recent loss,' Ellie blathered, welcoming the chance to round up the conversation and head off to Gordon Ramsey's. She'd had about as much of the obnoxious woman as she could stomach already.

'Loss? Oh yes!' Loretta quickly remembered herself, adopting an Oscar-worthy sombre expression, 'my dearest

Ramsey.' She clutched the overspill of her gigantic breasts, 'A terrible tragedy.'

'Indeed,' Ellie gave a sardonic smile. 'My condolences to you and your family . . . you have children?' She was intrigued to know if Loretta had ever embarked upon something as altruistic as motherhood.

'Oh no,' Loretta shook her fake glossy blonde mane that cost £7,000 a pop. 'No bambinos for me, darling; just *Bambino*.' She petted the tiny Chihuahua shaking in her clutches, rubbing its minute skull with the tips of her painted red nails.

'Left it a bit late I suppose,' Ellie remarked.

Loretta grimaced.

'Actually we have thought of adopting, you know, do a little Angelina and Brad and give a good home to some poor underprivileged orphan somewhere. Once we're married, of course'

'How terribly noble,' Ellie's tone was snarky, but she couldn't help herself. Mother Teresa herself would've had to hold her tongue. 'Marrying again so soon?'

'Yes,' Loretta replied, savouring the thought of what was coming next, 'you might remember him,' she said, pausing for great effect. 'His name is Tom; Tom Black.'

Ellie felt as if she had been winded by a blunt object. *Loretta and Tom?* But how? When? She had thought that particular union had long since dissolved. No, it couldn't be!

'You remember him, don't you?' Loretta remarked with a sardonic, self-satisfied smile, knowing full well that she did of course. 'You were step-brother and sister for a time, and lovers too, if my memory serves me correctly?'

Ellie glanced over at the assistant hovering nearby. The conversation was beginning to make her feel nervous.

'A long time ago now,' Ellie's voice trailed off into a low whisper. 'All in the past,' she added tightly, smoothing her dress with her hands, signalling her imminent departure.

'Well, congratulations to the pair of you,' she remarked with as much sincerity as a lie could fake. 'I wish you all the best.'

'Of course you do.' Loretta had seen the look of a wounded animal in Ellie's eyes and positively relished it. 'I would invite you to the wedding but, well,' she cast her a pitiful glance, 'it's not really the done thing is it? Former lovers and all that . . .'

'Oh, so it'll just be a small wedding then,' Ellie shot back, pleased by such a lightning-fast response. She was damned if this old bitch was going to get the better of her once again. Loretta laughed, her wide, plump lips pulling back from her cosmetically enhanced teeth.

'Touché,' she remarked with an asinine smile.

'You're forgetting I once knew Tom very well, Loretta,' Ellie found herself saying with temerity. 'I was there long before you . . . and the many others.'

Loretta visibly bristled.

'Well,' she said, her eyes narrowed, 'I will be sure to pass on your *good wishes*.'

'Goodbye, Loretta,' Ellie said, turning her back on her, lest she had to look at the woman's face a second longer.

'Ciao for now,' Loretta replied with a flick of her thick mane. 'Oh and dahling,' she turned to her, looking her up and down with a disdainful eye, '*Black* never was your colour.'

192

CHAPTER 38

Victoria Mayfield checked her diamond platinum Chanel bracelet watch with the lightest of impatience; Ellie was ten minutes late but she told herself to relax, it was no biggie. Fact was, it gave her the welcome opportunity to have a good shufty around the restaurant for any suitable candidates who might potentially assist her with the plan that had taken remarkable shape in her mind over the past few weeks. In fact, a likely suitor had attracted her attention already. He had been glancing over at her ever since she'd arrived and it had given her the lightest flutter in her belly as she'd caught his eye and coyly looked away again. He certainly ticked all the right boxes; late thirties perhaps, dark, well-styled hair with matching tanned skin and brooding mocha eyes. He looked smart and chic in a deep charcoal slim-fitting suit, clearly designer, a soft lilac shirt with matching grey tie completing the carefully considered ensemble. Just looking at him had made her juices flow with anticipation.

'Can I get you a drink while you're waiting for your friend, madam?' the waitress broke through her hundred mile stare as she approached the table.

'Oh, er, yes, I'll have a champagne cocktail, please,'

Victoria replied with a sense of purpose. She had as good as written the day off work-wise, and what the hell; she would need a little Dutch courage if she was to start turning her thoughts into reality. The stranger was alone but it was likely that he was waiting for someone. Some six-foot Victoria's Secret model with tits like zeppelins and a washboard stomach most probably.

Victoria audibly drew breath. God, she was so out of practice with all this romance business, after all, she'd been married since time immemorial. She would just have to think like one of the characters from her novels. Being so brazen might not be second nature to her but if it got her what she wanted in the end, then so be it. Desperate measures called for desperate actions, after all. She glanced over at the stranger once more and was pleased to meet his gaze in response. He really *was* flirting with her and she felt the lightest frisson pass between them like a bolt of electricity. She hoped that Ellie might be delayed a few more moments now so as to allow her to make some more headway, but as it was she saw her friend already storming across the restaurant towards her.

'I'm so sorry I'm late,' Ellie blustered, smoothing her hands down her Isabel Marant tie-dye bleach jeans that highlighted her perfect form and were incongruous to her seemingly stormy mood. She threw her bags down onto the floor, practically throwing herself onto her seat.

'Bad day?' Victoria enquired, stating the obvious.

'You don't want to know, Tor,' Ellie replied, signalling to the nearest waiter for a drink. 'Make it a large one, will you?' she nodded with a forced smile.

Victoria raised an eyebrow, suddenly glad she had worn Westwood today. Dame Viv always gave her a cleavage to die for and she hoped it would be enough to continue holding the man's attention.

The waiter duly brought a glass of Bombay Sapphire gin

to the table and began pouring Ellie a generous measure of the clear liquid which she promptly threw back in one hit.

'Jesus Ellie, when you said you had a bad day . . .'

Ellie caught the look of surprise on Victoria's face and made to speak. She wanted more than anything to tell her friend all about her chance meeting with Loretta Fiorentino, but in doing so would have no choice but to confess to a past she had long ago buried. Ellie was close to Tor; they had been through perhaps one of the most painful and arduous ordeals a woman could ever go through – infertility and IVF – and they had been through it *together*. The pair had simultaneously seen each other at their worst; strung out on hormones, exasperated by blood tests and daily injections, a monthly suspense story that, in their respective cases, had ended with the bitterest disappointments, periods that appeared as regular as a baddie in a fairy tale, and such consistent emotional felling had bonded them tightly as friends, as women with something in common who understood each other. Ellie knew that Victoria Mayfield was a non-judgemental woman; she had a heart the size of Manchester and her innocent, almost prudish façade, hid a fiercely high emotional intellect and an innate understanding of the human condition. You only had to read one of her novels to know that much. She was sure that while Tor might be surprised by Ellie's confessions of her less than salubrious former profession, she would hardly be shocked by it. If anything, she would most likely be intrigued. Yet still she could not bring herself to confess. It would undoubtedly cause Vinnie shame and embarrassment and this was something she had always been at great pains to prevent. Yet still there was a part of her that resented having to hide the truth about herself. Sometimes she wondered if in fact it had not been for her own good that Vinnie had insisted she keep her former occupation under wraps, but to save his own blushes among the sharp wagging tongues of society and his influential wealthy business associates.

God, *Vinnie*. He had just flown out to Australia for goodness knows how long to seal a very important deal and she wasn't sure she had the heart – or stomach to drop the bombshell on him that it was Tom, *Tom Black* above all people, who had outbid them at auction. All those years ago they had made a pact never again to speak the man's name and yet here he was back in *her* city, turning *her* dance school into a den of iniquity. And that was before she could even get her head around the whole business of him marrying the black widow that was Loretta Fiorentino. *Marrying her*! It was sick and twisted, absurd, wrong, unfathomable – and vintage Tom. Ellie couldn't understand why she felt quite so upset; the smug look on that ghastly woman's plastic face had made her want to throw up her breakfast. As much as she had not wanted it to, the idea that Tom Black was somewhere in London caused her heart to palpate. Tom was *here*. Somewhere in this city and, regardless of the bombshell Loretta had just dropped, she knew it would only be a matter of time before their paths crossed.

CHAPTER 39

'So, what's with the face then,' Victoria asked her friend. 'Don't tell me, they didn't have your size in Harvey Nicks?'

Ellie took Tor's joke as a welcome slice of light relief, but it wasn't enough to stop her sense of foreboding. Her past was coming back to haunt her and she didn't know what she should do about it.

Victoria glanced over at the handsome stranger who immediately met her eye. He was blatantly staring over at her now; practically standing in a bid to get a better view.

'Do you want to tell me about it?' Victoria asked, forcing herself to peruse the menu. She had rarely seen Ellie in such an uptight state, but the attention from the good-looking stranger was proving to be too much of a distraction.

'If I did I would have to kill you,' Ellie retorted, wondering why she was making light of the situation. It was nothing to joke about.

'Shall I order us a bottle of something cold and fizzy?' If Ellie fancied getting sozzled then she was right behind her.

'Actually Tor, do you mind if I skip lunch? I've had one hell of a morning and my appetite is slimmer than Victoria Beckham during fashion week. I'll make it up to you, I promise.' She was up and out of her seat before Victoria had a chance to respond.

'Of course, look, don't think anything of it,' she nodded profusely, admittedly a little relieved. 'We'll do it another time. If I can help at all . . . ?'

'I'll call you,' Ellie sang as she pushed her Martin Margiela python leather clutch bag up underneath her armpit and fled the restaurant.

There was no mistaking her, Tom thought as he watched Ellie strut from the table, a vision in tight jeans and a silky camisole, her long glossy hair swishing behind her with momentum, and yet still he could hardly bring himself to believe it. He felt compelled to run after her; chase her down the street. But what would he say? Besides, he'd promised her that night at the country house that he would stay away forever; let her marry her billionaire and be happy. Tom had the grace to burn with shame at the memory of that last night at Livedon but still felt the familiar stirrings inside his designer cut slacks. No woman had ever turned him on as much before or since – and there had been plenty of both. What he'd had with Eleanor O'Connor had been like nothing else; chemistry at its most potent.

Tom's iPhone 5 beeped, causing him to jerk back to the present with all the subtlety of a brick through a window. It was Loretta telling him that she wouldn't be able to make lunch after all due to a protracted visit to one of her many Harley Street friends. Relieved, he slipped his phone in his breast pocket and stood. He needed to know if she was happy; that her life had been what she had hoped it would be; that she'd made the right choices. It would be enough to see the look on her face; to know what she felt for him in an instant, a catch of the eye, a fleeting glance.

And he knew there was only one way to find out.

CHAPTER 40

Tess looked around the carnage that was her apartment and groaned. It had been one hell of an all-nighter and she was busy surveying the extent of the damage. If her daddy could see the state of the place he would throw an epic fit; empty champagne bottles littered the formerly pristine surfaces, overflowing ashtrays spilled out onto the floor, a mirror had been smashed though she could not recall how, or by whom, and someone had emptied their guts all over one of the matching rugs.

Tess half-heartedly pulled a black refuse sack from the kitchen and, with a look of disgust, picked up a bottle. *Screw this*. She couldn't be dealing with this shit now; not with such an epic hangover. She would hire in a cleaner tomorrow; pay someone else to do it. She fell back down onto the sofa, her head hazy and hurting. A party had seemed such a great idea; she had hoped that it might somehow help her feel herself again, forget the horrors of what had happened. She had arranged it primarily to see if she couldn't resurrect the old Tess again, the girl who liked to down shots and dance on tables, who was always the first to arrive at a party and the last to leave. But it had turned out to be a big mistake, because however much she tried to be, she wasn't the same girl. *Everything* had changed.

*

As soon as the guests had arrived Tess had wanted them to leave. It had all been too much. The noise, the revelry, couples kissing in the bedrooms, those bouji boys and their wandering hands. Hugo Rivington had been all over her like the proverbial rash the entire evening, something she would've revelled in a few weeks ago, but now . . . now his advances made her feel cheap and dirty.

'You're such a cock-tease, Tess,' he'd spat at her accusingly as he'd cornered her in the bedroom. 'One minute you're gagging for it, the next you're giving it the little Miss Virgin act, and believe me, we all know it's an act, so why don't you just drop it eh, and drop your knickers while you're at it.' Tess had pushed him away, disgusted.

'Sod off, Hugo.'

'Ah now come on babes,' he'd protested, pushing himself up against her, his hands crudely grabbing at her breasts, 'you know you want to . . .'

'Stop it, Hugo,' she attempted to slap his hands away but he didn't seem to be getting the picture, 'I don't want to . . . I said stop!'

'You heard the girl, she said stop,' a stranger's voice had interrupted, causing them both to look up in alarm. Hugo looked at the young man standing in the doorway and gave a little harrumph as he slunk off to join the merriment taking place next door.

'Thanks,' she'd turned to the stranger and took in his face for a moment. Big blue eyes and a mop of dark messy hair. She didn't recognise him as one of the usuals on her scene – or what had once been her scene.

'Don't mention it,' he'd smiled and Tess had found herself

returning it. 'Dan,' he said, holding his hand out. 'And you must be Tess, the hostess with the mostess.'

She shook his hand. It had felt warm and soft in hers.

'I'm a friend of Poppy's,' he'd explained, 'in case you were thinking I was just a passing gatecrasher,' he added.

'Poppy's friend,' she'd said. He had a nice smile. Genuine.

'Yes. We grew up together, summer holidays, Christmases, that sort of thing. Our parents are best friends. She's more like a sister really,' he'd added and she wondered if he'd felt compelled to. 'Are you sure you're OK?'

'Yes, really I'm fine,' she'd replied, suddenly feeling self-conscious around him.

'Good. Well then,' he'd paused. 'It was nice to meet you, Tess.'

'You too, Dan,' she'd replied as he turned to leave. 'And thanks again.'

*

Tess looked around her trashed apartment and felt a wave of self-loathing. Dan had seemed so decent. Far too good for a girl who already had a bit of a reputation as an easy lay with enough Tanqueray inside her. If Tess had learned one thing in Ibiza it was that she wasn't about to give it up so easily to any old Tom, Dick or Hugo. The next guy who came along would be made to wait for the goods.

Tess poured herself a glass of fresh orange juice and knocked back a couple of Nurofen in a bid to begin to shift her hangover. Dressed in a pair of pink Jack Willis track pants and a Juicy Couture cropped t-shirt, she caught sight of herself in the broken mirror and poked her tongue out. She looked as bad as she felt. Still, she supposed it had all been worth it. She had managed to fool everyone but herself. *Result.*

Marco DiMari looked up at the imposing building and felt the first flutters of adrenaline hit his nervous system. Number One Holland Park. So this was where daddy's little princess resided? Very fucking nice too, he thought as he stepped into the plush reception area.

It hadn't exactly been challenging to locate daddy's head offices in Berkeley Square. The enormous aluminium sign that read Great Scott Properties had been a dead fucking giveaway.

Under the guise of a motorcycle courier, Marco had struck up a regular little conversation with some receptionist who had gone onto to tell him all about daddy's little princess and what a stuck-up, spoilt little madam she allegedly was.

'He's just given her one of those luxury apartments, you know at One Holland Park. Have you seen them? I mean, Madonna can't even get one, they're that sought after, and yet madam clicks her little fingers and bang! Jammy fucking cow.' She had leaned in towards him from across the desk and lowered her voice conspiratorially. 'Rumour has it she drops her knickers for just about anyone though. Bet daddy doesn't know *that*, does he?'

Marco smiled at the suited security man on reception.

'I have an urgent delivery for Tess Scott,' he said with a disingenuous smile. 'Only they don't seem to have put an apartment number on the address,' he added with a bored sniff.

The security man gave Marco the once over and looked at the package. Parcelforce 24-hour recorded; addressee's signature only.

'Sorry sir,' he replied, 'I'm afraid I cannot give away that information.'

Marco blinked at him. He had expected some resistance and had his story ready prepared.

'It's a very important delivery, perishable goods by all accounts,' Marco launched into his well-rehearsed charm offensive. 'It's come directly from Mr Vincent Scott. I suppose his PA forgot to put the apartment number on the address label – maybe she thought it *wouldn't need it* . . .' he paused. 'But I understand totally, more than your job's worth and all that. How about I leave it with you then,' he suggested, continuing with the one-way conversation. 'I mean, it says addressee signature only but I won't tell if you won't tell.'

A double bluff. Marco was thoroughly pleased with himself.

The security guard looked at the package and began to weigh the situation up. If he turned the guy away and Mr Scott's daughter didn't get the package her father had urgently intended her to have, he'd find himself in hot water. Glancing up at Marco, he picked up the phone with a reluctant sigh, as if he was doing him a great favour, and dialled.

'Yes, Miss Scott, there's a parcel down in reception for you. Urgent apparently . . . no, addressee signature only I'm afraid . . . right . . . OK, very good Miss Scott. I'll send him up then.'

'Penthouse apartment seven, on the tenth floor,' he informed Marco without looking up, 'the lift's over there.'

'Thank you,' Marco said, and this time he meant it.

Hearing the buzzer, Tess dragged her aching body off the sofa and slowly shuffled towards the door.

The buzzer went again, a loud irritating sound that grated on her frazzled nerves.

'Yes, al-*right*,' Tess snapped, 'I'm coming,' she said as she opened the door. '*I'm coming.*'

204

'Funny, that,' Marco said as he watched the look of surprise, closely followed by fear cloud her pretty face, 'but that's *exactly* what you were screaming the last time I saw you.'

CHAPTER 41

Victoria rolled over onto her side, pulling the 1000-thread count cotton Egyptian sheets around her nakedness.

'Well, that was an unexpected way to spend an afternoon,' she surmised with a lightly arched brow, propping herself up with her elbow as she looked down at his handsome face. He really was quite exceptional up close; lovely bone structure, a strong jawline and a perfectly neat nose, though she suspected he might've had a little help in that department. And his smile was broad, displaying neat Hollywood white teeth. Aesthetically speaking he was perfect reproduction material.

'Wasn't it just,' Tom agreed, stroking her arm gently, enjoying the smoothness of her skin from beneath his fingertips as she gently rested her head on his tanned chest. 'Best dessert I've ever had in Ramsey's joint,' he added with a cheeky grin.

Victoria smiled, struck by how seemingly effortless it had been to cheat on her husband.

Ellie's early departure from lunch had given her the perfect opportunity to embark upon her seduction, only she hadn't needed to put in much effort. Seeing that she was alone, he'd made his way over to the table and requested to join her without any prompting whatsoever.

'Great minds,' she'd mused with her best provocative eyes, inwardly surprised by her own sexual temerity. She had gestured to the empty seat in front of her with a lightly shaking hand.

'Champagne?' he'd suggested, his dark intense eyes meeting hers.

'Why not?' she'd smiled agreeably, 'after all, looks as if we've both been stood up.'

He'd ordered a bottle of Krug, a 1998 Vintage; a gesture that had impressed her.

'To strangers,' he'd toasted her glass, the mellifluous ding resonating.

'Otherwise known as friends you have not yet met.' She was enjoying the obvious flirtation far more than she'd thought she would and the champagne had eased her nerves.

'Tom,' he'd announced, taking her hand and kissing it, an old-school gesture that she had found charmingly quaint and made her instantly realise that the option for them to go to bed was a case of when, not if. 'Tom Black.'

'Rachel,' she'd said, deciding on the spot that an alias was most definitely the best thing as far as this little liaison was concerned.

Less than an hour of small talk later, they had skipped dessert and she had found herself making love to him in the aptly named Writer's Suite at the suitably adequate Corinthia Hotel.

'So, how long have you been married?' Tom asked, glancing down at the Tiffany diamond solitaire and matching platinum wedding band on her finger.

'Fifteen years,' she said quietly, lifting her head to look up at him. 'And I have every intention of making it sixteen. Why, does it bother you?'

207

Tom smiled, stretching his tanned legs out beneath the soft Egyptian cotton sheets.

'Not at all, Rachel,' he answered honestly. A married woman up for a bit of clandestine sex with no strings was just the kind of woman Tom Black liked. She was attractive in a smart kind of way; reserved with an air of class and respectability about her. He figured she was probably married to some uptight toff who refused to go down on her, because she'd come like the proverbial train the moment he'd set his tongue to work in long deep movements.

'I don't want an affair;' she'd said softly, though her tone was quite matter-of-fact. 'I just want a man to be with every now and again. Do you understand?' *I just want a baby*.

Tom looked down at her, intrigued. Truth was, despite the obvious attraction between them, he had initially approached her to ask about the woman he had seen her with; the woman he had been sure was Eleanor O'Connor. Ostensibly he had wanted to pump her for information, but it was soon apparent that she had other plans.

'The woman you were with at the restaurant . . .' Tom carefully enquired, 'a friend of yours?'

Victoria felt her throat tighten. The effects of an afternoon's champagne consumption were beginning to wear off and she started to experience the lightest flutters of guilt settle upon her stomach like fresh snow on grass. Sweeping them aside, Victoria justified her actions by convincing herself that there was every chance that a child had been conceived this afternoon, which had been the sole purpose of such a premeditated act of betrayal after all. Tom had been a generous lover, taking his time to please her and bring her to orgasm not once, but three times in as many hours. She'd read somewhere in her vast collection of pregnancy books that you were more likely to conceive during sex if you orgasmed.

As he had wrapped his arms around her naked body,

gently lowering her to the bed, Victoria had gasped in a mix of shock at what she was doing and undeniable pleasure as he had begun to nibble at her neck and breasts, working his way down towards the curve of her belly and beyond . . . It was only as he had eventually slid himself deep into her that Lawrence's face had flashed up in her mind like a still frame and she'd squeezed her eyes tightly shut in a bid to erase it, telling herself over and over again that what was happening was not a true betrayal of her husband.

'Yes,' she replied. 'An old friend I was meeting for lunch, 'why the interest?'

His enquiry had sparked something rather odd in her: the lightest of jealousy.

'Oh, I just thought I recognised her, that's all,' he casually replied. 'What was her name?'

Victoria sat up then, suddenly self-conscious of her naked exposed breasts. She covered them with the sheet. 'Though I could be mistaken,' Tom quickly added, aware of her slight change in countenance. 'I've been in LA for fifteen years,' he said, 'but I was born here . . .'

'So what brings you back to these waters?' Victoria asked, avoiding having to answer the question. She made to get up then but he gently pulled her back down towards him, preventing her. He hadn't quite finished with her yet. He had to know about that woman she had been with over lunch; if it had been Ellie.

'Business, actually,' he replied, lightly circling her erect nipple with a finger.

'Oh really? What kind of business?'

'I've just bought a place in Soho. I'm planning to turn it into a casino and club.'

Victoria felt herself instantly sober up.

'The old warehouse on Swift Street?'

'Yes! That's the place. You've heard of it?'

She nodded.

'The woman I was with . . . we were at the auction together.' She glanced at him, keen to gauge his reaction. 'We watched you pay twenty million for it. You must've wanted it pretty badly.'

'Ah, so it was *your* friend who pushed the price up?' Tom's mind began to race. *Had Ellie been bidding for the warehouse too?*

'And you'll go back to LA once you've got the place up and running?' she had manoeuvred herself from his embrace now and was starting to dress. He studied her closely as she slipped her summer dress over her slim shoulders, watching as it slid over her neat curves and nude, expensive underwear that was both pretty and practical, indicative of the woman herself, he suspected.

Victoria shook her hair from the neckline of her dress, suddenly gripped by the desire to make her escape. Her champagne bubble had now well and truly burst; if this man somehow knew Ellie then it would be far too close for comfort.

Tom wasn't sure how to answer. He would like to have said yes, but he suspected Loretta had other ideas, namely some vulgar, ostentatious and over-the-top society wedding in Italy for starters. The thought instantly depressed him. He had less than a couple of months to get himself out of that particular predicament, yet so far had struggled to come up with anything viable that didn't involve his own incarceration and the ultimate subversion of his friendship with Jack.

'I have a wedding to attend in August,' he said, adding facetiously, 'an *Italian* wedding.'

'Oh, how lovely,' Victoria remarked, wondering if this was his way of asking her to be his plus one. 'Whose?'

'Mine,' he replied with a laconic smile.

Victoria involuntarily laughed. It was just as she'd suspected. He was obviously a player; an international one

210

by the sounds of things. It suited her fine to learn that Tom was intended to another; that he too had something to lose if their stolen afternoon should ever come to light.

'I think it would be a good idea if we kept this afternoon between us,' she suddenly felt compelled to say, adding, 'particularly if there is to be a next time.'

'A next time?' He raised an eyebrow. 'Who said anything about a next time?'

She laughed, though it belied the cheapness that was beginning to stick to her like a bad smell.

'You sure know how to make a woman feel special, Tom.'

Victoria felt like a completely different person. It was as if the past few hours had happened to someone else. Someone called 'Rachel'.

'You have children?' she casually enquired, smacking her lips together and wondering if she would burn in hell for all of this. 'None that I'm aware of,' he replied, giving nothing away. Tom preferred these kinds of encounters to remain largely impersonal. It was always better that way. Victoria was satisfied with this response. It had given her the answer to the question that had been paramount in her mind. As long as this man *could* have children, then there was the potential for her to conceive, and her mission would be accomplished.

CHAPTER 42

Tess looked down at the number on the scrap piece of paper, her iPhone poised between shaking fingers, deciding whether or not to dial.

'If you're ever in any trouble . . .' Monique's departing words throbbed inside her mind over and over like a migraine. Well, she was in trouble alright; big fucking trouble.

Marco was seriously pissed off. It had been such an unexpected shock to see him standing on her doorstep that it had taken a few seconds for his presence to compute, her epic hangover slowing down her reactions.

'I don't fucking think so!' he'd snarled, getting a foothold in the door as Tess had frantically attempted to shut it in his face. 'And don't even think about screaming,' he'd added menacingly, eyes like flint as he had bolted the door behind him.

'What the fuck do *you* want?' Tess's breathing was rapid. She sprang back from him, her eyes flicking towards the panic button located next to the light switch on the wall, just behind him.

'Now that's not the welcome I was hoping for, Miss Scott,' Marco had smirked, exposing his set of neat white teeth. Laughably he was still speaking with an Italian inflection, though the rest of the façade had somewhat radically slipped. He was unshaven and a little dishevelled looking; a far cry from the well-turned out, suited and booted look that had caught her eye in Ibiza.

Tess panicked; fear and confusion engulfing her. She had confined the whole unpleasant experience that had been their encounter to the deep recesses of her mind, where she had hoped it would forever remain.

'Nice place you've got here,' he'd allowed his eyes to wander around the apartment with obvious approval. 'Party last night, was it?' he enquired, noting the general state of disarray.

'P . . . pl . . . please leave,' Tess had stammered, her heart hammering hard against her ribs so much that it was a struggle to breathe. 'I'll call the police.'

'No, you won't,' he'd shot back. 'You'll sit down like a good girl and shut the fuck up.' Tess had immediately done as she was told. Marco cut a physically threatening figure for which she knew she was no match.

'How did you find me?' she found herself asking. The adrenaline that had crashed through her system with all the force of a tsunami had all but instantly cleared her hangover. 'It wasn't difficult,' he'd shrugged, affording her a waft of his sour body odour, 'seems like you've got somewhat of a reputation round these parts.'

Tess had glanced at the panic button again, wondering if she could make a run for it.

'I do hate it when people leave without saying goodbye,' he'd said, picking up a bronze Art Deco statue from a shelf on the wall and playing with it menacingly, holding it in his hand like a weapon. 'I was very disappointed that you deemed my hospitality in Ibiza to be unsatisfactory, Tess.'

She had blinked at him from the sofa wondering if she might somehow be able to reason with him.

'Look, I've got money,' she'd managed to say, reaching

213

for her handbag. 'I'll give you a couple of thousand right now if you leave me alone . . . here,' she said, taking a wad of cash from her Mulberry purse. It was supposed to be her living costs for the next month, but she'd gladly hand it all over to get him to leave and never come back.

Marco had started to laugh then, a truly sickening sound that caused Tess's terror to accelerate. Was he going to rape her? Beat her up; kill her even? Would her parents find her dead in a few days' time, rotting among the gubbins of last night's celebration? Whatever her fate, she just wanted him to get on with it; get it over with and leave. *Just please leave*.

Snatching the money from her shaking hand, Marco had thrown a USB stick down onto the sofa next to her.

'Yours, I believe,' he said with a raised thick eyebrow as he began to stalk the room, circling the sofa with slow, purposeful movements, enjoying her sense of fear. Tess watched him, petrified that he was about to pull a knife. He looked manic, like he was on something, his eyes wild and wide, his pupils like pin pricks. 'You really think I would only make one copy,' he lunged at her from behind, hissing the words in her ear, causing her to flinch. 'You and that filthy, junkie slag really thought you had one over on me, huh? Well, I'm afraid I'm going to have to put you straight.'

Tess, convinced he was going to kill her now, was too terrified to move. 'No one takes the piss out of Marco DiMari,' he'd said, eventually pulling away from her.

'Take the car!' she'd half screamed, pointing to the keys on the table. She'd tell her parents it had been stolen, or that she'd crashed it. Surely that would be enough to get rid of him. It was a top of the range Audi TT coupe after all. Thirty grand's worth.

'Don't mind if I do,' he laughed, momentarily appeased. His own Audi TT. Bit of a bird's motor but he'd get a good price for it. 'Aren't you going to offer me a drink then, I mean, manners Miss Scott?' His tone was suddenly lighter, almost jovial, like it had been the night she had first met him. 'Got any beer?'

She pointed towards the fridge with a shaking finger.

Marco made his way towards the kitchen and seeing her opportunity, Tess had leapt up from the sofa in a bid to reach the panic button. Marco, however, was too quick for her, and she had yelped in pain as he'd thrown her back down onto the sofa with excessive force, covering her mouth with his hand.

'You know, in different circumstances, I might've warmed to you, Tess Scott,' he'd snarled, baring his teeth at her like an animal, his disposition switching. 'I like a bit of spirit in a woman – more fun when you knock it out of her.' Tess's stifled screams went unheard. 'Now I think you know why I'm here,' he'd said in a low, malevolent whisper. 'So I want you to listen carefully.' He picked up the USB stick and waved it in front of her petrified face, 'How much is this little piece of celluloid worth to you? Fifty grand? One hundred and fifty grand? Maybe two hundred and fifty grand? Nice round little figure that, don't you think, and a drop in the ocean for someone like your old man.' He threw it back down onto the sofa. 'The car's a good start; it'll do for now. Anyway, I figured it shouldn't be too taxing to stump up some cash – just tell Daddy you want a new pony or something,' he'd laughed again then, tickled by his own repartee. 'Failure to come up with the goods and Daddy dearest gets a copy of this couriered directly to his desk.' He smiled nastily. 'Quite the little actress. I'm sure your old man would be *thrilled* to see you having such a *good time* on your holidays.' Paralysed with fear, Tess could only look up at him as he laughed manically. 'And it wouldn't just be your dear old pops who'd get a special delivery either; I'd make sure your whole family got to critique your acting

215

ability, before embarking upon a nice little global viral campaign. By the time your old man's put his injunctions in place, the world and his wife will have seen your Ibiza debut.' Marco's accent had slipped into a broad Cockney one now – and it sounded worse than ever.

'But . . . but I don't have access to that kind of money,' Tess's voice had been a dry, desperate rasp. 'My dad's rich, yes, but I can't just ask him for a quarter of a million pounds! He'll get suspicious. And I only get an allowance of five thousand pounds a month as it is.' She momentarily paused. 'Look, you've got the car – it's worth thirty thousand pounds – can't you just take that? Please . . .' she begged, 'please just leave me alone.'

Marco let out a little sigh of mock-sympathy.

'I wish I could, princess,' he sucked air in through his teeth, 'like I said, the car'll do, for now at least . . .' he pouted. 'You see, I'm not a complete tyrant. And anyway, I quite fancy an extended stay in London . . . see the sights . . .' his voice trailed off. 'You've got three weeks until your next payment is due. Try and fuck me over Tess and I'll organise your first screening.'

'But . . .' Tess had made to speak but he'd swooped down at her again, his eyes a set of menacing slits.

'Three weeks. And you had better hope I don't find that filthy whore who helped you escape, because her life is depending on you,' he looked at her then with dark, menacing eyes as black as onyx. 'That's right, babes,' he'd smirked, 'failure to make payment means you can kiss goodbye to your fucking fairy godmother.' His face distorted. 'OK,' Tess had nodded profusely. 'I'll get your money for you; I promise, I *promise* . . .' Marco had seemed instantly calmed by this, his whole countenance relaxing.

'Atta girl,' he'd said softly, leaning in to stroke her hair almost tenderly. Tess flinched but did nothing to prevent him. *Please God, just make him leave, make him leave.*

216

Marco had turned towards the door. 'And Tess,' he'd added sagely, his voice low with gravitas, 'no police. The slightest whiff of filth and I'll find that bitch Monique and slit her throat from ear to ear,' his eyes met with hers, 'before I come back for you.'

Tess was still nodding even after he had shut the door behind him, and she'd bolted and chained it shut. Her heart beating a painful tune in her chest, she had reached for her phone, her hands shaking violently as she attempted to press the digits.

'Oh dear God Jesus Christ, Monique,' she said as it had begun to ring, 'please pick up the phone. For fuck's sake, *pick up the phone.*'

CHAPTER 43

'Lionel, great to see you; come through. Can I get you something to drink?' Vincent Scott shook the man's hand amiably, already pouring him a generous measure of Highland Park 1948 single malt into a diamond-cut crystal tumbler.

'Don't mind if I do, Mr Scott,' Lionel Crosby nodded as he simultaneously took the glass and seat offered to him.

Crosby was a former police detective with an exemplary thirty year record on the force. Though now officially retired, he had struggled to adjust to a slower pace of life and had set up his own private investigation company. He cut a slightly rumpled and exhausted figure, though looks could be deceiving; when it came to professionalism, Crosby was in the premier league. Ostensibly, he'd been recruited by Vincent Scott to start digging up a little information on the new owners of the old warehouse.

Crosby sipped at his single malt, savouring the potent yet smooth afterbite of the expensive alcohol.

'So, what have you got for me, Crosby?' Vinnie asked, intrigued. It was obvious by the man's presence that he'd come up with something and he was keen to get straight to the point.

'Well,' Crosby swilled the contents of his glass, savouring the top vanilla notes of the Scotch, 'there has been some development.'

Vinnie's contacts in the trade had been suspiciously reticent about the new occupants of the warehouse on Swift Street, causing his interest to pique. He planned to arrange a face-to-face with whoever had acquired it and make them an offer they couldn't refuse, in a bid to buy it back for his wife. Hell, he'd strong arm them if he had to. He knew some powerful people in Soho who could make life pretty difficult for the occupants of that casino if he was pushed to. But first he wanted to know exactly who he was dealing with. Casinos were ten a penny in London and he would happily remind them of this fact; besides, Soho was full of old timers; no one spent money there anymore. Now Shoreditch, where Vinnie had unoccupied buildings himself to sell; that was a far safer bet . . .

Lionel Crosby pulled a piece of paper from the inside pocket of his tired-looking suit and downed the dregs of his crystal tumbler, unable to hide his cheer as Vinnie refreshed his glass with another generous measure of the good stuff.

'It seems as if your wife's warehouse was snapped up by a couple of middle-aged Americans; small time by all accounts. One of them is British-born, though he's lived in the States most of his adult life.'

Vinnie listened with interest, absent-mindedly adjusting his diamond Cartier cufflinks – a present from Ellie last Christmas.

'The pair of them had businesses all over the States,' Crosby continued, 'bars and strip joints mainly, nothing of significance. Debts in every state too, by the looks of it.'

Vinnie's mouth turned outwards. This was a surprise to him. He'd have put money on the new owners being Arab or oligarchs, but small-time Yanks with nothing of previous note . . . this would be easier than he thought.

'So you think they might be open to a little negotiation? You see, I want that venue Crosby,' he said, his tone leaving no room for negotiation. 'That venue was supposed to be my wife's . . .'

Crosby nodded sympathetically. The man was obviously in the dog house.

'I'd say you were in with half a chance, Mr Scott,' he conceded. 'From what I can tell, these two are little more than chancers; the interesting part is where they managed to scrape the funds from. Checking their respective credit history, neither man is what you might call solvent. One of them in particular is partial to a flutter and a rich older woman by the looks of things. Got a few press cuttings of him gallivanting with a few prominent society women and the like . . .'

'I see,' Vinnie said, digesting the information. If the man was as partial to the pound as Crosby was suggesting then he was in a strong position to bargain. 'And does he have a name, this American player?'

Crosby nodded, throwing the piece of paper down onto the desk with pride in his own efficiency. He really was cut out for this job.

'Yes,' he said, 'does the name Tom Black ring any bells?'

CHAPTER 44

'I'm really not so sure about this,' Tess said hesitantly as she looked up at the sign outside the club that read; *Black Jack's: Dancers' Auditions this way – 12.30.*

'You have any better ideas?' Monique turned to her, blowing the smoke from her Gitane into Tess's face. 'You need a job, I need a job, *et voila*!' she said, with a deadpan expression.

They had agreed to meet outside a nondescript café on Wardour Street earlier that day. It was a beautiful morning and the sun was shining, casting a whole new light over the city. The morning rays highlighted the vibrant, eclectic mix of cultures thrown together as they collectively welcomed the change in season.

'Do you think I should call Marco's bluff?' Tess had asked, sipping on a skinny soya macchiato with dry lips while Monique chain-smoked between mouthfuls of greasy pain au chocolat, 'call the police and tell them everything?' She'd hardly slept since Marco had paid her a visit and she felt strung out.

Monique had shrugged as she'd devoured her breakfast. She'd been off the brown for a week now and as always her appetite had returned with a vengeance.

221

'Are you prepared to take that chance?' she'd said between simultaneous mouthfuls of pastry and Gitane. 'You heard what he said; any police and he'll courier the footage straight to your father's front door . . .'

'But he said he'd slit *your* throat,' Tess had protested, incredulous. Monique seemed unmoved by Marco's threats. 'You didn't see him, Monique. The guy was manic!'

Monique had sighed with a shrug.

'This is Marco . . . like I told you, he's one sick fuck.'

'No shit, Sherlock – which is all the more reason to go to the police,' Tess had implored. 'I mean, aren't you worried he might find you too?' Tess was incredulous.

Monique had finished the remains of her pastry and instantly lit another Gitane. She'd spent the past seven days in a women's refuge, wired out of her mind on cocaine to help with the mother of all junk comedowns. Frankly, whatever Marco had in store for her it could hardly be any worse.

'Marco won't find me unless I want to be found,' Monique had snorted, with an air of defiance that belied her tiny frame.

'How can you be so sure?'

'Because he's not as clever as he thinks he is,' she replied, signalling to the waiter to bring her an Americano. 'Black and sweet, just how I like my men!' she'd laughed then.

'None of this is remotely funny,' Tess had swallowed hard. 'If my dad gets to see that video . . .' her smile had evaporated and she felt her guts twist. 'Jesus, it's all such a fucking mess.'

'Chill out, *cherie*,' Monique had run a hand subconsciously through her short dark cropped hair. She was through the worst of the itching stage now, when it felt as if a million lice were crawling over every inch of your skin, making you want to tear it off, but every now and again it returned with a spiteful malice. 'Look, if it makes you feel safer, I will come and stay at your place for a while,' she'd suggested, making out that she would be doing her a favour, when in fact it would be the other way round. 'I know how to deal with Marco, what to say to get him to back off and chill the fuck out.'

Tess had nodded her agreement.

'It's money he wants; give him what he wants and he will leave you alone. You say he took your car?'

'Yeah,' Tess had slumped further into the plastic chair, depressed. 'Thirty-thousand pounds worth of brand new soft top Audi TT, gone,' she'd clicked her fingers, 'like that. I'll have to tell the folks it's been stolen or something. They'll go fucking spare! I was hoping it would be enough to get rid of him for good, but it seems not,' she'd added, her voice filled with misery and despair.

'He said he wants more . . . a lot more . . .' Tess fought back yet more tears; she'd never produced so many in all her life as these past couple of days. 'He wants a quarter of a million pounds.'

'Savings?' Monique had suggested as she emptied four little packets of sugar into her coffee in quick succession. 'An inheritance perhaps?'

Tess had shaken her head ruefully.

'In three years' time I inherit a lump of cash that'll set me up for life,' she said, flatly. 'On paper I'm loaded, but until then, it's all tied up in bonds and shares . . . fat lot of good that is to me! *And* Daddy's expecting me to pay my way with bills and household shit and stuff. I'll be scraping by on my monthly allowance as it is.'

Monique had resisted the urge to lean forward and slap Tess's ungrateful face. She would never know of Monique's pathetic excuse of a life, dragged up in the poorest back streets of Paris by an alcoholic, promiscuous mother whose nefarious, often violent boyfriends had abused her since the age of five; how she had subsequently been pushed from one foster home to another only to suffer a similar fate, a never-ending cycle of abuse and neglect. Tess felt the familiar sting of tears prick the back of her eyes and rested her head in her hands in despair. 'I just want rid of him, Monique. I want him to give me that video and leave me alone . . .'

'So, pawn some of your jewellery,' she'd shrugged coldly. Tess blinked back at her, not sure how to take such directness. '. . . Stage a fake robbery at the flat or something.'

'You think I haven't already thought of that? The Number One building is like Big Fucking Brother, there's CCTV cameras everywhere, it's alarmed up to the hilt.'

'Well, then you'll have to get a job like the rest of society and pay him off that way. You know, *work* for a living.'

'Oh yeah, a job, doing what huh?' Tess had spat in response, watching as the waitress hurried past with a tray of empty glasses, a harried look of stress on her face. 'I'll not make twenty thousand a month waiting tables, that's for sure,' she threw herself back into her chair. 'Where am I going to earn *that* kind of money fast?' Tess whined, her voice a hopeless mix of sarcasm and despair.

Monique had grinned, a wide, proper grin, one that displayed her small, neat gummy smile and gap between her front teeth. 'Actually,' she said with an insouciant stare as she blew smoke from her thick pillow lips, 'I think I know just the place.'

CHAPTER 45

Vincent Scott slammed his fist down onto the antique oak and leather desk with such aggression that it genuinely shocked Crosby. Scott had never struck him as the violent type; but that was people for you, they never failed to surprise. He watched Scott carefully as he paced the room from behind his desk, dragging the skin on his chin with his thumb and forefinger, his face a mix of fury and concern. 'I'm sorry, Crosby,' Scott apologised, his initial shock subsiding a little.

'Someone you know, I take it?' he gently enquired.

Scott raised his eyes by way of an answer.

'You could say that.' He needed to think. He was due to fly out to Australia in a couple of days for what was to be one of the biggest property deals of his illustrious career, and he couldn't allow this bombshell to jeopardise everything he'd worked for. Black had been the only dark cloud on what had been an unblemished marital landscape and here he was again, out of the blue, and back to cause trouble, of that he was in no doubt.

Though he had never met the man in the flesh, Vincent felt as though he knew Black's character inside out. He was a beacon for discord, a magnet for upset and mayhem and that he had somehow managed to acquire the very property he had hoped to obtain for his wife had a terrible irony to it, something that greatly unsettled him. Were they somehow linked to this man for all eternity? Vincent wondered if Ellie knew anything of this and pushed away the idea that she might. She would have said something. There were no secrets between them now, *were there*?

'So,' Crosby took a tentative breath, 'is this man someone you feel you may be able to negotiate with?'

'Abso-fucking-lutely not.' Vincent dismissed the idea instantly with an incredulous laugh. 'Look, this Black character, Crosby, he's seriously bad news. He's an old . . .' he paused momentarily, '. . . an old associate of my wife's.' Vinnie glanced over at him and Crosby nodded. He didn't need to spell it out.

'The man's a tumour, Crosby. He needs cutting out.'

Vincent was transported to the morning of his wedding twenty years ago, the look on Eleanor's face as she told him what had transpired the night before at Livedon, and felt the pain all over again.

'I want you to tail him,' he turned to Crosby, nodding towards the decanter of fine malt on the desk, indicating that he should help himself. Crosby didn't need telling twice. 'I don't want that bastard anywhere near my family, you understand?' Crosby gave an effective nod. Whatever beef Scott had with this man, he could tell it was serious.

'I'll take care of it Mr Scott,' Crosby said with reassuring efficiency.

'I want to know everything; who he's doing business with, what he eats for lunch, hell, which side of the goddamn bed he sleeps on; the minute you get something of interest I want to hear about it, OK?'

'Of course, Mr Scott,' Crosby drained his glass. 'I'll get onto it with immediate effect.'

'Do whatever it takes, Crosby,' Vincent said in a low

voice. 'I want that man out of London and on the first plane back to the States, and if that can't happen, well, do whatever needs to be done.' Vincent met the man's gaze.

'Is that all Mr Scott?' Crosby enquired.

'Actually, no,' Vincent said quietly. 'There is something else . . .'

He paused.

'I want you to tail my wife too.'

CHAPTER 46

Standing in her private bathroom, her bare feet warm against the underfloor heating, Victoria looked down at the white stick and read the words in the digital window, 'Not Pregnant'. Staring at them as if they were foreign, she discarded the piece of plastic into the Brabantia bin with breathtaking self-denial. This was bullshit. She'd been screwing Tom Black like they were the last two people on the planet for the past few weeks, so what in hell's name was taking so fucking long? This is what happens to women who lie and cheat and deceive she told herself; they don't get what they want. They don't deserve to.

Holding her chin up in a forced act of defiance, Victoria audibly inhaled as she stared at herself in the enormous Venetian antique mirror. She wanted to see someone else staring back at her, someone she liked and respected. Instead she saw a desperate woman, prepared to deceive those she loved to get what she wanted. She quickly looked away, pulling her La Perla silk housecoat around her nakedness like a shield.

In spite of the stellar front she was putting up, Victoria was unravelling inside, and deep down she knew it. The strong, capable image she was projecting to the outside world was the antithesis to the broken woman inside. She felt like two different people; three if you included Rachel. Victoria felt the futility of her situation like a noose around her neck. She had started something now, something that needed finishing and she would just have to keep reminding herself of the end goal. Once she was pregnant then she could end it with Tom, forget him like he never existed but, torn between her rational and increasingly irrational mind, she knew that was impossible now. To justify her behaviour she had somehow convinced herself that she must have developed some sort of feelings for the man.

Unwrapping another test, she held the thin white stick in her urine stream for longer than was necessary, looking down at the digital window expectantly as the faint type slowly appeared: 'Not Pregnant'. The words seemed to mock her somehow.

Her emotions enflamed, Victoria took a Jo Malone scented candle from the glass shelf in front of her and threw it at the mirror, the antique glass shattering against the floor-to-ceiling marble.

'Seven years' bad luck,' she said aloud to no one, her chest heaving with adrenaline as she enjoyed a fleeting moment of release.

What the hell, make it ten.

CHAPTER 47

Every day in Paris was like fashion week, Ellie thought as she trotted along the Rue Du Faubourg, appreciating the warmth of the morning sunlight on her tanned, exposed shoulders.

She stole admiring glances at the Parisian women who flocked to the exclusive area in their achingly chic droves to peruse the windows of the exquisite boutiques, sucking nonchalantly on cigarettes and chatting in fast French on their cell phones.

'Everyone here looks like Emmanuelle Alt,' she observed, referencing the French *Vogue* fashion editor's signature style – all sharp shoulder blazers, soft t-shirts lazily tucked into the low waist-band of skinny jeans and of course, vertiginous heels. 'Hardly a scrap of make up on, perfectly glossy hair, so groomed yet so understated . . .'

'And *so* thin . . .' Victoria added. 'But then I guess you would be if you lived on a diet of cigarettes, coffee and laxatives.'

'Hmm,' Ellie replied lazily, her attention suddenly caught by an older man with a grey beard who was standing outside Chanel, looking to be admiring the impeccably styled shop window. He seemed somehow incongruously dressed in an ill-fitting, cheap-looking suit, there among the smart and fashion conscious in this exclusive part of town. For a split second Ellie made the briefest of eye contact with him. She couldn't be sure, but something told her that he was watching them.

'Shall we head off to Balmain after lunch?' Victoria suggested, hopeful that she might just find *the* perfect dress she was looking to wear to the imminent opening of *Black Jack's*. After all, it was the reason she had suggested a little shopping weekend in the French capital in the first place. Victoria wanted to find something devastatingly chic for her lover's opening night. *Lover*. Could she call Tom that? *Should* she? Much to her burgeoning self-loathing and wracked conscience, Victoria wanted to ensure she looked her best – and most desirable, for their clandestine sexual encounters. She bit her lip; she knew she was losing herself in the drama of it all but felt powerless to prevent it. Sex with Tom Black was like nothing she'd ever experienced in her entire life; the antithesis of the kind she had with her husband; with Tom it was base and dirty, fast and furious, a little crazy and passionate. Just reliving their last encounter in her mind caused her juices to stir.

*

Sipping on a strong espresso on the beautiful terrace of the Epicure restaurant in the heart of the 8th district, Ellie slipped on a pair of Stella McCartney aviators and sat back into her seat, wishing she could allow herself to open up to her friend about her troubles – and more importantly, her past. The whole thing was driving her to distraction. Deep down she knew she should tell Vinnie, yet she couldn't. Was a lie only what you said as opposed to something you *didn't say*? Jesus, she needed to purge herself of all this anxiety somehow. The threat of Tom's presence had cast a black cloud over everything. She gulped back her espresso, allowing the hot liquid to burn the back of her throat almost as punishment.

'*Plus de café, mesdames*? The impeccably dressed waiter approached the table with an air of Parisian insouciance.

'Actually, I fancy something a little stronger,' Victoria began perusing the wine list with alacrity, 'oh screw it, let's have the Louis Roederer Cristal 2004!'

'*Magnifique*!' Ellie replied enthusiastically. A glass of the good stuff was what she needed to take the edge off her troubled thoughts. The waiter nodded his approval and returned almost instantly with a chilled ice bucket and two glasses.

'*Salut*!' the two women chinked flutes. It didn't escape Ellie's eye that Tor had gulped half her glass back in one hit.

'Everything OK, Tor?' she carefully asked.

'Couldn't be better,' Tor replied, wondering just how many more lies she would have to tell before they began to trip her up. 'The book is coming along brilliantly and Lol is fab, phoning me as often as possible, though it can get tricky out in the jungle you know, dreadful reception . . . I do worry about him, all those strange animals and insects . . .' she pulled a face.

'You must miss him terribly. I know I miss Vin,' Ellie sighed wistfully, wishing how things could just go back to being how they had been a few weeks ago, when she had been none the wiser about the auction or Loretta and Tom and what could only be described as their ridiculous sham of a marriage.

'Oh I do,' Victoria gushed guiltily, 'but this is the price one pays for having a successful husband, no?'

Ellie sighed her agreement, trying to shake off the thought of Tom and Loretta sashaying up the aisle together, a look of love in their eyes as they exchanged vows. 'This

Australia trip is a big deal for Vin. If the Aussies sign on the line then I've pretty much lost him for the next six months. I've told him if he comes back with an Aussie accent I'll divorce him.'

Victoria laughed, though it struck her that on the very odd occasion, usually after a few glasses of fizz, that Ellie herself slipped into a soft stateside lilt. 'I wish I could be there with him but someone's got to be around to keep an eye on things . . . Tess being one of those "things".' Her daughter was behaving strangely and she could no longer put it down to her overactive parental imagination, especially given that ever since she'd moved into that damn apartment she had hardly seen hide nor hair of her. It was as if she was deliberately keeping her distance. She was a mummy's girl at her core, however much she liked to pretend otherwise. Ellie recalled the conversation she'd had with Tess the previous day over their weekly lunch. It had left her feeling so ill at ease that she'd been unable to sleep properly ever since.

*

'Here she is!' Ellie had stood, arms outstretched as her daughter had slunk into Bibendum a little over twenty-five minutes late. 'I was beginning to think you might have broken down on the way here,' she had said, hugging her only child tightly.

Tess gave her mother a weak smile as she threw her Mulberry Alexa onto the table and practically fell into her seat. She knew she would have to tell her about the car. She couldn't keep making excuses about MOTs and lending it to friends. 'Actually Mum, now you mention the car . . .'

'I took the liberty of ordering you a starter,' Ellie interrupted her, 'the Waldorf salad, that's OK isn't it?'

'Yes . . . about the car Mum,' Tess had continued a little

irritably, keen to get it over with. She wished her mother would just shut up and listen to her.

Ellie had looked up from the menu and studied her daughter's familiar face, so much like her own.

'What about the car, baby?' Ellie had said, gently this time. She knew better than to go in all guns blazing.

'I crashed it,' Tess said quickly, flicking her hair from her face, 'wrote the bloody thing off. It was my fault, went through a red light; wasn't concentrating,' she fiddled nervously with her napkin.

Ellie had absorbed this information as she cast a concerned eye over her daughter. Her roots were showing and her nails were bitten to the quick. Her usual carefully planned attire looked thrown together, like she'd picked the first thing up off the floor that morning, and she'd looked even thinner than usual.

'My God Tess, why didn't you tell me?' Concern dripped from Ellie's voice. 'You weren't hurt, were you?'

Tess had stared at her starter plate without meeting her mother's eye.

'A little whiplash, nothing major . . .'

'So how did it happen . . . I mean, was anyone else hurt? Where did it happen? When? Were you alone . . .'

'Jesus Mum, does it matter?' Tess had snapped, cutting her off. 'The fact is the car's totalled, which is why I was late meeting you. I had to get a cab . . .'

Ellie had blinked at her daughter in shock, the pause between them long enough for an awkward silence to develop.

'What's going on, Tess?' Ellie had eventually said, her voice low.

'Going on? Nothing's going on,' Tess had shot back unconvincingly, holding back a river of tears that were stinging the back of her eyes. She had never before in her life wanted her mother's love and help more than she did at that very moment. It was only now, now that she was faced with such terrible adversity, that Tess finally realised just what a constant source of love and security she had always been.

'You know you can tell me, sweetheart, whatever it is, whatever's happened, you know you can always talk to me,' Ellie had taken her daughter's hand in her own and held it tightly, silently pleading with her to open up, to talk to her. 'If you're in some kind of trouble . . . you know I'm your mother, Tess, I can help . . .'

Tess had swallowed back the lump that had lodged itself in her windpipe and pulled her hand away roughly. She just couldn't bring herself to do it; she was too ashamed.

'Look, I crashed my car that's all . . . I'd rather you didn't tell Daddy if it's all the same. And if you want to help, then you can lend me one of the Mercs because frankly, I'm pretty stuffed without a set of wheels. Now, please, can we just drop it, OK?'

*

'What do you mean by that?' Victoria was intrigued. She'd come to know Tess pretty well over the duration of her and Ellie's friendship and although she knew the girl was a little spoilt, she thought a lot of her.

'Oh I don't know . . . I can't put my finger on it. Ellie sighed. 'It's like I'm losing her, Tor. Like she's distanced herself from me. I think she's hiding something from me.'

'A romance turned bad?' Tor suggested, refreshing both their glasses and jabbing at a plump green olive before popping it between her nude painted lips.

'Maybe,' Ellie mused, 'but I feel sure she would tell me if it was something like that; she's always been pretty upfront about that sort of thing. And then she told Vin that she's thinking of going back to school and finishing her exams.'

235

'And that's a bad thing?'

'No! Not at all, that's exactly what I wanted her to do; it's just that, well, she was so dead against it a few weeks ago . . .'

'Don't knock it,' Victoria sipped her champagne, enjoying some respite from her own problems by listening to someone else's.

'Oh, I don't know,' Ellie sighed, 'She's got a reckless streak that one, seems to naturally attract trouble . . .' Ellie gave a weary sigh, 'she's just like her father.'

'Really?' Tor looked genuinely surprised. 'I've always been under the impression that Vinnie was quite the opposite of reckless.'

It had been a momentary slip of the tongue.

'What I mean to say is that she has his feisty determination . . .' Ellie quickly added.

There was a poignant moment's pause between them.

'I was thinking,' Victoria finally said, 'what with our men both currently working away and everything, if you would do me the honour of being my plus-one at an event I've been invited to . . .'

'Oh?'

'I realise there could be what you might call a conflict of interest, so feel free to turn me down.'

'Now I *am* intrigued,' Ellie said.

'It's that new casino in Soho, *Black Jack's* . . .' she said, measuredly. 'I've been given this ticket you see – rarer than one of Willy Wonka's according to the papers. Rumour has it that half of the States are flying in especially. Anyway, what do you say? I know you had that place pegged for your studio, but at least this way we get to have a good nose around, and bitch about how you would've utilised the space much more efficiently,' she grinned, hoping she had not offended her friend by asking.

Ellie's mind clicked into overdrive. As much as her

conscience told her to turn the invitation down, the other, more curious side of her nature told her that this presented her with the perfect opportunity in which to legitimately bump into Tom. She could always tell Vinnie about it afterwards, feign ignorance about not knowing who the host had been in advance. Ellie made a snap decision.

'I'd love to come with you, silly,' she said brightly, 'no point in bearing grudges . . . besides, you're right, I'm intrigued to see what they've done with the place – why not!'

They sealed the deal with a ding of their champagne flutes.

'It's a date!'

Both women were rather looking forward to it, though neither guessed they shared the same motive.

CHAPTER 48

Boarding her private jet – destination Milan – Loretta, dressed head to toe in Cavalli, extinguished her L&M and instantly lit another before turning to wave to Tom.

'Ciao, darling, I'll be back before you know it,' she called out to him, her voice inaudible above the loud roar of the jet's powerful engine. 'Be a good boy now won't you, *if you can*,' she added wryly, her zebra-print kaftan flapping in the wind. Tom smiled and waved back enthusiastically, grateful for the fact that she couldn't see his eyes beneath his mirrored Ray-Bans. Spending so much time with her had left him feeling drained and exhausted. As he watched the doors of the aircraft close, Tom couldn't help wishing for a little airborne disaster to take place. Loretta was on her way to Milan to hook up with some celebrity wedding planner she'd hired at an exorbitant cost of three thousand euros a day. Nice work if you could get it.

'I'm thinking of having a 'purity' theme,' Loretta had announced on the journey to the airport, oblivious to the ridiculous irony of such a statement, 'everything white. I want to launch a thousand white doves into the sky as we say our vows, have a pair of white tigers either side of the arbour and ride in on a pair of white stallions – what do you think, dahling?'

'I think I don't like horses,' Tom had remarked wryly and she had shot him a caustic look. 'Unpredictable things.'

'I do hope you're not going to start being difficult,' she snapped. 'This is *my* big day and I want it to be one hundred per cent *perfecto,* oh yes, Mummy does,' she said in a high-pitched baby voice as she stroked Bambino's head.

'Look, Loretta,' Tom said, the drop in his tone causing her to look up. 'Seriously, how do you expect this to work? We both know this is nothing more than a marriage of convenience. Why can't we just fly out to the Little White Chapel in Vegas and be done with it? I mean, all this expense – and for what? We're not even a real couple, at least not exactly,' he added. 'How are we supposed to keep up such pretence after the wedding? And what about the finer details, like are we supposed to live together, and if so, where?'

Loretta's eyes darkened.

'*Pretence?*' she allowed the word to roll off her tongue like a marble. 'Who said anything about pretence?'

'It's just that the press are already all over this and well, it's becoming increasingly difficult to lie.'

The paparazzi had been hounding him ever since the rumour of a wedding had somehow been leaked – Loretta tipping them off, no doubt. After all, Loretta was prime time gossip fodder thanks to the high profile Muldavey case, and her larger-than-life personality and outlandish dress sense.

'So, what first attracted you to the multi-millionairess, Mrs Loretta Hassan then?' one weasel-faced little gossip hack had nastily enquired, cornering him on his way into the club one morning. 'Is she bank-rolling this joint? Are you not worried you'll end up like her second husband?'

'Oh come come Tom, don't give me this bullshit,' Loretta

said now. 'You've turned lying into an art form. You could fib at the pearly gates and get away with it.'

Tom was growing tetchy. Was this his life from now on, being Loretta Fiorentino's bitch?

'I signed a contract of marriage, remember? Hardly the stuff of Mills and Boon is it? We can't very well pretend this is anything more than what it is – a business transaction, albeit with benefits.'

Loretta smirked. The 'benefits' were the best bits.

'Mummy is upset by what the bad man is saying,' she cooed to Bambino, who seemed to give a little sympathetic whine in response. Tom felt like snatching the hapless animal from her clutches and throwing it from the moving vehicle.

'I mean it Loretta,' his voice hardened. 'We need some ground rules, some boundaries if this shit is going to work. When I signed that piece of paper I agreed to marry you, not love you.' He was pushing his luck now and he knew it, but he needed to make things clear.

Loretta was visibly upset.

'Oh, how you forget so quickly, Tom,' she mused, her calm tone belying her anger as she blew smoke in his direction from thick glossy lips, 'if it wasn't for me, that delectable little *ass* of yours would be sitting in jail right now and Jack would have a price on your pretty head. I don't think you are in the best position to start calling the shots, no?'

'You're buying my name Loretta, that much I understand,' Tom said, careful to keep any malice from his voice, 'but the soul ain't for sale.'

'Ha! I would need to cut a deal with the devil himself for that!' she snapped back. 'If it is clarity you're after, then let me explain. After we're married, I want you to be on hand to accompany me to any social event I choose. I expect us to be pictured together regularly and for you to show me public displays of affection, especially when there are cameras present. We will spend at least half of the year together, shared between Italy, LA and London, although I appreciate this might not be consecutive due to respective business commitments,' she added, matter of fact. 'We will be seen holidaying together, and we will publicly support each other's business ventures. It will be a proper marriage in that respect.'

'And what about the other side of things?' he glanced sideways at her. 'You know, the *private* side?'

Loretta tutted.

'You are bored of fucking me already, Tom?'

Tom snorted with mirth, though it lacked any real humour. She was to the point, he gave the woman that much. Tom had never had a problem emotionally detaching himself from the physical, but the thought of conjugal duties with Loretta on demand turned his stomach.

'Boring in bed is one thing you're most certainly not,' he said. Such a backhanded compliment was lost on Loretta and her sexual ego.

'I am glad to hear it, darling,' she purred. 'Look, I hardly expect you to be faithful Tom, after all, I do not believe in miracles,' she smirked, 'and perhaps I will not even afford you the same courtesy, but if you publicly humiliate me with another woman, if you are caught by the paparazzo with your trousers down, then I will take back that casino faster than you can do your zipper up, do you understand?' Her tone was low and menacing, leaving no room for debate.

'You know me, Loretta,' he smiled that devastating smile of his, displaying his neat white teeth and dimples, 'discretion's my middle name.'

'So I remember,' she replied with an involuntary smile of her own.

Tom felt as if he was onboard a runaway train that he was powerless to stop. 'Unless of course you wish to tear up that contract and go directly to jail, do not pass go, do not collect two hundred dollars . . .' she glanced at him, her feline eyes dark as coal, mocking him.

'It's pounds, actually,' he corrected her. 'Two hundred *pounds*; Monopoly is an English game – and no, I don't want to tear it up,' he said, feeling utterly defeated. 'If you want a big wedding, well then, whatever the lady wants . . .'

'*Bueno*,' she smiled, never happier than when she was getting her own way.

CHAPTER 49

'You! You filthy, fucking, dirty, junkie whore!' Marco screamed into the receiver, his voice hoarse with aggression, eyes bulging manically from of their sockets in protestation. 'You'd better have an explanation for me, Monique – and it had better be the life-saving kind, because so help me God, if I so much as find out where you are . . .'

'Oh relax, Marco,' Monique sighed with such insouciance that Marco thought he might combust with rage. 'I would hardly be calling you if I didn't have something worth saying, would I? Look, I realise I fucked up in Ibiza, ruined your evil plans and everything, but you know, the girl had been howling, banging on the door for God knows how many days . . . it was starting to give me a headache! Besides, you might not have thanked me for it then, but you will when you've heard what I've got to say . . .'

Marco breathed deeply, trying to stop himself from imagining his hands around this fucking snide bitch's throat, shaking every last miserable breath from her rancid bones.

'Nothing you could say would please me, you treacherous little cunt,' he spat. The fucking nerve of this bitch! 'After everything I've done for you, you fucking betray me at the first opportunity . . . stabbed me in the back, well . . .'

'Oh spare me,' Monique huffed, 'you needed me just as much as I needed you – and deep down you know it, Marco. Now cut the victim crap and listen; it's about Tess Scott.'

The mention of her name was enough to momentarily silence him.

'What about her?' he said after a pause.

'Well, for one thing, I know you're blackmailing her.'

'Oh yeah? And how the fuck would you know that?'

'Because she told me so herself.'

Marco's interest piqued though he was careful to disguise it.

'I know *everything*,' Monique continued. 'How you threatened to slit my throat unless she pays you your ransom, fund your *lifestyle* while you're in London. You took the girl's car . . . and by all accounts that's just the start of it . . .'

Marco snorted, as if on cue expelling a little coagulated white mucus, remnants of last night's coke and hooker marathon.

Thanks to Tess's generous gift in the form of an Audi TT which he had promptly sold to a dodgy dealer in Leyton, Marco had checked himself into a decent hotel in Bloomsbury where he'd promptly ordered up a couple of hookers and a bag of coke.

'What the fuck do you want, Monique? You must have a death wish calling me, bold as brass.'

Monique snorted.

'You think I am scared of death, Marco. Death is something beautiful; a chance to be reborn. Another life. One that isn't shit, filled with misery and pain.'

Marco gave a nasty laugh.

'Hear that, Monique? That's the world's fucking smallest violin playing a tune just for you,' he sneered.

Monique smiled. She would enjoy screwing Marco over,

this time even bigger and better than before. He had been the one to introduce her to heroin. She had been so young, so naïve when they had met ten years ago and he had shown her the one thing she had been starved of her entire life: love. Or at least she had thought that's what it had been. When they had taken drugs together and made love it had been some of the most happy and memorable moments of her entire life, at least it had felt that way at first. In Marco, Monique thought she had found her saviour, her soul mate, a man who would love and cherish her, make all the bad things she had seen in her life good again. But he turned out to be worse than all of them put together. He sucked her into his nasty world. And once he'd been sure of her unwavering faith, he had set about pulling her apart, piece by piece, until he had destroyed what little there had been left of every fragile human emotion she possessed.

'What would you say if I told you that Tess Scott is my new best friend, and that we're going to be working together?' There was a pause on the line before she continued.

'And what if I also told you that currently I'm living at her luxury apartment – the very same apartment you visited just a few weeks ago?'

'I'd say you were lying,' he scoffed.

'There's money here, Marco,' she said, tempting him. 'Much more than the quarter of a million you're after. There's a safe here that contains all her jewellery – and it's just as you would expect of a billionaire's daughter, enough ice to sink the Titanic. And then there's the designer bags and clothes . . . her shoe collection alone must be worth treble figures . . .' Monique had his attention now and she knew it. 'I have access to all of it. If we play our cards right we could split the lot and be set for life. Look, it's simple,' she said, her voice low, 'I get her hooked on

245

the powder, pump her full of the stuff until she's a zombie who wouldn't have a clue what was in her fridge, let alone her safe, then we siphon it off, bit by bit until we've fleeced the lot. In the meantime, we'll start working at Black Jack's, the new casino that's due to open, you know the Soho place? We've got jobs there as a couple of lap dancers – well, the girl has got to find some way of paying you, *non*? You'll get your weekly payments and a cut of the rest of it.'

'*Half* the rest of it,' Marco interjected, already sold on the idea.

'Obviously, you could always just sell the video now and make what, maybe fifty thousand at most? But this way, *my* way, we're potentially looking at ten times that amount.'

'Why are you telling me all this Monique? Marco eventually replied. 'You could've just gone ahead and taken the lot for yourself . . .'

'You're right,' she sighed, 'but I owe you, Marco. You've been good to me over the years.'

Yeah, he'd been good to her alright; destroying what was left of her pathetic excuse for a life.

'I'd like the chance to repay you, make up for what happened in Ibiza.'

'Why should I trust you, Monique? After all, you've already proved yourself to be nothing more than a treacherous, two-faced whore.'

'Oh come on,' she lamented, 'a girl's allowed one small mistake, *mais non*? But if that's the way you feel . . .'

'OK,' he interjected, 'I'm in.'

'*Bon*!' she said, lighting a Gitane between her small gummy teeth.

'But I'm calling the shots on this one, Monique,' Marco warned her, 'if I find out you're fucking with me in any way, I swear that this time I *will* kill you.'

He hung up then and Monique stood, the phone still

pressed to her ear as she listened to the loud purr of the dialling tone.

'Not if I kill you first,' she said, quietly replacing the receiver.

CHAPTER 50

'You're kidding me, right?' Jack blinked at Tom from behind
the shiny spanking new cocktail bar of their casino, where
he was busy sampling the vast array of exclusive imported
spirits and assortment of mixers. His smile soon faded
when he caught the look on Tom's face. 'Tell me you *are*
kidding . . .'

Tom sipped at his 'Vegas Sunset' – a signature cocktail
one of the new bartenders had come up with for the
launch night, a cucumber and pink gin-based Martini,
finished off with a dash of Cristal. A little on the dry
side for him, but not bad, he thought, not bad at all. He
was silent for a moment, allowing the cucumber aftertaste
to linger on his tongue. He only wished it was all a big
joke.

'Six weeks' time,' he said, matter-of-factly, 'a castle in Capri;
belongs to the Armani dynasty, beautiful apparently.'

Jack was dumbfounded.

'You're *marrying* Loretta Fiorentino?'

Tom slid a large hologram-embossed black and gold
envelope across the bar towards him.

Jack narrowed his eyes suspiciously as he opened it.

248

Ms Loretta Fiorentino and Mr Tom Black request the pleasure of your company . . .'

It had taken Tom weeks to pluck up the courage to come clean about his forthcoming 'arrangement' with Loretta. It would be easy enough to fool strangers into the belief that he was looking forward to becoming Mrs Loretta Fiorentino, but he knew that fooling Jack would be quite another task altogether.

'. . . Are you fucking mad?' Jack turned his back on him and, grabbing a fresh glass from the stack, he poured himself a single malt from one of the optics, throwing it back in one hit, spluttering as the contents met his gullet.

'What the fuck's going on, Tom?' Jack demanded. 'You had better start talking to me buddy . . .'

Tom inwardly sighed. This was going to be even harder than he'd thought.

'What can I say?' he deadpanned, 'we were meant for each other.'

Tom's facetious response caused Jack to explode in a mix of laughter and rage.

'*Meant* for each other? Jesus fucking Christ Tom, that woman is a Goddamn pariah! Everything she touches she destroys. I mean, screwing the bitch is one thing . . . but *marrying* her?' He shook his head. He didn't need a fucking bombshell like this right now. The casino was due to open in a week and Jack was really beginning to feel the strain. It was all he could do to drag his sorry ass up and out of his pit each morning. He felt zapped of strength, his bones heavy and cumbersome, this persistent cough driving him to distraction. He'd put off an appointment with the quack until after the launch, then he would go see one of those flash doctors in Harley Street. Afford himself the soft touch.

'Actually, I was hoping you'd be my best man,' Tom broached the subject quietly. He had expected a showdown and had decided that the only way to play it was to remain calm. Just tell Jack his news, ask him to do the honours and leave it at that.

'This is about money isn't it, pure and simple?' Jack stated. 'I mean, she's just got a big lump from that dead husband of hers, hasn't she?'

'It's not about the money, Jack,' Tom said quietly. At least not quite in the way he thought it was.

'Seriously, I don't understand,' Jack threw back the rest of his Scotch and poured another from the optics. 'It's not as if she can be in the family way or anything . . .' he sneered. 'She's pushing fifty if she's a day . . .'

'Yeah well, that's not likely to happen; I've had the snip, remember? Besides, I love her,' Tom lied unconvincingly. It sounded so disingenuous and ridiculous that they had both laughed.

'Yeah, but you love her newly inherited millions more huh?' he shook his head. 'Jeez Tom, I don't give a fuck how much bread that broad's got, it still ain't enough to get *me* to walk up the aisle with her, you know what I'm saying?' Jack turned to him then, his expression softening slightly. 'Look, we're sitting on a fucking goldmine here – the press have said so themselves. You don't need a cent of that woman's money. Whatever she's giving you, you know you'll end up paying it back with interest one way or another.' Jack was almost pleading with him, 'you don't need her, not now we got this place,' he gestured around the palatial bar area. 'This is our dream right here, dude,' he held back the need to expel the contents of his lungs into his hands, 'our own casino – our own place! I mean, look at it! It's gonna be limo and yacht season for us all year round . . . just like we dreamed of as kids.' Jack's lungs finally exploded into an epic and violent coughing fit that saw him bent double. Tom went to him and slapped him on the back.

250

'Fuck me, Jack,' he cursed, 'you been to the quacks about that cough yet? You sound like an afternoon in Iraq.'

Jack forced himself not to smile. Tom always had such a way of disarming anger in a person; a skill that was as admirable as it was irritating. 'Never mind the goddamn doctor . . .' he wheezed, the sharp pain in his chest causing him to wince in agony.

'Look,' Tom's voice was low and reassuring now. 'I realise this is a bit unexpected,' Jack shot him a look that suggested he was stating the obvious, 'but I know what I'm doing here bud – just trust me on this, OK?'

Jack shook his head, smirking.

'You're un-fucking-believable Tom, you know that?' he said, and threw back the dregs of his Scotch in a bid to prevent another attack from taking hold.

Tom grinned. Jack's bark was always worse than his bite.

'So does that mean you'll be my best man?'

Jack wearily shook his head; he couldn't believe what he was agreeing to. 'But I mean it Tom; you keep that crazy fucking Italian bitch away from the casino and away from me . . .'

'Thank you my friend,' Tom's grin belied his inner despair; 'you don't know how much it means to me. Shall we crack open a bottle of the good stuff?' he nodded in the direction of the champagne chiller, 'celebrate.'

Jack snorted derisively.

'Now you're pushing your luck,' he said, reaching for the bottle anyway.

CHAPTER 51

'Look, I realise it's a bit of an ask, and I really wouldn't be doing this unless I *had* to . . .' Tess looked up at Tom with a set of pleading eyes, curling a piece of her hair around an index finger as she stood in his office.

Tess had already given Marco her car and every last penny in her bank account but now he was demanding more and had made it perfectly clear what would happen if she didn't deliver.

The look on her new boss's face was not pleasing her; Tess was so used to getting what she wanted, whenever she wanted it, that the thought that someone might actually say no to her was an alien concept. 'I can see you're a decent man,' she continued, instinct telling her to play up to his ego, 'it would just be an advance on my wages . . . you'll get it all back ten times over once we're up and running next week, I swear. I'll even throw in a bit of interest,' she added; well, he was a businessman after all.

Tom swivelled around in his brand new leather and chrome chair – the kind he'd always wanted to own. It gave him a real sense of importance to be sat behind the kidney bean-shaped glass Conran desk in his very own bespoke designed office that was nothing if not a shameless homage to masculinity; furnished with zebra rugs and monchrome framed photographs of semi-naked Vegas showgirls.

'Drink?' he lightly suggested, happy to have the opportunity to indulge himself. 'A Martini perhaps? You look like a Martini girl.' Tom smiled at his own reflection in the glass. He liked what he saw; the face of a man who was finally going places.

Tess pulled a face.

'Can't stand the stuff. I'll have a vodka tonic though.'

Tom couldn't help smiling as he began to pour her a generous measure of Grey Goose. For some reason he liked the young girl. She had a directness about her that appealed, coupled with an air of class and respectability. He handed her the crystal tumbler and watched as she threw half of it back without flinching. He noticed her hands were lightly shaking.

'Like I said,' Tess continued, 'I really need this money or else I wouldn't be asking of course . . .'

'*Of course.*' Tom eyed the girl standing before him and resisted the urge to laugh out loud. Quite how she had had the nerve to bowl into his office like this and demand an advance on wages she had not yet even earned – three grand's worth of wages no less – was almost commendable, were it not so impertinent. Tom paused, absorbing her natural young beauty for a moment. He didn't doubt for a second that she would make a lot of money for him at the club. He knew men who would sell an eye for an hour with a girl like this. She was exceptionally pretty, maybe even beautiful; all emerald-green eyes and long honey-coloured hair, a perfect plump rosebud pout and a young, coltish body with full breasts. She reminded him of someone, only he couldn't quite decide who. 'I'm sorry but it's completely out of the question, Nicole. It is Nicole, isn't it?' Tom said, snapping himself out of her spell. Tess nodded. 'The club doesn't even open until next week!'

'For Christ's sake it's *only* three grand!' she screeched, her raised tone causing his eyebrows to rise. '. . . I mean, my fath—' she stopped herself from saying anything more and the pair of them stood blinking at one another.

Tom rubbed his temples with a thumb and forefinger in a bid to prevent the makings of a stress headache from further taking hold. He knew it was risky getting involved with lap dancers; women were women at the end of the day and he'd never yet met one who didn't come with a whole heap of fucking aggravation.

'Look, you'll get your money as soon as you've earned it, understand sweetheart?' Tom's tone switched. 'I can't be seen to be giving hand-outs to all the girls that work here; if I do it for one then I'll be expected to do it for everyone. And three grand *is* a lot of money Nicole, despite what you might think.' He shook his head, 'Brasses, I don't know; you're all the same at the end of the day . . .'

Tess glared at him, indignant.

'Brass?' she said, pulling her chin into her neck, outraged by such an assumption. She was sure she'd read somewhere that the word 'brass' was slang for prostitute. Tom shook his head, immediately apologetic.

'Look sweets, I'm sorry, I didn't mean . . .'

'You think I'm a *prostitute*?' Tess felt her hackles rise, weeks of pent-up stress and worry culminating into anger and frustration, 'after all, a girl who takes her clothes off for money *obviously* must fuck for it too.' The sarcasm dripped from her vexed voice. 'Well, it's a good job there *are* girls like me,' she sneered, 'otherwise your fucking casino wouldn't even get off the ground, would it?' It was all too much. Not only wasn't he going to loan her the money she desperately needed, but he had insulted her too. 'You can stick your three grand – and your sleazy job. I'm sure there'll be no shortage of other willing *prostitutes* to take my place,' she spat between her tears, realising she'd really gone and fucked it all up for herself now, resigning from a job she hadn't even started.

Tess had never felt more lonely and desperate in her entire life and the futility of her predicament finally caused her to break down and sob uncontrollably.

Tom blinked at her in alarm, unsure of how to react. There was something about this girl; she wasn't your usual common-or-garden lap dancer, that was for sure. He wondered what her story was.

Tom handed her a tissue from the silver box on his desk.

'Tears have no truck with me, lady,' he found himself saying, only to instantly regret it when he saw her snot and mascara-stained face. The girl was *really* crying now, great rasping sobs that seemed to have taken over her entire body.

'Jesus,' he found himself saying, lightly touching her arm, 'it's not that bad, is it?' Tess practically launched herself at him, throwing her arms around his neck as she sobbed into his clean, white Ralph Lauren shirt. She felt so desperate for any kind reassurance, even if it came from a virtual stranger.

'No,' she spluttered, her face a contorted, crumpled mess, 'it's *so* much worse . . . you don't understand.' She shook her head. '*You don't understand.*'

'Try me,' Tom cocked his head to the side, watching her carefully, and suddenly realised who it was she reminded him of. She was a young Ellie. It was the eyes; large haunting green eyes, just like he remembered.

Tess buried her head into his chest and enjoyed the scent of his smooth clean skin. In a rash moment of madness she pressed her lips against his and opened her mouth.

'What the fuck are you doing, Nicole?' Tom sprang back from her, taken aback at his own reaction. Women had been making advances at him his entire life, and usually, if they were young and beautiful like this one was, he welcomed their attention with the proverbial open arms. Only this somehow felt different.

'I'm sorry,' a mortified Tess stood back, wiping her eyes as she took a deep breath, composing herself. In that moment she wondered despairingly if her life could possibly get any worse. 'I didn't mean . . . look, I'm sorry to have bothered you.'

She made to leave, throwing her expensive bag over her shoulder in a defiant swoop.

'Hang on,' he opened the drawer of his desk, 'look, take this,' he said as an afterthought, wondering if he was going soft with age, 'there's a thousand pounds here,' he said as he placed a wad of notes on the desk. 'I don't know *why* you need it so badly, but I'm sensing that you do. But that's *all* I'm prepared to give you.'

Tess looked at the money on the table, then back up at Tom. His company was oddly reassuring for a complete stranger. She almost didn't want to leave.

'Thank you,' she said tremulously as she reached to take it. 'You'll get it back . . . every penny of it. I promise.'

Tom nodded.

'And not a word of this to anyone, OK?' he said. 'If this gets out they'll all come with a begging bowl . . .'

'Yes, of course, thank you Mr Black,' her voice was almost a whisper as she turned to look back at him, her face stained with black tear tracks.

'It's Tom,' he smiled at her gently, 'the name's Tom.'

'Thanks Tom.'

Hair swishing, she flounced from the room leaving the sweet feminine scent of her Viktor & Rolf Flowerbomb perfume behind her.

Flicking the venetian blinds, Tom watched her make her way out onto the street where she was promptly greeted by some swarthy-looking dude in low-slung Evisu jeans and a Superdry hoodie. He watched with careful interest as the guy hovered over her menacingly, his eyes darting left to right as he snatched the wad of notes from her hands. He had

256

whispered something in her ear, and judging by the way she'd flinched, Tom suspected it wasn't exactly sweet nothings. He felt an unusual compulsion to fly out there and confront the man – fucking bully that he was. The girl had an air of vulnerability about her and he suspected she was mixed up in something way out of her depth. Tom sat back down at the desk and poured himself a slug of Courvoisier, throwing it back in a bid to dislodge the strange feeling that had settled upon his chest. Truth was, he didn't *want* to know.

CHAPTER 52

Driving back through Notting Hill in the late afternoon sunshine, her silver BMW 3 Series convertible purring as she sat in the waiting traffic, Victoria looked down at the fruits of her shopping spree: a divine Lanvin draped, belted, crepe jersey dress in a deep russet colour; a Roberto Cavalli floor-length, one-shoulder, silk number, and a daring sequin and lace Alexander McQueen mini with a plunging neckline that was far too revealing for a woman of her advancing years, or so all the bloody magazines would have it. She'd dropped thousands of pounds in Agent Provocateur and La Perla too; pounding her credit card on a colourful array of tulle and silk matching bra and panties, lace-topped stockings and a darling silk kimono, perfect for a little post-coital glamour. Then of course there had been the matching shoes; Jimmy Choos and Louboutins mainly; six inches of heels and straps and buckles to elongate the leg. He liked her to keep her shoes on during sex, something *Victoria* would have once considered a little on the perverted side of things, but *Rachel* had loved it!

Victoria flipped the interior mirror and briefly checked her reflection. She could barely stand to look at herself. She had spent an absolute fortune on a mission to look *sexy* as Rachel and despite the dreadful nagging guilt that was gnawing at her conscience like a starving beaver, she could barely wait to get the chance to test the goods. This week, she was convinced, was the week she would make a baby. She could *feel* it.

Her mind wandered back to their previous encounter. The glass had felt cool to touch as she had sipped at the expensive chardonnay in a provocative fashion and wondered what he thought when he looked at her; did he feel lust and desire?

'Are you looking forward to the opening night next week?' she'd enquired. 'Everything ready to rock and roll?' *Rock 'n' roll*. She even spoke differently when she was with him. It was as if she changed shape in his presence, became someone else entirely.

A naked Tom had risen from the bed and she had watched him as he had begun to shower.

'It will be by next week,' he'd called out from the bathroom. 'It has to be.'

She'd continued to sip at her wine, enjoying her nakedness stretched out across the high king-sized bed, appreciating the decadence of alcohol in the afternoon combined with 4000-thread count Egyptian cotton sheets. 'Will you be coming?' he enquired, rubbing his head with the complimentary Aveda shampoo.

Wild horses and Apache Indians wouldn't stop me.

'I'm thinking about it,' she'd replied casually. Tom had smirked beneath the powerful jet of the shower. Jesus, it was a bit late in the day to start playing hard to get, wasn't it? If he was honest, Tom was growing complacent with his and Rachel's little *arrangement*. A bit of no-strings sex in the afternoon with an attractive woman had been all well and good to begin with but now he felt its appeal was on the decline. It wasn't so much the sex; that had been progressing rather nicely now that Rachel had allowed that

guard of hers to slip. It was what he'd seen in her eyes
that had made him decide to call time on their dalliance. That
fleeting flicker of emotion as he'd lain on top of her and
thrust himself deep inside her; it was a look he was all too
familiar with and one he didn't much care for. Rachel was
getting attached and the last thing Tom wanted, or needed,
right now was another woman demanding his time and
energy. He was struggling as it was, what with the force of
nature that was Loretta planning their forthcoming nuptials
like a manic despot, sending him fabric swatches and menus
to approve – not that she would've taken the slightest bit
of notice if he didn't.

Tom decided it would be best to tell her now, let her
down gently.

With a fluffy white towel wrapped around his torso, toga
style, he had exited the shower room, rubbing his wet hair.

'I was thinking of bringing my husband along,' Victoria
said, deliberately playing devil's advocate, 'to the launch
night I mean.' She was keen to gauge his reaction. Would
she see a flicker of jealousy perhaps?

'By all means,' Tom replied amiably, sitting down on the
edge of the bed, the heat from the shower emanating from
his smooth, tanned body.

Victoria's smile dropped to a thin line.

'That doesn't bother you?'

'Why should it?' he'd shrugged. 'I've always known you
were married. Fifteen years you said, "and I'd like to make
it sixteen . . ."'

She watched him as he discarded the towel, his dick
swinging between his legs. She felt the pull of him once
more. She needed to remind herself why she had started all
this in the first place. *A baby, remember?*

'Thing is, Rachel . . .'

'Actually I'm not planning to bring my husband at all,'
she'd interrupted him. 'I'm bringing a girlfriend, if that's

OK?' She watched him provocatively from behind her wine glass, lowering her eyes coquettishly.

Tom's interest was ignited. Girlfriend? Could she be referring to Eleanor O'Connor perhaps?

'Sure,' he said, his stateside lilt suddenly more apparent than ever. She had noticed how his accent slid across the spectrum from broad cockney and cut-glass English gent, right through to American street slang – and she found it quite fascinating. 'Someone I know?' he'd casually enquired, reaching for the room service menu. 'Oh I doubt it,' Victoria had responded. 'Though you might have heard of her husband, Vincent Scott, Great Scott Properties, you know; the *billionaire*,' she'd raised an eyebrow. She was being far more candid than she'd intended but the chardonnay had loosened her inhibitions – in every sense.

'Not that you'd ever know it; he's the most unassuming, least ostentatious billionaire you'll ever meet.'

Tom had felt a shot of adrenaline mainline to his heart. She *was* talking about Eleanor.

'Scott . . . yeah the name rings a bell, now you mention it,' he nodded casually without looking up from the menu.

'So it should; he's the man Hollywood goes to if they want a house. He built the Beckham's new place you know . . . they're personal friends . . .'

'Will they both be coming along?' Tom was careful to keep his interest light, in keeping with the tone of the conversation, 'the Scotts I mean, not the Beckhams, although frankly they'd be more than welcome too.'

Victoria smiled. 'I shouldn't think so,' she'd sniffed, reaching out with a playful foot and gently pushing him in his back. 'He's in Sydney working on a new deal . . .'

'I see.'

'That is OK, isn't it, if I bring her I mean? Poor thing's been on her own all summer . . .'

'Sure,' Tom's heart was beating a tattoo in his chest and

he'd instinctively put his hand up towards his chest as if to calm it. 'The more attractive women that turn up, the better I'll look,' he'd grinned.

'How do you know she's attractive?' she'd shot back lightning fast, digging him in the back with her toes once more, his flesh feeling soft beneath them. The comment had jogged her earlier memory back to their first encounter at Gordon Ramsey's restaurant.

Hadn't he asked after Ellie then too, like he somehow already knew her?

Jesus, there was no flies on this broad, Tom thought, deciding that he was maybe being a little hasty in calling time on their relationship. Ditching Rachel now could very well jeopardise his chances of seeing Eleanor O'Connor in the flesh once more, and this was not something he wanted to happen.

'Beautiful women like you don't have unattractive friends, Rachel.' His response had disarmed her and she'd smiled, pulling him between her willing open legs. It had been the right answer.

CHAPTER 53

Situated high upon the cliff tops, above the picturesque Marina Piccola and impressive bougainvillea-drenched pergolas, the vast Villa Amore sat like a giant white diamond carved into the rock face, a veritable jewel in the crown of the picturesque, historic island of Capri.

Built by the Romans and eventually taken over by a prominent eighteenth-century artist who enjoyed well-documented debauched sex and drugs orgies there, the infamous villa had stood derelict for many years until a member of the Bahrain royal family discovered it and proceeded to, debatably, restore it back to its original magnificent glory. Today it was by far the most exquisite example of jet-set decadence upon the notoriously glamorous island. With a grand white-pillared entrance, accessible only by climbing some 230 stone steps, the Bahrainian regal had transformed the inside into an Arabian palace, complete with priceless gold chandeliers, pre-Raphaelite-esque high-vaulted ceilings and giant glass windows that allowed the omnipresent sunlight to stream through the rooms like laser beams. It was a testament to sheer grandiosity and opulence that some might, and *did*, deem to be vulgar. Loretta, however, adored it.

Stretched out upon a white padded sun lounger, next to a perfectly still azure-blue swimming pool that overlooked the Tyrrhenian Sea, Loretta, wearing a tomato print triangle D&G bikini and matching turban, threw her copy of Victoria Mayfield's latest tome, *Mirror Mirror*, down onto the glass table and peered over the edge of her Yves Saint Laurent cat-eye printed sunglasses at the woman beside her. Lighting an L&M cigarette with a solid gold Cartier lighter, she tickled Bambinos head with her blood-red nails and began flicking through the pile of photographs.

'No . . . too ugly . . . too feminine-looking . . . too pale . . . too British . . . no, no . . . oh, he's a maybe,' she handed the picture to the woman opposite. 'No . . . no . . . definitely not . . .'

Felicity Montgomery-Philips, wedding planner to the stars, resisted the urge to roll her eyes in exasperation. She had been in the wedding business for nigh on twenty years now and had helped orchestrate some of the most lavish and extravagant ceremonies in the world. This one however, was her most ostentatious and ambitious yet. The bride-to-be had insisted on selecting the entire male waiting staff for her big day by hand – all 200 of them.

'It's all in the detail, dahling, all in the detail,' Loretta had chastised her.

'Oh I quite agree,' Felicity had nodded, her enthusiasm long since having waned.

'Have you sorted the private jet transportation for some of the more salubrious guests yet?'

'All arranged, Mrs Hassan. And the limo transportation back to their hotels is all in order. The cars will arrive around midnight and wait until the guests decide to leave.'

'*Bueno*. Ah yes, the hotels. Five-star, I'm assuming?'

'Goes without saying,' Felicity forced a smile.

Loretta sipped at her kumquat and ginger martini, wincing as she swallowed.

'I'm not really feeling this,' she said, tipping the excess from her glass into the swimming pool beside her. 'Have the team come up with something else, yes? Something more refined on the palate, something that compliments the caviar canapés and steak tartare amuse bouche.'

The wedding planner nodded, furiously tapping notes into her iPad.

'Consider it done,' she said without looking up. 'Now about the flowers, Mrs Hassan . . .'

'Please Felicity, call me Loretta,' she insisted, clicking her fingers high in the air to catch the attention of the private butler. Felicity pasted on a forced smile.

'A bottle of Cristal, Luca darling. Nice and chilled, yes.' Luca nodded before disappearing into the villa. 'You'll join me, won't you?' she enquired.

'Not while I'm working thank you, Mrs Has – *Loretta*,' Felicity shook her head with professionally pursed lips, 'got to keep a clear head and all that . . . wouldn't want to forget any *details* now, would I.'

Loretta smiled as she reclined back onto the lounger, throwing one lazy mahogany-tanned leg over the other. 'If the weather remains this glorious for the big day I shall be a very happy woman indeed.'

Felicity hoped so too, otherwise she suspected she might be held to account for that as well.

'The flowers are going to be jetted in on ice the night before. All 100,000 of them, including the rare orchids from Hawaii, if we can get hold of them that is.'

'*If*?' Loretta didn't bother opening her eyes but her tone had said it all.

'Well,' Felicity shifted uncomfortably in her rattan chair, 'we're still working on it; the supplier's asking for three times the amount than we know is reasonable and—'

'—I don't care!' Loretta barked, 'I *have* to have those orchids.'

265

Felicity nodded, swallowing hard. 'Right . . . OK well, the good news is the trumpeters, the 50,000 white Diptyque candles, the thirty-six-piece orchestra and the flights for the chef and his entire team are all booked. And I'm having a meeting with the security firm this afternoon to discuss police presence and how we're going to handle the whole press intrusion. They're thinking about your request to close the airport to the public for the day so we'll see what they have to say about that.' Felicity glanced down at her iPad, 'Oh and ABC are battling it out with MTV over viewing rights. At the moment we're gridlocked at 3.7 million dollars but it's only a matter of time before one of them budges . . .'

Loretta smirked from beneath her shades, sipping her Cristal with satisfaction.

'Splendid,' she remarked, which was the closest she'd come to giving any kind of praise so far. 'And the fireworks display? I want the entire sky lit up across the ocean at midnight, *si*?'

'Si . . . I mean, yes, yes, I'm onto it . . .'

Loretta sat up then, exposing her enormous fake breasts without a hint of modesty, or thought for Felicity, who wasn't sure where to look. 'This is the most important day of my life and it *has* to be the most spectacular. Every part of it, every detail, must be perfect, and if it isn't I will hold *you* and your team personally responsible, do you understand?' Her tone sent an icy rod of fear running from Felicity's neck down to her sphincter.

'Yes Loretta, I understand completely,' she said tightly. No doubt she'd said the same about her last two weddings. Stupid deluded old bitch, she thought as she made to stand. If she quit right here and now Loretta's wedding would collapse faster than a house of cards in a hurricane.

'Ciao darling!' Loretta called out to her. 'And don't forget to order the Lamborghini; Black, it has to be black – it's my wedding gift to my husband!'

266

Felicity raised her hand to signify it was on her ever-burgeoning list of impossible tasks to complete before the big day.

Loretta reclined back onto the sun lounger. She had a limo picking her up in a couple of hours to take her to see a plastic surgeon friend on the island where she planned to have a little of the fat sucked from her backside and injected into her face. She wanted to make sure she looked her absolute best for this wedding, a wedding which was costing her in excess of five million pounds. But it would all be worth it, she assured herself as she began to drift off into a light slumber. Loretta had waited a long time for this moment and she was going to wring it out like a wet towel. Tomorrow she flew back to London for the opening night of her fiancé's casino and then she was straight on a plane to LA to begin filming with Guy Bentley. Then it would be back here to Capri for the big day. To the outside world, life couldn't really get much better, she concluded. But subconsciously it was a slightly different story.

As Loretta slipped into a deeper slumber she saw a vision of Miranda Muldavey appear before her; the once-beautiful actress's face a mass of shiny scars and disfiguration, her malevolent smile crooked, her eyes boring holes into her skull as her features continually distorted out of shape like a house of mirrors.

'What . . . what do you want? Please leave me alone . . . it . . . it wasn't my fault . . . I had nothing to do with it . . .'

Miranda started laughing. It was a slow snigger at first that gradually developed into a manic, sinister cackle. Loretta put her hands over her ears and closed her eyes, but still she could see the woman's face staring back at her, mocking her, and then slowly it morphed into someone else . . . Eleanor O'Connor.

Loretta woke with a violent start that had her gasping for breath.

'*Merde*,' she breathed, her heartbeat galloping inside her rib cage. She reached for her glass but deciding against it, lit a L&M instead. She'd clearly had too much champagne and sun. Rumours that Miranda was planning to make an entrance at the opening night of the casino had persisted for weeks now – after all, the actress was still skulking around London incognito, visiting family allegedly, although Loretta was convinced it was more than that. She was sure that Miranda had chosen to stay in the British capital simply to rain on her fucking parade, the threat of her presence a deliberate ploy to make her feel ill-at-ease. And as for Eleanor O'Connor, well, she would just have to keep a very close eye on *that* one. Loretta was many things, but stupid she wasn't; she knew Tom still held a torch for the woman and the idea of her being in such close proximity only further added to her sense of discomfort. She looked down at the time on her Prada LG phone with shaking hands. The limo would be arriving shortly.

Frankly, it wasn't a moment too soon.

CHAPTER 54

Pulling up outside her stucco-fronted house just off Westbourne Grove, Victoria switched off the BMW's engine and dragged her mountain of shopping bags through the front door. She shouldn't even have been behind the wheel, what with the half a bottle of chardonnay she'd sunk earlier that afternoon, and it suddenly struck her what might have happened should she have been pulled over by the police. Already an adulteress; now a drink-driver? What in God's name was she becoming? She honestly didn't know. What she did know however was that as she switched on the large antique lamp at the console table, she saw her husband's familiar frame standing in the doorway, his silhouette illuminated in the low glow.

'Lawrence!' she physically sprung backwards in alarm, her myriad bags clattering to the parquet floor in a heap. 'I . . . I thought . . . you're supposed to be in . . . what are you doing here?'

She watched as her husband's adoring face broke into a huge warm smile that lit up the remainder of the room.

'Now that's no way to greet your old man, is it?' he said, arms outstretched wide in welcome. She was smiling now too, nervously. She smelt of booze and sex, another man fresh on her skin, the light scent of him reaching her nostrils as she walked. Jesus, she could still *feel* his hotness inside her. Lol would notice; *he would know*.

'Well, aren't you going to come and give me a hug?' he enquired, a little crestfallen by her lukewarm reception.

She went to him tentatively, wrapped her arms around his slim waist.

'I . . . it's a bit of a shock that's all,' she stammered, her heart racing inside her chest fast enough to make her feel lightheaded. 'You didn't call . . .'

'I wanted to surprise you!' he said, his voice pitching. 'I wanted to see the look on your face when you came home to find me here – as it is I'm beginning to wonder if I did the right thing, travelling halfway around the world simply for one night with my wife!'

She pulled away to look up into his face. 'One night! You came back from Africa, all that way, just for one night?'

He nodded slowly.

'The slave-driver of a client gave us all twenty-four hours off – generous bugger – and I thought, what better way to spend it than to come home to my wife. So now we've got exactly . . .' he looked down at his Patek Phillipe watch, 'seven hours and thirteen minutes before I have to fly back again.'

'Oh Lol,' Victoria said, fighting back tears; her darling Lawrence, her husband, the man who had been father to their adored child, her rock and her best friend. He had come all this way just for her, his cheating, adulterous, treacherous whore of a wife. Burying her face deep into her husband's warm encompassing embrace, his familiar smell causing a granite lump to form in the back of her throat, Victoria had never hated anyone as much as she despised herself in that moment. No wonder God had seen fit not to bestow her with something as innocent and pure as a child. She wasn't worthy.

'Can I fix you a drink? Ask Marney to prepare you something to eat perhaps? You must be famished,' she quickly wiped the corners of her eyes, beginning to make her ascent towards the kitchen.

'Ah, now steady on,' he grabbed her wrist and gently pulled her back towards him, his eyes shining mischievously in the low light. He brought his lips down upon hers and she felt the familiar smoothness of his tongue as it slipped between her lips. 'You're right, I *am* hungry,' he said with a lascivious grin, taking her hand and he began to lead her upstairs towards the master suite. 'Only it sure ain't for food . . .'

CHAPTER 55

Loretta threw her paperback copy of *Mirror Mirror* down onto the bed a little forcefully.

'Easy tiger,' Tom remarked, 'I thought you said you couldn't put the book down.'

He began adjusting the cufflinks on his one-off, bespoke white Eton shirt. Both the studs and cufflinks were encrusted with white and coloured diamonds that caught the light with every movement. Only the best for tonight Tom thought, as he stepped into a pair of black wool voile made-to-measure Armani slacks. Loretta had insisted on him choosing an Italian designer for his grand opening apparel and who was he to argue? After all, she was paying for it.

'Touché darling,' Loretta smirked. 'Now do me up, will you?' she commanded, turning her back on him. She'd been in a frightful mood ever since her return, thanks to her little ill-thought-out surgical procedure.

'They will take a few days to settle, Mrs Hassan,' the surgeon had reassured her as she had inspected them coldly in the mirror, adding tremulously, 'you did say you wanted them filled out as much as possible.'

'I look like Jackie fucking Stallone!' Loretta had screamed

in the man's face, causing him to spring back from her in alarm. 'Do you realise I have a very important opening to go to tomorrow and then I am flying out to LA to begin filming? I can't turn up on set looking like this!' The doctor had nodded apologetically, figuring it was the least of her worries. To add insult to injury, Tom's reaction when he had met her from the plane had left Loretta fuming.

'Jesus, Loretta!' he'd recoiled as she'd stepped from the Lear jet. 'You look as if you've been ten rounds with Cassius Clay.'

Loretta had pulled her enormous Prada shades past her nose.

'When I want your opinion Tom Black, I'll ask for it, *capisce*?' she had brushed past him defiantly, towards the waiting limo, but even she could see how utterly ridiculous she looked.

Tom obligingly began fixing the lobster clasp around Loretta's neck.

'Jesus, that's some piece of bling you got there, honey – that thing weighs a tonne.'

'*That thing* is worth 4.5 million dollars, I'll have you know. It's the De Beers Marie-Antoinette necklace; over 180 carats of mixed cut diamonds; pink, yellow and white,' Loretta's eyes glazed over as she caught a glimpse of it in the mirror. 'A spectacular piece, wouldn't you agree?' Tom couldn't argue with that; at least it might detract from the set of marshmallows on her face where her lips had once been. 'It was a gift to myself after Ramsey died,' she sighed ruefully, 'something to cheer me up.'

Tom raised an eyebrow. 'And did it make you happy, spending so much of your poor dead husband's hard-earned cash on diamonds?' he was humouring her, attempting to lighten her dark mood.

'It's like Marilyn once said; a girl's best friend . . . Diamonds *always* make me happy,' she shot back, 'which is more than can be said of any man I've ever met,' she turned away from him sharply. 'I consider them to be my children,' she fingered the necklace lovingly '. . . As well as Bambino of course,' she added, reaching out to pet the tiny Chihuahua, resplendent in a bespoke tuxedo outfit complete with a diamond-encrusted collar in the shape of a bow tie that she'd had made especially for the occasion. 'Doesn't baby look adorable . . . yes he does, give Mummy a kiss,' Bambino began to lick Loretta's swollen mouth as she made grotesque kissing noises. Tom pulled a face, barely able to conceal his disgust.

'Anyway,' Loretta strutted across the hotel room, stark naked save for her McQueen power tower heels and diamond necklace, 'I'm afraid I won't be able to stay for tonight's duration,' she stated. 'I'm in LA first thing. Of course, I will do the whole press thing for tonight, give those snivelling bastards what they want,' she reassured him with a casual shrug, '. . . but I've ordered a limo to pick me up before midnight. I wouldn't want to get off on the wrong footing with Guy.' Although frankly, Loretta didn't much care if she did. She was already planning her seduction of the Hollywood heavyweight-in-the-making. She'd get her legs wrapped around him before the week was up.

Tom nodded, absent-mindedly picking up the copy of *Mirror, Mirror* from the bed and flicking through it. He scanned the back cover blurb – usual schmaltzy chick-lit with a hefty dollop of gratuitous sex thrown in for good measure. Every woman he'd ever met went in for this kind of crap, even those high-flying, ball-breaking business types. In fact, they were the ones who seemed to suck it up the most; escapism he supposed. Tom stopped as he surveyed the inside cover. Jesus fucking Christ! He recognised the author's face. Tom's heartbeat began to accelerate as he read the biography with interest. 'Victoria Mayfield is a bestselling author whose debut novel, *Broken Glass,* reached number one in the *Sunday Times* top ten bestseller list. To date she has sold over six million books worldwide. Victoria currently splits her time between her London and Surrey residences with her husband. *Mirror Mirror* is her seventh novel . . .' Tom stared at the photograph, perplexed. Unless she had an identical twin sister then he was sure as shit it was Rachel.

'Tom?' Loretta was staring at him now, her dark eyes examining him closely.

'What? Yes, sorry . . . of course,' he placed the book back down on the bed. If Loretta was planning to leave the party early then that was fine by him. The idea that Loretta, Rachel – or whoever she really was – and Ellie would all be in the same room together at the same time unnerved him. It had the potential to be explosive. Tom's eye wandered back to the photograph inside the book. Why would Rachel lie about her true identity? It was obvious they both wished to keep their little affair secret and Tom had certainly never given her reason to believe otherwise. He was puzzled, and a little pissed if he was honest. She had deceived him.

Tom poured himself a glass of Cristal to steady his nerves. Tonight was going to be epic and he wanted to make sure it all came off without a glitch, yet still he had a nagging sense of foreboding that he just couldn't seem to shift.

Loretta slipped into her dress and after a little adjusting, turned to face Tom.

'So,' she asked with a finely arched thin brow and a hand on her hip, 'what do you think?'

Loretta grinned in anticipation of Tom's reaction. This dress was going to snatch all the headlines – she was convinced of it, even if that freak-show Miranda Muldavey did show up like all those goddamn rumours in the gossip rags suggested.

Tom only hoped his expression didn't betray his inner

thoughts. He was in no doubt that on another woman, a much younger woman, one with class, who hadn't meddled so much with what God had given her, the undeniably stunning dress would've looked the million bucks that it no doubt cost. Only somehow Loretta managed to make it look cheap, gauche and vulgar, like she'd ordered it from a K-Mart catalogue.

'Well, what can I say? You look . . . amazing.'

Tom's lukewarm reception made Loretta want to give his face a cold, hard slap. This dress was supposed to have blown him away! As it was, it had barely elicited a smile.

'Just remember, Tom,' Loretta sneered, her eyes turning to slits, 'there would be no opening night without me,' she stabbed her breast bone with a sharp manicured nail. 'No casino to open, no paparazzi to pose in front of and no showgirls to flirt with . . . so I would appreciate a little more effort on your part, if it's all the same to you.'

Tom hid his tetchiness with a smile. As if he needed reminding of the fact – it stuck in his throat like a blade.

'Well then, let me see,' he said, moving his body in closer to her, running his hand up the inside of her short, slim leg, his fingers meeting with her soft, moist flesh. It was no surprise to learn that she wasn't wearing any underwear. 'You of all people should know actions speak louder than words,' he whispered, pressing his lips against her heavily scented neck. Loretta flicked her hair back sulkily, unable to prevent a small smile from creeping across her painful, swollen lips.

'Be careful,' she groaned softly as he pulled her dress up above her waist and pushed her down onto the bed. 'The fabric is *incredibly* delicate . . .'

CHAPTER 56

'Christ alive! Have you seen the amount of paparazzi?'
Lindsay was practically bouncing in her seat like an excitable puppy as the Bentley pulled up alongside a fleet of chauffeur-driven luxury cars and limos. The entrance to Black Jack's was awash with photographers, jostling with each other to get the best views of the arriving glitterati, cameras firing like machine guns going off in every direction, lighting up the night sky like strobes. 'Oh my *God*! I might even make the papers tomorrow!'

Ellie cursed underneath her breath. *Shitting hell.* The last thing she wanted was the paparazzi in her face. She didn't want to rub Vinnie's nose in it, her face splashed all over tomorrow's *Daily Mail*.

Meanwhile Victoria felt sick. Physically sick. In fact she had felt so nauseous at one point during the journey that she thought she might have to stop the car and throw up on the curb. Nerves, she told herself. She was chancing her arm coming here tonight, knew she would see Tom – and his fiancé – and she also knew that there was every chance her cover would be blown. After all, Victoria Mayfield was the biggest selling female author in the UK and as much as she liked to largely eschew the whole glitterati London social circuit, her face was still recognisable. It would only take one person to call out her name and for Tom to over-hear, and she would be exposed. Then what? She hadn't really thought that far ahead. In fact Victoria suddenly realised with striking clarity that she hadn't really thought at all. For once in her regimented and highly organised life she had lived firmly in the moment. Now she was beginning to think that coming here tonight had been a very big mistake indeed.

'For the love of God, who the *hell* is *that*?' Lindsay cried, breaking Victoria away from her thoughts.

The three women simultaneously turned to look at a small dark-haired woman who had seemingly caused a media meltdown as she exited from a sleek, shiny black Lamborghini. Her see-through dress that scarcely covered her intimate regions was causing an absolute explosion among the paps who were jostling and elbowing each other in a bid to get the best shot as she turned to the side and leaned forward to blow a kiss, one arm linked proprietarily through the arm of a very good-looking man dressed in a slick, well-cut suit, the other clutching a tiny teacup Chihuahua in a tuxedo. Victoria held her breath.

'*That*,' Ellie said, unable to disguise the bitterness from her voice, 'is Loretta.'

*

'Loretta! Lorettta! G'is a smile babes . . . that's it . . . over 'ere . . .'

'Where's the dress from, Loretta?' a young female jour-nalist shouted out.

'Me; turn to me, towards me, *bella* . . . *bella* Loretta . . . over here!'

Loretta was in her element; the press were going wild.

'The dress is Valentino, dahling. Italian of course,' she

278

lowered her eyes provocatively, swishing the train of her revealing haute couture gown behind her, turning to give the paps a full rear view. 'And I would like to introduce you all to my fiancé, Mr Tom Black,' she looked up at him, resplendent in a slick cream tuxedo-style suit, complete with dark Wayfarer Ray-Bans. 'Tom's the man of the night; he's the proprietor of the casino – he *is* Black Jack's!'

Tom attempted to free his arm from Loretta's vice-like grip but she wasn't letting go.

'How are the wedding plans coming along guys, got a date, a venue?'

Tom felt his sphincter muscle contract as Loretta's sharp elbow dug into his ribs.

'Tell them . . .'

'Hell yeah, good!' he grinned. 'We're thinking maybe August . . .'

'Tell them it's in Capri . . . in a castle,' Loretta hissed into his ear. 'And that you're the luckiest guy on the planet . . .'

'Congratulations guys . . .'

'We can't wait, can we dahling?' she said, wrapping herself around him like a viper.

Tom nudged her. 'Tonight is about the *casino*, remember,' he said through a closed mouth. 'Not our fake fucking romance . . .'

'Relax, darling,' Loretta smiled sweetly as the cameras continued to pop around them. 'Plenty of time to sell yourself as the next big hot shot . . .'

Tom's eyes darted through the crowds, searching out Ellie and Rachel. They were here somewhere, *together*. Tom felt irritation prickle the back of his neck and dug a finger into his collar to alleviate it. Three women; one his past, one his present and one his future, all somehow interlinked and in the same room together. It was going to be a tricky evening. He could feel it.

CHAPTER 57

'*That's* Loretta Hassan, the one who was married to the surgeon who butchered Miranda Muldavey's face?' Lindsay stared at the woman in disbelief.

'The very same,' Ellie nodded, unable to take her eyes off Tom as he disappeared into the casino with Loretta in tow. She had seen him. It had been the most fleeting of glances but enough to cause her guts to twist over.

'How do you know?'

Ellie remembered herself, shaking her thoughts back to reality.

'Oh, I've seen her in all the magazines; recognise her face that's all.'

'She's marrying the guy who runs the casino, Tom somebody or other,' Lindsay remarked. Lindsay was the oracle on this kind of stuff, devouring every celebrity and society magazine with regular alacrity as she did. Victoria's interest in the conversation resumed. So *that* was Tom's wife-to-be, the one he'd been so reticent about during their stolen afternoons together. She wasn't sure how she had imagined her; young, blonde and fiercely attractive she'd supposed. This woman however, was much older and moreover, ageing pretty disgracefully by the looks of it. Victoria had never really been sexually jealous of anyone her whole life; never had cause to be, and it wasn't a nice feeling at all.

*

The party was rammed; the cream of London's social scene were out in full effect dressed in their finest attire. Everywhere you looked it was wall-to-wall designer; Gucci, Dior, Marchesa, Alexander McQueen, Balmain, Burberry, Stella McCartney, Givenchy . . . a cacophony of heels, lace, silk and chiffon, tanned, toned bodies were on display as guests mingled in what was little more than a thinly veiled catwalk show.

Inside the main gaming room Ellie, Victoria and Lindsay stood next to the enormous gold fountain that was surrounded by semi-naked fire-breathers dressed in loincloths.

Swiping a Black Jack's cocktail that had been furnished with edible, gold leaf-encrusted marshmallow dice from a passing bikini-clad showgirl – a sublime little touch – Ellie took in her surroundings. Credit where credit was due, in a matter of months the old disused warehouse had been completely transformed and was now unrecognisable. Positioned over four levels, Black Jack's uber-swish gaming room, boasting a selection of slots, roulette and craps tables was nothing if not impressive. All black and gold detailing, with a distinct *Great Gatsby* 1930s feel, it was old-school Vegas meets modern-day Soho. Guests were encouraged to explore the four levels at their own leisure and had each been given chips to the value of 200 pounds to spend on the tables, as well as VIP passes to the exclusive member's only nightclub below. Vegas-style showgirls wearing barely-there bright G-string bikinis sauntered around the venue with never-ending trays of champagne and a rainbow array of cocktails, while male models in white slim-fitting suits and sultan's turbans distributed amuse bouches of tuna tartare and confit duck canapés on enormous gold platters.

In the centre of the high-ceilinged room, a vast gold fountain depicted the scene of Narcissus looking into the lake and falling in love with his own reflection. Very apt, Ellie thought, unable to help herself from smiling as she watched up-lit jets of water fire up into the air. She could see touches of The Player here, Tom's favourite casino in Vegas, somewhere he had spent far too much time frequenting during his youth, if she remembered rightly.

'I'll own this place one day, Ellie,' she recalled him saying. 'Be the biggest player in Vegas!'

Victoria placed her champagne glass onto the bar. Tonight she had worn a strapless, fitted Maria Grachvogel floor-length silk chiffon gown in a pastel green that offset her chestnut brown hair and dark eyes to perfection, and had finished off the look with a pair of delicate silver Jimmy Choo six inch sandals. She'd already turned a few heads and was feeling good about herself, at least on the surface. Underneath however, Victoria was cracking up, and it seemed her fragile state of mind was now having an impact on her physical well-being. She had never felt more ghastly. She needed to see Tom. Talk to him. Maybe even slip off for a little clandestine sex in his office to escape her demons . . .

'Are you OK, Tor? You look a little peaky,' Ellie observed, glancing at her friend with a look of concern.

'Yes, I think I'm just going to nip to the ladies,' Victoria replied, distracted. 'I'll meet you girls up by the pool terrace. I've heard it's spectacular and I think I could do with a little fresh air.'

'Good idea,' Ellie nodded, watching her disappear into the swinging crowd. Victoria was acting a little strange tonight; she seemed distracted. In fact, she hadn't seemed her usual self at all these past few weeks. Tess, and now Victoria; Ellie wondered if there was something in the air lately.

'These canapés are amazeballs,' Lindsay sighed, greedily stuffing another crab claw between her glittery lips. 'I won't need to eat for a week!' She grinned manically.

*

Standing on the mezzanine level, looking over at the swelling throng of guests below, Tom and Jack raised their glasses.

'Well buddy, here's to what's looking like one helluva successful evening!'

'I'll drink to that,' Jack agreed, downing a Belvedere cocktail as though it were a shot. He was enjoying himself; even that persistent cough of his seemed to have calmed down a touch. 'We did it, Tom,' Jack said, clapping him hard on the back. 'We finally hit the jackpot! And do you know what my man? It's all thanks to you. I'm sorry I ever doubted you bro'.'

'Don't be soft,' Tom said, swallowing down his conscience. If only Jack knew the real score he certainly wouldn't be apologising. Tom tried to appease his nagging guilt by telling himself he had done all this for his oldest friend. He'd compromised everything to make sure Jack got this place; hell, he was even marrying a woman he didn't love – now *that* was friendship for you. The fact that it was his gambling habit that had put him in such a predicament in the first place seemed to have escaped Tom's mind. 'Look at the place!' Jack beamed. 'It's heaving with celebrities. Heaving with famous fucking pussy man! And boy am I gonna get me some of that later!'

Tom grinned at him as he looked out into the crowd, his eyes desperately trying to search her out. Ellie was here somewhere and he was damned if the night would end before he got to see her in the flesh.

'You can have my cast-offs if you like,' Tom joked, though he was hardly in the mood for wisecracks.

'Cast-offs my ass; besides, you're a one woman man now remember?'

'Don't remind me,' he shot back.

'Where is the lucky lady anyways?' Jack asked. 'That was some outfit she was wearing,' he raised a dubious eyebrow. 'You could've got a tan from all those camera flashes.'

'Yes, well, that's Loretta for you. Always was the shy, retiring type.'

Jack smirked. 'Yeah, a regular wallflower. Well, at least the dress detracted from her face. Those lips of hers look like a couple of canoes.'

The pair began to laugh as a tall redhead in a purple split-to-the-thigh sequinned Cavalli gown came striding towards them, a look of purpose on her heavily made-up face.

'Well if it isn't the men of the moment!' It was Hilary Austin-Hugh, London society queen and gossip maven extraordinaire. A vociferous woman in her late forties, all red hair and lipstick-stained teeth that people were too frightened (or mean) to tell her about, Hilary had all the right friends in all the right places, and no party was complete without her. 'Congratulations darlings,' she sing-songed, arms outstretched, bingo wings flapping in greeting. 'The place looks *amazing*, and the canapés are divine – Nomad? They're the only caterers to use,' she explained earnestly, snatching some sashimi from a passing waiter and popping it between her pouting red lips with an appreciative groan. 'Better than sex,' she licked her lips provocatively and laughed like a drain.

'I'm off to mingle,' Jack whispered from the side of his mouth. 'This one looks like a job for Tom Black.'

'Great to meet you, er, Hilary, enjoy the rest of the evening.'

'Oh I intend to,' Hilary beamed, her Grey Goose vodka cocktail sloshing as she smiled at Tom, displaying her lipstick-stained teeth.

'You're an asshole,' Tom whispered, as Jack disappeared into the crowd, chuckling.

'You look sensational, Hilary,' Tom turned his attentions to her, slipping effortlessly into full-on charm offensive – it was a default setting and one he'd had a lot of practice at. 'I hear you're a very prominent woman on the London society circuit; do a huge amount for some very worthy causes.'

Hilary Austin-Hugh thought she was in love. There had been a whisper among the female society fraternity that the new American owner of the Soho casino was something of a dish, but no one had warned her just how seriously hot he really was. And charming too. What an absolute bloody shame he was marrying that ghastly Loretta Hassan woman! She could only assume she must have hidden talents.

'Oh, you know, I do my bit,' Hilary giggled coquettishly with a hefty dose of false modesty, wondering if he was marrying the Italian woman for her money. If so, then she might have to reliably inform him that *she* was in line for a fat inheritance herself any day now. Poor Daddy was on his last knockings and as his only daughter and heir . . . 'You simply *must* come to my garden party next week,' she gushed, curling a piece of her Titian-red hair behind her ear in a deliberate attempt to showcase the Boucheron baubles she was wearing. 'The theme is *A Midsummer Night's Dream*. You could be Demetrius to my Helena,' she exclaimed. *And the rest*!

'I'd be delighted to,' Tom replied, touching her glass lightly with hers, a gesture that made Hilary feel instantly aroused. Out of the corner of his eye, Tom spotted Rachel from across the room. She had a grave expression on her face and appeared to be in a hurry somewhere.

'Oh look!' he said, nodding in her direction. 'There's . . . oh, what's her name now?' Tom rubbed his forehead.

'. . . Victoria Mayfield,' Hilary helpfully explained, 'famous novelist.'

'That's right!' Tom nodded.

'Don't tell me you've read any of her novels,' Hilary exclaimed, wondering if the man could be any more perfect. Tom shook his head, smiling. 'I'm afraid not, though I have heard she's very popular.'

'Indeed,' Hilary agreed, turning to watch as Victoria hurried through the crowd, oblivious to their eyes upon her. 'She writes with genuine pathos, really gets to the core of her characters, you know?' she banged her chest in a dramatic fashion, sloshing more of her cocktail down her Cavalli '. . . Exceptionally talented little thing. Still, I suppose that's what comes with experiencing personal tragedy yourself.'

'Personal tragedy?' Tom had subtly yet expertly steered the conversation exactly in the direction he had hoped it would go.

Hilary exploited the opportunity to move in a little closer towards him. 'She lost a child you know . . . a daughter, a couple of years back now. It's common knowledge,' she added, not wanting to expose herself as the frightful shit-spreader she really was. 'Cot death. Little mite lived for a fair few months first though,' she mused. 'Poor woman was naturally devastated . . . some say she had a breakdown afterwards . . .' She allowed her voice to trail off for dramatic effect. 'And then of course to add insult to injury it transpired that they – she's married to some rather handsome documentary producer – couldn't have any more children,' she leaned in even closer and whispered the last part conspiratorially, 'according to some she would do *anything* to replace the one she lost, just between you and I of course,' Hilary sucked air through her teeth, enjoying the sense of importance it gave her imparting such salacious gossip to the new boy in town.

Tom nodded, 'Of course.' His mind was revving in fifth gear. *Desperate for a child . . . would do anything to replace the one she lost . . .*

'Would you excuse me, Hilary,' Tom suddenly said, cutting her off mid-sentence. 'There's someone I need to see. It was great talking to you,' he added, smiling at her from over his shoulder as he disappeared into the milling crowd.

'Oh! Well yes, forgive me, you must mingle, can't keep you all to myself now can I?'

More's the bloody pity. '. . . Bye for now,' Hilary called out to him, utterly crestfallen at having had their conversation cut short. 'And don't forget the garden party! It's next week and . . .'

She watched him disappear from view, swiping another consolatory Grey Goose cocktail from a passing waitress with a look of disdain and a little harrumph.

CHAPTER 58

In the exclusive private member's only club, oblivious to the fact that her mother was two floors above sipping cocktails, Tess swished her golden hair behind her shoulders and pouted provocatively at the balding, older-looking gentleman who watched as she shook her bejewelled hotpant-clad buttocks in his delighted face to the sound of Usher's *Yeah*. This stripping business was proving to be much more fun than she had anticipated. In fact, she didn't know what she had been so worried about. Tonight she felt like the old Tess, the Tess she'd been before Ibiza and she was positively loving the attention, never happier than when she had the eyes of an audience upon her. The fact that her audience consisted of a man who was old enough to be her grandfather didn't seem to bother her one iota, especially since she was flying off her tits on grade-A coke that Monique had supplied. Tess glanced over at Monique, who was busy shaking her tiny tits in some Japanese businessman's face. She gave her a knowing nod and Monique gave a conspiratorial wink back.

'Beautiful,' the old man wheezed, his watery grey eyes devouring Tess's smoking hot young body as she gyrated herself around the pole, grinding her crotch against the shiny metal in time to the music. 'Absolutely stunning . . .'

Tess smiled to herself. She'd already made a little over 500 pounds in a matter of minutes . . .

'You do private dances?' the man subconsciously licked his papery thin lips, unable to take his eyes from Tess's pert young breasts that were barely contained by a tiny gold Bond girl-esque string bikini.

'Of course,' Tess shot back obligingly, enjoying the sense of power she had over him. 'It's 100 pounds for ten minutes.'

The old man reached for his Cartier wallet without hesitation, bewitched, as Tess slunk off towards the private booths, her peachy backside rotating in time to Usher's creamy vocals.

She felt her spirits lift; the way things were going she would be able to pay Marco off in no time – and then she saw her. Tess's heartbeat accelerated inside her chest as she watched the familiar face scan the room. *Shitting hell*. It was only Victoria Mayfield, her mother's best friend for God's sake! What was *she* doing here? And then it struck Tess that if Victoria Mayfield was at the opening night of the casino then there was every chance her mother was here too . . . Seized by panic, Tess quickly slipped behind a long purple drape, lest she be spotted and her cover blown.

'Well,' she said, peering out at the old man from behind the velvet curtain, 'do you want a private dance or don't you?'

CHAPTER 59

'My office, *now*,' Tom sidled up to a startled Victoria grabbing her roughly by the upper arm.

'And it's nice to see you too, Tom,' she said, feeling the panic rise inside her like a tsunami. She knew she'd been risking it coming here tonight. Too many people knew her face; too many people had read her goddamn books.

'Jesus Christ Tom, you're hurting me!' she protested as he forcibly dragged her down the stairs. 'Has something happened?'

'You tell me,' Tom shot back, opening the door to his office and practically throwing her inside. Victoria straightened herself out, blinking at him, the adrenaline coursing through her in waves, mouth watering with nausea. 'There had better be a good reason for you man-handling me like this,' she added tremulously in an unconvincing bid to act the innocent.

'You had better start talking, Rachel,' he growled. 'Or should I say *Victoria*?'

*

'. . . And so there I was, at the Met Gala, when who should come over and ask me if I had a spare safety pin?' the woman paused for dramatic effect . . .

'Liz Hurley?' Lindsay breathlessly suggested, hanging off the woman's every word.

'Oh no, darling, not Liz, someone much more *fabulous* . . .'

Victoria had been right Ellie thought, only half-listening to the conversation going on around her, the rooftop swimming pool *was* stunning. With a platinum-tiled bottom and mosaic sides up-lit with ultraviolet lighting, it invited you to strip off and jump right in, which incidentally, was what some of the guests had begun to do. Ellie looked on as various recognisable raconteurs on the scene de-robed to join the topless showgirls who were frolicking in the water, inciting as much bad behaviour as possible.

With Victoria having been missing for over an hour Ellie was in half a weary mind to go looking for her, and tell her she was leaving. Instead however, she had somehow managed to get stuck with Lady Jemima Macclesfield and Hilary Austin-Hugh; two of the most pretentious, tedious women in society who were busy critiquing every piece of couture that sashayed past, and surveying the decadent scene unfolding in front of them with barely concealed delight. Just as she thought it couldn't get any worse, Ellie spotted Loretta striding towards them, her enormous breasts arriving a few seconds before the rest of her. There was no time to make a run for it.

'*Donne, Donne,*' Loretta greeted the group of women with a forced smile as she blew smoke and air kisses into the cool inky night air, her eyes sweeping critically over Ellie's undeniably impressive attire. The sight of her looking nothing short of stunning in cream Armani one-shoulder couture was sending Loretta into a green-tinged meltdown. 'I trust you're all enjoying *my fiancé's* hospitality?'

'Oh absolutely,' Lady Macclesfield smiled, unable to keep

herself from staring at Loretta's lips and tits, in that order. 'The casino is totes amaze, darling. Just what Soho needs to liven the place up a bit.' She held her hand out. 'You must be Moretta?'

'It's *Lor*-etta,' she sharply corrected her. These English women were so thick, hardly a brain cell between them. Hadn't they read all about her?

'I do beg your pardon,' Lady Macclesfield apologised profusely. 'Lady Macclesfield, Jemima Macclesfield,' she shook Loretta's diamond-encrusted hand, eyeing the elaborate jewels around her neck approvingly. 'And this is my good friend, Hilary Austin-Hugh.'

'A pleasure.'

'All mine,' Loretta remarked disingenuously, checking out the redhead's purple gown with thinly-veiled disdain; it was far too young for her. 'And of course, *we've* already met,' Loretta turned to Ellie, a thin, sinister eyebrow twitching manically. 'How *are* you, Ellie?'

'Oh! You two know each other?' Hilary's gossip radar sprang to immediate attention.

'Yes,' Loretta smirked, 'we go back a long way don't we, darling? Ooh, now let me see . . . it must be what, twenty years or so now . . . ?'

Lindsay looked up at her boss in surprise. She'd never mentioned ever having actually *met* Loretta Hassan before.

Ellie fixed Loretta with a cold, hard stare. If she even *dared* . . .

'We met in Las Vegas, didn't we?' Loretta explained to the women, 'I had a bit part in a movie and Ellie here . . . well, she was . . .' She deliberately paused, '. . . *just passing through*, weren't you?'

Ellie silently exhaled. 'I can barely remember now,' she said tightly, 'it was so long ago and I was so *young* at the time.'

Loretta gave her an amused smile that belied her true malice.

'No husband this evening?'

'He's away on business; busy adding to his billions, you know how it is?' Ellie hated the way Loretta brought out her bitchy side but it was almost instinctive.

'How delightful,' Loretta's eyes narrowed. 'Though of course I'm a millionaire in my own right these days,' she boasted, flicking her hair behind her, 'no need for a husband's money.'

'Not one who's alive, anyway,' Ellie shot back.

Hilary Austin-Hugh, Lady Macclesfield and Lindsay were staring at the pair of them with barely-concealed glee. These two women had form! How utterly thrilling!

'Tell me, have you seen the *lap dancing* club yet?' Loretta asked Ellie with a snide smile. 'The *strippers* are amazing, hand-chosen by Tom, every one of them. Still, I guess he knows a good one from a bad one, with all the practice he's had. Good job I'm not the jealous type, isn't it? After all, why dine out on hamburgers when you've got filet mignon at home.'

'Mutton, more like,' Ellie muttered under her breath.

'Ooh a lap dancing club,' Hilary cooed, clapping her hands together, the idea appealing to her voyeuristic nature. 'Not that I could do anything quite so bold as to take all my clothes off in front of a complete stranger!' Though she would certainly consider it if Tom Black made a special request, she thought. Hilary glanced at the pretty topless showgirls who were busy frolicking with various male guests in the swimming pool. 'Oh to be so young and body confident again,' she sighed. 'It's been years since I had sex with the light on,' she threw her head back and snorted with laughter.

Loretta gave her a pitiful look.

'Tom *worships* my body; says it's better than that of a woman half my age.'

Ellie made to say something but thought better of it.

'Well, I think it's all little distasteful myself,' Jemima Macclesfield pulled a face. 'Hardly flying the flag for feminism, is it?'

Loretta stifled a laugh. The English were such prudes. It was a wonder they hadn't all been wiped out they were so sexually retarded.

'Yes, I suppose it must take a certain *sort* of girl to take her clothes off for money,' she agreed, shooting Ellie a disdainful look. 'Don't you agree, Ellie?'

If Loretta was trying to make her feel uncomfortable then she was succeeding.

'Can't say I've ever given it much thought,' Ellie gave a casual response, 'but then again I suppose we're in an enviable position; for some women it's their only chance of making money to survive. Besides, it's just naked flesh at the end of the day; if we're talking about starring in a *porn film* however, that's another matter altogether.' She batted her eyelashes at Loretta in an over-exaggerated manner and watched delightedly as her smug smile rapidly dissolved. 'Would you excuse me for a moment, ladies?' Ellie said, unable to stand breathing the same air as this vile woman any longer. 'I really need to check on my friend.'

*

'Well, someone seems to have found her voice,' Loretta smirked, following close behind Ellie as she left.

'Oh sod off, Loretta. Why don't you go and ruin someone else's evening, hmm?' Ellie shot back, nodding and smiling at various guests in recognition as she continued to walk.

Loretta snorted. 'Touchy darling, touchy . . . PMT is it?'

'Well, that's no longer something *you* have to worry about, is it Loretta . . . ?'

Loretta's smirk morphed into a thin line.

'Hear this, Eleanor O'Connor—' her voice was low and menacing now.

'—It's Scott,' Ellie corrected her.

'Well, whatever your name is now,' Loretta spat, her dark eyes disappearing like black holes into the back of her skull. 'I want you out of here and away from my husband, *capisce*?'

'Husband?' Ellie stopped and turned to face her then, smiling sweetly at her, 'Oh, but I thought the poor man was dead?'

'You know who I'm talking about.'

'You're getting ahead of yourself Loretta.' It was Ellie's turn to smirk and she felt the feisty East End girl buried deep within her rush to the surface in a show of defiance.

Loretta pulled a face as if she'd just chewed a nettle.

'Stay away from Tom,' she hissed, 'or the world will know all about your sordid little secret past, something I'm guessing your very rich and well-respected husband wouldn't exactly be thrilled about.' Loretta's fat top lip curled in contempt. 'Just imagine, all that unwanted press attention, all those friends looking at you in a whole new light – not to mention that daughter of yours . . . it is a daughter, isn't it? Not exactly setting her the greatest example is it . . . her mother an ex-stripper . . .'

Ellie felt something inside her explode like a mushroom cloud.

'I don't know why my presence is such a threat to you, Loretta,' she said, turning on her heel to face her. Ellie towered above the woman and yet somehow Loretta had always managed to make her feel small. 'It's really quite flattering, but I assure you I'm a very happily married woman with no interest in your husband-to-be. It was all a long time ago and I have long since moved on; maybe it's time you did the same – now, won't you excuse me,' she shot her a look of contempt as she pushed past her, forcing Loretta to take two steps backwards – straight into the swimming pool behind her.

'Oops,' Ellie smirked as she strutted defiantly from the terrace, the clacking of her six inch Louboutin sandals drowned out by the sound of Loretta's splashing and screeching, the gasps of onlooking guests punctuating the warm night air like birdsong.

CHAPTER 60

Fleeing barefoot down the staircase of the fire exit, her cream dress hitched up with one hand, Ellie bit her lip and stifled the urge to laugh out loud. She had not exactly meant for Loretta to end up in the pool dressed in her finest Valentino but it had been a sweet moment nonetheless. She would almost certainly have to leave the party now though. Loretta would be baying for her blood and her smile began to fade as it suddenly struck her that she would probably have announced her secret past to the whole of the roof terrace by now.

'Shitting hell!' she cursed. 'That damn bloody woman!'

Pushing the fire exit door, Ellie began searching for a way out of this goddamn maze. She needed to find Victoria.

The sound of raised voices and a door slamming in the near distance caused Ellie's heartbeat to quicken, and she looked up to see the flash of a green dress disappear from a side room.

'Tor?' she called out after her but was halted dead in her tracks by a shadowy figure standing in the doorway. Ellie visibly jumped like she'd just been given 240 volts.

'Hello Ellie,' he said as she instinctively dropped her Louboutins to the floor.

Tom and Ellie stood opposite each other, eyes wide, both of them paralysed to the spot.

'I . . . I was looking for my friend . . . I got lost . . .' she said, gesturing behind herself as if to demonstrate it had been the truth and that in no way had she been looking for *him*. Her chest was so tight she could barely squeeze the words out. 'What on earth are *you* doing here?' she did her best to feign ignorance.

Tom surveyed her with barely-concealed delight. Two whole decades had gone by and yet it seemed like only yesterday, the memory of her face still clear in his mind as if it had been etched onto glass. In that moment Tom felt something erupt inside him like a volcano, showering him with the debris of a thousand memories; of holding her young teenage body tightly against his own, the sound of their heartbeats in unison, the noise of the squeaky oscillating fan above the bed they had come to share, the satin feel of her hair, soft against his skin as she rested her head on his bare chest. Everything they had shared; the day before her sixteenth birthday, the day he had taken her virginity . . .

He struggled to stop himself from embracing her.

'You're looking good, kiddo,' he eventually said.

Ellie felt light-headed with adrenaline. *Kiddo*. It had been years since anyone had called her that. 'You're back in London,' she said, her voice crackling like an old radio, feigning surprise.

'Oh, didn't you know?'

'Why would I?' she shrugged convincingly. The last thing she wanted was for him to think that she knew all about the club and Loretta and that she had been unable to keep away, unable to resist tempting fate. Tom's ego had always been big enough to eclipse the sun and she had no reason to believe that it had shrunk with time. Egotistical, vain, a gambler and a cheat – it was hardly a fantasy lover's CV and yet Ellie knew there was so much more to him than that; or at least, there had been once. 'This is my casino, Ellie. *I* am Black Jack's.'

Tom was pleased as punch to be able to legitimately lay down such a line. The potential to impress her would not pass him by unrealised. 'I always said I'd make it, didn't I?' he met her eyes with his own, wondering if she could really see what was behind them.

Ellie forced herself to remember what a bastard he had been to her. How he had deserted her, discarded her without a thought the moment Loretta offered her ample charms on a platter. And then of course there was the night at Livedon, the night before her wedding . . .

'Modest as always, Tom,' she looked away from him, careful to conceal her shaking hands. 'Some things never change.'

'Oh, but I *have* changed,' he objected, his initial shock giving way to a surge of adrenaline now, the emotional barriers he'd always used as shields shooting up around him once more.

'I'm a rich man now Ellie,' he said cockily, thinking it only a half a lie. Well, he had this place after all, didn't he? It was only a matter of time.

'I didn't realise all this was *yours*.' Now it was her time to lie. 'If I'd known I wouldn't have . . .'

'. . . Come?' he finished her sentence for her.

'That's right,' she replied with forced defiance, trying not to look him in the eye, to observe the changes that had taken place in his face. She couldn't deny that he still looked good, better than good in fact; he was still ridiculously handsome, sophisticated even, dressed immaculately as he was in a made-to-measure Armani suit that offset his deep mocha tan and matching eyes. He had aged well and it suited him, gave him a distinguished air. Tom had always been blessed in the looks department. It was as if his features had been hand-carved by God himself.

'I didn't think you would ever come back to London,' she said, the tension between them almost tangible.

'I know,' he eventually said, '. . . but that was a long time ago now.'

Ellie wished she had not said anything.

'Of course; all in the past,' she fleetingly met his fixed gaze.

'We were just kids back then,' he said, regretting each word as he spoke them. Why was he being so goddamn glib? He wanted to tell her how good it was to see her; how she had haunted his thoughts and dreams . . . only his words betrayed him.

'Yes,' she managed a thin smile, '. . . kids . . . I hear congratulations are in order.' Tom felt his heart sink. He guessed she already knew. 'You and Loretta Fiorentino,' she raised an eyebrow, 'so it stood the test of time after all.'

'It's not like that, Ellie . . .'

'Oh, you don't have to explain to me!' she said, her very countenance suggesting otherwise. He watched as she touched her chest lightly, her fingertips making contact with her soft skin. 'I always thought you two were a good match – the perfect couple in fact,' she said. It sounded churlish but she couldn't stop herself.

'You don't understand, it's—'

'Tom! Tom! Are you up here?' the sound of Loretta's garrulous voice cut him off mid-sentence.

'I have to go,' Ellie said quickly, snatching up her Louboutin sandals hurriedly. She pushed the fire exit open.

'Ellie, wait!' he said, 'I need to talk to you . . .'

'Goodbye Tom,' she said, turning to look at him, their

eyes connecting for the briefest of moments. 'And good luck,' she added, tipping her head in the direction the shrill voice had come from, before closing the door behind her, adding, 'you're sure as hell going to need it!'

CHAPTER 61

She stood in his office, her face streaked with black mascara, false eyelashes falling from her lids like macabre spiders on the run. Her hair was dripping wet, matted into messy clumps that hung from her shoulders like old rope and her $10,000 Valentino dress now looked like a cheap bit of catalogue tat. She was incandescent with rage, her enormous chest heaving in protest as she struggled to regain composure.

'Jesus Loretta, what the fuck happened to you? You look like you've been dredged from the bottom of the sea!'

'I'll tell you just what the fuck happened to me! That *cazzo cagna stupida* ex-girlfriend of yours, that's what the fuck happened! That fucking skinny-assed crazy bitch! She pushed me in the swimming pool – humiliated me in front of everyone. And look!' she tugged at her hellishly expensive gown, watching in dismay as some of the hand-sewn Swarovski crystals fluttered to the floor, 'she has destroyed my Valentino!' Loretta looked as if she was about to spontaneously combust; even her botox looked angry.

'Ex-girlfriend? I'm afraid you're going to have to narrow it down a little more than that . . .' Tom joked.

'Eleanor O'fucking Connor, that's who I'm talking about,

you stupid man,' she snapped aggressively. Tom gave her a deliberately blank stare, as if he had absolutely no idea who she was talking about. 'The English stripper you were shacked up with in Vegas all those years ago . . . oh, don't pretend you have forgotten, Tom,' she spat the words from her inflated lips like broken teeth. 'She was here, tonight, bold as gold . . .'

'It's brass, Loretta,' he corrected her, 'bold as *brass*.'

'Gold, brass, my fucking ass Tom!' she finally exploded then, coming at him with her fists. 'I knew it was a mistake telling her about tonight . . .'

Tom's eyes flickered with interest as he attempted to restrain her.

'You've seen her before now, before tonight?'

Getting nowhere, Loretta gave up her assault and reached for an L&M, struggling to light it with a huge marble desk lighter, her hands shaking with indignation.

'A few weeks ago, in Dior,' she forcibly blew smoke from her pursed lips into his face.

'And you told her about us?'

'Of course . . . and the casino,' her eyes turned to slits. 'Why the sudden interest, Tom? A second ago you had no idea who I was talking about. You'll go up in flames if that torch you're carrying gets any bigger.' She shot him a disdainful look, adding, ironically, 'you never did have any class . . .'

'Don't be ridiculous,' he shot back, turning his back on her lest his eyes betrayed him.

'That was all a lifetime ago. I've never given her a second's thought until now.' He poured them both a glass of Cristal from the bottle he had on ice, as a means of distraction. 'Here, it'll help calm you down.'

Loretta snatched the glass from him without objection.

'Do you realise I am supposed to be halfway to the airport by now? Thanks to that bitch I will show up in LA

303

looking like something that has been dragged from Lake Placid,' she attempted to run a hand through her hair but was met with some considerable resistance.

'Look at me! The press will have a field day!'

Tom had stopped listening. So Ellie had known about the opening of the casino all along; known that it was his place, and yet she had still made an appearance tonight. A triumphant smile crept across his lips. She had *wanted* to see him.

'Screw the press, Loretta,' Tom said twirling round to face her; suddenly feeling like a million bucks. 'You'd look beautiful in a paper bag.'

Loretta's expression softened a little then. It was exactly the sort of thing she wanted to hear.

'You mean it?' she pouted in a brief moment of insecurity.

Tom humoured her with a frown that suggested she didn't need telling twice.

'Forget about that bitch Eleanor O'wassherface. You've got a movie to make, remember, a movie that won't happen unless you get your ass on that plane pronto.' His words were enough to make Loretta snap out of her maudlin moment of self-pity.

'Darling, you're right,' she said, inhaling deeply on her cigarette as she drained her glass.

'Call down to reception and let the car know I'm on my way!'

Tom fought back the urge to ask her what her last servant died of but instead obligingly did as she asked. Anything to get her out of there.

*

As the last of the guests finally made their way out into the harsh glare of morning light, Tom slumped back into one of the plush velvet cube banquettes and signalled to the lone

304

barman to fetch him a Courvoisier. Loretta would be halfway to LA by now and the thought brought him a small modicum of comfort.

'One for the road, eh?'

Tom's head fell back on his shoulders and he allowed himself a small smile as he sipped at the smooth warm liquid, resting his polished Gucci leather shoes on the low glass table. Exhausted yet elated, everything about the evening had been a roaring success. The press had gone wild for Black Jack's almost as much as the guests had appreciated his sublime hosting skills; from the catering to the cocktails to the showgirls and free gaming, it had gone down the proverbial storm. Attention to detail and authenticity, that was the key, and the London glitterati had lapped it up all night long – literally – it was 4.48 a.m. and he was exhausted. Most of the dancers had called it a night now and Jack had left some time ago with a nameless blonde with fake tits and fake smile in tow. Tom thought he'd recognised the girl but he'd been distracted by that awful Hilary woman before he'd been given the chance to get a proper look.

'I don't know about you, but I would say that tonight has been a resounding success.' Tess, appeared from nowhere and plonked herself down onto the seat opposite Tom, folding her long, slim legs up underneath her in a manner that suggested she was incredibly supple. Still dressed in her gold bikini and buzzing on coke, she was in no mood to call it a night. Pulling her glossy hair to one side provocatively she giggled at him, her green eyes wide and manic, pupils dilating wildly. Tom could see the girl was on something and the thought depressed him.

'What are you still doing here, Nicole?' he asked wearily. 'It's five a.m., why don't you get yourself off home.'

Tess grinned.

'But the night's only just beginning!' she protested, barely

305

able to string the sentence together coherently. Tom watched her sadly.

'You wanna lay off the gear, Nicole. If you wanna keep this job – and those good looks of yours,' he said coolly, unsure as to why he even gave a shit. 'Time for bed,' Tom smiled at her kindly from across the table, though it was more an instruction than a request, 'call it a night, eh?'

Tess could barely focus and was swinging one leg manically over the other, her heart-rate and adrenaline pumping as she attempted to lick her dry lips. God she fancied her new boss. He was hot, hottie, hot!

'Bed! I like the sound of that!' Tess shrieked in drunken coked-up delight as she began pulling random twenty and fifty pound notes from her handbag and throwing them up in the air like confetti. 'I made three grand tonight – three fucking grand! Can you believe it?' Her euphoric smile was quick to dissolve. 'Only it still won't be enough, will it?' she shook her long glossy blonde mane ruefully, uncrossing her legs as she attempted to stand. 'He'll still want more . . .' She met Tom's eyes with her own. 'He's never going to go away, is he?'

She was swaying on her feet now, her fingertips balancing on the edge of the banquette to stop her from toppling over. 'You'll make him go away, won't you?'

'Who are you talking about Nicole?' Tom stood then, placing his arms around her to support her. 'And what won't be enough?' The girl wasn't making any sense.

'Take me home and make love to me,' she breathed, hanging from his neck, her knees buckling beneath her. 'I know you want to really,' she flicked her hair from her overly made-up face that somehow only served to highlight just how young she really was, 'everybody does.'

Tom shook his head but couldn't stop a small smile.

'Let's get you a cab, shall we?' he said resignedly. 'You do remember where you live, don't you?' He scooped Tess up into his arms and was struck by just how feather-light she was. He looked down at her smooth young face and wondered why he felt inexplicably drawn to her; she was incredibly beautiful, even shit-faced on coke and drink, but he sensed the girl was trouble – and opening night aside, he would have to give her a serious talking to if she wanted to carry on working in his club; he couldn't have the girls openly taking drugs on the premises. Tom decided he would get her home, let her sleep it off and sober up before reading her the riot act.

'Give us a hand,' Tom said to one of his burly doormen outside who sprung to attention, opening the door to his private limo and helping to pour a catatonic Tess inside, a mass of coltish limbs and gold lamé. A camera flash went off behind them and Tom spun round in alarm. 'Jesus Christ!' he glared at the bearded man who hastily disappeared down a shadowy side street. 'Freakin' paps! Don't those motherfuckers ever sleep?' He shook his head. 'Take this one home will you, Reggie?' Tom instructed.

'Where's home, sir?'

'Good question,' Tom sighed as he reached for Tess's handbag and began to search for some kind of ID, something with her address on it. He was beginning to lose patience as he rifled through her belongings. It had been a long night and he didn't need to deal with this shit now. 'Bingo!' he said finally locating her driver's license. It was only when he read the name on it that his heart stopped dead in its tracks.

CHAPTER 62

In what was fast becoming Groundhog Day, Victoria sat on the toilet seat in her bespoke designed private bathroom, heart knocking violently against her ribs and stared down at the white applicator. 'Pregnant 2-3 weeks.' Had there been some kind of mistake? She blinked down at the small digital grey window, unsure whether to laugh or cry. Had it really happened; was she actually pregnant? This was what she had wanted all along, wasn't it? The reason she had compromised everything, risking her marriage and sanity, trading in her moral fibre and everything she had always believed in? So why didn't she feel elated? Why did she feel like her whole life was collapsing around her like a house of cards?

Discarding the applicator, a terrible ache inside her chest, Victoria ripped open a fresh test from the stack of boxes and proceeded to re-take it, the three minutes passing like hours as she watched the results slowly repeat themselves on the small digital screen: 'Pregnant 2-3 weeks.' Holy shit. She was carrying Tom Black's baby.

Victoria blinked at her reflection, her mind buzzing loudly in her ears as she cast her mind back to the previous evening. Tom had taken her into his office and summarily dismissed her like she was some sort of incompetent employee.

'Look er, Rachel, Victoria, whoever the fuck you are, I don't really care,' he'd said, coldly. 'I think it's time we called it a day on our little get-togethers, don't you?'

She had blinked at him; his lack of emotion rendering her speechless.

'Tom, I'm sorry I lied about who I was . . . it . . . it just seemed easier to adopt an alias, you know . . . I wanted to tell you the truth . . . I was planning to tell—'

'Save it, honey,' Tom shot back. 'I'm not that interested. You can call yourself Queen Elizabeth for all I care . . .'

Whatever this crazy bitch's game was, Tom wanted no part in it. He had good reason to suspect that 'Rachel' had used him as nothing more than a freakin' sperm donor, only she had no idea that while the gun was always loaded, these days it only fired blanks. Well, he had half a mind to bring her up to date on that little important fact, really rain on her fucking parade! Whether she had planned all along to leave her husband, or if she'd just wanted his sperm, it was more than a little fucked up.

'It's been fun,' he'd said quickly, in a bid to get the whole thing over with and back to the party before anyone noticed him missing. 'But you're married, and I'm about to *get* married and . . . well, I think you know what I'm saying Rach— *Victoria*, it's not like it can go anywhere, is it?'

Victoria had swallowed down the lump of emotion that was threatening to block her oesophagus as well as her pride.

In that moment it was as if someone had lifted the blinkers from her eyes and she saw Tom Black for who he really was; a shallow, soulless, cowardly player simply out for himself. Victoria realised her uses had run out; he probably had a replacement lined up already, keeping the bed warm as they spoke. Painfully, she realised she meant absolutely nothing to this man, a man who probably wouldn't even mourn her passing if she died tomorrow. In fairness to him, Victoria could not have ever expected anything else, after all, he had promised her nothing; it had been *she* who had been using *him* to get herself pregnant. So why did she feel so bereft? And why wasn't she cartwheeling across the marble floor of her bathroom?

Victoria looked at herself in the mirror and briefly wondered if she might be better off dead. At least that way she would be reunited with her beloved CeCe. It had been nothing short of complete madness to have thought she could embark upon an affair with no consequences. She had betrayed her darling Lol and their daughter's memory, and she had betrayed herself. She was a faithless slut. And now she was pregnant with another man's child. A child she had thought she so desperately wanted. But it was only now, now that she knew she had achieved what she'd set out to do that she finally understood that it wasn't just any child she had wanted; it was *their* child, hers and Lawrence's. She pictured her husband's handsome smiling face on the night he had returned home some weeks ago from his African trip just to see her for a few hours, remembered how he had held her in his arms, stroked her face with tender fingers, looked into her eyes as he told her over and over again how much he loved her and missed her . . .

A silent tear escaped Victoria's eye and slid down the back of her neck. Lawrence was such a strong, proud man; he'd always been her rock, keeping his own emotions in check while hers ran amok. She had made such a diabolical mistake, a terrible, abhorrent error of judgement.

Victoria threw the white applicator despairingly into the waste bin. Was this how utter blackness and crippling despair felt? How could she ever begin to forgive herself? How could she carry another man's child inside her belly, a belly that Lawrence would stroke and kiss and love? How could she have ever thought for a second that she could stand back and watch as he raised the child as his own,

310

knowing the truth? She had tainted the unblemished landscape of their marriage with a torrid affair that had produced a pregnancy and now they would all have to pay; herself, Lawrence and the tiny clump of cells buried deep inside her.

Victoria felt the tears of her despair sting her eyes like broken glass. She had to say goodbye to Rachel once and for all; forget such a faithless, selfish person had ever existed and bury her for good. Wiping her face with the back of her hand and taking a deep breath, Victoria splashed her tear-stained face with cold water and took a deep breath.

She knew what she had to do.

CHAPTER 63

LA was hot. 110 degrees hot.

'*Merde*, will someone get me a glass of champagne before I catch fire?' Loretta was relaxing between takes on a sun lounger by the private pool at her exclusive Chateaux Marmont villa while a personal butler stood over her with a large white ostrich feather-and-bamboo fan. 'Yes Mrs Hassan,' he stopped fanning, 'though may I suggest you have some water instead? The alcohol will only dehydrate you and—'

'You may *suggest* what you like my dear,' Loretta replied tartly, 'but be a good boy and fetch me a nice chilled bottle of Cristal, chop chop.'

The butler nodded, duly silenced. Vile old diva. Who did she think she was anyway, Elizabeth fucking Taylor?

'Back on set in ten minutes, Loretta,' a young female runner called out to her from across the pool.

'It's Mrs Hassan to you,' she shot back. 'Actually Black . . . it's *Mrs Black*!' Or it soon would be, Loretta thought with a self-satisfied smirk.

The runner rolled her eyes, giving Loretta's personal servant a sympathetic nod.

Loretta had held up the filming schedule with her diva antics and impossible demands ever since she'd arrived.

What she hadn't quite realised however was that the joke was on her; her part in this movie was simply an opportunity to make a fool of her and the irony was she was just too vain and stupid to realise it.

Adjusting her leopard print and gold beaded Heidi Klein Montenegro bikini and pulling her Gucci visor down over her eyes, Loretta fully reclined onto the lounger and gave a satisfied exhalation.

'Speed it up a bit,' she commanded without opening her eyes. She was practically translucent since she'd been in London and couldn't wait to top up her tan when she got to Antigua – her honeymoon destination of choice. She had hired her and her husband-to-be a luxurious state-of-the-art yacht called 'The Blue Angel' to celebrate their marital bliss in style, and had fallen in love with it so much that she'd decided to buy it outright. Money; it really did get you everything: houses, boats, jets, jewellery, couture, even a husband! Loretta grinned from underneath her Gucci visor. And oh my, what a husband she had bought herself! Tanned, toned and hotter than July. She hoped he was behaving himself. It was partly the reason she'd tipped off the paps, anonymously giving them his daily schedule so that they could relentlessly pursue his every whereabouts, keep an eye on him on her behalf. An inspired idea . . .

'Your copy of the English newspapers have arrived, Mrs Hassan, as requested . . .'

Loretta squinted up at the butler.

'*Meraviglioso.*' She was keen to see what the British press had made of the casino's launch, and more importantly, her appearance in that delectable Valentino creation. Tearing the pages back enthusiastically, glass of chilled champagne in hand with Bambino at her feet, Loretta scanned the pages with an impending sense of elation, a feeling that, as her eyes met with page seven, was rapidly short-lived. Springing

313

to a seated position on the sun lounger, practically dropping her champagne in the process, she cursed loudly.

'. . . Ageing B-list actress, Loretta Hassan . . .' there was no picture, no homage to the dress or her latest film, and only the briefest mention of her wedding to Tom – paltry consolation. Instead it was all about that bloody bitch Eleanor O'Connor. 'Undeniable beauty,' that's what those bastards had written, while describing Loretta like she was some sort of figure of ridicule. She furiously ripped the offending newspaper into shreds before setting fire to it with her Cartier lighter.

'Mrs Hassan!' the butler began frantically banging the flames in a futile bid to put them out. 'Please be careful!'

'Every time they humiliate me!' she screeched, her voice as sharp as cut glass as she stood, wobbling, on her seven inch Miu Miu glitter patent sandals. 'These people wouldn't know talent if it came up to them and slapped their ridiculous faces! They call *her* a beauty and me an 'ageing has-been'! How *dare* they! I will have my lawyers onto this! Get me Artie Maynard right away!'

Her butler nodded, careful to keep his secret smirk in check as he handed her the phone.

CHAPTER 64

He ran his hands up underneath her dress with a sense of urgency.

'I love you, Eleanor and I want you, God I want you; I've never wanted anyone else like it.'

'Never?' she asked biting her lip as his lips touched her neck. She felt the tips of his fingers reach the softness inside her Agent Provocateur lingerie.

'Never. Never before or since. It was always you; only ever you.'

Expertly undoing the zip on her dress with one deft move, he reached inside, his fingertips lightly circling her nipples beneath the thin, delicate lace of her bra.

Ellie stifled a moan.

'No Tom, don't,' she weakly protested but he pressed his lips against hers to prevent her.

'Shhh . . .' She felt the smooth hotness of his tongue as it gently slid into her mouth and met with her own, a slow, soft, sensual kiss that quickly escalated into something more frenzied and urgent. Resistance where Tom Black was concerned was futile and they both knew it. She could feel his hardness beneath the thin woollen fabric of his expensive designer suit and had a feeling it would soon be on the floor, alongside her expensive underwear. He had stood then, removing his shirt, exposing his tanned six-pack, the result of many hours spent at the gym tweaking and toning his lithe, strong body to perfection. She struggled not to look impressed and he smiled provocatively, sliding the Gucci belt from the waistband of his jeans, unzipping his trousers and stepping out of them. He was naked now and she leaned across the bed, taking the chilled bottle of vintage Krug rosé from the Tiffany ice bucket and pouring them both a glass in matching flutes by means of distraction. Naked and hard, he was an impressive sight.

'I've waited a long time for this moment, Ellie – a lifetime,' he said, the genuine pathos in his voice causing an ache inside her chest. 'I've been so lonely without you,' he took both the glasses from her hands and taking a mouthful, lent in to kiss her, depositing its contents between her lips. Ellie swallowed breathlessly, enjoying the creaminess of the champagne mixed with his saliva, the bubbles tickling her lips. 'Leaving you was the biggest mistake of my life and not a day has passed by without my thinking what a regular schmuck I was.' He was on top of her now, his hardness hot against the smooth skin of her thigh. She felt him; wanted him like she had never wanted anyone her entire life and she groaned in ecstasy as he made his descent from her breasts, gently nibbling and licking, covering them in kisses until he reached the small curve of her flat stomach. Ellie squeezed her eyes tightly shut in a futile bid to block out what was happening. There was fire between them, a passion that had a life of its own, that neither could own nor control. It had always been Tom; from the moment they had met she had known it, just as she knew it now.

'You can't fight physics, Ellie,' he spoke softly, as if reading her thoughts and she felt the hotness of his breath between her thighs. 'What we've got, it's special. You know it, and I know it.'

His tongue began to explore her then and she gasped, arching her back as he buried it between her legs, enjoying the sweet softness of her, the intimate scent of her skin. After a while she could bear it no longer and guided him up towards her, crying out as the tip of him gently nudged against her.

'It should have been me you married,' he said as she dug her fingernails into his back, pulling him inside her, moaning in pleasure as he sank himself into her over and over and over again. 'I should've been your husband,' he breathed, feeling his orgasm rush to the surface and willing it back, 'I should have taken care of you . . . loved you . . . I love you Eleanor O'Connor, God help me I love you . . .'

'I loved you, Tom,' she cried out, her orgasm building to a crescendo as she felt him deep inside her, 'I loved you so much and you betrayed me, us, everything we were . . . everything we could have been . . . but there's something I need to tell you . . . it's about Tess and . . .' the sound of a door opening caused Tom to slow down almost to a stop.

'Jesus Christ!' Ellie shrieked, sitting bolt upright as she scrabbled to pull the covers around her nakedness. 'Vinnie!'

Ellie awoke with a start, her chest heaving in short sharp bursts, tiny beads of sweat forming a glistening sheen across her brow.

'Jesus fucking Christ,' she breathed, reaching for the glass of water on her bedside table and gulping back the contents like her life depended on it. She pulled the bed sheets up around her tightly, resting her head on top of her knees, attempting to catch her breath. Eventually she made her way into the en-suite marble wet-room. The dream had left her feeling dirty and unclean and she needed to wash away all memory of it. Disgusted with herself, she squeezed a generous dollop of Jo Malone nectarine blossom and honey body wash onto a pouf and began angrily attacking her skin. How could she have allowed herself such thoughts, unconscious or otherwise? Seeing Tom had affected her far more than she was ready to admit. The dream had been so graphic, so intimate and so . . . passionate it felt as if she had already betrayed her husband. She allowed the hot water to prickle her tanned skin. God how she wished Vinnie would hurry up and come home. She had not been herself last night; she had allowed that gargantuan bitch Loretta Fiorentino to get the better of her, forcing her to act out of character by getting embroiled in a catfight! Deep down Ellie knew the reason for such an outburst. Loretta was marrying Tom. And as loathed as she was to admit it to herself, the very idea caused her to feel something she hadn't in a long time: jealousy. *Jesus, Eleanor*! She chided herself. What had she been thinking? What business was it of hers if Tom wanted to betroth himself to that vile creature anyway? It was his funeral. Her actions last night had not been those of the upstanding lady she was supposed to be. But that was just it, Ellie thought as she switched off the shower and wrapped herself in a new fluffy cotton white towel. The lady she was *supposed* to be. Had she ever really existed? On the outside Ellie presented herself as the veritable society wife, always immaculately dressed, a social delight full of wit, beauty and charm, but underneath she was just a simple girl from the East End of London, a streetwise former stripper who knew how to take care of herself when the situation called for it. It was this girl who had made an appearance last night and what's more, Ellie had realised just how much she had missed her.

Slathering her skin in matching highly scented silky body lotion she began to dress, opting for a pair of Isabel Marant skinny jeans and a simple white Helmut Lang vest. There was a knock at the door.

'Your morning paper and post Mrs Scott, and some black coffee and wheat-free toast as requested,' Angelika, a new and efficient addition to the Scott staff household, said, bringing the tray towards her.

'Just leave it on the bed thanks, Angelika,' she smiled at the young Polish girl.

'Oh and these flowers just arrived for you, Mrs Scott. Shall I put them in some water?' Slicking some mascara over her eyelashes, Ellie stopped and turned round. The bouquet was enormous, white hydrangeas and akito roses, her absolute favourites.

'Gosh, they are beautiful aren't they?' she said, admiring them, 'yes, please do. The Lalique vase – the green one.' Vinnie, she thought as she picked up the small card that had accompanied them. He always knew how to cheer her up. As Angelika hurried off, wondering what in the hell a Lalique was, Ellie turned her attentions to the newspaper. Pouring the hot black liquid into a delicate bone-china cup, she tentatively snatched it up and began flicking through the society pages until she reached that dreadful stuffed shirt, Richard Rollins' column.

She almost dropped the hot coffee down her Helmut Lang as her eyes fixed on the photograph of herself. She read the copy with a knot of dread in the pit of her stomach, even the bit about Loretta being an 'ageing B-movie actress' failing to raise a smile. The only small consolation was the fact that there was no mention of her former occupation. Ellie squeezed her temples with a thumb and forefinger in despair. If this got back to Vin . . . if he saw it . . . she necked her coffee and poured herself another with a shaking hand. She needed caffeine to take the edge off her nerves. Tomorrow's chip paper, Ellie told herself firmly. It was unlikely he would even see it, she attempted to reassure herself. She'd come clean about everything when he came home; minus the little part about actually knowing in advance who was hosting the event in question. There she went again, planning more lies to tell her husband. Ellie threw the paper down in despair and looked at the small envelope that had accompanied the beautiful flowers. 'Oh Vin,' she sighed aloud. 'What's happening to your wife?' Carefully opening it, she began to read:

Lunch Friday? I will send a car at 2pm. T x

Ellie threw it into the wastepaper bin like it was on fire. Tom. She felt her hackles rise. The man's ego was bigger than ever. 'Dream on, Tom,' she muttered underneath her breath as her eyes wandered back to the discarded card. As if she would just drop everything and meet him for lunch! Who did he think he was? She was a married woman now, twenty years a married woman. She had made the mistake of allowing her curiosity to get the better of her last night, but she wasn't about to make the same mistake twice, *was she?*

CHAPTER 65

'Jesus guys,' Tom attempted to sidestep the paparazzi as he made his way from his car towards the casino. 'Don't you people have lives . . . homes to go to?' Ever since the opening night the paps had been stalking him unrepentantly. Like, WTF? He wasn't even famous – yet.

'Yeah, and a living to make,' one cocky little oik shot back as they snapped away at him like a pack of starving wolves. Tom glanced down at the young man's wedding band on his finger. 'Beautiful, is she?'

'Who?' the good-looking paparazzo said, puzzled.

'The wife, buddy, the wife . . .'

He grinned. 'She'll do for now.'

'Yeah, well, maybe you should spend more time with her, know what I'm saying. Girl's got needs and shit, or so she says . . .' He watched as the young man's smirk faded.

'You know my wife?'

Tom smiled to himself as he made his way into the building.

'Hey! I said how the fuck do you know my wife?'

The casino was busy and Tom gave a sanguine smile as the punters fed the slots with vigour, the whirr of the roulette wheel on constant spin filling him with satisfaction. Black

Jack's was only in its second week of trading and already the place was packed out with diners and groups of businessmen making the most of the lap dancers' goods on offer. Tom felt a rare moment of accomplishment. If only it hadn't come at such a high price he thought, realising with dismay that his wedding to Loretta was fast looming and time was running out. It was this place that had got him into all this mess in the first place and ironically, he'd decided it would be this place that got him out of it too. Once it started making a healthy profit he would have enough to buy back his liberty and debt at The Player and get rid of that poisoned chalice from around his neck once and for all.

But it wasn't only his impending nuptials that were giving Tom sleepless nights. His mind drifted back to what he had learned about Nicole on the opening night of the casino. Turns out the young lap dancer with a penchant for snorting too much coke wasn't 'Nicole' at all, forcing Tom to wonder if anyone in this godforsaken city was who the fuck they said they were. *Nicole was Ellie's little girl.* It had been staring him in the face all along. It was there in her smile, in the way she carried herself; she was a bonsai Ellie, the mirror of her mother as she had been at her age – and Tom was at a loss as to what the hell he was going to do about it.

The question troubling him most was why? Why in God's holy name would the beautiful young daughter of billionaire parents be stripping for money? It was hardly something she needed to do to make ends meet. By all accounts Tess had been educated at the best schools money could buy, and was taking a gap year out before 'contemplating' university. He'd found pictures of the Scott family on the internet; snapshots from various society and business magazines, smiling onboard the family yacht in Portofino last year. Eleanor had looked stunning in a black and gold bikini, her husband's arm casually draped around her brown, slim shoulder as Tess stood, hand on hip, posing for the camera – the ultimate rich and beautiful family on holiday together. The shot of them looking so happy had caused an ache to form inside Tom's chest. The notion that it could have been him in the photograph, had he played his hand differently, had not escaped him. Even more troubling however was the fact that the picture, taken the previous March, had claimed that Tess was just about to turn seventeen years old, something that had set alarm bells ringing inside Tom's head. If his calculations were anything to go by, then that meant the girl had been conceived at some point in the July of 1993, around the time of Ellie's wedding to Vincent Scott; around the time he had paid one last visit to her that night at the country house . . . Could it be that Tess was in fact *his* daughter? He had to admit that it *was* a possibility. It would certainly begin to explain his unnatural desire to look out for the girl. Tess was a very beautiful young woman and yet even when she had blatantly propositioned him he had uncharacteristically refused. Was it nature's way of letting him know that she was his own blood?

The very idea caused him to shudder. Jesus, one way or another he had to know. He would confront Ellie when he took her out for lunch on Friday, and her reaction would tell him everything he needed to know. But first he had to deal with whoever it was who was driving Tess Scott to drink and drugs. At the very least he owed it to Ellie to watch out for her daughter.

CHAPTER 66

'Pregnant! Oh my God, Tor that's amazing!' I can't believe it!' Ellie clasped her hands together excitedly, her collection of Aurelie Biderman charm bracelets clanking in celebration on her arm. 'Oh darling, I'm *so* happy for you . . . no one could be happier – except Lawrence I imagine! He must be thrilled!' Ellie giggled ecstatically, genuinely elated by her friend's welcome news. 'You see!' she exclaimed, 'all that patience finally paid off! This calls for champagne – you could have a little sip couldn't you, or maybe not? Anyway, I'll have your share! Oh God, Tor, this is such *amazing* news . . .'

Seated at her usual table – the best in the house – at L'Etranger restaurant, Ellie, dressed in a light cornflower-blue Acne Mallory dress and white strappy Tibi sandals had been waiting for Tor to turn up. She had sounded pensive on the phone, like she had something important to say. Now she knew what that something was. This piece of news was like music to her ears. It was just what she had hoped for, something wonderful to celebrate after the disaster that was the press coverage from the opening night of the casino. Ellie was still undecided on what she was to do about Tom. In fact, she had thought about little else all week. As much

324

as she had wanted to ignore his brazen lunch request, she could not deny that she was intrigued by it.

'Can we order a bottle of vintage Dom Pérignon, the 1998 please, and some homemade bread and Nocellara Del Belice DOC Olives as well?' she smiled happily, placing her concerns about Tom to one side. It had not escaped her notice that Tor seemed remarkably subdued for someone who had such fantastic news to impart. She had scarcely raised a smile since she'd got here. In fact, her whole countenance suggested she was carrying the weight of the world on her shoulders.

'So, come on then,' Ellie prompted her enthusiastically, 'tell me *all* about it; how did you first find out? What made you think you were pregnant . . . come to think of it, you said you were feeling a little nauseous the other night on the way to the casino opening . . . was that why you left early? I knew it! I had my suspicions you know . . . got a sixth sen—'

'Ellie, please!' Victoria raised her voice sharply, instantly silencing her.

Ellie's expression changed to one of concern as she slid her arm across the table, gently resting it on top of her friend's. 'What is it, hun, what's wrong?' She had never seen her friend like this before. 'Is everything OK, with the baby I mean?' Ellie put her hand up to her mouth, 'Oh God, there's nothing wrong is there?

'No,' Victoria shook her head, tears silently rolling down her cheeks as she spoke. 'There's nothing wrong with the *baby*. It's me who is the problem.'

Ellie shook her head in confusion.

'I can't have this baby, Ellie,' Victoria's voice was so low that it didn't sound like her own.

'Please Tor,' Ellie stared at her in bewilderment, 'you're scaring me,' she said quietly.

Victoria threw back the remains of her champagne and poured herself another.

'Darling, do you really think you should?' Ellie said gently. 'I mean I'm hardly the pregnancy police but it might be wise not . . .'

'A beautiful, talented, successful author with an adoring husband, right?' Victoria snorted the statement derisively. 'Well, you can add adulteress to that list as well!'

Ellie stared at her blankly.

'Adulteress?'

'That's right,' Victoria said, attacking her glass of champagne with avidity. 'This *amazing* woman, with her *amazing* husband and *amazing* life has been having an *amazing* affair!'

Ellie's hands automatically covered her mouth. She couldn't contain her shock. 'An *affair*?' she breathed through open fingers.

Victoria dropped her head in shame, a shaking hand wandering to her flat stomach.

'This little thing inside me,' she croaked, overwhelmed by the enormity of everything that she had done and everything that would now take place as a result, 'this tiny clump of cells, that with every passing day becomes more of a human being . . . everything I ever wanted since CeCe was taken from me,' she looked up at Ellie's horror-stricken face, 'it isn't Lawrence's.'

Victoria began to silently sob and Ellie instinctively reached for her hand again to comfort her.

'Oh God, Tor . . .' If it wasn't Lawrence's baby then whose the hell was it?

'I'm so sorry to burden you with this, Ellie,' Victoria looked up at her, mascara streaking her pale, shame-wracked face. 'But I had to tell someone . . . I thought I might *die* unless I told someone . . .'

Ellie fought back tears of her own.

'It's OK . . . it's OK,' she attempted to soothe her. 'I'm your friend, aren't I? And that's what friends are for. I'm here for you, hun, I'm here . . .'

Victoria stared at her through her culpable despair.

'And you don't judge me? You don't think I'm a terrible person?' She had sounded so desolate that Ellie signalled for the waitress to bring the bill. She needed to get Tor out of here, go somewhere more private where they could talk properly. This was L'Etranger after all; the walls had ears and eyes and she was conscious of their fellow diners who had begun to look over at them with interest.

'Of course I don't judge you,' Ellie lowered her voice. Hell, who was she to judge anyone; a former stripper who had kept her past secret for the best part of twenty-one years? But this had been so unexpected. Tor. An affair. It was so . . . so out of character.

'I've made an appointment at the clinic this Friday,' Victoria said stoically, drying her eyes with a starched linen napkin as the waitress hovered nearby with the bill. 'There's no other way.'

'Are you *sure* this is what you want, Tor?' Ellie implored, realising what a ridiculous question this was to ask. 'I mean, have you thought this through – there are other options,' she said, casting her mind back to the very same situation she had found herself in eighteen years ago. 'You don't have to go down the . . . *abortion* route,' she whispered the word as though it were unclean. 'Perhaps if you talked to Lawrence . . .' the futility of her words made her want to sew her mouth shut.

Victoria buried her head in her hands.

'I've been so stupid Ellie . . . I thought if I took a lover . . . if I could just have a baby . . . oh, I don't know what I thought . . . I have screwed everything up, not just for me and Lawrence, but for this poor innocent little thing growing inside me! An adulteress *and* a murderer!'

Ellie absentmindedly threw a wad of notes down onto the table and, taking Victoria's shaking hand, dragged her from the restaurant.

'Holland Park, please,' she instructed, flagging down a black cab. Once inside, Ellie allowed Tor to fall onto her shoulder and sob, deep rasping primeval cries that shook her small diaphragm and brought a lump to Ellie's throat.

'Shhh, it's OK, it's OK,' she stroked her tear-stained face with a soothing hand and pulled her friend close to her. 'If it's really what you think is for the best,' she said gently, 'then I will come with you on Friday. You don't have to face this alone, Tor. I swear I will be here for you,' she looked down at her face and saw the raw despair in her eyes, 'every step.'

'You're a great friend, you know that?' Victoria managed to say through her pain, 'but this is something I have to do alone. I created this whole mess, I'm culpable and now it's down to me to sort it out, live with the consequences, live with the guilt and the shame . . .'

Ellie could do no more than hold her friend tightly as she continued to sob for the entire journey home.

Jesus. And she'd thought *she* had troubles.

CHAPTER 67

'Gone? What the fuck do you mean, *gone*?' Marco was so close to Tess's face that she could feel the flecks of his rancid spittle on her cheeks.

'When I got back to the apartment . . . she wasn't there . . . all her stuff was gone too,' her voice was tremulous, '*my* stuff.' She thought it prudent not to tell him about the note she'd found pinned to the fridge door.

> Dear Tess, For what it's worth, I'm sorry. It was nothing personal. Say au revoir to Marco for me. Tell him I hope he rots in hell. M x

'And the jewellery?' Marco was pacing the pavement outside the casino now, anger coming off him in waves. His eyes were bulging out of their sockets and the veins in his neck were throbbing vermillion. He wanted to hurt someone, hurt them really bad. 'Did she take the jewellery?'

'She took *everything*,' Tess said quietly wondering how he knew about the missing jewellery. Oh God! Tess felt sick. Had Marco and Monique planned this all along – *together*?

'The door to the safe was open when I came home; it was empty.' Monique, her only friend left in the world, or at least so she'd thought; the girl who had saved her from a terrible fate in Ibiza had been planning to fleece her all along, and now she'd gone and fucked Marco over – again.

'What are you crying for you stupid bitch?' Marco viciously snapped as Tess broke down. 'Aw, don't tell me you actually thought that filthy junkie whore was your *friend*?' He mocked her derisively. 'You're even more stupid than I thought. She's a *junkie*. That lot would prostitute their own kids for a hit.' Marco's manic pacing was beginning to really scare her now. He was so angry he looked fit to combust. 'And there was no note, no letter . . . nothing to let you know where she was going?'

Tess sheepishly shook her head. As devastated as she was by the fact that Monique had done a moonlight flit with virtually the entire contents of her apartment, she somehow managed to feel some small empathy for her. Monique had seen an opportunity to start her life over. Tess was simply collateral damage, a pawn in her and Marco's twisted little game.

Marco lit a cigarette and sucked on it noisily. He'd been a fool to ever trust that rancid bitch. She'd got one over on him *again*, and for a narcissistic maniac like Marco, this was way too much to bear. Someone would have to pay for this monumental fuck-up, big time.

'You realise what this means, Tess?' Marco's eyes had practically disappeared into the back of his skull. Tess shook her head without looking up from her feet, too scared to make direct eye-contact. 'It means that you had better get to work, because *her* debt just became *your* debt . . . are you hearing me, you little bitch?' he grabbed Tess by the chin, forcing her to look up at his twisted features, contorted with rage and objection. He was going to kill her, she knew it. There was no escaping this man now, and no Monique to help her any more.

'Yes, I hear you,' she nodded profusely, blinking back tears. She would do whatever he asked, because in that moment Tess Scott genuinely feared for her life.

*

Tom watched the scene unfold from behind the blinds of his office with growing anger. It was clear that whoever this dude was, he was one nasty piece of work. Tess looked half-blind with fear, cowering away from him, flinching with every word he spoke. Tom resisted the urge to immediately go to her rescue – or at least send the security guys in to do the job for him. He forced himself to hang back. He would get the measure of the man first, find out what his game was and what kind of a hold he had over Tess, before deciding on a suitable course of action. Snapping the blinds shut, Tom straightened the lapels on his ink-blue Ralph Lauren suit and marched from his office with a sense of purpose.

'Nicole,' he said, stopping Tess in her tracks as she hurriedly made her way into the casino. She was dressed in her 'civvies' as the girls called them, white skinny jeans and a thin cotton vest bearing the name of some unfamiliar rock band on the front, neon pink toenails peeping out from her towering gold sandals. She stared at him in surprise, eyes wide like a rabbit caught in the headlights, tear tracks marking her youthful skin.

'I'm . . . I'm not late, am I?' she stammered, absentmindedly looking down at her wrist, at the delicate Chanel platinum diamond timepiece that was no longer there; another item Monique had kindly relieved her of.

'Can I see you in my office?' Tom asked, though it was more of a command.

Tess nodded, using every last bit of emotional strength to raise an affable smile. She didn't like the sound of this

331

and her heart sank. She really couldn't afford to lose her job, not on top of everything else, not now.

Closing the door softly behind him, Tom stared at the young woman opposite and searched for himself within her face. He was sure they shared a similar bone structure; sharp, high cheekbones and an angular, prominent jawline. She had her mother's colouring, that was indisputable, but in a certain catch of the light, he was convinced that looking at her was like looking in the mirror.

Tess glanced around the office, wondering if it might be inappropriate to ask her boss if he had any coke. She wanted to get as out of it as quickly as she possibly could, anesthetise herself in a bid to try and forget what was happening to her.

Tom decanted two large measures of Remy Martin cognac into enormous bulb glasses and offered her one. He sensed they both might need it.

'Thank you,' Tess gratefully accepted, silently throwing the strong-tasting liquid back in one and willing the alcohol to hit her bloodstream as quickly as possible. In the absence of any grade-A on offer it was a suitable consolation.

'Am I in trouble?' she asked, savouring the warmth of the alcohol as it hit her empty belly. The strain in her young voice moved Tom.

'You tell me,' he responded gently, head cocked to one side, his eyes questioning hers. The kindness of his tone was enough to undo Tess completely and she felt herself unravel before him like a ball of wool.

'Oh God,' she cried, her legs almost giving way as she began to crumble, unable to stop the fat tears spilling from her eyes, 'it's all such a horrible, *horrible* mess.'

Tom came round from behind his desk and went to her, instinctively pulling her into his embrace. He felt her body sag, small and vulnerable in his arms as she buried her head into his shoulder, the wetness of her tears against the skin of his neck. This girl was his blood; as a gambling man, he would lay money on it.

'It's OK, honey,' Tom said, surprised by the tenderness in his own voice. 'I'm gonna help you, OK? It's all going to be OK.' He cupped her face with his hands and looked down at her, her lovely young face a broken mess of tears and mucus, despair in the emerald-green eyes that were so much like her mother's that for a moment he felt like crying himself.

'Now,' he said, wiping away one of her tears with his thumb as he stood back from her, 'I want you to tell me everything from the beginning . . .'

CHAPTER 68

Sometimes the gods were smiling down on you, and today, Marco decided, was one of those days, as he strutted through Hackney town centre with a self-congratulatory swagger. The past twenty-four hours had been a total gift, and thanks to such a sublime stroke of fortune he was now able to make his escape from this cesspit of a country and fuck off back to the sun where he belonged. Only this time round, he was going to have a fair few quid in his sky rocket, thanks to some gullible Yankee-doodle who had more money than sense.

Marco laughed aloud as he felt for the plane ticket in the inside pocket of his jacket and thought about what had gone down just a few hours earlier. It had been such a touch that he couldn't have made it up even if he'd tried.

He'd been at the club, Black Jack's, ostensibly to pick up his takings from Tess, but then something magical had happened. At first, when the two security guys had collared him outside and frogmarched him through the building, he had thought he was in line for a good kicking, after all, he'd been pimping and dealing right under the proprietor's nose for weeks, but it soon transpired that in fact a good kicking couldn't have been further from the truth.

Marco had nodded at the man sitting behind the desk, wondering what the hell the flash fucker was going to do with him. He'd glanced around Tom's office, careful to conceal the fact that he was somewhat impressed.

'What can I help you with?' Marco had said matter-of-factly. He would rather have cut off his own cock than let the man see he was a little nervous. 'No offence, but I'm a very busy man.'

Tom had weighed up the young man standing opposite him with the cautious eye of an expert poker player. Marco's Paul Smith shirt was opened just one button more than necessary, exposing a tanned smooth chest and an expensive-looking platinum chain that was very probably hooky. The shoes were the latest Gucci offerings, waffled brown leather with a horsebit buckle, currently retailing at about $800. Tom had thought about ordering a pair himself but seeing this spiv in them had put him right off. He knew exactly what he was dealing with; a plastic gangster with zero class who wore his wealth like a badge and attracted all the wrong kind of attention. He was a nasty piece of work; it was all over him like his strong aftershave. Empty eyes like black slits with nothing going on behind them. It made Tom feel physically sick to think of what he'd done to young Tess – and God knew how many other vulnerable young women. He would have to play this one extremely carefully indeed. From what Tess had told him, Marco was a psychopath, and their lack of conscience made them the most dangerous, cunning fuckers of all.

'Drink, er . . .'

'Marco . . . Marco DiMari.'

'A Courvoisier perhaps, Marco? Or are you more of a Scotch man?'

'Courvoisier's fine,' Marco had nodded, sizing his opponent up.

'The thing is, Marco,' Tom had poured them both a large

measure and taken a generous sip of his brandy, pulling his teeth over his lips, 'I've been keeping a close eye on you these past few weeks – and frankly I like what I see.' Tom paused for effect. 'I'm looking for someone like you . . . someone smart, sophisticated, someone who knows the score on the street, yet can hold his own with the big guns, you know what I'm saying?'

Marco nodded though in fact he didn't have a clue what this prick was on about.

'How do you know I can hold my own?' he answered facetiously.

Tom had laughed.

'The name's Black, Tom Black, and I'm the proprietor here.' They'd shaken hands. Marco's skin was clammy to touch.

'Like I say, what can I help you with Mr Black? . . .' Marco flicked his cuff back to display his Breitling for Bentley timepiece, a deliberate gesture that did not go unnoticed.

'I'll cut to the chase then,' Tom had fixed him with a stare, adding, 'I'm looking for someone to make a drop for me; someone reliable, who knows the city well. You see, I'm unfamiliar with these parts . . . another?' Tom nodded at Marco's near-empty glass.

'I'm not going to bullshit you, Marco,' Tom had smiled affably, 'I know that the girls who work in this club like to, how can I put it, use a little help to get them through the night, if you know what I mean?'

Marco's interest piqued.

'Now, I'm not a big fan of the old Persian rugs, as I believe they're referred to round these parts, but I'm of the thought that if it's a necessary evil, then I'd rather be the one in control of the supply.'

'I couldn't agree more, Mr Black,' Marco had given an unctuous smile that Tom had wanted to instantly erase, ideally with his fist.

336

'I've got a guy over in Hackney, runs a rather aptly named strip joint called Charlie's Angels. Have you heard of the place?'

Marco hadn't – must be new he thought, but not wanting to lose face, he'd given a little familiar nod.

'Rings a bell.'

Tom had taken a large package from the top drawer of his desk and thrown it down in front of him.

'There's ten kilos of pure top-class powder there Marco, uncut. My friend is expecting the delivery in a couple of hours. I trust you can clear your schedule, for say, $70,000?'

Marco looked down at the package and back up at the flash-looking Yank.

'100,000,' he said flatly.

A small smile had spread across Tom's lips. Marco's type were all the same; greed blinded them. It was more effective than mace.

'OK, Marco. Let's call it a round hundred.'

'Up front,' Marco said coldly. The Yank didn't know him from Adam and yet here he was, handing over ten kilos of yay-yo and one hundred fucking grand to a virtual stranger. Marco had forced himself not to allow a chuckle to escape the corners of his mouth. He would shaft the stupid tit for the lot of it. Take the gear, offload it for a decent profit to one of his contacts and double his money before getting on the first plane out of there!

'Anyway, how do I know if this geezer's kosher?' Marco had thought it best to offer a few platitudes, make it sound authentic.

'I can vouch for Charlie,' Tom had smiled, 'anyway, I'm the one who should be worried here. How do I know I can trust *you* with the cash up front?' He began taking bundles of notes from the safe behind a large Andy Warhol print of Elizabeth Taylor, and Marco had felt his confidence replenish as he spun round on the Aresline Xten Italian leather swivel chair. He could hardly believe his fucking luck. 'You can't,' Marco said, 'until I've come back from doing the job right that is.'

Marco smirked to himself as he made his way to meet an old 'business' associate who was more than happy to help him offload his newly acquired stash. Of course, he had absolutely no intention whatsoever of honouring his part of the bargain with the stupid Yank and felt chuffed in the knowledge that later that day he would be on a plane heading for Marbella with £500,000 in his pocket and there would be fuck all anyone could do about it. What an absolute result. Marco had it all planned; a new stomping ground where no one knew him, a little change of ID and a new MO, yeah, that should sort him right out. No trails, no ties, a clean slate.

As Marco made his way through the busy marketplace, engrossed in thoughts of the new life he planned for himself, he didn't notice the two dark-suited men approach.

'Tarik, Tarik Valmir?' one of them said.

Marco took a step back in surprise.

'Who the fuck wants to know?' he said, as a surge of adrenaline hit his bloodstream and exploded. No one knew his real name, save for that cunt Monique and those bastards he called parents. He spun around, gearing up to make a run for it, but was suddenly blocked by two more of them.

'Tarik Valmir, I'm arresting you for the possession of cocaine with the intent to supply, you do not have to say anything but if you . . .'

Marco felt his throat contract and his fury rush to the surface as his face impacted with the cold pavement, his arms roughly pulled behind his back as the men began to search him. Jesus fucking Christ, he'd been set up.

'Planning on going somewhere nice, are we?' one of the plain clothes coppers asked as he pulled the plane ticket from Marco's pocket for inspection.

Marco looked up at the man, hatred and contempt

emanating from him like a force field, his dreams of another new start in the sun rapidly diminishing with each passing second.

'Well,' the copper smirked, as they roughly pulled him to his feet and threw him into the back of the unmarked car, 'you are now.'

CHAPTER 69

'I knew you would come.' Tom stood, smiling at her as she approached the table.

'Curiosity,' she shrugged breezily, wishing she didn't find his arrogance so attractive. Tom really was the antithesis of her modest, demure husband. 'I was at a loose end . . .'

Tom laughed, the banter had begun. 'Well, you know what curiosity did to the cat . . .' he replied with a self-assured smirk. 'And incidentally, while the cat's away . . .'

Ellie shot him a look that suggested he had already overstepped the mark and Tom cleared his throat, suitably subdued. 'Seriously Ellie, I'm glad you came.' He went to take her hand, to kiss it, but she took her seat quickly. She didn't want to feel the touch of his lips against her skin; no physical contact, that's what she'd told herself, in no uncertain terms. She was sailing dangerously close to treacherous rocks coming here today as it was. She didn't trust Tom; and worse, she wasn't sure she trusted herself either. Ellie smiled thinly, placing her studded Alaïa clutch down onto the table as she looked around Black Jack's busy restaurant, a magnificent homage to old school Vegas with its plush velvet banquettes, low lighting and gilt furnishings.

'You look . . . you look beautiful,' Tom struggled to find the words and wondered why he found it so much easier to be disingenuous. Words with genuine meaning behind them always left him tongue-tied. Despite his earlier display of self-assurance, he had not been quite so convinced that Ellie would come. In fact, he had been mentally preparing himself for a no-show all week. Now that she was here, it was his big chance to make amends. Besides, he really needed to talk to her about Tess . . .

'Thank you,' Ellie replied graciously, with a look of casual acceptance. He would never know how much she had agonised and deliberated over her choice of attire for today, how she had stood in her private dressing room for three hours solid this morning, trying on myriad ensembles, only to discard them in frustration. She had wanted her outfit to flatter her without being provocative, to be subtly sexy without saying 'I'm available.' She'd finally settled for a smart Jay Ahr two-tone crepe shirt and skirt dress combo, the unbuttoned shirt giving the lightest glimpse of her lacy 'Love' Agent Provocateur underwear beneath. She hadn't been able to help herself.

'I took the liberty of ordering the Ruinart . . .' he smiled as the sommelier wheeled the silver champagne bucket towards them and made a rather grand fuss of opening the bottle, before decanting it into two chilled slim flutes.

'To old friends,' Tom said carefully, watching her facial expression in a bid to try and read her thoughts. Their glasses lightly touched and Ellie allowed herself to look at him properly. He was wearing a dark grey suit, the cut precise, the cloth, expensive. His shirt was a pale soft pink, his tie a slightly lighter shade of grey with an iridescent sheen; the cufflinks were diamond and the watch peeking out from beneath his cuff appeared to be a Rolex. Every move he made afforded her a subtle waft of his Tom Ford cologne. He looked ridiculously handsome, a thought that made her feel guilty. She heard her husband's words ringing in her ears, '*We never mention that man's name ever again* . . .' and did her best to silence them.

Blinking at him from across the table, Ellie wondered just what it was he wanted from her, and moreover what *she* wanted from him. He gently smiled at her, causing the burgeoning ache inside her chest to swell. Looking into his eyes was like looking into her daughter's. It wasn't so much a physical likeness, more a disposition, and it felt like a vice around her heart.

'It's beautiful here,' she remarked, glancing out across the plush restaurant. 'You've done well, Tom. I'm almost impressed.'

'Almost?' he said, keeping his eyes firmly upon her. 'The view from here is pretty good too.'

She gave him a cursory look.

'Platitudes; you know none of that bullshit ever worked on me.'

He looked a little crestfallen and she wished she'd not been so dismissive. 'But I appreciate the gesture.' She glanced at her watch. Tor would be at the clinic in a couple of hours and the thought instantly depressed her. The idea of her friend going through something so traumatic on her own, especially given her fragile state of mind. She had tried talking her out of it; after all, Vinnie had forgiven her indiscretion with Tom all those years ago, why wouldn't Lawrence do the same? All Tor had wanted was a child, and she had been prepared to go to any lengths to get one – even by taking a lover, a lover whose identity remained tightly under wraps. Ellie would be lying if she said she wasn't intrigued but Tor was keeping schtum.

'It's been a big hit with the Londoners,' Tom said. 'The restaurant, I mean.'

Ellie raised an eyebrow.

'You don't refer to yourself as a Londoner anymore . . .

342

old East End boy like you? You've sold out, Tom, abandoned your roots.'

He laughed, though she wasn't far off the mark.

'London was a long time ago now,' he said. 'I can barely remember . . . me and Ray . . . we were always doing a moonlight flit from some woman or the other.' He smiled wanly at the memory.

'So, what brought you back, besides the casino, I mean?' She hoped it didn't sound like she was fishing for compliments.

'It was Jack's idea,' he shrugged. 'I much prefer the States to be honest. LA is . . . sunnier for a start and London . . . well,' he looked down at his napkin, brushed away crumbs that weren't there.

'Sunnier . . . and full of attractive young blondes I should imagine,' Ellie added. Now she just sounded as if she was jealous.

He flashed her a smile, amused.

'Coincidentally, you do know that I had my eye on the place as well, the casino, I mean.' She was being way more candid than she'd planned. She hadn't wanted to allow him the satisfaction of having got one over on her.

'I had plans to turn that place into a dance school before you got your grubby hands on it and turned it into a den of iniquity.'

Tom's eyes widened.

'A dance school, of course . . .' he nodded.

'But *you* scuppered my grand plans, Tom Black,' she added, mock-accusingly.

'Blame Jack; he was the one doing the bidding.' His eyes fleetingly met with hers. 'Anyway I'm surprised . . .'

'By what?'

'By the fact that you were outbid, I mean, come on . . . you're Mrs Vincent Scott after all . . .'

Ellie swallowed hard. Like she needed reminding. 'Well,'

she sighed, returning his fleeting glance as her cheeks began to flush, 'I guess it's my own fault for not being brave enough.'

He smiled. She had always been the more cautious one; quite the antithesis of himself. She would've been so good for him. He knew it.

'Well, you know what they say about luck?'

'And what's *that*?'

'It favours the brave,' he said, daring to wonder for the most fleeting of moments if the afternoon might end in him making love to her. The idea caused an ache inside his ribcage and a hardness inside his trousers.

'I wanted the place but not badly enough to pay twice its worth,' she shot back derisively.

'Something's worth is only measured by what you're prepared to pay for it.'

'So profound!' she mocked him. 'You know you were stung and that's the end of it.'

He watched her bristle and wondered if it was possible to love anyone any more in that moment than he loved her. Tom's phone rang, shattering the moment and abandoning his thoughts.

Holy fucking shit, it was that crazy broad Victoria, whatever her name was. What in hell's name did *she* want?

*

Victoria looked down at her phone. The bastard wasn't answering. Pressing redial, she looked at the imposing building, squinting up at it in all its neoclassical glory, struggling to reconcile how something so horrible could take place somewhere so beautiful. She wondered if the walls inside were haunted with the cries of a million unborn babies, unwanted and unloved, brutally scraped from the comforting walls of their mother's wombs and discarded. She placed her Mulberry overnight bag down onto the steps and tried to banish such gruesome, maudlin thoughts. It was a beautiful day; the sun was glowing, bathing the well-kept grounds of the clinic in its bright white light, the pretty floral borders belying the horrors that took place inside. She heard the sound of birdsong, cheerful and vibrant, so alive that it was heartbreaking. Victoria took a deep breath; she had to stop this, and pull herself together. This was the right thing to do; the *only* thing to do. And yet she knew just one kind word from Tom would be enough to see her halfway home. Instinctively touching her slightly swollen belly, Victoria placed the phone to her ear and listened as it rang out.

CHAPTER 70

'Don't you think you ought to answer that?' Ellie said, perusing the menu. 'Sounds like someone's pretty determined to get hold of you.'

'It's just business; they can wait,' he pressed the decline button and switched the phone to silent. 'Anyway, where were we?'

'You were just about to tell me all about your wedding to Loretta,' she teased him. Tom felt his heart sink. Just the woman's name was enough to kill his good mood in a flash.

'Ah yes, well, that's a real long story, kiddo.' *Kiddo*. It still made her heart jump, even after so much time had passed.

'You think you'll be living in London after the wedding?'

He shrugged. 'We'll be between homes I guess; LA, Milan, London . . .'

'Nice.' She pretended to read her menu.

'Actually, I have to thank you.'

'For what?'

'For pushing her in the pool the night of the opening . . .' he grinned, and Ellie found herself joining in. Tom had always brought out her playful side, a side of her she had long ago tempered when she had become Mrs Vincent Scott.

'It was an accident,' she looked at him with a

346

mock-innocence that made him want to lean forward and kiss her.

'It reminded me of something. Do you remember the time we went skinny-dipping in Laurie Mancini's pool, the summer of 1997? Her folks lived off the Strip and had given her the run of the place.' Ellie pulled a bemused face. 'You remember, you accused me of flirting with her, went nuts and pushed her into the pool and stormed off . . .' he laughed. 'You were so feisty back then . . .'

'You *were* flirting with her . . .' Ellie replied, her memory jogged. 'Besides, I didn't *push* her, she *fell*!' The recollection made her blush. 'And I am *still* feisty,' she added. 'Anyway, you were always such a terrible flirt.' Their eyes met for a second. 'All so long ago now, Tom,' she said quietly. 'We were so young back then . . .'

'Aw, c'mon Ellie, you make it sound like it was a hundred years ago. We're still young now.'

'Speak for yourself,' she shot back, 'you're what's deemed middle-aged, Tom. Bet you thought you'd never get there, huh?'

'You don't feel young?' he questioned her.

'Well I don't feel old if that's what you mean but, hey, I'm not twenty-five anymore – and neither are you! I'm forty next year – forty! Jesus Christ!'

'It's worse if you say it aloud,' he joked. 'Besides, forty is the new thirty apparently. Old enough to know better, still young enough not to care . . .'

'Bullshit,' she sipped from her water glass. 'That's just some crap the media and retailers feed you to make you feel better and buy their products.'

'Cynic,' he poked her hand with a finger.

'Anyway, it's different for women. Once you hit a certain age you become invisible; it's deemed 'unattractive' or 'inappropriate' to wear your skirt above your knee, dance like you're enjoying yourself, or wear a bikini on the beach.'

'And you believe that shit?' Tom pulled his chin into his neck. 'I mean, seriously? Some dried-up old hack telling you how to live your life, making up the rules as she sees fit – and it's always a she, because only women put this kind of crap on each other.'

Ellie laughed. He was so right.

'Besides, a woman like you doesn't need to worry about that stuff anyway. I mean look at you, kid!' He saw the chance to pay her a compliment, say something memorable, something romantic even, but the words just wouldn't come.

'Yeah, look at me,' she said with a self-deprecating sigh.

'I bet you can still party with the best of them.'

'I have my moments, I suppose,' she said, trying desperately not to flirt with him.

'I'm sure you do . . . how about we find . . .' he made to finish the sentence but the waitress appeared and his phone vibrated again. Tom hit the decline button once more and smiled up at the young waitress.

'I'll have the scallops followed by the pork loin and lobster ravioli, please,' Ellie said.

He raised an impressed eyebrow.

'Good choice. I'm going for the ox cheek and what the hell, I'll have the beef and truffle macaroni.'

'And there was me thinking that mutton was more to your taste,' Ellie smirked.

Tom raised a smile of his own.

'If it means anything, I don't love her you know,' he said, and the tone of his voice led her to believe he meant it.

'It doesn't,' she shot back with a light shrug, '. . . mean anything I mean.' Although they both knew that it did.

There was a long silence, though not an awkward one.

'Jesus, Ellie, we've come a long way,' he said eventually, suddenly struck by a melancholic sadness at the years that had separated them. 'Look at us now. A million miles away from that damp room on Parkway Boulevard . . . me, a casino owner and you the wife of a billionaire . . . who'd have thunk it, eh?' His eyes met hers. 'Does your husband know you're here?

Ellie shifted uncomfortably in her seat.

'What's it to you whether he knows or not?'

'I'll take that as a no then.'

'He's in Australia,' she said quietly.

'And your daughter?' Tom said, attempting to bring the conversation round to Tess.

After listening to Tess's gut-wrenching sobs over the events of the last few months, Tom had arranged for her to stay in his hotel suite where he could keep an eye on her, get her seen by a private doctor, a stint in rehab if she needed it. She was suffering pretty badly with the effects of cocaine withdrawal and he wanted to do all he could to help her get back on her feet. She was his blood after all, he was sure of it.

'Why are you being so kind to me?' she had asked him as he'd replenished her water and gently placed a clean pillow underneath her head. 'I'm just a stranger to you . . . you're just some good-looking American guy . . . my boss from the club . . .' She'd been quite delirious, drifting in and out of consciousness, feeling the effects of the doctor's prescription drugs to aid her sleep. 'Why do you even give a shit?'

Tom had smiled. 'Shhh,' he'd said. Truth was he hadn't known how to answer her. As for Marco, Tom had called in a favour from an old gambling contact in the Met – a *big* favour. The rest was simply a case of lulling Marco into a little trap. A trap he had walked into like a blind man walking into a lamppost. Greed; it really was a man's downfall.

'Tess?' Ellie sighed as she thought of her wayward teenage offspring. 'Tess is a law unto herself – just like her father,' she found herself adding. He held her gaze. 'She never returns my calls, not unless she wants something. But that's kids for you,' Ellie reasoned. 'You never had any?' The waitress brought their starters to the table and Ellie pretended to look interested, though her appetite had been completely obliterated by the sexual tension that was so potent it was almost visible. Adrenaline that was coursing through her like a river.

Tom shook his head.

'None that I know of,' he said carefully, searching her eyes for clues. *Tell me, Ellie, tell me the girl is mine . . .*

'I'm surprised,' she mused, 'the way you used to spread your DNA about . . .'

He laughed, stabbing an ox cheek with his fork.

'I had the snip about ten years ago. Paternity suits are like fast-food flyers through the front door in LA . . .'

'Clever.'

'Oh I don't know. I just never wanted to inflict my DNA on another human being. Life's tough enough, right?'

She looked up at him. It was the first time she'd ever heard him say anything self-deprecating and she wondered for a moment if he really had changed.

'Don't you ever wish . . .' she looked down at her plate of food, suddenly thinking better of finishing the sentence.

'. . . Wish what?' *That I had never ever left you? That I had married you and we'd lived our lives together, happily ever after with our daughter. Yes, I do . . . I do . . .* 'Not my style, Eleanor, you know that.'

She gave a wry smile.

'So what *is* your style, Tom? Marrying ageing old porn stars? Is that the whole deal with Loretta, a second chance? Help the aged?' Ellie tried to hide the contempt in her tone but it was evident.

Tom's phone buzzed again and he placed his forearm over it to prevent her from seeing it flash.

'Shall we skip dessert?' he suddenly said. 'How about a

350

little spin on the roulette wheel instead?' Ellie narrowed her eyes at him. 'No money involved, Eleanor,' he raised his palms. 'For old . . .'

'. . . Time's sake? Oh come on, Tom, you can do better than that, surely?' She shook her head and laughed lightly, forgetting herself. 'Just a little spin?' she narrowed her eyes.

'The smallest.'

Tom was already signalling to the waiter, before Ellie had a chance to change her mind.

CHAPTER 71

'Thirteen red,' the croupier said evenly as the ball bearing rattled around the roulette wheel.

'Yay! That's twice in a row!' Ellie was enjoying herself and Tom watched her intently, savouring her presence as she clasped her hands together, animated. 'I haven't gambled in years. I'd forgotten how much fun it is.'

It was funny how the years had not dulled his familiarity of her; the way she flicked her soft hair from her face as she spoke, the slight upturning of the corners of her mouth that made her look as if she were smiling, even when she wasn't. Even now, as she bent over the roulette table, her eyes wide with joy, lost in a simple moment of pleasure as the tiny ball bearing flicked across the wheel, Tom realised that his whole life had been nothing more than a series of gambles. You threw the dice, you spun the wheel and you played your hand. It was the thrill of chance. Mostly you lost, but sometimes you won. And right then, with Ellie next to him, the scent of her delicate perfume in his nostrils, the warmth of her body so close to his, Tom felt like the biggest winner of all.

'Beginner's luck,' he sniffed, teasing her.

'You wish. I'm on a roll!' she squealed, forgetting herself, forgetting her husband, forgetting Tor . . . being with Tom always forced her to live in the moment. She looked down at the roulette wheel as though it were indicative of her life. Sometimes she wondered who she might be now, had the ball hit a different number. Vinnie had saved her from a life of strip joints and sleaze, but she couldn't help but wonder just who she might've been without him.

'So, you want to up the stakes?' Tom said, his eyes meeting her own; mischievous, dark, deadly.

'What did you have in mind?' she replied, already in the game.

'A little one-on-one bet?'

'Go on . . .'

'I win and you have a drink with me up in my suite.'

She looked up at him, green eyes wide, and held his stare for a moment. He was serious.

Ellie paused as she thought over the odds in her head.

'One number? One spin? One *chance*.'

He nodded.

'Just a drink?'

'Just a drink, kiddo.'

She stood back, signalling for him to go ahead, her nerves jangling so furiously her hands were shaking. She was playing the game. Tom's game. And she knew it was a dangerous one.

'Black number one,' he nodded at the croupier, who smiled at his boss with a knowing nod.

As the wheel turned and he released the ball, Ellie asked herself what she wanted the outcome to be. The tension between them mounted and she resisted the urge to seize his hand, like they'd done as kids. Her brother, her lover, her friend: Tom Black.

The ball jumped onto red, nineteen and Ellie felt her heart drop, but at the last second it flicked across to black; number one.

'Well,' she said, turning to him, unable to stop a smile from creeping across her lips, her heart hammering against her ribs through the thin fabric of her dress. 'You always were a lucky bastard.'

CHAPTER 72

Ellie stared out of the huge glass window on Berkeley Square. It was a hot afternoon and the square was awash with suited men on their mobile phones, jackets lazily slung over their shoulders, and smart women in pencil skirts and heels, oversized handbags proving cumbersome in the heat. London was such a smart, vibrant city; she knew people grumbled about overcrowding and hostility, but on a day like today, it seemed like the most exciting place on earth, a place where anything was possible.

'Palm Beach?' she said 'You're staying right near another casino,' Ellie remarked. 'Isn't that putting money into the pockets of the competition?'

'I don't gamble anymore,' he replied, which was not strictly a lie. Ever since Vegas, he'd not even picked up a deck of cards. 'But I'm more than happy to watch those who do lose their money in my casino.'

'The house always wins,' she said.

'Damn right.'

'You used to say that was bullshit. You just had to be one step ahead of the game, that was all.'

'I told you, I've changed. Shall I order champagne?'

Ellie gave a tentative nod as she continued to stare out

onto the busy square below, scared to look at him. Lunch had been one thing, but coming back to his hotel suite, she knew, was quite another.

'One drink,' she reiterated nervously. 'And then I must go. I have a friend who's going through a tough time right now and I need to be there for her.' Ellie checked her watch. Tor would probably be at the clinic by now and the thought clawed at her conscience.

'I wanted to talk to you about Loretta,' he said, phoning down to room service and ordering a bottle of Cristal. 'You see, I wanted to explain to you on the opening night but you disappeared before I had the chance.'

'Explain what?'

'Explain why I'm marrying her.'

'You don't need to,' Ellie turned away from the window to look at him. He'd removed his jacket now, a small gesture that unnerved her. Tom was a master seducer, she above all people knew this; he was the type of man who took a woman from zero to sixty in three seconds flat, making you wonder, as you lay naked in his bed, just how you had got there so quickly. Of course, it had not escaped her thoughts that there was a possibility they would end the afternoon making love, a thought that sent shockwaves through her heart, but she could not allow herself to entertain such thoughts of betrayal.

'It's a marriage of convenience,' he felt compelled to tell her the truth. He trusted Eleanor, always had. What they'd had as kids, what they'd been through together, it had bonded them for life. He would tell her about Vegas, about the debt and the deal he'd struck. Then he would talk to her about Tess. As the girl's mother she had a right to know what had been happening to her daughter. Maybe she wouldn't thank him at first, maybe she would scream and shout and cry, but for the first time in his life, Tom decided he wouldn't run away.

'Whose?' Ellie remarked. 'You ought to be careful, Tom,' she mocked, 'you know what happened to her last husband!'

'Don't remind me,' he said flatly.

'What was all that business with her dead husband and Miranda Muldavey anyway?' she asked, keen to get the gossip while she had the opportunity. 'Did he really deliberately slice her up?'

'No one really knows,' he replied 'and if Loretta does, she's not saying. You can't even mention the woman's name without her exploding.'

'Does she now?' Ellie raised an eyebrow.

'Well anyway, the marriage; it's nothing but a business deal.'

'You old romantic you . . . what kind of a business deal?'

'You wouldn't believe me if I told you . . .'

'Try me.'

He smiled.

'I screwed up in a game of poker at The Player; I gambled Jack's money that was meant for the casino and I ended up in debt to the house to the tune of a few mill.'

Ellie gave a little whistle.

'All this from the man who says he no longer gambles.'

'I don't,' he shot back. 'Not after that monumental screw up, let me tell you . . . anyways, the house was gonna call the cops and have my ass thrown in the clink, and then who, in a twisted stroke of luck should I run into, quite literally . . .'

'. . . Loretta Fiorentino.' Ellie was still as a statue now, enthralled. 'And she bailed you?'

Tom nodded slowly.

'And . . . oh my God! The deal was that you *marry* her?' Ellie's eyes widened in shock.

'I hadn't seen the woman in a little over eighteen years . . .'

Tom felt a little of his tension ease. It felt so good to tell someone, but particularly her.

357

'Jesus Tom, that's fucked up, even by your standards. And you're going through with it?'

'What choice do I have?' he replied, miserably.

'Oh Tom,' she sighed. She felt the familiarity, the heat of him as he moved closer and she willed him to stay back but it was too late. He embraced her then and she felt the strength of his arms across the small of her back, the outline of his chest as it lightly touched her own, the electricity passing through them, a pair of conductors.

'Never a dull moment, eh?' Her lips were millimetres from his.

'I was never any good without you,' he said. He wanted to drink her in, to touch every inch of her, taste her; bury himself between her legs and never leave.

Such a candid admission from Tom was rare and it caused a pocket of air to catch in her throat. Jesus, this was Livedon all over again Ellie thought, as she felt her body naturally respond to his. Some fight you're putting up, girl, she thought angrily as he began to push her legs apart with his knee, his breath shallow and hot in her ear . . . oh Jesus, she would go to hell for this . . .

The loud trill ring of Tom's phone caused Ellie to spring back in alarm.

'That damn bloody thing!' he cursed, visibly angry this time; he thought he'd turned it to silent.

'Saved by the bell.'

There was a knock at the door and they both laughed, breaking the palpable tension between them.

'The champagne.'

Ellie nodded, looking down at his phone on the side table. It had been ringing all afternoon. Who was so desperate to get hold of him? Loretta perhaps? In a moment of uncharacteristic madness, she picked it up while he wasn't looking and checked the number on the screen. Oddly, it seemed familiar. Ellie surreptitiously

358

scrolled through to Tom's text messages and began to read.

I need 2 tell u something. It's v. important. Pls call me asap.

It had been sent earlier that day. And there were more.

Your hotel? Same time? Cant W8 2 C U. Usual time?

It was obviously a hook-up of some sort. She stared at the messages; there were dozens of them sent over a period of time, all pretty much saying the same thing. But the number; Ellie absentmindedly tapped her lip . . . 7719 . . . it looked so familiar to her but why . . .

An ice-cold rod of fear travelled the length of her spine to her sphincter as it came to her. It was Tor's number! Jesus fucking Christ, *Tom* was the other man! Ellie felt her heartbeat accelerate so rapidly that she instinctively put her hand to her chest in a futile attempt to steady it. It was all beginning to make sense; the way Tor had been acting recently, and on the night of the opening . . . the fact she'd been able to get tickets so easily . . . and then it occurred to her, that if Tom was the other man and he'd had the snip ten years ago then that could only mean . . . Ellie gasped aloud as she dropped the phone, causing Tom to spin round in alarm.

'You!' she hissed at him, snatching up her clutch bag and pushing through the door past him, 'you bastard!'

The room service guy, champagne in hand, blinked at her in shock.

'What the . . . Ellie wait – please!' Tom called out to her in confusion.

'Go to hell, Tom Black,' she shouted over her shoulder, halfway towards the lifts already. 'I should have known better.' She shot him a look of such cold contempt that it stopped him dead in his tracks. 'Men like you never change. Once a womanising bastard, always a womanising bastard. I must've been half crazy to come here . . .' The room service guy looked on in barely concealed delight. A bit of drama made his otherwise mundane job so much more exciting.

'Ellie please . . . I don't understand . . . don't go . . . I need to tell you something . . . I . . .' But the door to the lift closed in his face before he had the chance to get a foot in it.

. . . *Love you*, he added. But the words never quite reached his lips.

CHAPTER 73

'I need you to take me to Harley Street please – and I need you to be quick.'

The cab driver snorted. 'Everyone's in a rush, lady. This is London.'

'Will a hundred do it?' she shot back, practically showering him with twenty-pound notes.

He sniffed.

'Buckle up then, girl.'

Ellie's chest was so tight she could barely breathe. She had to get to Tor before she made a dreadful mistake. She pictured her friend lying on the operating table of a clinical white room, her feet in stirrups; the glint of the surgeon's knife flashing inside her mind like the scene of a horror movie. Tor was about to abort her own child; *her and her husband's child.*

Perched on the edge of the seat, her face practically squashed against the plastic barrier between herself and the driver, Ellie tried to call Tor for the fifth time in as many minutes. The phone rang out yet again and Ellie fought back the urge to throw it out of the window in sheer frustration.

'Roadworks, innit?' the cabbie commented as they ground to a halt, before launching into a diatribe about the ubiquitous digging up of the capital. 'You're better off on one of Boris's bicycles these days darlin'', though not in those heels,' he chuckled, glancing down at her legs in the rear-view mirror with unconcealed appreciation.

Hitting the redial button again, Ellie held her breath.

'Answer the phone Tor, *please*,' she begged aloud. 'For the love of God, pick up the phone!'

*

Victoria was feeling a little woozy. The pre-med had kicked in. Dressed in a gown, she lay on the thin uncomfortable bed and stared at the innocuous picture of a bunch of flowers on the wall. She wondered if any thought had gone into the choice of painting. Had someone at some point had a conversation about appropriate artwork to adorn an abortionist's operating room?

'Nothing to remind the women of babies,' she imagined someone sensitively suggesting. 'Nothing that could possibly signify birth, life or death,' and yet ironically, flowers signified all three of these things. She stared at the crude painting and wondered how the unknown artist might feel should he or she know where their creation had ended up.

The doctor had told her that she would be able to go home 'about an hour or so' after it was all over. She could hardly believe it; she'd had facials that had required more down-time! 'You might experience some discomfort for a few days, much like a heavy period, but after that you should be fine.' *Fine?* Victoria wondered if she would ever be 'fine' again.

The pre-med was making her sleepy now and she closed her eyes and waited for the nightmare to begin.

CHAPTER 74

'Please tell me I'm not too late!' Ellie was so out of breath – having finally abandoned the cab and run the last five minutes of the journey – that she could barely speak. 'Victoria Mayfield,' she had the presence of mind to whisper her friend's name, 'you *have* to let me see her!'

The nurse behind the desk of the plush Harley Street clinic looked upon her with kind eyes.

'Oh yes, Mayfield . . . third floor – only I'm afraid that's not possible. She's already with the doctor.'

'Noooo!' Ellie thumped her fist on the desk, causing the nurse to look up in alarm, 'you don't understand! I *have* to see her as a matter of extreme urgency, *please*,' she begged. 'What I need to tell her . . . it could change everything.'

The nurse nodded in a gentle but patronising fashion. She'd worked at the private gynaecology clinic for fifteen years and had seen every type of hormonal woman alive. Hysterics were all in a day's work for her. Jealous lesbian lover perhaps, she wondered, eyeing Ellie with interest.

'She'll be done in half an hour or so and then you can see her,' she explained slowly.

Ellie could see she was getting nowhere.

'Screw you,' she said, discarding her Lanvin sandals and making a run for it.

'Excuse me! Madam! You can't just . . .'

Ellie took the stairs three at a time, her long dancer's legs powering her towards the third floor. She would never forgive herself if she was too late.

'What the . . . excuse me!' The surgeon and his team looked up at Ellie in surprise as she flew through the door, chest heaving in short, sharp bursts, perspiration dripping down the sides of her face. 'Oh thank God,' she sank to her knees as Victoria sat up, blinking at her through woozy confusion.

'Tor,' she panted, throwing her Lanvin shoes to the floor in exhaustion, 'the baby; it's not Tom Black's.'

CHAPTER 75

On the whole, Lionel Crosby loved his job, but it was occasions such as this that made him wish he was busy enjoying his autumn years fishing on a quiet little river somewhere near Devon. Instead, he was suffering with chronic jet lag and facing the unenviable task of imparting some particularly unwelcome news. Still, it was all part of the service.

'I appreciate you coming all this way again, Lionel,' Vincent Scott said, signalling to the waiter.

'Some champagne perhaps, or would you prefer a nice single malt?' He'd remembered how much the man had appreciated it from their initial meeting in London. 'And bring us some mineral water will you, Aubrey? I don't know about you,' he smiled affably at Lionel, 'but I always find myself terribly dehydrated after such a long flight.' The waiter smiled obligingly.

Scott was on first name terms with all the staff here at the Sydney Harbour Marriott hotel, a five-star waterfront establishment that boasted unrivalled views – and there was no lengths they wouldn't go to in pleasing such a highly regarded guest. Not to mention a very generous one. Scott's tips were legendary.

'Scotch and water, in that order, would be wonderful,'

Lionel sat back in the raffia bistro chair and admired the breathtaking view of the world-famous harbour. As the bearer of bad news, he only hoped it wouldn't be a case of shooting the messenger.

'Good man,' Vinnie nodded at the waiter who disappeared with a sense of purpose. 'I think I might join you in an aperitif before lunch; the lobster and shrimp salad is really something else. None of your piddly little excuse for prawns like you get back home; these are what the Aussies call, "real beauties". I can highly recommend it.'

'Business going well I take it, Mr Scott?' Crosby said, thinking how tanned and relaxed his client looked in a pair of Lacoste white tennis shorts, aqua-blue polo shirt and Ray-Ban Wayfarers.

'Couldn't be better, Crosby, just got a few more loose ends to tie up before I head back to the big smoke, to catch up with that beautiful wife and daughter of mine. I've spent far too much of the summer without them already. And please, call me Vinnie, won't you?'

Crosby forced himself to smile as he gulped back some Evian and willed the waiter to be hasty with his Scotch. He sensed he was going to need it before this meeting was out.

Vinnie eyed Lionel Crosby carefully, attempting to gauge the man's countenance. He obviously had some news on Tom Black, important news, he suspected, as the man had insisted on flying all the way over from the UK to brief him in person.

Finally the waiter arrived with his Scotch.

'So, what have you got for me?' Vinnie asked a little ominously, meeting the man's eye as he raised his tumbler. 'I take it you're here to talk to me about the casino . . . about Tom Black?' Crosby nodded. The Scotch slid down his neck and he savoured the moment, knowing it was soon to be replaced with a very bad taste indeed. 'So, what's the slippery bastard been up to?'

Lionel inwardly sighed as he tentatively retrieved a pile of photographs from a brown envelope inside his battered old briefcase and silently placed them down onto the bistro table like a deck of cards.

'I'm afraid, Mr Scott . . . Vincent,' he said with a heavy heart, 'it's not exactly good news.'

*

Driving through the London traffic in a silver soft-top Mercedes-Benz SLS, Tom pulled up at a set of traffic lights and caught his own reflection in a glass shop window. In spite of all his woes, he still couldn't help but feel buoyed by just how good he looked in such an awesome piece of machinery, the sun's rays bouncing off the top of the bonnet, his mirrored Ray-Bans glinting in the sunlight. It was the type of vehicle that took luxury to another level; sleek and sophisticated, with a throttle that begged to be pounded. He had hired it for the week in a bid to cheer himself up, only it wasn't quite proving to be the tonic he had hoped for.

Tom roared away from the lights like he was Lewis Hamilton in pole position with Jenson Button up his rear. He was furious at himself for having screwed things up with Ellie, but as usual he was looking to lay the blame elsewhere. Ellie had been there, in his hotel suite of her own accord, and he had felt the heat between them. A few more minutes, a 'do not disturb' sign and she would've been his again, he'd felt sure of it. If only she hadn't seen those goddamn text messages from that crazy writer bitch.

Despite the fact the lunch date had culminated in her walking out on him, a tiny part of Tom couldn't help but feel a little frisson of excitement by the assumption that Ellie must still have some kind of feelings for him; after all, why react like that? He desperately needed to see her, to explain, but time was running out. He was due to fly out to Capri tomorrow ready to prepare himself to become Mr Loretta Fiorentino, a thought that caused his chest to constrict. And he'd not even been given the chance to speak about Tess.

Tom had encouraged Tess to go home back to her apartment and start enjoying her life again.

'I don't ever want to see you in my club again,' he'd said, only half-joking as he'd watched her pack the last of her things into her bag, 'at least, not as an employee anyway.'

She had smiled and it had lit up the whole room.

'Maybe I can bring some friends down to the casino; we could hang out.'

'Come on, you don't want to "hang" with an oldie like me,' he'd laughed, thinking how he had never before referred to himself as 'old'. It was as if everything he did around her was instinctive somehow, intuitive. 'But I hope you'll keep in touch . . . if ever you're in any trouble . . .'

Tess had shot him a look of mock-horror.

'I plan to stay out of trouble for the rest of my life!' she rolled her eyes and he'd watched her young face, full of expression, with carefully concealed affection. He only wished that it were true. He could tell Tess was attracted to drama. She was feisty like her mother and a risk-taker just like him; the poor girl had no chance.

'You know, it's not what happens to you in life, Nicole,' he'd said with genuine pathos, 'it's how you deal with it all that counts.'

He'd watched her as she'd visibly digested his choice words, a pensive half-smile across her lips.

'Thank you,' she'd said, throwing her arms around him, closing her eyes tightly as she squeezed him, 'for everything you've done for me. You've been the greatest boss I've ever had; in fact, you've been the *only* boss I've ever had.' They had both laughed and Tom was struck by just how much he would miss her company.

'You don't need to thank me,' he'd shaken his head,

modest for once in his life. 'I was just doing what any . . . really there's no need.'

'Without you I don't know what I would've done . . .' she lowered her head for a second, the memory of the past couple of months' events marring her good mood. Fact was, whatever he had done, it had worked a treat because by all accounts that freak Marco was locked up behind bars, never to bother her again. And to top it all off, Tom Black had even managed to recoup a little of her money.

'Listen,' Tom had taken her by the shoulders. 'I want you to stay away from the coke, you hear me?'

She had nodded solemnly.

'I promise.'

'And talk to your parents. You know, they were young once too, just like you. They'll understand more than you think, I'm sure.'

'Maybe,' she'd sighed, looking up at him, her smile returning as she perched on the end of the bed, her face free of make-up, her hair a little mussed up. He wondered what she had looked like as a small child and suddenly felt the pain of having missed so much of her life; so many milestones been and gone.

Tess had looked down at her chipped nail polish and made a mental note to book an emergency pedi at Urban Retreat, a thought that suggested she was already on the road to making a full recovery. Tom Black had saved her life; he'd made everything right, without the need to involve her parents or the police – and for that she would be eternally grateful.

'Oh and Tom,' she'd added as she picked up her bag and made to leave, suddenly sad to say goodbye, 'call me Tess. My real name is Tess.'

CHAPTER 76

Jack Goldstein sat down at Tom's desk and attempted to write his best man speech for the fifth time in a row.

'Ladies and gentlemen . . . on this auspicious occasion . . .' He snorted aloud, *auspicious my ass*, 'it is with great pleasure . . . no,' he scribbled out the words in frustration.

'Ladies and gentlemen, it is *my honour* to introduce to you the bride and groom (cue applause etc.) . . .' He blinked at the words on the page, a thin spidery scrawl of black ink, and screwing it up, he aimed it at the wastepaper basket across the room and missed – again. His mind was a blank, the words refusing to come. Truth was, he couldn't think of any positives to say. If he'd been writing a speech giving reasons why Tom *shouldn't* be marrying Loretta Fiorentino, well then that would be an altogether different story. That shit would write itself.

'Jesus Tom, this is bullshit,' Jack muttered underneath his breath as he felt the familiar embryonic tickling at the back of his throat that suggested a coughing fit was imminent. He willed it back. The attacks had got much worse recently; they were lasting longer and had become increasingly painful. He was coughing up more blood too; expelling great dark clots, like parts of his vital organs were coming apart and making a run for it. He'd finally bitten the bullet and booked himself an appointment with a quack for that afternoon. He'd head off just as soon as he'd got a start on this goddamn sham of a best man's speech.

Although Jack wasn't looking forward to the wedding, he *was* looking forward to visiting Capri, beautiful little island that it was, with its turquoise-blue waters, secluded unspoilt beaches and stunning views over the med, not to mention all that young fit Italian eye candy. It was just what the doctor would order he reckoned. Bit of sun on his bones and fresh air in his decaying lungs. This London smog wasn't doing his chest any favours at all.

He took a fresh piece of Smythson notepaper and started again. 'Ladies and . . . oh for fuck's sake!' Now the frickin' pen had run dry! He threw it down onto the desk in fury and sighed, attempting to open the top drawer of Tom's desk. It was locked. Immediately suspicious, Jack began attacking it with a letter opener until it finally relented. So, what did his dear old buddy have hiding inside that he didn't want his business partner to see, he wondered. What was this then? He pulled out a large A4 envelope with the words 'Important Documents Enclosed' emblazoned on the front and without thinking twice, opened it.

Pushing back the swivel chair, Jack scanned the documents inside, his heart beating fast inside his tight chest. It was some kind of legal agreement by the looks of it, an agreement between Tom and Loretta. A pre-nup perhaps? A bead of sweat tickled his cheek as he began to read with interest. This was a contract! Jesus, he knew it! He'd suspected there had to be some kind of incentive for Tom to hitch himself to that woman and . . . wait . . . his hands began to tremble, his clammy palms leaving oily imprints on the paper as he gripped it tightly. It said that Tom had agreed to marry Loretta in exchange for paying off debts to the tune of . . . eleven million dollars . . . eleven million frickin' dollars!

What the . . . ? Jack stared at the typed words in disbelief, his heart knocking violently against his ribs. According to this, *Loretta* had bought the casino! Black Jack's belonged to . . . her! Jack speed-read the remainder of the document and saw that he was named as 'temporary manager,' whatever the fuck that meant.

'. . . this agreement should cease to hold any legal weight should Mr Black forfeit any part of the aforementioned . . . forfeiting the legal arrangement could potentially result in the business immediately transferring back to Mrs Hassan's full and open ownership.'

Dumbfounded, his mouth slightly agape, Jack made his way over towards Tom's fancy drinks cabinet, clutching the A4 document in his hand and, feeling a little lightheaded, he went for a crystal Lalique tumbler but thought better of it, and swiped a bottle of fifty-year-old Dalmore, a snip at eight thousand dollars a pop, instead. Taking a large swig directly from the bottle, he willed the expensive amber liquid to quickly deaden his frazzled nerves. If Tom had been in debt to the tune of eleven million dollars, then what the fuck had happened to his money? He'd ploughed his entire life savings and everything he owned into this casino, so where in God's name was it? Jack went to pick up the phone, his initial instinct to call that slippery fucker he called a friend and demand to know what the hell was going on, but at the last minute he resisted. Lies fell from Tom's lips like lemmings. No. He would skip the monkey and go directly to the organ grinder: Loretta. He would confront that conniving bitch head on; catch her off-guard. Picking up the phone, Jack started to dial but was besieged by a sudden and violent shooting pain in his left arm that was so acute it forced him to drop the receiver and sit back down onto the chair. Stunned and breathless, he reached for the bottle of Scotch, his heart knocking like a shed door in a hurricane.

'Jesus,' he said, clutching his chest, struggling to catch his breath as he went to take a swig. The second instalment, when it came, stopped his heart dead and, with the Scotch emptying itself out over the desk, Jack slumped forward, eyes wide in a mix of disbelief and confusion.

CHAPTER 77

'Jesus fucking Christ, what now?' Tom muttered underneath his breath as he approached the casino to see blue flashing lights. He had more drama in his life than a series of ER right now.

Shooing away the gaggle of paparazzi, who had become a permanent fixture these past few weeks, and walking through the plush entrance to his casino, Tom began to experience a trickle of unease.

'Mary,' he shrugged at the pretty receptionist, 'are you going to tell me what the fuck's going on? Why is there an ambulance outside? Is someone hurt?' It suddenly struck him that one of the girl's might have OD'd on all that shit they liked to put up their noses. That was just the kind of headache he didn't need, not to mention all the bad press that would follow.

Mary Milford swallowed hard and brought a shaking hand up to her tear-stained face as she watched her boss make his way towards his office.

'Please Mr. Black, I wouldn't go in there . . .'

Ignoring her impassioned plea, Tom's heart began to gallop inside his chest as he realised the source of the drama was coming from *his* office. The place was awash with paramedics, a hive of green-shirted activity buzzing in and out, their expressions rueful, pensive, fixed in concentration.

'Can you stand back please, sir,' one of them commanded authoritatively, as Tom made to enter the room.

'This is my office!' he responded, 'I'm Tom Black, the owner!'

A harried-looking paramedic pulled him to one side as Tom strained his neck to get a better view of the situation. The room was full of people, equipment; a red blanket covering a bulk.

'Mr Black?'

'Yes, that's me.' Tom couldn't keep his eyes off the blanket. He was worried now, really worried. 'Is someone going to tell me what the fuck's going on here or am I supposed to play guessing games? I just hope to God that's not a stiff,' he said, pointing to the red blanket. The young man shook his head. He looked exhausted; a shimmering sheen of oily sweat highlighting his smooth youthful brow.

'I'm sorry, sir,' he said, his expression sombre. 'There was really very little we could do . . . the coronary was fatal . . . it would have killed him outright.'

'Him?' Tom pulled his chin into his neck in momentary bewilderment. And then he realised.

'Oh no . . .' he said, sinking to his knees, clarity and despair coming at him in equal brute force, 'not Jack!'

CHAPTER 78

Tearing through the London rush-hour traffic in her soft-top Mercedes SLK, one hand precariously on the wheel, her foot hard against the metal, Ellie ran her spare fingers through her hair in nervous anticipation. Vinnie was home, and she wanted to see his face more than she'd ever wanted to see anyone's in her life.

Now that her husband was back, normality could resume, and she could put the unsettling events of the past few weeks behind her. The thought of his presence alone was comforting, especially given the tense and awkward, not to mention depressing, conversation she'd had at the private hospital with Lawrence Mayfield.

'An *affair* Ellie . . .' Lawrence's tone had slipped from angry questioning to one of imploring desperation – and it had broken her heart to hear it. 'An *affair* . . .'

They had both looked through the clear glass at a sedated Tor with heavy hearts, and finally at each other.

'. . . I . . . I can't understand it . . .' he'd stammered, 'I tried to do my best . . . to be there for her and . . .' Lawrence Mayfield had been on the first plane home the moment the call from Ellie had come through, explaining that Tor had been taken to hospital with 'exhaustion.'

Truth was, he had been expecting such a phone call for weeks, maybe even months. His wife's mental state had been in gradual decline since CeCe's death, only he had buried his head in the sand, had not wanted to face what was happening in front of him.

'Listen, Lol,' Ellie had said his name with familiarity and kindness, taking his hand as they had stood behind the perspex glass, watching Victoria. 'This whole baby obsession . . . she was suffering more than any of us realised.' Victoria had confessed her affair to her husband while under heavy sedation, told him all about Tom Black as he'd cradled her at her bedside, every word from her dry lips shattering his heart.

'It's OK baby,' he'd said, wiping the tears away with his thumb as they slid down her temples onto the pillow. 'I'm here now; it's all going to be OK . . .'

'I'll understand if you hate me . . .' Tor had croaked, her mouth dry and dehydrated, 'if you want a divorce.'

'Shhh . . .' Lawrence had stroked her hair gently, 'till death us do part, remember?'

'But I broke out vows, Lol . . . I hate myself . . .'

'I love you Victoria. I'll always love you. And I'm going nowhere, OK? Now, come on,' he had spoken to her gently, 'the doctors say you must rest; we've got a little life in there, baby,' his hands had lightly touched the sheet over her stomach, 'we've got to be strong . . . together.'

'It's like I don't know who she is anymore, Ellie,' Lawrence had wailed, 'like I've lost her . . .' The despair in his voice caused Ellie's lips to quiver with emotion.

'This bastard Tom Black; who is he Ellie? How did she meet him?' he clenched his teeth, his eyes narrowing, 'whoever he is, I'm going to kill him; do you hear me?' He shook his head, his face a grim mask of anger and grief.

'This was never meant to happen, Lawrence,' Ellie spoke gently, 'she did a crazy thing, yes, but you can't let this destroy you . . . please don't let it destroy you.'

Lawrence snorted. He'd been gentle with his wife because he couldn't risk upsetting her, not in her condition, but the anger inside him was bubbling up, and it was close to boiling point.

'That baby is yours, and when Tor wakes from this nightmare she's going to need your support. This whole thing has broken her; look at her!' They both simultaneously turned to the window. Even heavily sedated, Victoria looked visibly anguished. This final thread had caused her to unravel completely.

Lawrence stared at his wife, his fingers lightly touching the perspex glass.

'We had everything, Ellie,' he said, his voice was low and filled with pain. 'The homes, the cars, the holidays . . . the success! I guess it just wasn't enough . . .'

Ellie quietly closed her eyes. 'There are some things in life money can't buy you, Lol,' she said softly, not wanting to add to his obvious distress.

'Tell me about it.' He dragged his hands down his cheeks again, audibly sucking in air. 'It's going to be OK, right?' he'd turned to her.

'You know it will be,' Ellie raised a small smile. 'You'll *make* it alright. You love her, don't you?'

Lawrence Mayfield hadn't needed to answer her. His impassioned look had said it all.

*

Ellie swung her SLK around the corner of Holland Park with a deft move. She could hardly believe how close she'd come to betraying her own husband in that hotel suite and the thought caused her to bite her lip and groan. Yet even now, after everything, she couldn't quite bring herself to hate Tom. He hadn't known that she and Tor were friends, at least not initially, and could only have discovered this fact on the night of the casino opening. Jesus, what did it matter anymore? He was still a womaniser; a leopard doesn't change its spots, and yet she had sensed there was more of a softness to him now, an understanding that had come with the passing years. He had confessed to her about Loretta and she had felt there was more he wanted to say, much more. Well, whatever it was, she guessed she would never know now. Vinnie was back, and whatever chance she might've had to solve the problem that was Tom Black was over.

*

'Oh Vin!' Ellie practically ran through the door of her immaculate home, so desperate was she for the safety of her husband's arms. She wanted to feel him; to breathe him in and hold him close, reassure herself of her integrity which was, by the skin of her teeth, still intact.

'You're back! I can't tell you how happy I am to see you, darling!' she threw her arms around her husband's neck and felt the stiffness of his shoulders as she embraced him.

'What's wrong?' she said, immediately pulling back from him, her heart beginning to accelerate. Vinnie looked at his wife and felt the coldness that had built within him on his journey home begin to thaw. He loved her so much that for a split second he felt like striking her. How could she have done this to them? She was his girl, his wife. Twenty years . . . twenty beautiful, amazing years together, and the second that piece of shit had re-entered their lives it had all been undone in a second.

It would not be an overestimation to say that Vincent Scott's journey home to the UK had been the worst of his entire life. Twenty-four hours on a private Lear jet, sinking neat Scotch and poring over those candid shots Crosby had provided had been like Chinese water torture. The pictures themselves weren't damning, no suggestion of anything inappropriate, but her face, it had never looked happier; her green eyes bright and smiling, alive with endorphins. The rest had simply compounded his misery; Ellie and Black having lunch, their faces animated, eyes locked upon one another; his wife's arms risen in triumph as she stood at the roulette wheel, Black inches away from her, their bodies dangerously close, to the point he could feel the heat between them. And the worst one of all; a nervous-looking Ellie as she turned to follow Black inside his hotel suite . . . These pictures had taken Vinnie to a place inside his mind where he had sworn he would never go.

But it was the images of Black and his daughter that had left him a broken man. There were reams of them. His baby girl all dressed up like a hooker . . . looking terrified as she talked to a swarthy-faced stranger . . . inside the casino, swinging around a pole, laughing, enjoying herself, her eyes wide and vacant as she writhed up against a small, androgynous-looking girl . . . he didn't recognise her; she had morphed into someone else completely. And then there was Black again. Tess and Black together, animated in conversation, his arm on her shoulder, touching her, his face dangerously close to hers. And finally, all the evidence he'd needed; a dishevelled-looking Tess going into Black's penthouse suite at the Berkeley hotel. Crosby had told him that she had re-emerged some days later; *days*. Vinnie knew what days meant; days also meant nights. And it was this that caused his guts to twist and his heart to turn to stone. Interestingly, there were incriminating shots of Black with Victoria Mayfield too, plenty of them, and Vinnie's heart went out to her husband. Another of Black's casualties.

Vinnie had thrown back another Scotch as he replaced the photographs back inside the manila envelope. Tom Back had certainly had a busy summer, make no mistake. Two families destroyed because of one man's inability to keep it inside his trousers. He wondered, what was it about that man? He couldn't speak for Victoria Mayfield, a woman he had always considered to be a thoroughly decent, loyal, loving wife by all accounts, but his Ellie? He had thought she was above all that.

'You don't seem pleased to see me,' Ellie said tremulously. She had never in her life seen such a cold look in her husband's eyes and it was scaring the shit out of her. She watched him as he silently turned from her and began to fix them both a drink, a Scotch for himself and a gin for her, and felt his palpable disdain as he slowly placed the brown envelope of photos down onto the large glass table. She accepted the glass of clear liquid with her heartbeat thudding in trepidation, not daring to glance at them.

'What are these then, holiday snaps?' her stab at lightening the atmosphere was unwise and fell instantly flat. Vinnie sipped his drink as he watched her coolly. He wanted so much to hear that there had been some dreadful mistake . . . that there was some kind of reasonable explanation for all of this.

Tom Black had destroyed his family; he'd destroyed his life. And boy was he going to pay for it. Of that, Vincent Scott would make damn sure.

'You're really scaring me, Vin,' Ellie said, in an attempt to get him to break his deathly silence.

'Sit down, Ellie,' he said evenly, his voice was tight and authoritative. 'There's something I think you ought to see.'

CHAPTER 79

Tom peered at the BA clerk behind the desk and pasted on a smile as she checked him into the first-class lounge at Gatwick.

'Thank you, sir,' she flashed him a friendly smile as he handed over the necessary documents. 'The flight leaves at 13.25. Is there anything else I can do for you?'

'Actually yes, there is,' Tom nodded, sliding an envelope towards her across the desk. 'I need a courier to deliver this for me as soon as possible, can you arrange it?'

'Of course, sir,' the heavily made-up clerk nodded, batting her fake eyelashes at the handsome older man. 'I'll have it done right away.'

'Thank you . . .' Tom cocked his head to get a better look at her name badge, '. . . Salina,' he winked at her and she felt herself flush. 'It's really quite important, Salina,' he added, sagely.

Making his way through to the first-class lounge, Tom's smile instantly evaporated.

'A Courvoisier,' he said, giving the barman a cursory nod and the man poured him a large measure in silence, sensing not to attempt to engage in conversation.

Throwing it back and immediately requesting another,

Tom wondered how long it would be before the alcohol started to numb the pain. He felt so wracked with anguish that he physically ached. Jack was dead. *Dead*. His only true friend, his best man – in every sense – gone for good. It just seemed so . . . so unreal. He'd seen him less than twenty-four hours ago; Tom had been telling him all about the honeymoon in Antigua, how Loretta had bought some fancy boat to add to her inherited collection. Jack had seemed in good spirits, despite his reluctance to endorse his friend's nuptials. He was even planning to bring some broad as his guest, some little LA blonde who'd been at the casino opening, the one Tom had seen him go home with . . . the one he'd thought for a fleeting moment that he'd recognised. Jack had seemed pretty enamoured with her. 'She's a little on the young side, you know,' he'd almost apologised, 'but hey, a man's gotta do what a man's gotta do, right?' They had both laughed.

Tom struggled to comprehend just how someone could be walking and talking, larger than life one moment, and then the next . . . gone forever. For the first time ever in his life, he blamed himself; he should've insisted his buddy go to the quacks when he'd started coughing like a seal pup all those weeks ago. He should've been looking out for him, like brothers do. And now it was too late; he'd suffered a massive heart attack, one that had killed him instantly. Stone cold dead.

Pressing his fingers into the flesh on his face, Tom felt the wetness of his tears behind his Ray-Bans. There was nothing left for him here now; he'd lost everything. The casino meant nothing without Jack; it had been a shared dream. Jack had found the documents in his desk drawer, the contract Loretta had blackmailed him into signing, and it caused Tom's guts to twist to learn that he'd died with that information in his hands. Was Jack's final thought one of hatred for him, of rage, of disappointment? Had this

383

discovery been the catalyst for his heart to give out? What was it they said; for every action there's a reaction?

A voice came over the intercom system and distracted him from his maudlin thoughts. In a poignant moment of grief he suddenly remembered something his father had once said to him. 'If you don't want to be found, son, make sure you hide in the most obvious place.' Picking up his flight case, and straightening himself out, Tom made his way towards gate number seven with a sense of purpose, oblivious to Lionel Crosby who was watching him from a safe distance.

As far as he was concerned, now that Jack was dead, the deal with Loretta was off.

CHAPTER 80

Loretta attempted to stand, which, thanks to the hand-sewn diamond, gold and crystal embellishment of the heavy, white, crepe-satin Versace couture wedding gown she was wearing, was something of a struggle. It weighed the equivalent of an adolescent child and was so tight that even she debated whether she might make it through the entire occasion without passing out. Strapless, with a plunging bodice that stopped short of her navel and a twenty-foot-long train, the exquisite dress gave the illusion of being entirely back-less thanks to the fine sheer mesh that had been hand-dyed to match her exact skin tone – and it left very little to even the most vivid of imaginations.

'Have the acrobats arrived?' she turned to one of her many assistants, Giordana.

'*Si, si*, Mrs Hassan, please do not worry . . .'

'And the fire-eaters . . . the orchestra? What about the ice luges? Have those edible gold macaroons surfaced yet?'

'*Si, si* . . .' the girl sing-songed as she continued to primp and adjust Loretta's gown, picking at imperfections in the fabric that didn't exist in a bid to justify her position on the payroll as chief dress-fitter. 'It is all under control; please try and relax.'

'Relax!' Loretta roared so loudly that the girl almost swallowed the pins balanced between her lips. '*Cazzo!* You tell me to relax? Do you realise the entire world's press are outside and that there are 500 extremely important guests waiting to experience the finest cuisine and the most sublime entertainment money can afford!' Loretta's make-up artist stood by, brush poised in hand, waiting for the right opportunity to go in and add more mineral powder to her already flawless complexion. She gave Giordana a sympathetic glance.

OK then. Stress yourself out all you want you silly bitch, give yourself a fucking heart attack if you like, see if I give a shit anyway, Giordana silently thought, returning the make-up artist's look with a clandestine roll of the eye.

'Where's the head planner?' Loretta snapped, shooing them both away with a flap of her hands. 'Get that bloody Felicity wassherface woman here right now. And open a bottle of Cristal. I need something to steady my nerves.'

*

Loretta gulped back her champagne like water and continued to stare at herself in the full-length antique Venetian mirror. The dress really was incredibly heavy and cumbersome but who gave a shit when she looked as divine as this? Donatella had created a masterpiece for her and she would thank her by starring in every glossy magazine and newspaper on the planet; the exposure would be worth what the dress cost a hundred times over. She looked like an angel walking on air and Tom wouldn't be able to resist her in such a sublime creation, she felt sure of it. The entire island of Capri was overrun with journalists and TV crews, all scrabbling to get an exclusive on her widely anticipated nuptials, and it was beginning to make Loretta feel uncharacteristically nervous. She wondered if Tom was feeling just as jittery.

She pictured him getting ready in his palatial hotel suite a little further along the island, slipping into his morning suit, his freshly showered body, firm and tanned, and she looked forward to the moment they would be alone together, onboard the Blue Angel, moored on the crystal-blue waters of a private beach in Antigua.

In a rare moment of inner reflection, Loretta realised that deep down this day was all she had ever really wanted. She had the money, and the fame was on its way, and yet it was the day she was to become Mrs Tom Black that gave her the greatest satisfaction of all.

Loretta lit an L&M, her fifth in half an hour, as she opened the old shutters to the enormous rustic villa, and attempted to breathe the warm Italian air into her restricted lungs.

It was an undeniably beautiful day; the cloudless sky a rich azure-blue, the sun high and fierce, perhaps a little too fierce she decided, the lightest of perspiration instantly beginning to form a light oily sheen on her newly botoxed, brushed and polished skin. In the distance, behind the gated enclosure to the castle, she could just about make out the reams of paparazzo, swarms of them, the buzzing hum and screech of their scooters punctuating the almond-scented air as they made camp outside the heavily patrolled castle, and she stood back from the window, lest their long lenses spotted her. She had spent a small fortune on security for today and was pleased to see the helicopter circling above, keeping a close eye on proceedings and making sure no one managed to slip through the net to get a sneak preview of what she intended to be her biggest show-stopping entrance yet.

Blowing smoke rings into the air, Loretta wondered how long it would take before Tom fell back in love with her. She figured it wouldn't be long before some of that Fiorentino charm worked its legendary magic on him once more. Sure, she was older now, but then so was he, and this time she wanted things to be different; this time she vowed that she would allow her husband to see the real her. Loretta closed her eyes in a daydream of her and Tom's future, but the image was instantly replaced by one of Miranda Muldavey instead. Jesus, would that woman's face ever stop stalking her? Loretta sighed. She could not quite dampen the flickering of paranoia that the actress might have been saving herself for an occasion such as this to spectacularly unveil any revenge plan she might be harbouring. No, she wouldn't dare show herself today, not today, of all days, *would she*?

She checked her Cartier watch; Artie Maynard, whom she had asked to do the honour of giving her away, would be on his way over now. In a few moments' time, just after dusk descended, he would link his arm in hers and escort her up the aisle (an aisle that, incidentally, would be scattered with hand-painted, gold-leaf rose petals and lit with over a hundred thousand scented tea lights), and say her carefully chosen vows in front of the crème de la crème of Hollywood and European society. This wedding would make her a household name; set a benchmark in chic, luxury nuptials – the name Loretta Black forever synonymous with style and panache.

Extinguishing her cigarette and scooping up a tuxedo-clad Bambino, she swallowed the dregs of her champagne and took a deep breath; it had been a long day already and she was exhausted, but now it was her time to shine. Loretta Fioretino was ready.

CHAPTER 81

'Oh Artie darling, you're here!' she said, arms outstretched, genuinely thrilled to see her agent looking ever flamboyant in a gold lamé Alexander McQueen suit and couture Philip Treacey hat in the shape of a giant sea creature, balanced precariously on top of his purple rinse.

'What do you think?' Loretta attempted a 360-degree twirl but could only manage 180.

'Darling you look . . . *Magnifico* . . .' he clasped his papery hands together and fought back a tear. The dress was so over the top it made Elton John and Lady GaGa combined look positively demure. But it was spectacular.

Loretta preened, 'You over-emotional old queen, you,' she playfully chided him, 'you'll start me off. Anyway, we have to get a move on, darling,' she continued, 'we're already half an hour late and Tom will be getting worried . . . besides we can't keep the guests waiting too long, or the press for that matter. TMV have paid a small fortune for the honour of watching me say *faccio*.'

*

'You! Lady, what in hell's name is going on?' a rankled guest collared Felicity. 'We've been here over an hour

389

already,' she remarked sourly, adjusting the lapels on her cream YSL tuxedo jacket which displayed the blatant fact that she wasn't wearing much else underneath. She was half hoping they'd be enjoying the first course and entertainment by now; after all, that was the only reason she had come.

'Not long now,' Felicity said, trying to remain upbeat, her sense of impending dread doubling with each passing second. 'Help yourself to more champagne and canapés!' She haphazardly punched Tom's hotel number into her mobile. Where in God's name was he? Maybe he'd had an accident on the way there . . . If the groom was a no-show, she would happily kill him herself. 'Come onnnnn . . .' she said tightly into the receiver as she hit the redial button, 'come onnnnn.'

*

Loretta nervously stood outside the entrance to the pergola and took a sneak peek inside. Even if she said so herself, it really was a breathtaking sight to behold. Two white tigers sat regally either side of the entrance like proud feline security guards, and her harem of white tuxedo-clad hotties stood on display, handing out chilled flutes of vintage Dom Pérignon. Loretta surveyed the collection of guests with unconcealed satisfaction.

'All these wonderful people, Artie,' she gushed, over-whelmed by the sense of occasion. 'Here to watch me take my vows . . . speaking of which, shouldn't I think about making an entrance now? Tom will think I've got cold feet if we leave it much longer.'

'Shouldn't we wait for Felicity?' Artie suggested. 'She said she would give us the cue when it was time . . .'

Ignoring him, Loretta pulled the curtains back and gave the nod to the conductor to begin playing.

'About bloody time too,' a disgruntled guest grumbled

as she made her grand entrance to the rapturous sounds of applause and cheers.

Hearing the sound of the orchestra kick in, Felicity Montgomery-Philips' sphincter muscle nearly fell out of her backside. She sprinted through the seated guests, tearing her Alice Temperley dress as she went. She'd given Artie Maynard strict instructions not to allow Loretta into the venue until she gave him the nod – stupid old poof! This was nothing short of catastrophic.

Loretta had never felt more radiant and happy as she did walking past the adoring eyes of her guests.

'Stop!' Felicity said, causing Loretta to recoil in alarm and drop Artie's arm. 'Please, Loretta, stop!'

'What in hell's name are you doing?' Loretta hissed, baring her teeth at the woman. What was the meaning of this, accosting her as she made her grand entrance, in front of all the guests! She would fire her on the spot, not pay the damn bitch a cent of her fee for this outrage.

Felicity signalled to the conductor to cut the music by running her hand vertically across her throat. The guests began to twitter, straining their necks to see what was occurring.

'You had better tell me what the fuck is going on, Felicity,' Artie whispered, his eyes bulging from their sockets. They were halfway down the aisle now, the white marble pillared altar that Loretta had specially commissioned to be made, almost in sight.

'What is your fucking problem?' Loretta cursed the woman while simultaneously smiling graciously at the line of seated guests opposite, who were gawping mawkishly.

'It's Tom,' Felicity said tremulously, biting down on her bottom lip so hard that she actually drew blood. Loretta's initial fury had dissipated and had now escalated into a seizure of abject panic, with hysteria hot on its tail.

Felicity blinked at her client with watery eyes. The woman

was an absolute nightmare on legs, but she didn't deserve this. What she was about to say, no bride should ever have to hear, even an ageing, garrulous one like her.

Loretta instinctively grasped on to Artie for support. 'What *about* Tom?' she snapped, her eyes narrowing, her enormous chest heaving up and down like an accordion.

Artie felt his stomach lurch as Felicity took a deep breath. 'I'm afraid he's not coming.'

CHAPTER 82

'Jesus Mum, you look like shit!' the words had left Tess's lips before she'd had a chance to realise what she was saying. Ignoring her, Ellie pushed her way into her apartment, clutching a large brown envelope between her shaking hands. Her mother's face was pale, her expression ashen, and suddenly Tess was genuinely worried.

'What's happened? Is it Daddy? Is someone sick?' Tess's eyes searched her mother's for clues. 'You're scaring me . . .'

Ellie's eyes darted around the apartment for clues, anything to suggest that Tom had been there. It was pristine, save for the odd stain on the sofa and a few suspect marks on the rugs. Tom had helped Tess organise an industrial clean-up, restoring it back to its former glory after the mess she and Monique had made of the place, and she had vowed she would never treat it with such disrespect ever again. It was a shame really, Tess thought, if only Monique had hung around a little longer, then she too would have been free of Marco for good. She wondered where her French friend might be in the world right now and despite the fact that Monique had betrayed her, she couldn't help but wish her luck.

Ellie blinked at her daughter and tried not to imagine what had taken place between her and Tom in this very apartment; she imagined them on the sofa, tearing at each other's clothes in haste; Tom's naked body, a body she herself was familiar with, as it blithely pumped away on top of Tess . . . Ellie thought she might throw up. *Her own flesh and blood, her blood father*. Because deep down, Ellie knew that's what Tom really was. She didn't need some DNA test; she had known all along.

She swallowed back bile. It was all so sordid, so disgusting . . . This was what became of secrets and lies, she told herself, desperately trying to banish the sordid images from her mind. *What goes on in the dark always comes out in the light*, that's what her mother always said, and now Ellie understood.

'What have you done, Tess?' Ellie said, tears streaking her face as she seized her daughter roughly by her arms and began to violently shake her, 'what in God's name have you done?'

CHAPTER 83

Ellie tore through a red light, hearing the sound of cars honking their horns in objection, her hand on her daughter's knee as she accelerated.

'You have to tell your father everything you've told me, Tess. About what happened in Ibiza, about Monique and Marco and . . . Tom.' Her mother's voice was desperately urgent and she wiped away the tears that hadn't stopped flowing since Tess had confessed everything to her. Tess silently nodded.

'I'm not angry with you, Tess,' Ellie said, fighting back her own tears and losing the battle.

'Even if you were I would deserve it,' Tess replied. 'What I did in Ibiza . . . what happened . . . it was disgusting Mum. And now I'm no good, a used-up slag that no one will ever want.'

Ellie felt a little whimper escape her lips involuntarily.

'Oh baby, please, you mustn't say things like that, please. You are none of those things. Promise me you will never say anything like that again?'

Tess began to sob into her hands. Confessing everything to her mother had opened the floodgates and now she couldn't seem to close them again.

'Listen to me,' Ellie took one hand from the wheel and grabbed her daughter's wrist.

'Listen to me, we are going to get through this, OK? Me, you and Daddy, I promise you, look at me, Tess – I swear. I just wish . . . oh Tess, I just wish that you'd come to me, talked to me. I knew that something had happened, that there was something wrong . . . I could've helped you baby . . .'

'I was ashamed!' Tess cried. 'I brought it all on myself Mum, the drink, the drugs. And then after that night at the villa, I couldn't see a way out, I had to get a job at the casino to try and pay him off. He said he would send you and Daddy the tape . . . and then Tom, Tom was like a knight in shining armour, he *saved* me, but we were never lovers. I swear it.' Tess had wondered why it was that her mother had been so vehemently insistent on knowing all about her relationship with Tom Black, whether it was purely platonic or otherwise. The age gap, she assumed.

Ellie listened to her daughter's impassioned words with a heavy heart.

'Believe me darling, you're not the only woman to have made mistakes – Lord knows I've made a few myself – and believe me, you won't be the last either.' They pulled up at a set of traffic lights and Ellie looked over at her. 'You've made mistakes too, big ones? Really?' Tess looked over at her mother. She couldn't imagine her mother had ever put a foot wrong her entire life.

'Yes, honey,' Ellie softly snorted, 'really.' She only wished she could tell her the truth about Tom but she knew that would mean destroying everything they had together as a family. 'You want to hear one of my secrets?' She turned to her daughter, her heart breaking over the hell she must've been though at the hands of that evil fucker Marco and his depraved friends. Her darling baby . . . she never wanted to let her out of her sight again.

'Yes,' Tess croaked.

'I used to be a stripper,' Ellie said, keeping her eyes straight on the road, 'in Las Vegas, before I met your father.' She quickly glanced sideways at Tess. 'In fact, it was while I was dancing in a club that I met him.'

Tess was so dumbfounded that she instantly stopped crying.

'You? *You* were a stripper?'

'Don't look so surprised,' Ellie managed a small smile. 'I had the figure for it back then, and actually I was bloody good at it. Made half a decent living on a good week.'

Tess was shocked into submission.

'Your grandmother and I, we lived in Vegas for a time. She was a stripper too and I ended up in the clubs, just like her,' she paused for a moment as if to give Tess time to digest what she was saying. 'I was in love with a man, a man who broke my heart into a thousand little pieces. And then I met your father and he helped me put them back together again . . . so you see, Tess, I know what it is to make mistakes. I was just like you once; young, feisty, thought I knew everything there was to know. I never listened to my mother either, but I tell you one thing; everything that woman ever said to me was right. She may have ended up a washed-up old drunk, but by God, she was always right.'

397

CHAPTER 84

As she drove and Tess gently slumbered on the passenger seat, Ellie thought about the earlier conversation she'd had with Vinnie back at the house.

'I've loved you for twenty years, Eleanor. Two decades . . .'

'Loved?' her voice was tremulous, conscious of the past tense.

'I trusted you, God help me but I did.'

'It's not what it looks like, Vin . . .' she'd realised how pathetic it had sounded, but it was still the truth.

Vincent Scott snorted derisively.

'Please Ellie, have a little dignity, at least,' he'd thrown the photos across the floor, the sound of them sliding along polished wood setting her teeth on edge.

'You were spying on me?' she'd said, her hurt audible. This was Vincent Scott, the hard-nosed powerful businessman, the man from the boardroom she never got to see. 'You didn't trust me.'

'I didn't trust *him*, Ellie,' he'd responded coldly. 'And it seems I had good reason to listen to my instincts.'

'I haven't betrayed you, Vin.'

He'd laughed then and it was as if he'd chopped her in half.

God how her mother had been right about the Blacks; 'ruiners,' that's what she'd called them all those years ago.

'I should have dealt with this years ago,' he'd said, his voice loaded with painful resignation. 'I should have put a bullet through that man's head after that night . . . after Livedon . . .'

'Don't say things like that, Vin,' she'd pleaded. He felt like a stranger and it scared her.

'That man has blighted our entire life,' he'd shot back. 'And I'm not going to stand by and let him do the same to our daughter, Ellie. I'll see him dead first. You hear me, dead!'

'Vin please,' Ellie had begged him.

'I'm not your equal,' she wasn't sure if she was making any sense, but the words were escaping from her lips, the truth finally revealing itself to them both. 'I was a working-class girl from the wrong side of the tracks and you were an upper-class billionaire . . .'

'And Tom Black . . . where does he fit into all of this?' Ellie had sighed.

'Tom was my brother . . . my first lover. Seeing him again . . . it reminded me of who I once was, who I might've been.'

'"Might've been"?' Vinnie snorted in derision, 'what, a ravaged old soak like your mother?'

He didn't understand. Hell, she didn't really understand herself.

'Some people were born great, Vin,' she'd said quietly, 'but some have greatness thrust upon them,' she'd looked up at him, her emerald eyes glassy with tears. 'Maybe I just wasn't born to be great.' Her voice cracked with emotion and it had taken Vincent Scott every fibre of strength in his body not to go to her. 'What do we do about Tess?' he'd eventually said, his tone softer now, more resigned. 'You do realise what this means? If these pictures tell the truth then our daughter . . .' he turned away from her, poured himself another Scotch to try and distract himself from the unpalatable truth. 'It's *incest*, Ellie.' The words made him feel physically sick.

'You don't think I know that!' she'd shrieked, not wanting to even entertain such a repulsive thought. Ellie felt a silent tear escape from her eye. Finally, the elephant in the room had been acknowledged. It was something they should've faced years ago, but instead they had buried their heads in the perfect golden sands of their privileged existence.

'I have to talk to Tess,' she'd said quietly, feeling a strange sense of relief, almost like a weight had been lifted. 'Those photos of me are misleading, I did not betray you. You have to believe me, please.'

Vincent, his whole world in tatters, his entire being flooded with bitter thoughts of hatred and revenge, heart hardening like fired clay, nodded at his wife.

For Tom Black's sake, he hoped that she was right.

CHAPTER 85

'Vinnie,' Ellie called her husband's name with a sense of urgency as she walked into the empty living room of their Holland Park home. The TV was on, which was unusual and she went to switch it off but something caught her attention. A picture of Loretta Fiorentino in a ghastly-looking wedding dress.

'It was billed as the celebrity wedding of the year,' the pretty presenter explained, making it sound more like a trailer to a film than a news link, 'with over 500 VIP guests waiting for the procedure to start, the bride looked increasingly distressed as she stood at the altar in a Versace couture dress, waiting for her groom to appear . . .' She paused for effect. 'As hundreds of catering staff prepared the six-course gastronomic wedding breakfast, London casino owner, Tom Black was nowhere to be seen . . .'

'We just can't imagine what went wrong,' an unnamed female guest spoke directly to the camera, her silk, lime-green Cavalli gown flapping almost gleefully in the Capri breeze. 'I mean, one minute we were all enjoying the amuse-bouche, well, tolerating it to be fair, when the bride turned up *sans* groom. I mean, can you just imagine the humiliation?'

Ellie gasped at the TV screen, mouth agape as she watched the drama unfold in real time, a shaky camera picturing

Loretta, flanked by security guards and her infamous agent, Artie Maynard, as they attempted to shield her from the media furore that had exploded around her.

Ellie turned to look at her daughter and Tess shrugged.

'He never said anything to me about getting married,' she proclaimed. 'Please Mum, will you tell me exactly what the hell's going on?'

Ignoring her, Ellie stalked from the room.

'Ah, Mrs Scott,' Angelika, one of their housekeepers said with a smile as she almost ran into her. 'There's been a special delivery for you,' she handed Ellie a small white envelope and instantly recognising the handwriting as Tom's, clumsily tore it open.

Jack's dead. I have to see you one last time. The Blue Angel; St John's Bay, Antigua. Please be there, Ellie. One last time. Tx

Jack's dead! Ellie felt her heart bounce around her rib cage as she placed the envelope in her back pocket. 'Have you seen my husband, Angelika? Is Vinnie still at home?'

'No, Mrs Scott,' Angelika replied casually, 'he's already left. I thought you knew . . .'

Ellie turned to her sharply, '. . . left for where?'

'Mr Scott . . . he . . . he chartered the plane,' she blinked up at her boss, wondering if she was now in some kind of trouble.

'Do you know where to?' Ellie's voice caused Angelika to panic. She shook her head. 'I'm, I'm sorry Mrs Sc—'

'Think, Angelika!' Ellie screamed, causing the young housekeeper to bite her lip and take a step back. 'Where did he say he was going?'

'I . . . I overheard him saying something to Mr Mayfield about Antigua . . . some business to attend to . . .'

'Mr Mayfield? Lawrence Mayfield was here?' Ellie's heart was galloping like a racehorse, the adrenalin surge making her feel giddy.

'Yes, Mrs Scott. The pair of them left together in a bit of a hurry . . . is everything alright?' It was a stupid question judging by the look on her boss's face but Angelika felt compelled to ask nonetheless.

Ellie tore down the stairs into her husband's study and picked up the phone, a terrified and confused Tess two steps behind her.

'What's going on, Mum?' she pleaded once more.

'Yes, hello, is that Malcolm . . . yes, Malcolm it's Mrs Scott. I need you to book me on the next flight to Antigua – urgently! Oh that's brilliant, thanks,' she said breathlessly as she abruptly hung up.

'I'll help you pack,' Tess said. She could tell by her mother's face that it was futile asking questions.

Ellie nodded. She only prayed she wouldn't be too late.

CHAPTER 86

The sound of fabric ripping caused Artie Maynard to wince and he could do no more than watch as Loretta began tearing at her hideously expensive wedding dress, crystals and diamonds flying through the air in a glittery shower.

'*Io sono gong di ucciderlo*, Artie, *uccidilo*!' she was ranting in her mother tongue, Bambino yapping at her heels as she attacked the dress, the bodice ripping like flesh. 'Get this hideous thing off of me, Artie, for God's sake get it off me!'

Artie jumped to attention and began wrestling with the heavy fabric. It took every bit of strength he had to undo the myriad buttons until she was standing there in her lace Myla underwear, the dress a crumpled pool of shredded cream couture at her diamond-encrusted Jimmy Choo-clad feet.

'I will *kill* him!' she screamed so loudly that Bambino shot underneath the bed for cover. 'I will have him lined up against the wall and executed!' Loretta tore open a packet of L&M and lit one with a visibly shaking hand.

'How could he do this to me, Artie?' she wailed. 'How could that bastard do this to me in front of all those people . . . all those press . . . ?'

'Look at it this way,' he was busy pouring them both a large brandy from the extensive bar, 'at least they'll stop using the "ex-porn star" prefix now.' Artie inwardly winced, wondering if he'd actually just said what he thought aloud. To his surprise, Loretta began to laugh.

'Every cloud, eh Artie?' she snorted as they both collapsed into hysterics, albeit Artie more nervously.

'They'll replace "ex-porn star" with "jilted bride" instead, or maybe they will simply use both! "Ex-porn star turned jilted-bride, Loretta Hassan!"' Loretta's mirth had tipped over into hysteria and she was cackling manically, her raw emotions unravelling. 'I bet they will still spell my name wrong as well, *those bastards*!' Her tone suddenly switched to demonic, eyes bulging from their sockets, her airbrushed make up now reminiscent of something from a Bacon painting. Loretta swiped the brandy from Artie's hands and began swigging it straight from the bottle. Her phone beeped suddenly, alerting her to a text message, and she sprinted across the room, snatching it up.

I'm sorry, Loretta, the deal's off. No hard feelings. I'm just not the marrying kind. T.

Artie Maynard watched through pitiful eyes as his client collapsed to the floor in a heap. She was wailing, rambling and cursing in Italian, teetering on the edge of a complete meltdown. She looked her age now, he thought, old and small, less threatening, and he saw a desperate vulnerability to her for the very first time. He guessed by the looks of it the text had not been welcome news.

'Get it down you, darling,' he said softly, watching as she threw back more brandy, spilling it down her face as she drank from the bottle, 'it'll do you good.'

The internal phone rang again and he picked it up.

'. . . It's off,' he whispered into the mouthpiece, '. . . the groom's a no-show. I don't know . . . tell them the groom's been kidnapped by aliens, there's been a plane crash . . .

405

anything! Just get rid of them. No . . . I'll deal with the press, leave those bastards to me . . . and send a doctor, will you? I've a feeling we're going to need one before the night's out.'

Loretta heard the media circus taking place outside her bedroom window. They were screaming her name, calling out to her, desperate for an update, a quote, anything to satisfy their thirst for the unfolding tragedy.

She had promised them a show today, and boy, had she delivered. Her life, and reputation, what there was left of it, was in abject ruins; she would be a laughing stock the world over, a figure of ridicule and pity – even more so than she already knew. Loretta's thoughts turned to Tom. Had he planned to humiliate her all along? Did he despise her so much that he would see fit to destroy her in the worst way imaginable? Loretta felt her anguish dissipate into a white-hot anger; a hatred so intense it felt acidic in her guts.

'Make them go away, Artie,' Loretta's voice was hoarse from screaming . . .

'Leave it with me,' he said gently, careful not to say anything that might push her over the edge. He'd seen some shitty tricks in his time – infidelities with minors, straight married guys being outed by their gay lovers on TV – but this was a first. Still, if they played their cards right they could turn this mess round to their fiscal advantage. He knew Loretta wouldn't see it right now, but given time she may well warm to the idea that all this could prove very lucrative for her career. After all, who didn't love a tragedy, and more importantly a victim? Women would empathise with her after this, giving her the potential to earn herself a whole new legion of fans. Every chat show host on the planet would want her in the hot seat, recounting the gory details of her brutal abandonment at the altar . . . hell, it might even breathe a new lease of life into her acting career.

'So then my darling,' Artie said, his mood suddenly lifted by such prospectively lucrative thoughts, 'anything you want me to say? You know they'll never fuck off without a quote . . .'

Loretta had stopped crying now, her eyes narrowed into menacing slits, dark as onyx, blazing with thoughts of retribution. Picking up her tiny dog and simultaneously lighting another L&M she looked at her flamboyant agent, her lips forming a cruel thin line.

'Tell them there's been an accident,' she said coldly, 'and that the groom is dead.'

CHAPTER 87

'Thank you,' Ellie said, tipping the porter as he placed her Louis Vuitton trunk down onto the decked wooden floor of the luxury villa. It was dawn and she threw open the wooden plantation shutters, squinting as shards of sunlight beamed into the room, bouncing off the white walls like lasers. The view was astounding; miles of ocean stretched out before her, seamlessly blending into a sugar-white shoreline.

Inside the villa, the perfectly made bed with its 300-count cotton sheets looked inviting, but she knew attempting sleep would be futile. She would have time for sleep later; once she'd seen Tom and once she was sure her husband hadn't made good on his threats.

The plane journey had given Ellie time to reflect, and no matter which direction she came at it from she couldn't believe her husband was capable of hurting another human being, let alone murdering one. But she had seen another side of Vinnie back at the house; a darker side that had scared her.

She struggled to dampen her own anger at the thought of how Vinnie had put a PI on her tail. How dare he! Someone had been *watching* her, taking clandestine shots as she'd gone about her daily business, and the very idea made her feel violated. She figured the PI must still be on Tom's trail too; after all, how could Vinnie possibly know he had been headed for Antigua? With a heavy heart she wondered if any of them could come back from this; her and Vinnie and Tess. She had not wanted to leave her daughter in London, not after learning the horrors she'd endured, horrors that Tom incidentally, had pretty much single-handedly put a stop to, but what choice did she have? She had to get to Vinnie before he got to Tom, before he made a dreadful mistake . . .

Ellie buried her head in her hands. There was an unborn child mixed up in all this, an innocent, and she only hoped that Lawrence Mayfield wasn't about to become complicit in something he too would later regret.

Ellie thought of the Capri footage she'd seen on the TV and imagined Loretta, alone up in that castle, her panic rising with every passing second of her groom's absence. A woman like Loretta Fiorentino wouldn't take this lying down, she would be baying for Tom's blood. A spiteful and envious woman Loretta might be, but Ellie knew that underneath it all she'd truly loved Tom Black. They all had. Like a pied piper, he had led them all in a merry dance down a path of destruction. A path she was now convinced would lead to his own.

CHAPTER 88

'There's got to be a hundred boats out there,' Lawrence Mayfield said, dropping the binoculars to his side, a little crestfallen. 'How the hell will we know which one is which? We're going to need to get closer.'

Vincent Scott murmured his agreement.

'We will just have to hire our own yacht for the day, won't we? See if we can't do a little *fishing* while we're at it.'

'Hmm,' Lawrence agreed, peering through the binoculars once more. 'Such a beautiful place,' he mused, 'shame we're here on such unpleasant business.'

Lawrence Mayfield had been shocked to the core as he'd looked through the wallet of photographs Vincent Scott had handed him.

'It brings me no pleasure for you to see these, Lawrence,' he'd said gravely, 'but as one man to another I think you have a right . . .'

'Jesus, no . . . not Ellie as well, *and* Tess?' Lawrence had shaken his head in dismay. Lawrence tried to banish the images of his wife and Tom Black together. Images that had tormented his vivid imagination ever since he'd discovered the dreadful truth. His wife, his Tor, and another man; *fucking*. He felt physically sick, like someone had punched him full force in the stomach. That bastard had sullied his wife, sullied his whole goddamn life! What they'd had, him and Tor, it had been good and right and pure. And now, thanks to that filthy philandering bastard, it was dirty and diseased; destroyed.

By way of self-protection, Lawrence had decided to lay the blame for all of this squarely at Black's treacherous feet. Tor had been ill, depressed and vulnerable, and that slimy, good-for-nothing piece of shit had sniffed her out like a wounded animal; he'd sensed an opportunity and exploited it in the worst way imaginable. A bastard like that needed to be taught a lesson. It was for this reason that Lawrence Mayfield was prepared to leave his wife behind in a hospital bed and join Scott on his crusade to even the score; after all, he had to be seen to do *something*. Anyway, Tor was tanked up to the eyeballs on tranquilisers and would be out of it for days. Enough time for him to meet the man who had detonated a bomb in his life . . .

Scott had sounded cold and calculated as he had revealed the plan he had in mind. Listening to him had hardly been a revelation; Lawrence had always suspected that Scott could be a ruthless bastard himself when the situation called for it.

'We'll have lunch down at the harbour, the seafood place,' Vinnie suggested. 'Maybe see if we can't get ourselves a boat for the afternoon and pay our friend, Mr Black, a little visit. I get the feeling he's the type who appreciates surprises . . . Do you like the sound of that?' He was smiling, but it did not reach his eyes, and Lawrence Mayfield suddenly felt a little sliver of fear settle upon his stomach.

'Right you are.' Lawrence agreed with a tremulous smile. After all, it was too late to back out now, wasn't it?

CHAPTER 89

'Under no circumstances am I to be disturbed,' Loretta addressed the desk clerk. She was incognito, dressed in a dark wig and oversized sunglasses, a colourful Hermès head scarf tied underneath her chin, Jackie O-style. 'I've had a long flight and would like to be left alone if that's possible. I will phone down if I need anything.'

'Of course Mrs . . .' the young desk clerk looked down at the woman's check-in details, '. . . Smith. We pride ourselves on our privacy and discretion here at La Marina. If there is anything I can do for you . . .'

'Thank you,' she said.

The wedding might be off, but Loretta had decided that the honeymoon was definitely still on. No one would think to look for her here, least of all the goddamn paparazzo. No one besides Tom, and now Artie Maynard, knew of their honeymoon destination and she was happy to keep it that way. She had entrusted Artie with her location in case of emergency – though frankly she couldn't imagine there being a greater emergency than the one she currently faced.

'It's the best idea, darling,' Artie had vehemently nodded. 'Go into hiding . . . give me a chance to get to grips on a little damage limitation. It'll be yesterday's news by the time you're back.'

Loretta knew he was soft-soaping her. The press would be all over this news story like a cheap suit for weeks, maybe even months, to come. She would never live it down. Loretta wondered where that snivelling little bastard, Tom, was right now. Unaware of Jack's sudden demise, she imagined the pair of them had snuck off together somewhere in the States. Perhaps it had been Jack who'd talked Tom out of marrying; maybe he'd forgiven him for his costly flutter much more readily than Loretta had given him credit for.

The idea of such pre-meditated treachery caused her already hot blood to reach boiling point. They were no doubt laughing themselves hoarse right now, sniggering at the wretched TV footage of her total public humiliation; enjoying a sweet moment of schadenfreude at her expense.

'Could you arrange for my luggage to be taken up to my suite?' Loretta enquired politely.

'Of course, Mrs Smith. If you wouldn't mind signing the guest register . . .'

Loretta nodded with a small smile as she took a Mont Blanc pen from her Mui Mui purse – she always preferred to use her own ink – and went to write her pseudonym in the book. And then she saw it; her eyes widening in disbelief as she read the name.

'*Io non credo che cazzo*! I don't fucking believe it!' Loretta whispered underneath her breath, clutching the edge of the desk for support as her entire body flooded with adrenaline, her heart knocking against her ribcage like a demented animal in a cage. A small smile crept across her lips as she read the signature again.

Tom Black was a dead man walking.

CHAPTER 90

'Wakey-wakey,' Vincent Scott walked through the door with a self-satisfied grin on his face. 'Get up, get showered and get your stuff, I've got us a boat for the afternoon.'

Lawrence Mayfield scratched his bare chest and sat up, trying not to think about what the day might have in store. He had awoken with a terrible sense of unease, as if they were on the precipice of some dreadful event taking place. Following Black to Antigua had seemed like such a grand idea the day before when his grief and anger had been at its peak, but now, after a decent night's sleep and his emotions slightly less frenetic, Lawrence wondered whether it had been such a good idea to come here after all. He'd done exactly the same thing that had arguably contributed towards this whole momentous fucking chaos in the first place; he'd run away in the opposite direction from Tor when she'd needed him most, deserted her in that hospital bed, distraught, alone, and pregnant with their child. What the fuck was wrong with him?

Lawrence got up from the bed, naked save for his black boxer shorts, and took a slug of Evian from the bedside table.

'So what's the plan, Vinnie?' he said, padding over

towards the bathroom. 'I mean, once we've found Black . . . what then?'

'Then we talk to him,' Vinnie called back to him, making his way out onto the sun terrace, the gentle breeze blowing the thin muslin curtains, causing them to flutter in a ghostly manner. Lawrence turned the power shower on and began searching through Vincent's wash bag for a razor. He had come to Antigua in the clothes he stood up in and little else. Vincent, however, seemed far more prepared.

'I'm going to make Tom Black disappear,' Vinnie said, adding, 'this time for good.'

Fishing around in the wash bag, Lawrence finally located a razor. And that's when he saw the gun. He stared at it for a moment, and rubbed his bleary eyes, just to make sure it was what he thought it was. Lawrence looked up to see Vincent Scott standing in the bathroom doorway, watching him carefully.

'So, Mayfield,' he said coldly, 'are you in, or are you out?'

CHAPTER 91

Lunch around the pool had been a disaster. Despite the plush sun lounger, her own private butler, and platter after delicious platter of Caribbean cuisine, Loretta could not relax.

She looked out across the bay at the myriad boats and yachts moored on the crystalline, sun-dappled water. That bastard was out there somewhere, on the boat she had bought for them, she felt sure of it. That he even had the audacity to come here made her want to run a knife through him a thousand times over, and watch him bleed out in front of her like a stuck pig. This was supposed to have been *their* honeymoon! Tom must've thought he'd been so clever, she thought sourly; after all, no one in their right mind would ever suspect he would actually have the gall to skip the wedding and come straight on his honeymoon. Loretta, however, wasn't surprised.

The man's hardiness was mind-blowing. Did he expect to get away with this? Was there no end to his arrogance and audacity? Well, if there wasn't, there soon would be. Loretta was going to make sure of it.

Loretta strutted from the sun terrace and made her way back to her hotel suite. The heat was beginning to get to

416

her and besides, she needed to prepare. That evening she was planning a surprise for her runaway groom, one that would shock him to his very core.

*

'*Merde*,' Loretta hissed as she fashioned her wet hair up into a turban with a fresh white towel. Who was that knocking at the door? She had specifically instructed the desk clerk that she was not to be disturbed. Did these imbeciles not understand English?

'I'm coming,' she snapped, swinging the door open, the L&M falling from her lips as her eyes widened in shock.

'Hello Loretta,' the voice said. 'Well, aren't you going to invite me in?'

CHAPTER 92

'How did you find me?' Loretta stumbled backwards into the hotel room as if she had been winded by a blunt object. Jesus Christ, what was *she* doing here?

Miranda casually brushed past Loretta into her sumptuous island retreat, as if she were an expected guest, and promptly admired the view from the vast, open shutters.

'I've always loved Antigua,' she wistfully announced. 'My ex-husband and I had a place on the island for a while, not far from here. I gave it to him in our divorce settlement and he promptly sold it. He never did have an appreciation of true style . . .' her voice trailed off into a whisper.

Loretta's chest felt tight, her hands shaking violently as she dragged heavily on a cigarette. They were face-to-face at last. And what a face it was, she observed, unable to prevent herself from staring at her dead husband's horrific handiwork.

Unable to stand it any longer, Loretta looked away sharply. She had been expecting this visit for months; but here, now, when she was at her most vulnerable and prone? *Mamma mia*! The woman's timing was impeccable. She would have Artie Maynard's balls on a plate for this – treacherous old poof. He was the only other person who knew where she was hiding out and he had given her up to Miranda Muldavey in the blink of a watery eye. Was there no one left on this earth who wasn't prepared to betray her?

'I'll call security . . .' Loretta warned her tremulously, edging towards the phone, cigarette ash falling to the floor.

'And why would you want to do that?' Miranda turned, looking genuinely surprised.

'What do you want, Muldavey?' Loretta asked coldly, her tone masking the fear she felt in the pit of her belly. 'Have you come to gloat at my misfortune, revel in my humiliation? Well, take a good look!'

'May I sit down?' Miranda asked. It was hard to deny that even with the face the way it was, Miranda Muldavey still had inimitable presence. She filled the whole room somehow, diminutive though she was. It was the kind of presence that demanded respect.

'I didn't know he was going to do it you know,' Loretta blathered, picking up her dog and squeezing him to her voluminous chest tightly, for support. 'You have to believe me. Ramsey . . . it was entirely his sick little idea . . .'

Miranda sat on the rattan sofa, still as a stone. There was a long pause before she spoke.

'How do you feel right now, Loretta?' Miranda asked from underneath the brim of her wide straw hat. 'I'm interested to know; truthfully.'

Convinced that had Muldavey been here in an assassin's role she would've done the job by now, Loretta sighed heavily. So the woman wanted a little schadenfreude. She supposed she could hardly blame her.

'I have been stood up at the altar, Miranda, by the only man I have ever genuinely loved in my lifetime. A man, incidentally, whose company I practically had to *buy* before he would have anything to do with me,' she swallowed hard and turned towards the actress, facing her. 'I am not young anymore, Miranda,' Loretta remarked, her candidness proving surprisingly cathartic, 'I cannot keep bouncing back . . . Loretta Fioretino, former porn star and jilted bride . . . I am a laughing stick . . .'

'Stock,' Miranda gently corrected her. 'It's laughing *stock*.'

Loretta shook her head; she had no fight left in her.

'He's humiliated me in front of the world . . . so if it's revenge you are after, I can think of none better than that, can you?'

'So you're filled with hatred? Wracked with thoughts of revenge?' Miranda nodded sagely, like a doctor debating a patient's symptoms. 'I understand,' she said. 'After what your late husband did I thought *my* life was over too.'

Loretta lowered her head.

'You know, we are not so different, you and I,' Miranda stood now, removing her hat and sunglasses, forcing Loretta to look at her face, 'we are both women who have traded on our looks, women for whom beauty and youth has meant everything. Please look at me, Loretta,' the actress implored, and it sounded so heartfelt that Loretta felt she had no choice but to meet her eye. 'I bear the scars of your late husband's evil, abhorrent crimes. This is what I see every day when I look in the mirror. I am a stranger to myself.'

'Would it make any difference if I said I was sorry for what he did?' Loretta asked. It was as close to a genuine apology as Loretta had ever come to make. It had been a truly appalling crime against an innocent woman and she only wished she could go back in time and ensure it had never been committed. 'Ramsey, silly old lovesick fool that he was . . . he would've done *anything* to make me happy . . . you see he thought . . . I always said . . .'

'I am not here for explanations,' Miranda cut her off.

'Then please, tell me, why *are* you here?' Loretta felt herself drowning in despair. She wasn't emotionally strong enough to handle this right now.

420

'Actually, I'm here to thank you . . . well, to thank your former husband, really.'

'Thank me . . . thank *him*?' Was she insane? The woman was clearly disturbed, and for a second Loretta wondered if she might suddenly be about to whip out a weapon in a moment of frenzied madness after all.

'Before this . . .' Miranda drew a circle around her face with a pointed fingernail, 'I had success, huge success, but I was lost to vanity,' she made her way over to the window, looking out towards the magnificent view of the bay from the balcony once more. 'I felt I needed the adoration of strangers just to stop myself from feeling worthless. I was obsessed with growing older, looking older, of missing out to someone younger.' She swiftly turned back to face Loretta. 'You see, in the end I didn't even care about the scripts, or whether my performances were particularly noteworthy, just so long as I looked beautiful and got my face in the papers. I was a narcissist, self-obsessed, an empty shell. And then your husband did this to me and it changed my life – for the better.'

Loretta was listening intently, gripped by the actress's impassioned speech. 'I can tell by the look on your face, Loretta, that you find this difficult to believe, but trust me; this 'tragedy' or however the press refer to it, has been the making of me. It has forced me to accept myself for who I am on the inside, and worry less about the outside. It's been the greatest lesson I have ever learned; the most humbling, and undoubtedly the most important.'

Loretta was lost for words. For once in her life she had no idea what to say next.

'I understand your pain,' Miranda continued. 'Above all people, I know the agony of humiliation and rejection, how it feels to be a figure of ridicule and pity. All I ask of you is that you hold onto those emotions, understand them, allow yourself to experience them, *feel* them . . . because you are going to need them.'

'Need them? You think they will make me a better person, like you?' Loretta snorted, unable to keep the disdain from her voice.

Miranda smiled softly, her kaftan gently lifting in the breeze that was blowing in through the open shutters.

'Artie said you were a jaded woman, just like I used to be . . .'

Loretta lit another cigarette and rolled her eyes.

'Yes, well, I'll be giving him his marching orders when I see him, treacherous old queen. After everything I've been through . . .'

Miranda's smile developed into a laugh.

'Don't be too hard on him,' he wanted to come here himself, impart the good news in person, but I insisted on coming, to see you face-to-face.'

'Good news?' Loretta squawked. She was growing tired of all this talking in riddles. She had something far more important, far more pressing to attend to and now that she suspected Muldavey probably wasn't here to cause her any immediate harm, she wanted to get on with the job in hand. 'And ask me what?'

'. . . To ask you to be me.'

Loretta shut her eyes and shook her head.

'I'm sorry but you are not making any sense . . .'

Miranda smiled.

'They are making a film of my life, Loretta,' she slowly explained, 'a biopic. A big production that myself and Ridley Scott are jointly directing, and I want *you* to play *me*.'

Loretta blinked at her, incredulous. Had she heard this correctly?

'I can think of no one better; after all, we are of a similar age, physical build . . . and now, after this experience, this humiliation and despair, I feel you have the depth of understanding you'll need to give a convincing performance.'

Loretta was so dumbfounded she had to hold onto the edge of the Lloyd Loom chair for support.

'I realise it might have come as a bit of a shock, but I do hope you'll give it due consideration. This could make your career, Loretta, buy back some of that adulation and respect you so desperately crave. It may even help you to realise that you don't actually need it to be truly happy . . .' she glanced at her stunned expression and smiled. 'Of course I thought about playing myself, but all things considered, I think I would prefer to be behind the camera rather than in front of it this time. It'll be my swansong, before I retire gracefully. I have enough money and like I said, I no longer feel the desire for public adulation . . .'

Loretta's mind was spinning like a top in all directions. A role like this would propel her into instant A-list superstardom and certainly shift the focus away from her newly acquired 'jilted bride' tag. Ridley Scott was directing; Ridley fucking Scott! Miranda Muldavey, the feted actress, whose life and career she had unwittingly helped destroy, had come here today not in the guise of her enemy but as her guardian angel, offering to breathe life into her shattered world with a wave of her magic wand. It didn't seem real, or possible, and for once in her life Loretta questioned whether she deserved such a turn in fortune.

'I've given the contracts to Artie to look over and discuss with you, when you're ready that is,' Miranda added matter-of-factly. 'I'm having a late supper at the Bay House restaurant this evening – the views are some of the best on the island. I will be there from around eight p.m. I do hope you will decide to join me.'

Stunned, Loretta could do no more than nod.

'Splendid; we can talk more then.' Replacing her hat and glasses, Miranda made to leave.

'Why are you doing this, Miranda?' Loretta suddenly

felt compelled to ask. 'What's the catch?' She had been around long enough to know that in life when something sounded too good to be true, it usually was.

Miranda's lips formed a small crooked smile.

'I don't do revenge, Loretta,' she said, turning to her one last time as she made her way out of the plush suite, her Missoni kaftan billowing behind her as she looked her up and down. 'That kind of thing can make a person ugly, wouldn't you say?'

CHAPTER 93

Ellie slipped into a Stella McCartney sun dress and lightly spritzed herself with Estée Lauder's Sun Goddess skin scent. Snatching up her woven leather beach bag and Linda Farrow vintage sunglasses, she wrapped a silk pashmina around her shoulders – she was ready . . .

She had spent every moment searching for Vinnie since arriving on the island, but to no avail. And now real panic had set in. Vinnie was going to kill Tom. She'd seen it in his eyes; years of bitter resentment, jealousy and rage finally unleashed. This wasn't just retribution for the here and now; it went way back, back to that night at Livedon, back to the night Tess had been conceived . . .

Ellie pushed such thoughts from her mind as she made her way towards the jetty. Whatever Vinnie had in store for Tom she had to stop it, and not just for his own sake. No matter who or what Tom Black was, she could not allow her husband to hurt him and in turn hurt himself.

The evening air was sultry and almond-scented, the sand soft as cashmere underfoot as she padded across the bay. Ellie had arranged for a boat to take her to the Blue Angel; she felt she had no choice but to go to him. 'The heart wants what the heart wants,' she heard her mother's voice once more as she remembered Tom's note back in London, the desperation in his words. Tonight she'd put an end to this once and for all; she would see Tom Black for what she knew in her heart would be the last time.

Approaching the jetty Ellie saw shadowy figures, policemen milling around talking on cell phones, their expressions earnest. They were signalling to each other, talking in broken English, and she heard them say something about gunshots on a boat . . . She began to pick up speed, and soon she was running towards the jetty, her dancer's legs powering her across the sand, her hair flying back from her face as her heartbeat quickened with her pace.

The men were cordoning off the area now, the sound of radio microphones crackling in the descending darkness. It was the police. Something bad had happened. It was as she drew closer that she saw them; first Vinnie and Lawrence and then . . . Loretta and . . . Jesus, was that . . . Miranda Muldavey?

'*Ellie?*' Vinnie's shock at seeing his wife approach, breathless, her pashmina and bag long since discarded somewhere on the sand, was tangible.

'Please,' she said, her voice a desperate plea as she sank to her knees on the sand, 'please tell me I'm not too late.'

CHAPTER 94

Tom heard footsteps along the jetty; the unmistakable click-clack sound of a woman's stiletto, and he smiled gently. She was here. She had come.

He made his way up towards the top deck, conscious of every step his Italian hand-stitched loafers made.

He saw her approach through the darkness, her figure barely visible in the low illumination of the moonlight. A little myopic, Tom struggled to make her out in the gloom. As she drew closer however, he realised that it wasn't who he was expecting; it wasn't Ellie.

She was on board now, walking towards him, her outstretched arm holding what looked like a gun. 'What the . . .' Tom squinted, his brain searching for some kind of recognition, an explanation. His heart was pumping furiously inside his chest, rendering him almost paralysed.

She was familiar to him, of that he was sure, but it was dark and – and then it came to him suddenly. The long blonde hair that couldn't possibly be all her own . . .

'*Candy*?' Tom's voice sounded low and detached, as though it didn't belong to him.

'So, you remembered my name then?' she said, pulling her mouth into a downwards slant. 'I'm impressed, Tom.'

Tom's brain furiously scrabbled to adjust; his mind a buzzing hive of questions and confusion, underpinned by blind fear. Mary mother of God, what was *she* doing here; and why was she pointing a gun at him? Was this some kind of sick joke? Had Loretta put her up to it?

He studied Candy's face with confusion. The girl looked demented, totally different to how he remembered her, what little he could recall of her. She appeared older somehow; those youthful apple cheeks of the girl he'd picked up on the sidewalk in LA now looking a little sunken and hollow and her eyes were wide and manic, practically bulging from their sockets. Her teeth were clenched and he saw the muscles in her jaw flexing in the warm soft glow of the candlelight.

'You're a piece of shit, Tom Black, you know that . . .' she was edging towards him slowly, the gun shaking in her hand. Tom gradually began edging himself towards the side of the yacht. His fight or flight survival instinct had kicked in and his eyes scanned the immediate area for potential means of protection or escape.

'You left me in Vegas . . .'

Tom blinked at her.

'Woah, now hang on a minute, baby,' he shakily protested, 'I didn't leave you . . . I can explain . . .'

Candy started to laugh then, a horrible girlie giggle that sounded incongruous coming from someone holding a lethal weapon.

'*Baby*?' she grimaced, her sneer dissipating into a thin cruel smile. 'I ain't your fucking baby you fucking asshole . . .' her face was contorted with contempt, 'men like you . . .' she spat at him venomously, 'you're just a taker, a user . . . you care about nuthin' and no one . . . I should shoot your dick clean off!'

Tom, who was used to such invective from women he'd

428

scorned in the past, recoiled. He could almost taste her hatred on his tongue.

Was this the reason she was standing here pointing a gun at him? He could understand a woman being pissed with him for leaving unannounced, but hellbent on murder? It was a little fucking extreme, wasn't it?

'Just listen to me, Candy . . . I can explain,' his voice had a new air of authority about it.

'Sure you can, shithead,' she spat back. 'So let's hear it huh, hear what excuses Mr Hot Ego himself has got . . . you promised me . . . you promised me diamonds and Dior . . .'

'I had to skip town; I gambled away what I'd won . . . I had no choice. There wasn't any time for goodbyes. Anyway, Loretta . . . the Italian woman, you remember her? She sorted it. Gave you the means to get back to LA, right?'

'Wrong, Tom!' Candy took a step towards him and instinctively he put his hands out in front of him. He was weightless with adrenaline now; light as a feather.

'Wrong, wrong, wrong!' she screamed in that high-pitched, shrieking noise she'd incessantly made in Vegas, the one that had eventually grated on his nerves . . .

'She booted me out onto the pavement like a piece of garbage. I didn't even have a dime to my name . . .'

Tom inwardly cursed. That bitch Loretta. She said she'd taken care of things . . . Frantically he wondered where all this was heading. His eye darted towards the eight arm solid silver candelabra on the table, the perfect dinner setting that he'd organised for him and Ellie on the top deck. Jesus Christ, Ellie. She could turn up at any given moment . . .

'Some frat guys picked me up,' Candy continued, 'bunch of college kids really, five of them.'

429

She was waving the gun around now, gesticulating wildly with a .9 mm in her hand. 'They said they would take me back to LA . . .'

Tom was still as a statue, his eye flicking back towards the candelabra.

'But they didn't . . . they took me deep into the desert and . . .' her voice faltered to a rasp, '. . . gang-raped me.'

Tom blinked at her.

'Jesus honey . . . I . . . I'm sorry . . .'

'They violated me,' she continued, her eyes rolling back into her head now, as fat tears tracked her smooth face. He wondered if she was on something. 'One by one . . . you wanna know what they did to me Tom? What those depraved sick fucks did to me because of you . . .'

'Candy, baby, listen,' he cut in, 'I realise you're pissed but you got me all wrong; I came back for you . . .' In fact if Tom thought about it, he could trace all the shit that had gone down in the past couple of months right back to her. If his damned conscience hadn't gotten in the way he would never have returned to Vegas that night, and he might never have become reacquainted with Loretta and been forced to strike a deal with the devil herself. Fuck man; the irony hit him like a titanium fist. He had looked upon Candy as a lucky talisman but truth was, she'd been the very antithesis of it.

'Don't call me baby!' she screamed.

Tom heard the sound of the gun as it discharged and lightning-quick, he sidestepped her and went for the candelabra. She made almost no sound as he brought it down across the side of her head, his chest heaving in slow heavy movements as the gun went off again. And then she was gone.

Tom peered over the side of the boat with some trepidation, his heart knocking furiously against his ribs.

Candy's body was floating face down in the water, her arms and legs outstretched, a human starfish; her blonde hair splayed out, like a mermaid. He stared at her for a second in ghoulish shock. And then he threw up.

CHAPTER 95

'They've found a body,' Vincent Scott said grimly as he placed a round of drinks down onto the table. *A body! Oh please dear God, not Tom . . . not Tom!*' Ellie brought her hand up to her mouth to stifle a gasp.

Vincent glanced at his wife, adding quietly, 'a woman's.'

Ellie tried not to let the relief show on her face. But if the body wasn't Tom's then where in God's name was he? *What had happened to him?*

'A woman,' Loretta sighed resignedly, 'there is always a fucking woman where that bastard is concerned . . .' For all Loretta's bravado however, she felt the tight knot of dread inside her guts loosen. She had come to Antigua with murderous thoughts swirling through her mind, and had been given a golden opportunity to act upon them thanks to that philandering man's stupidity, but would she really have been capable of killing Tom?

'Do they know who she is?' Miranda Muldavey asked, 'the dead girl I mean?'

Vincent shook his head.

'If they do they're not saying . . . at least not yet.'

The five of them sat in the foyer of the magnificent Hermitage Bay House hotel, a group of weary-looking faces

432

brought together by one man and his actions, a man who was now, by all accounts, missing, presumed dead.

'The inspector wants to talk to us all in the morning,' Vinnie responded, automatically taking charge, 'individually. He will want to know why we were all down at the jetty, why we're all here. So I suggest we all have our stories prepared.'

'What *were* you doing down at the jetty anyway?' Loretta addressed Vinnie with a clinical eye. 'Why are *you* even here? No one knew our . . .' she hesitated, barely able to expel the words, '. . . honeymoon destination, other than myself and Tom.'

Vinnie glanced at Ellie again. She looked pale and bereft.

'Black and I had business to discuss,' he replied shortly, 'personal business.'

'I see.' She turned her attention to Ellie. 'And how did *you* know where Tom would be?' Ellie looked up at her. It was five a.m. and she was exhausted.

'I didn't,' she lied. 'I came here for my husband.'

'You mean you came for *my* husband,' Loretta's response sounded more barbed than she had meant it to, but she just couldn't help herself. 'I wouldn't be surprised if he was up in your suite, hiding under the bed,' she turned to Vinnie. 'You have looked under the bed, haven't you, Vincent?'

Ellie leapt up from her seat.

'Bite my ass, you fucking bitch!' she screamed. This was Loretta's fault, all of it. Tom was missing, probably dead, all because this wretched bitch had forced him into some ridiculous, sick-minded contract of marriage. If only he'd never met that woman, then Tom would still be alive.

'Why you . . .' Loretta stood now and the two women faced each other, eyes narrowed, hissing like geese.

Miranda Muldavey stood. 'Now is not the time,' she cut in, sharply. 'We're all very tired, and a little emotional. I think we should retire to our respective suites and resume

433

after a few hours' sleep, don't you agree? Whatever questions we might have can be answered then.'

'I'll second that.' Lawrence Mayfield said.

As shocking as it was to hear about the woman's body, he couldn't help but feel a deep sense of relief. The events of the previous evening had left him feeling incredibly shaken and he wondered just what the hell he would say to the police when it came round to his turn to talk.

He and Vincent had made their way down to the bay just before sunset the previous evening. The marina had been empty, closed for business for the day, and Lawrence had been struck by how eerie and silent the place was, now that it was void of bustling holidaymakers and honeymooners.

The plan had been to secretly take a boat out from the jetty and locate the Blue Angel, to find Tom Black, and Lawrence was in no doubt as to what Scott had had in mind once they did.

'Look, Scott – Vincent,' he addressed him as a friend, 'I have a very bad feeling about this. I mean, seriously, you're not going to shoot the man, are you?'

Vincent Scott had met Lawrence's eyes with his own. He hadn't needed to reply.

'For God's sake, Vinnie,' he rubbed his forehead in frustration, 'he was fucking my wife too you know. But is he worth doing time for? *Fuck*, is anyone?'

Vincent Scott had begun to laugh, the kind of laugh that went right through a man, and it had made Lawrence nervous as hell.

'You think I'm stupid?'

'Of course not, but I think you're upset, and I think you're not thinking with your head. This is madness Vinnie, and deep down you know it. Jesus,' he rubbed his head with his palm, 'there are other ways of dealing with this.'

434

Vincent had fixed him with a stare that did little to assuage Lawrence's grave sense of foreboding.

'Oh really, and what do you suggest, Mayfield? I suppose we could always put him on the naughty step and give him a good telling-off, hope that he learns his lesson.' He shook his head. 'Do you really want to spend the rest of your married life, whatever there may or may not be left of it, tortured by images of them together? Believe me Mayfield, I know what that feels like . . .'

Lawrence turned away from him. He didn't want to be reminded.

'Black's a narcissist,' Vincent continued, a man who ruins lives, and simply walks away from the emotional detritus he leaves behind, without a backwards glance. Well, not this time.' Vinnie was pacing up and down now. 'This time he's hurt too many people. This time he *will* be held to account.'

It was futile to argue with Scott while he was like this and Lawrence had known it. Whatever score Scott had to settle with Black, it ran much deeper than he'd realised; fact was, he suspected he only knew the half of it. So then it had been somewhat of a stroke of luck, in his opinion at least, that the boat Scott had agreed to hire from a local fisherman that afternoon was nowhere to be seen.

'We've been screwed over,' Vincent had banged his fist against a moored catamaran with a furious thud.

'Perhaps it's for the best,' Lawrence had offered.

Before Scott had been able to answer him, they had both been alerted by a figure approaching; a woman. On closer inspection, Lawrence was shocked to see that it was Loretta Fiorentino. She'd adopted a rather flimsy disguise of a dark wig and glasses but thanks to the ubiquitous media footage of her face, currently beaming out across the globe, she was unmistakable. It would've been fair to say that she didn't look best pleased to see them.

435

'*Loretta*?' Vincent Scott watched as she'd strutted along the wooden jetty towards them in gold heels and a Missoni kaftan, carrying a small clutch purse underneath her arm. Her lips formed in a grim line.

'And who the fuck might you two be?'

Loretta had planned to meet Miranda for supper that evening as discussed, and impart the good news that she would humbly accept her highly generous offer; one she knew deep down that she probably didn't deserve. That Miranda had such capacity to forgive had struck a chord in Loretta's largely cold heart, forcing her to reflect on some rather unpleasant facets of her own nature. Miranda's words had resounded in her mind, '*I don't do revenge, Loretta. That kind of thing can make a person ugly . . .*' Her offer was a real second chance and she knew it. First, though, she'd had some unfinished business to attend to.

On closer inspection Loretta had vaguely recognised one of the men; the billionaire, Vincent Scott. That damn Eleanor O'Connor's husband.

'I could ask you the same question, Loretta,' Vinnie had fired back in response. 'Call me old-fashioned, but I thought a wedding was supposed to take place *before* the honeymoon started . . .' Before Loretta could come back with a suitable caustic retort however, they'd been stopped dead in their tracks by a sudden ear-splitting crack that had rung out through the descending darkness, small strobe flashes of light briefly igniting the sky. Two more had followed closely in quick succession; the unmistakable sound of gunshots.

Missing. Presumed dead. The words looped around Loretta's mind over and over again like a mantra. Well frankly 'presumed' wasn't good enough, as far as she was concerned. 'So there's no body, nothing?' she fixed Police Inspector George with her dark eyes.

'Just the girl's so far . . .'

'Does anyone know who she is?' Lawrence asked. A young girl washed up on shore like human detritus; the thought turned his stomach.

'I don't suppose the name Candy Wilson rings any bells?' Inspector George scanned the guests' faces hoping to see a flicker of recognition

Despite the fact that everyone here had an alibi for last night, he was not convinced that any one of their motives for being in Antigua was entirely innocent.

Loretta felt a jolt to her heart. *Candy* . . . the name did sound familiar and, my God, now she thought about it, wasn't that the same name of the little tramp she'd turfed out of The Player that time in Vegas?

Loretta prudently held her tongue. She would say nothing, not without speaking to her lawyer first.

'So she drowned then, the girl I mean?' Vincent enquired.

'Yes, though it looks like she had a pretty sharp blow to the head first,' the inspector explained. 'Blunt trauma to the skull.'

'So, a murderer as well as a philanderer,' Vinnie remarked, throwing back a neat Scotch on ice. He'd been drinking with impunity ever since his arrival on the island, Ellie had noted.

She squeezed her eyes tightly shut in a bid to maintain some composure. Tom was capable of many things, but murder? She refused to believe it.

'What was the girl even doing there in the first place?' Lawrence asked.

'Oh for goodness' sake, Mayfield, what do you think?' Vinnie snorted. 'I doubt they were planning on a game of scrabble . . .'

Inspector George cleared his throat.

'Mr Black was clearly waiting for someone to arrive; that was pretty obvious. There was a dinner setting for two, candles, music playing . . .'

Ellie sat silently on the padded rattan armchair opposite the inspector, her heart thudding so loudly in her chest she was sure that they could all hear it.

'Who the hell was he expecting?' Loretta screeched. 'No one could possibly have known he would be there . . .'

'No one except you of course, Loretta,' Ellie added.

She felt Loretta's glare like a laser beam on her skin.

'Is there any chance that Black could still be alive?' Vinnie began to pace the room, glass of Scotch in one hand, a half-full bottle swinging in the other. He was barefoot, chinos rolled up to his shins. 'I mean; could he have made a swim for it?'

The inspector gave a light shrug.

'We think one of the bullets probably hit him and that he fell into the water.'

'So where's the body then?' Lawrence piped up. 'Hers washed up alright . . .'

Ellie turned away. She tried not to picture it; Tom, white and water-bloated, covered in seaweed as the tide carried his lifeless body to shore. She saw him then, inside her mind; his well-built toned stomach, his smooth tanned skin and that bright smile, laughing. The night at the casino when they'd played roulette. The look he had given her when they'd met face-to-face for the first time in twenty years. Livedon . . . against the tree with the light breeze on her naked skin. And that day; the day before her sixteenth birthday all those years ago, when she had gone from girl to woman, when she had lain with him for the first time . . . It wasn't possible that he was dead; she couldn't believe it. *Wouldn't*.

'It could've drifted,' the inspector offered, 'dragged by the current, taken further out to sea . . . there's even a possibility that, well, you know,' he lowered his eyes, 'a shark took him.'

Lawrence Mayfield grimaced and Ellie instinctively put her hand over her mouth.

Loretta raised an eyebrow. The idea of Tom meeting such a gruesome end cheered her up no end.

'I suppose there is a slim chance that he could've made a swim for it,' the inspector added, 'but the whole island is on red alert. There's no way he could make it off the island without capture.'

Vinnie held back the urge to clap his hands together triumphantly. Tom Black wasn't coming back.

CHAPTER 96

The only rest she'd had that night was the kind that tricked you into thinking you were asleep, a cruel, shallow half-slumber, hovering between the conscious and sub-conscious; a twilight zone. With her mind constantly turning over, Ellie was unable to erase the horrifying images of Tom struggling to breathe underwater; his panic in the darkness of the deep eventually becoming her own.

It was nine a.m. and, finally surrendering to her insomnia, Ellie had risen, careful not to wake her husband as she made her way out onto the marbled patio, inhaling the scented Antiguan air inside her lungs, the first of the morning's rays breathing life into her shattered body.

Her emotions upon finding Vinnie down at the jetty the previous evening had been bittersweet; a deep sense of relief, accompanied by abject disappointment as she realised that she was too late; she would not get to see Tom.

Ellie wondered if Tom had been already dead when he hit the water, or if he had spent his last moments desperately gasping for breath. Had he died thinking that she hadn't come for him? *Oh but I did come, Tom, I did.*

Ellie tilted her head back and closed her eyes, her mind

turning to the previous evening and the conversation she'd had with Vinnie.

'How did you know I'd come to Antigua?' he'd asked her, pouring them both a Scotch once they were back inside the villa. Ellie had always hated the stuff, but she had accepted it gratefully. She'd needed it.

'One of the housekeepers overheard you and Lawrence talking . . .' She'd glanced at him, hoping that her eyes did not betray her anguish over Tom. 'I had to come . . . I thought you were going to . . .' she'd paused, unable to finish the sentence.

'. . . Kill Tom Black?' Vinnie had given a little derisive snort, throwing back the dark brown liquid and pouring himself another from the crystal decanter.

'I didn't want you to do something stupid, Vin, something I knew you would later regret, especially since you'd got it all so wrong about Tess and Tom . . .'

'Wrong?'

She'd sat up then, folded her long dancer's legs beneath her and fixed her husband with an earnest stare. 'It's not what you think. Tom was not Tess's lover. He was her friend. Jesus, Vin, he *saved* her . . .'

Vinnie had listened with a rapid heartbeat, glass of Scotch shaking in his hand as Ellie had imparted the truth about what had happened to their daughter in Ibiza, about Marco's blackmail, and consequently how Tom had come to Tess's rescue.

'If anything, we should be grateful to him . . . he looked out for her, made sure that evil piece of shit got his comeuppance.'

Vinnie had to stop himself detonating like a bomb.

It was a lot to take in but . . . *Grateful*.

Vinnie had little choice but to accept the fact that Black had protected Tess, but he certainly didn't have to like it. How he managed to come out of everything looking like a hero made him want to run a knife through the man's spleen. Tess was his daughter, *his*! What his poor little girl must have gone through didn't bear thinking about. But it hurt that she hadn't seen fit to come to him and ask for help. Instead she had inadvertently given Black the chance to play the shining knight. It was enough to send him off the edge.

'Jesus Christ, Ellie,' he'd sighed, looking to the ceiling, 'what a goddamn mess.'

She had looked up at him with impassioned eyes.

'Oh Vin.'

He had gone to her then, held her in his strong arms, arms that had always made her feel so safe and protected, and yet still she couldn't help but wish that they were Tom's arms. What she wouldn't have given to see his handsome, cocksure face walk through that door right there and then. 'I'm so sorry,' she had said, over and over again as she'd sobbed. 'I'm so, so sorry.' And she *was* sorry, only not for the reasons her husband assumed.

'Who'd have thought we'd end up here, eh?' Vinnie had spoken gently to her, like a father to his child, 'not quite the holiday I had in mind . . .' he had laughed softly and she had attempted to join in, but it got caught somewhere between her diaphragm and her throat.

'Let's go home, Vin,' she'd finally managed to say. She couldn't stand to be in Antigua a moment longer.

'Yes, back to the real world – *our* world,' Vinnie had nodded.

She didn't know it yet but he was one step ahead of her; a plane had already been chartered and was waiting for them.

It was over.

CHAPTER 97

Ellie stood on the balcony of the luxury villa and looked out towards the bay, at the landscape of perfect blue ocean, still as a bath. The collection of boats moored at the marina now looked like children's toys gently swaying in the distance. Vinnie was downstairs in the lobby, clearing up a few loose ends, and she welcomed this private moment to herself.

Tom was out there, somewhere . . .

Ellie brushed away a tear that had unwittingly escaped down her cheek with a swift movement. She didn't want Vinnie to see that she'd been crying. She stared down at the piece of notepaper, at Tom's handwriting. He had requested to see her, *one last time,* it said. Had he somehow known he wasn't coming back? She sensed the urgency behind his words. He had wanted to tell her something, something important. And now she would never know what that something was.

Ellie closed her eyes. If Tom was dead she would have known it in her bones, for they were inextricably linked; bound together by the love they had; a love she knew would never be replicated, nor understood. He was part of her soul and although she knew that life had led them along different paths, he would forever remain a part of her that she could never let go . . .

'The heart wants what the heart wants,' she whispered her mother's words aloud as she stared out across the beautiful blue blanket before her.

'Goodbye, Tom,' she said, blowing a kiss into the warm, perfumed air. 'I always loved you . . . I always will.'

CHAPTER 98

8½ months later

The girl's name was Candice Wilson. A twenty-four year old from California with a history of mental health problems. She'd been with Tom in Vegas, on the night of the Big Win, and subsequent Big Loss. The newspaper article had said that Tom had abandoned her after taking a big hit on the tables, forcing her to hitch-hike her way through the Nevada desert in a bid to get back to LA. Apparently she had been picked up by a bunch of fraternity guys who went on to . . . Ellie squeezed her eyes tightly shut, she could barely bring herself to read the rest.

'Oh God,' Ellie put her head in her hands as she let the newspaper fall to the ground. *That poor girl . . .*

It transpired that Candy had spent a stint in a psychiatric unit, sectioned by her own parents no less. 'A former drug user, bipolar, prone to bouts of depression and outbursts of aggression,' the paper had said. According to a former employer at the Rib Shack in Melrose where she had once worked, he'd been forced to sack her when she'd 'threatened a disgruntled customer with a steak knife for complaining about tardy service.' Jesus.

445

Ellie stared at the photograph of the girl, her young, exceptionally pretty face smiling back at the camera as if she hadn't a care in the world. She looked so innocuous, so innocent, but it was clear from what she'd read that Candy wasn't as harmless, or stupid as some might have believed. Following her ordeal in Vegas, she had kept a diary, extracts of which had been printed in the article; the incoherent ramblings of a disturbed young woman determined to take her revenge upon the man she held responsible for the desert atrocities. 'He plucked me from the street,' one of the excerpts had read, 'he put me on a pedestal, told me I was special, that I was his 'lucky talisman' and then discarded me like a piece of human trash . . . threw me to those depraved fuckers . . .'

Candice had made a trip to London in a bid to begin what she'd called her 'divine retribution', even attending the opening night of the casino. There was a photograph taken from the event in which her pixelated face was vaguely recognisable in among the bustling crowd of party-goers, of which Ellie herself had been one. According to the reporter, Candy had left with Jack that night, gone back to his hotel and had sex with him before grilling him about Tom. Her initial plan had been to turn up unannounced at Tom's wedding, but as that hadn't taken place she'd had to revert to plan B. She had followed Tom to the airport, watched him board the plane . . . it was all there, in black and white, documented by Candy herself in the childish scrawl of her diaries, next to a picture of her bereft-looking parents.

'She thought she had won the lottery that night, the night she met him [Tom],' her mother was quoted as saying, 'only it turned out to be the opposite; it turned out to be the worst night of her whole life.'

Ellie stared at the photograph of Tom on board a boat, goodness only knew where. It was an old photograph; he looked younger, tanned, his toned body proudly on display as he rested an elbow against the side of the boat, the other hand holding the edge of his Ray-Ban Wayfarers. He was smiling that cocky, perfectly neat smile, and he looked so handsome; so alive. 'Renowned playboy and casino owner, Tom Black, on board a friend's yacht in 2009. His body has never been found.'

Ellie read the caption before abruptly shutting the newspaper; her emotions beginning to get the better of her once more.

'Ah, there you are darling!' Vinnie popped his head around the bedroom door. 'Best get a wiggle on, the Mayfields are here . . .'

'Oh!' Ellie quickly discarded the newspaper and ruffled her hair in the mirror before following her husband downstairs.

'Tor! Lol! Oh my God, here she is . . . !' Ellie went forward to greet her friend who was holding her tiny new baby girl in a soft cashmere blanket. 'Let me look at her! My God Tor, she's adorable! She has Lawrence's eyes, and look at all that hair!' the two women began to coo.

Vinnie clapped Lawrence Mayfield on the back. It was as if the man he'd seen in Antigua, the one set on murder and retribution, had never existed. Scott had never mentioned it, and Lawrence certainly wasn't about to bring it up. Fact was, the man he'd seen that night at St John's Bay had scared the shit out of him.

'How about a drop of the good stuff for you my man? Wet the baby's head . . .'

Lawrence nodded eagerly as he followed Vinnie into the large reception room of their beautiful home, 'leave the girls to it,' he winked.

With the men gone, Ellie looked at her friend.

'You did it, Tor, she's so perfect . . .'

Tor glanced at the tiny bundle in her arms, her eyes and heart filled with love.

447

'And it's largely thanks to you,' she said. 'This little one might never have been born if it hadn't been for Auntie Ellie, hey?' she lightly touched the child's face with soft fingertips.

Ellie shook her head and squeezed her friend's shoulder. She didn't want to bring up the past, what had been and gone. Tor was on the mend, gradually getting back to her usual self, and she was finally a mother once more. They would never mention Tom Black's name again.

'So,' Tor said as she handed Ellie her little bundle of joy. Ellie's heart melted as she looked down at her. 'I can't believe the news about the casino . . . about Loretta giving it to you.'

Ellie raised her eyebrows.

'*You* can't believe it!' she retorted. 'No one was more shocked than I was!'

In the weeks that had followed that fateful night in Antigua, Loretta had surprised Ellie by inviting her to lunch at Hawksmoor.

'I realise we've never been the best of friends, nor are we likely to be, but I have a proposition for you,' she'd announced in an unexpected telephone call. 'One I think you will be interested in.'

Ellie would have been content never to set eyes on Loretta Fiorentino again. The woman was nothing less than a painful reminder of everything that had transpired between her and Tom, of everything she had lost. But her intrigue had got the better of her once more.

'I'll cut to the chase,' Loretta had said, getting straight to it as the waiter brought over a bottle of Krug without prompt. Loretta was a regular at Hawksmoor.

I want to get rid of the casino. It's of no interest to me now,' she'd waved her diamond encrusted hand in the air dismissively. 'Never wanted the damn thing in the first place . . . and now it holds nothing but bad memories. So, I'm offering you first refusal on it.'

Ellie had almost choked on an olive.

'You want me to buy the casino?' her suspicions were heightened. After all, this was Loretta Fiorentino she was dealing with.

'Turn it into that damned dance school or whatever hair-brained idea you had for it.'

Her dark eyes met with Ellie's briefly.

'And how much would you want for it?'

Loretta had shrugged, 'You can pick up the lunch cheque if you like . . .'

'You're *giving* it to me?' Ellie was dumbfounded. 'And why would you do something as generous as that, Loretta? Like you said, we've not exactly been what you could call the best of friends over the years, have we?'

Loretta had given a sanguine smile. Ever since that night in Antigua, the night she'd learned the truth about Candy Wilson, her conscience had gnawed at her like a rat through a cable. She had been the one who'd seen the girl off in Vegas, telling her in no uncertain terms that her time was up. At the time she had thought nothing of it; had instantly forgotten her, just another of Tom's little pick-ups. How was she to know that Candy was fresh from the nut house?

Loretta was now convinced however that her own actions had helped spark a diabolical chain of events that had resulted in the girl's death, and that of Tom's too. Tom. The man she had paid to marry her; the man who had conse-quently betrayed and humiliated her in the worst way a man ever could. She had wanted him dead. And yet now that a little time had passed and it had become apparent that he really wasn't coming back . . . Miranda Muldavey had been right. Revenge made a person ugly on the inside. And now Loretta wanted to appease her nagging conscience. Of course, she knew she would never be a candidate for the Nobel Peace Prize, but a little of her caustic edge had softened slightly.

'I've had the contracts drawn up,' Loretta had slid the documents towards her across the table. 'Sign them and the place is yours.'

'What's the catch?' Ellie had said, eyeing her cautiously. There was always a catch where Loretta was concerned.

'Call it a peace offering.'

Ellie had blinked at her in surprise.

'We may never be the best of friends, Eleanor, but we will always have one thing in common,' she'd said.

'Really? And what's that?' Ellie had tentatively taken the documents in her hand, daring to look at them.

She had given a wan smile.

'We both loved the wrong man.'

*

'So, you'll be coming to the opening of Ellie's Angels then?' Ellie said. 'The place is almost finished now. I'm hoping to have it up and running in less than a month. Lindsay was beside herself when I told her the good news!'

'I wouldn't miss it for the world!' Tor smiled. 'In fact I'm thinking of enrolling this little one in a ballet class just as soon as she's old enough, aren't I poppet? She has the look of a ballerina, don't you think?'

Ellie smiled, revelling in her friend's happiness.

'Tess is helping me design the interior,' she said, 'she's halfway through her first year of her interior design degree and is loving every minute. The teacher says she has 'natural artistic flair'.

'Takes after her mother,' Tor grinned.

'She's in Sardinia at the moment with the Kennedy-Ling's and Monique. They've just Skyped. Looks like they're all having a ball onboard the yacht.'

Monique, it turned out, had had an attack of conscience too and had, perhaps somewhat surprisingly given her

450

track record, returned Tess's jewellery in its entirety, with a handwritten message explaining how she was back in Paris, in a rehabilitation programme, attempting to rebuild her shattered life. Tess had told Ellie all about it and her mother had suggested that they invite her to come and stay.

'Everyone deserves a second chance, Tess.'

Tess had hugged her mother tightly, grateful for her understanding in such a delicate situation. Monique's life had been so terribly difficult, one Tess finally realised had been quite the antithesis of her own, and now her mother was granting her the opportunity to help make sure her friend didn't slide down that slippery slope again.

It would be fair to say that Tess had been initially blindsided by her mother's revelation that she had once been a Las Vegas stripper. But her shock had eventually given way to a strange kind of pride; she was proud that her mother had finally come clean and trusted her enough to take her into her confidence. And in a way it had been a relief to Tess to discover that her mother wasn't perfect; that she too had made mistakes and bad choices in her life. It had humanised her somehow, and in doing so brought them closer together.

'I've been asked out on a date,' Tess had nervously explained to Ellie, biting her lip.

'And?' Ellie had been cheered to hear this news. It was what Tess needed, some normality in her life, 'have you agreed?'

'I really like him, Mum,' she gave a coy smile, something the pre-Ibiza Tess wouldn't have known how to do. After everything she'd been through, she wasn't sure she was ready to put herself back out there again.

'Dan's different from the other guys; he's not flash or showy, he's just . . . normal, I suppose.' She thought back to the night at the house party, when Dan had intervened between her and Hugo, and she smiled.

'But I don't know if I'm ready to . . . well, you know, get close to someone.'

Ellie had taken her daughter into her embrace. Held her slim body close and buried her face into her soft shampoo-scented hair. She would always be her baby, no matter how big she got.

'I know my darling, I know . . . but you know Tess, if he's decent, he'll understand, and he'll wait until you're ready . . .'

'I'm seeing him tomorrow night,' she'd said and Ellie saw a flicker of excitement in her young face. 'He's taking me to the cinema, maybe for a coffee afterwards . . . take it slow, you know?'

Ellie had waved her daughter off that night with butter-flies jiggling in her own belly, as if it were she who was going on a date. A couple of hours later she received a text message from Tess that had made her smile and given her hope for the future.

Having a Gr8 time, Mum! I checked my boot; no snakes 2 b seen! Don't wait up! Luv Tx

*

'Oh to be nineteen years old again,' Tor said. 'I wonder what this little one will be like when she's that age.'

'Beautiful like you, I'm sure. And no doubt worrying you into an early grave, but that's kids for you!'

The two women stared at the baby, a thousand silent words exchanged between them.

'Have you decided upon a name yet?' Ellie enquired. 'It's been over a week now; you can't keep calling her "Angel".'

'Ah well, that's where you're wrong Auntie Eleanor, because she is our little Angel, our perfect miracle.' She looked up at her friend, 'we're calling her Angel Eleanor

452

CeCe Mayfield. What do you think?' she asked, gently kissing the tip of her tiny baby's new nose.

'I think,' Ellie said with tears in her eyes, 'that it suits her perfectly.'

CHAPTER 99

'You look . . . you look beautiful . . .' Vinnie wrapped his arms round Ellie's neck from behind, leaning in to kiss the side of her soft cheek.

'Thank you my darling,' she giggled, giving him a twirl, affording him a 360-degree view of her exquisite Stella McCartney evening dress, a birthday present to herself. 'I want to look my best for the big occasion!'

'The guests will be arriving soon,' he said, wondering if there was enough time to get her out of it and back before they began to descend en masse.

It was Ellie's fortieth birthday and Vinnie had planned a no-expense spared party, a celebration for family and close friends; a tribute to his talented and beautiful wife.

Ellie smiled.

'I can't wait,' she said, spritzing herself with Chanel Beige perfume. 'It's going to be a night to remember! Help soften the blow of turning the big four-oh!'

'It sure is my darling,' Vinnie beamed, watching her with loving eyes. Forty years old today, it didn't seem possible. She'd practically been a child when they'd met. They had been through so much together during the past twenty-one years, and not least in the past twelve months. But slowly they were putting all that behind them. They had come through the events of the past few months and were subsequently stronger, with a better understanding of each other as a result. There would be no more secrets; no more lies and above all, no more Tom Black.

'Happy Birthday Mrs Scott,' Vincent said, wrapping his arms around her small waist and kissing her soft nude glossy lips, 'I love you.'

'I love you too Mr Scott,' she beamed, the light catching her emerald-green eyes. He may not have set her heart racing whenever he walked into a room and their marriage would never be the rollercoaster of intense thrilling passion and pain like it had always been with Tom, but he was her rock; familiar and comforting – and there was a lot to be said for that she supposed.

'Now go and see to those guests for me while I finish making myself beautiful . . .' She watched as her husband left the room, smiling to herself as she began to inspect the pile of birthday cards that had dropped through the letter box that morning.

Shuffling through the various coloured envelopes, an assortment of shapes and sizes,

Ellie's attention was caught by a small white one. It had been franked, the red ink a little too faint to make out its provenance. Odd, she thought, discarding the rest of the pile in haste as she tore it open. Inside was a postcard; a picturesque scene of the infamous Ipanema beach in Brazil. Flipping it over, she recognised the familiar scrawl, 'Wish you were here, kid . . .'

Ellie gasped loudly, holding the card to her chest, squeezing her eyes tightly shut as adrenaline and relief poured through every fibre and crevice of her being. *Tom.* He was still alive! She steadied herself against the dressing table, fighting back tears. In Brazil! The instinct to go to him was so strong that it was all she could do not to pick up the phone and charter the first plane to Rio.

She heard voices downstairs now, the first of the guests arriving.

'Ellie!' Vinnie called up the stairs to her, 'are you almost ready? Get yourself down here – I've got a surprise for you!'

'I'm coming!' she called out to her husband, checking her reflection one last time. Knowing that Tom was still alive was the best present she could've asked for.

Ellie buried the postcard deep inside her lingerie drawer and felt her heart soar inside her chest. 'Happy birthday to me,' she whispered, smiling to herself, before making her way downstairs to greet her guests.

EPILOGUE

Wearing nothing but a tiny pair of swimming shorts, Tom strutted along the soft white sand of Ipanema beach, admiring the vast assortment of women of all shapes and sizes in the smallest bikinis he'd ever seen in his life.

He made his way up towards Ponta Do Arpoador, a rocky point of the beach that juts out into the water and serves as a superlative place to watch the magnificent sunset, the beach stretching off towards the towering peaks. Sheltered and secluded, away from the crowds, it was his favourite spot in Rio, bar none.

Tom nodded at one of the fishermen as he sat down, resting his forearms lightly on his knees, his tanned body glistening in the dying rays.

Why had he never thought of Rio before now? As far as hunting grounds went it was beyond perfect, rich pickings indeed. Pushing the wedge of lime into the neck of the bottle, Tom took a swig of ice-cold beer and looked out onto the horizon.

As usual, he played the sequence of events in his mind on a loop, trying to establish if he might've done anything differently.

He saw her standing in front of him, her shaking hand

and the gun it had held. She was supposed to have been Ellie; he had been waiting for Ellie to return . . .

For reasons unknown to him at the time, Tom had watched Candy Wilson's body float lifelessly in the water for some moments before jumping in in a futile attempt to save her. But he had known the girl was already dead – and that he had killed her.

Tom remembered momentarily debating whether to alert the authorities, tell them the truth. It was self-defence. The crazy bitch was pointing a gun at his head, what's a guy supposed to do? But the truth was something Tom Black had never had too much faith in. It had never done him any favours in his life . . .

Instead, Tom had made the decision to swim away from the boat and out into the darkness. He was a good swimmer, strong and powerful; if he swam through the night he might just make it to Barbuda by sunrise, if the sharks didn't get to him first. The island's warm steady winds would carry him along the coastline towards the safe harbours, the nearly unbroken wall of coral reef protecting him from the coast-guards that would no doubt be on the lookout for him soon.

He had reached Barbuda a little before sunrise, collapsing onto the deserted beach where he had promptly passed out. He was exhausted but couldn't rest for too long. He needed to find a way off the island without risking capture. And as it turned out, he hadn't had to wait long.

'A crab will crawl into your mouth if you leave it open like that!' the young woman had laughed, gently nudging him awake. 'You look like you've just washed up on shore,' she'd smiled. 'Are you shipwrecked?'

Tom had rubbed his dry eyes awake and looked up at the girl; well, woman actually, maybe early-thirties, long flowing dark hair, a pretty face in a natural kind of way, and a great set of tits scarcely covered by her red bikini top.

'No,' he'd replied with a bright smile and outstretched hand, 'I'm Jack; Jack Gold.'

*

It had been a long ride to Rio; airports were not an option for a man on the run, so it had been a slow chain of connecting boat rides, some it had to be said, more comfortable than others. He had lost count of how many days it had taken him to reach Brazil's capital city. That was a little over eight months ago now, and despite having arrived in Rio with no more than seventy real in his pocket (less than thirty pounds) it hadn't been long before Tom had worked his charms and had found a five-star hotel suite with his name on it, courtesy of a rich older German woman by the name of Anita.

Tom watched the dazzling sunset with unmasked appreciation, nature's vibrant colours bringing the sky to life and making him feel alive. It was the simple pleasures in life he thought; if the past eighteen months had taught him anything, it was that.

He took another slug of beer and wondered if this ubiquitous dull ache inside his chest would ever leave him. He didn't think so, at least not until he saw her again. Eleanor. She flashed up inside his mind, that familiar look on her face, slight disapproval mixed with mischief; no one had ever looked at him in the way she had, never before or since.

'Jack! There you are darling, I've been looking for you all over,' Anita panted, out of breath as she sidled up next to him, instantly destroying his sanguine moment of reflection. 'I told Frieda I would find you up here, you old romantic you!' her eyes lightly scanned his semi-naked bronzed body with delicious approval, 'such a perfect, secluded spot.'

459

'Isn't it just . . .' he gave her a cursory smile in return, wishing she would just fuck off and leave him in peace with his thoughts to enjoy the sunset.

Anita was a Berlin-born woman in her late fifties, though it had to be said she was wearing pretty well, and, like most of his previous women, had recently inherited her late husband's 200 million dollar estate. She would have to do for now. Needs must.

'I came to ask you if you think we should eat at the Café de la Musique this evening?' She lit a Vogue cigarette and adjusted her brightly-coloured kaftan over her chunky legs. 'You know how much I adore the view there . . . not to mention the steak!'

'Whatever you desire, *liebling* . . .' Tom gave a cursory reply.

'Great, I'll tell Frieda the good news . . .' she looked at him expectantly, 'so, are you just going to sit here eyeing up all those beautiful young girls or are you coming?' she forced a smile. 'You think I can't see what you're up to behind those dark sunglasses . . .'

Tom laughed.

'Don't be crazy, you know you're the most beautiful woman in Rio. I'll be right behind you.'

Tom watched the sun as it made its gradual descent into the ocean, disappearing like a gold disc behind a sideboard. He thought of Tess then. Bright young Tess; the vivacious girl he was sure he had fathered, how beautiful she was, just like her mother, her whole life ahead of her . . .

Even though Tom Black was dead, he knew that one day he would see Eleanor O'Connor again. One day, somehow he would find a way back to her. And when that day came he would look her in the eyes and tell her that he loved her, finally do what he should have done all those years ago . . .

'Don't leave it too long!' Anita called out from behind him, her harsh accent cutting through the balmy Rio breeze as she disappeared down the steps behind him. Tom gave a low groan as he looked out across the water, his attention suddenly caught by a figure approaching in the distance – a female figure. He watched with mounting interest as she emerged from the sea in a white bikini. As she drew closer a surge of adrenaline propelled him suddenly to his feet.

'Jesus . . . what the . . .' instinctively he made his way towards her, his walk increasing to a jog. '. . . *Eleanor*?' For a moment Tom wondered if she was simply an apparition, a result of too much sun and cerveza, but she was here, in front of him, wearing a white and gold string bikini and the gentlest smile, her bronzed skin shimmering like gold in the heat. He was stunned into silence.

Ellie knew she should not be here – she was still a married woman after all – but she knew that she had no choice. The heart wants what the heart wants. And hers wanted Tom Black. It always had. Any guilt or regret she felt, the pull of him outweighed all of it.

Ellie had not had a proper moment's rest since the events in Antigua. More than anything, she had wanted him to know that she had come for him that night on the boat, just as he'd asked her to.

Thinking that Tom could be dead had given Ellie emotional clarity. While she knew they could never be together, not while Vinnie was alive and Tom was wanted in connection with Candy Wilson's death, the idea that she would never see him again had been like a weight on her heart.

Tom Black; gambler, womaniser, vigilante. She loved him regardless.

'Just couldn't keep away, huh?'

She smirked. It was vintage Tom; cocky and irresistible. 'How did you find me?'

Instinctively he drew her to him, their skin touching as

they embraced. He pulled her down onto the powder-soft sand, his hardness pressing against her as she wrapped her legs tightly around his back. She wanted him now. God help her, she had always wanted him.

'The postcard . . .'

'Ah,' he pressed his lips against hers, soft at first, then harder, more urgent. She tasted even sweeter than he remembered. Their eyes met. 'I can't believe you came, kiddo.'

He couldn't hold back any longer as he pulled at the side ties of her bikini, abandoning it behind him. Cradled in his arms, he carried her to a secluded part of the beach, sheltered by rocks. Placing her naked body gently onto the sand, he looked down at her face. She was wearing the same expression she had worn all those years ago, the night before her sixteenth birthday, the night he had taken her virginity. She was beautiful then, now perhaps more so.

'I had to come,' she breathed, her throat tight, 'I had to see you one last time . . . to say good . . . goodb—'

His smile lit up his face, the sliver of remaining sunset casting a warm glow on his handsome features.

'You never could quite say goodbye to me, could you?' he said as he slid deep inside her.

'And you could never tell me that you love me,' she gasped, back arched in pleasure.

'Well,' he met her eyes then, his fingers brushing grains of white sand from her face as their bodies fused, 'I love you, Eleanor O'Connor.'

His words sounded like birdsong to her and she smiled.

'Goodbye, Tom Black.'

WHY DOES IT FEEL SO GOOD
BEING BAD?

It's a question I have asked myself many times over the years! I have to admit that I have always had an endless fascination with wicked women or 'femme fatales' as I prefer to call them. You know the type of women I mean, effortlessly glamorous, whose presence can be felt long after she's left the room (in a cloud of expensive perfume, naturally). The kind who leaves a trail of broken hearts and promises behind her; a strong, sensual and independent woman who's not afraid to get what – or indeed, who – she wants while managing to retain an air of vulnerability and femininity about her.

While the female protagonists in *Wicked Wives* are sometimes feisty, occasionally fierce and, I hope you'll agree, always, *always* glamorous, they are never truly wicked, at least not in the traditional sense of the word (although Loretta does have her moments!). Being wicked for me is an attitude; it is being unapologetic for taking no prisoners, and of course, for looking fabulous while you do it!

I think it is essential that all women should indulge their inner bad girl at least once in their lifetime. I've certainly had my moments; abandoning an ex-boyfriend one New

Year's Eve to hitch a ride in a Portuguese pop star's Porsche springs to mind, as does almost being arrested for throwing a pair of shoes at a man during an argument in a very posh London restaurant – what *was* I thinking? They were brand new Jimmy Choo's after all!

So, paying homage to wicked women everywhere, I have compiled a list of my favourite luscious lovelies (both real and fictional, in no particular order) who, naughty by nature, put the oh-so-good into being bad . . .

Eve: The naked temptress! Arguably the girl who kicked it all off by taking a forbidden bite out of the serpent's apple, thus creating the original sin and giving women a bad name the world over. The moral here? Never trust a snake!

Bonnie Parker: One half of the infamous 1930 outlaws, Bonnie and Clyde. She may have been diminutive in stature but this bad girl bandit had balls the size of space hoppers, particularly when brandishing a weapon, which she was want to do on occasion, incidentally.

Cleopatra: The ultimate seductress who not only ruled Egypt, but also the hearts of the world's most powerful men at the time, Julius Caesar and Mark Anthony. She also liked to bathe in ass's milk to keep her skin in tip-top condition, as you do, and looked pretty damn hot in a headdress to boot.

Elizabeth Taylor: No surprise then that luscious Liz, Hollywood legend and herself a successful seductress, was cast as the sensual Egyptian queen in the epic film adaptation of Cleopatra's life. Liz went through marriages like pigs through bone, walking up the aisle no less than eight times in her lifetime. Her tempestuous yet wildly passionate relationship with Richard Burton (whom she married twice) was the stuff of legend.

Mae West: The undisputed queen of the caustic one-liner and a true bad gal to the core. Although she was most famous for being a Hollywood sex symbol, minxy Mae was once prosecuted on moral grounds for writing a risqué play entitled *Sex* and was sentenced to ten days in prison. 'Is that a gun in your pocket or are you just pleased to see me,' is just one of her many unforgettable quips.

Nancy Friday: Author of the controversial *My Secret Garden* (or should that be *My Secret* Lady *Garden*?'), which caused a right old uproar when it was first published 25 years ago, proving to the world (i.e. men) that – shock horror – women have sexual fantasies and are a little bit naughty too!

Nancy Dell'olio: Something in a name perhaps? She's the loud, louche, striking Italian diva who seems to have been the same age for ten years and had a high profile affair with one-time England football manager Sven-Göran Eriksson. Ever modest, the unrepentantly sexy Nancy once quipped during an interview, 'of course other women are jealous, I mean, look at me!' Plus she also wore a red rhinestone-encrusted jumpsuit to Number 10. A guilty pleasure.

Joan Collins (as Alexis Coly in *Dynasty*): The finely arched sardonic eyebrow, the blood-red lips, the omnipresent champagne flute, the shoulder pads! Alexis Colby (perfectly played by Joan, another wicked woman in her own right), connived, corrupted and colluded in a bid to get her revenge on her ex-husband, Blake Carrington and his fragrant (yet not nearly so much fun) wife Crystal. Although she was portrayed as ruthless, using her sexuality as a deadly weapon, there was a vulnerable side to Alexis, making her one of the most iconic and best loved TV bad girls of all time.

Joan Rivers: Unapologetic, award-winning motormouth US comedienne and talk show host, Ms Rivers is certainly no stranger to controversy. A self-confessed lover of cosmetic surgery, Rivers once handcuffed herself to someone's shopping cart in Costco because they refused to stock her *NY Times* bestselling book while shouting 'I hate everyone . . . starting with me,' through a megaphone. You tell 'em Joanie.

Madonna: No list would be complete without the original Material Girl. The queen of the shock tactic needs no introduction, from her crucifix days gyrating on a gondola while singing about virginity, to *that* book, to *that* bra, to the lesbian flings and failed marriages and countless controversial stage shows. The list goes on and looks like it has every intention of continuing still . . .

Other wonderfully wicked women worth a mention include Courtney Love, Lady Gaga, Tania Turner in *Footballers' Wives* (brilliantly portrayed by Zoe Lucker), Angelina Jolie, Joan Jett, Pam Grier, Dita Von Teese, Bettie Page, Kate Moss . . .

*

I would love to hear from you. Tweet me at @annaloulondon or find me on Facebook/ChelseaWives.

And finally, in the inimitable words of Mae West, remember this:

"There are no good girls gone wrong – just bad girls found out."

Prologue

Detective Inspector Mitch McLaren glanced around the magnificent library, casually perusing the literature that was neatly stacked inside the antique wooden bookcases. The fact that he had been kept waiting seemed to irk him more than usual, so much so that he had helped himself to a cheeky nip of cognac from a decanter on the sideboard. Something told him he was going to need it.

You could tell a lot about a person by the books they owned, he thought, as he threw back the cognac in one hit. Somehow he hadn't had Sebastian Forbes down as a Jane Austen man. Must be his wife's, he thought, smiling as he came across Milan Kundera's *The Unbearable Lightness of Being*. Exhaling softly as he pulled it from the shelf, it immediately evoked a strong memory of her; her long, dark hair, shyly falling over her face like a silk curtain as she pretended not to notice him looking at her . . .

'Detective Inspector McLaren?' Sebastian Forbes's clipped tones sliced through Mitch's thoughts with all the subtlety of an axe as he stormed into the library, his face a crimson colour, veins protruding in his neck in what looked like protest.

'Pleased to meet you, Mr Forbes,' Mitch said, his hand outstretched in greeting.

Sebastian did not take it.

'The Commissioner said you're the best he's got,' Sebastian said, matter of fact, casting the Inspector a rather disdainful glance. 'Well, I hope for your sake he's right because I want this case solved pronto, do you understand me, Inspector? I said *pronto*.' Sebastian poured himself an extra large champagne cognac and threw it back without offering Mitch one.

'It's a fucking disaster, that's what this is,' he growled, pulling his lips over his teeth as the alcohol hit the back of his throat. 'That diamond is worth more than the national debt, and somehow those bastards knew exactly how to get inside my bank and get their thieving hands on it.' Sebastian was incandescent, his hands shaking with rage. 'I want them *found*, Inspector. I want you to find the scum that did this and I want you to throw the bloody book at them, do you hear me?'

Mitch watched Forbes carefully. It was immediately obvious that the man was a tyrant. It was written right through him like a stick of Blackpool rock. He hadn't even asked about the unfortunate security guard, currently fighting for his life in hospital.

'Mr Forbes, I need to ask you a few questions if that's OK.' Mitch cleared his throat. 'Questions you might find impertinent, but are necessary nonetheless.'

Sebastian didn't care much for the DI's abruptness but given the circumstances had little choice but to comply.

'You say you were the only one who knew the codes to the security system, that is right isn't it?'

'Yes,' Sebastian snapped back, the irritation in his voice tangible. 'I changed the codes myself, a few hours before leaving to catch the plane. Look,' he said tightly, 'that system is infallible, Inspector; it's one of a kind, pioneering technology from America which *I* helped create.' He thumped his chest, indignant. 'Only *I* knew the codes to gain access to the vault and only *I* have access to the room where the diamond was kept. The Interlocking System has an in-built scanner that relies on facial recognition. *My* face, Inspector, is the key that unlocks it.'

'Is there somewhere I can play this?' Mitch asked, producing a CD from his inside pocket. 'I think it might be of some interest to you,' he said as Sebastian nodded towards the flat-screen on the wall. 'It's CCTV footage taken from last night. I want you to look carefully at it, Mr Forbes,' Mitch instructed him. 'Tell me if you recognise any of the men.'

Sebastian downed another cognac, squinting at the images as they came into view.

'Good . . . good God . . .' he said after a moment, taking a step back in alarm, pointing at the screen in shock and confusion. 'That man . . . it's . . . it's me! But . . . it isn't *me* . . . that's impossible. I told you, I was on a plane to Rio last night. I was on a goddamn plane!' Sebastian's voice was high-pitched in protest. 'Surely you're not stupid enough to think this really *is* me? A hundred or more people can vouch for me!'

Mitch nodded. 'We will have to check all your alibis, of course,' he said with an even smile.

'Jesus fucking Christ!' Sebastian slammed his glass down onto the antique desk with such force that it was testament to the quality of the crystal that it didn't break.

'I'm going to need to speak to your wife, Mr Forbes,' Mitch said after a moment's pause. 'Ask her a few questions, if that's OK.'

Sebastian looked up.

'My wife?'

'It's merely a formality,' he reassured him.

Sebastian sighed heavily, his temper dissolving into self-pity.

'As you wish. Though I can't imagine she'll be of much help.' He picked up the internal line. 'Jalena, ask Mrs Forbes to come down to the library immediately will you? What? I don't care if she's still sleeping, goddamn it, this is important!' he bellowed, slamming the telephone down.

Muttering under his breath, Sebastian reached for the cognac decanter once more, this time having the decency to pour the Inspector one.

Accepting it, Mitch turned away from him and wandered towards the bay window, looking out onto the pristine terrace at the pruned topiary and expensive Lloyd Loom furniture.

He was still looking out of the window, cognac in hand, as he heard the door to the library open. It was only as he slowly turned round that he felt the glass suddenly slip from his fingers and his heart stop dead.